Knight of the Jaded Heart

The Eglinton Knight series
Book 1

Margaux Thorne

Dragonblade Publishing, Inc. is an imprint of Kathryn Le Veque Novels, Inc.
P.O. Box 23
Moreno Valley, CA 92556
ceo@dragonbladepublishing.com

Produced in the United States of America

First Edition January 2023
Trade Paperback Edition

ARE YOU SIGNED UP FOR DRAGONBLADE'S BLOG?

You'll get the latest news and information on exclusive giveaways, exclusive excerpts, coming releases, sales, free books, cover reveals and more.

Check out our complete list of authors, too!

No spam, no junk. That's a promise!

Sign Up Here

www.dragonbladepublishing.com

Dearest Reader;

Thank you for your support of a small press. At Dragonblade Publishing, we strive to bring you the highest quality Historical Romance from some of the best authors in the business. Without your support, there is no 'us', so we sincerely hope you adore these stories and find some new favorite authors along the way.

Happy Reading!

CEO, Dragonblade Publishing

CHAPTER ONE

London, England August 1, 1839

GEORGIANA SPENCE SCOWLED up at the gray dollop of storm clouds. Rain and bad news. Two things she was perpetually destined to catch on the back foot.

"He told me he had tickets for us!" Minnie Carmichael cried. "I can't believe he let them slip through his fingers! If I don't get tickets, I'll just die, I tell you. Just die!"

Georgiana tore herself away from the ominous firmament and offered a consoling expression to her best friend, who looked close to tears, patting her arm for extra measure. Minnie was anxious at the best of times, and this, certainly, was not one of those.

"Of course we'll get tickets," Georgiana said, softening her voice as if speaking to a newborn kitten. "Your father tried, and that's what is most important. We have a few more weeks. There's nothing to worry about."

As if on cue, lightning streaked a jagged edge across the sky, the corrugated line threatening to crack open the very heavens. In hindsight, a walk with Minnie along Hyde Park's fashionable Rotten Row wasn't the smartest idea with the weather as it was, but Georgiana had thought the rain would hold—*and* she'd desperately needed to get away from her family. Gossiping about the Eglinton Tournament was her one and only escape. With each day that passed, the atmosphere in her father's townhouse grew more and more suffocating. Her summer had been stuffed with unrelenting expectation and innuendo, the kind that a subtle shift of pressure could burst at any moment.

But Georgiana refused to think about *all that*. She was so very tired of worrying and planning a way out of *all that*. So she would walk with Minnie and ruminate over more pressing things…like ancient coats of arms and long velvet draping sleeves, pretending the weather was sunny and fine and her future was hers to control.

Unable to find the same motivation, Minnie let her shoulders slump even further. "How can you say that?" she whined. "The knights are almost done practicing and are leaving for the country soon. What's the use of having a rich father if he can't even get tickets to the most important event of the year? Nay, the century. Nay, *my life!*"

Georgiana fought to keep a placid smile on her face as she nodded to the few passersby on their strolls; it proved difficult, as it seemed Minnie had lost all strength in her legs and was not only using Georgiana as a shoulder to cry on but also a cane. "Please control yourself," she pleaded, nudging Minnie upright. "Just this morning my father told me he had a lead on some tickets, so we still have a chance. I'm absolutely positive our fathers will come through."

Minnie sniffed, raising her eyes to her friend. The perfect English rose, Minnie was so fair and her eyes so glassy she could have been a doll in a store. "You swear?"

"I swear."

"Swear on something you hold dear."

"Like what?"

Minnie's doll eyes narrowed. "Your mother's grave."

"Why on earth?" Georgiana exclaimed. "You know my mother's not dead!"

Her friend had the grace to look contrite. "I know. I was

trying to add to the dramatic effect."

Georgiana frowned. "Well, you hardly need to do that. I am fully aware of the gravity of the situation, but if you need me to swear on something then fine. On my signed copy of *Ivanhoe*, I swear we will go to the Eglinton Tournament. There. Are you happy?"

For the first time that afternoon, Minnie's pouty lips warped into a wide smile, *and* she resumed using her own legs. "Yes, thank you. You're such a good friend. The very best. I'm sorry I'm being such a baby; I just don't want to miss it." She sighed dramatically. "Can you believe it? A real medieval tournament in England—"

"Scotland."

"—with knights and ladies, jousting and balls. It's just so...so...romantic."

It *was* romantic. Even though Georgiana was playing the calm, rational friend on this walk, she was just as excited as Minnie. And they weren't the only ones. Ever since Lord Archibald, Earl of Eglinton, announced his tournament, the entire country had been crazed with anticipation. The expanse of his vision for a medieval spectacle had never been considered before in Britain. Over three days at the end of August, it would feature a joust, melee, banquet, and ball on his grand estate just over the English border. Anyone who was anyone would be there. However, Lord Archibald had not realized the magnitude of people's enthusiasm, and tickets for the grandstand seats had been snatched quickly, creating an overzealous demand for more. The ones that remained were difficult to find and going at a premium.

"We'll just have to be patient. In the meantime, we can console ourselves by watching their final practice tomorrow," Georgiana replied. The wind, thick and heavy with late-summer heat, picked up with such a gust that she had to grab hold of her wide-brimmed bonnet to keep it from flying away. "Do you want to go together?"

"Naturally," Minnie replied at once, keeping her hand on her own straw bonnet. Riders thinned out on the sand and dirt bridle path next to them, leaving mostly carriages passing down the row. "What a smart idea for the knights to host practices before the big day. It's absolutely wonderful that they are open to the public." Her lips pursed to stifle a giggle. "Though I did hear Jerningham still can't get his horse to run the lists and keeps flying off his saddle. I'm sure he didn't like having an audience for that."

Georgiana laughed. "Isn't he the Knight of the Swan?"

"Indeed."

"Apt name."

"Indeed."

Snickering at their joke, they made their way to Queen Elizabeth Gate, where the eighteen-foot-tall statue of Achilles stood poised and menacing in all its naked splendor. Well, not quite naked. After an uproar at its debut, a fig leaf was added to maintain a modicum of respectability for the hero of antiquity. Georgiana couldn't help but think Achilles would be pleased with the fig cover. As far as leaves go, it *was* on the larger size.

The women took their time, appreciating the magnificent display of bronzed man, lost in the rippling muscles and bulging...courageousness.

"Oh, that reminds me," Minnie said, dragging her focus away. "I can't believe I haven't asked. Has your father settled the betrothal yet?"

Georgiana was dumbfounded how the statue's near-naked gorgeousness and all-around chivalric display could remind Minnie of her impending doom. Any sort of fire building within her from gazing at Achilles's massive, valiant thighs dampened in a hurry. "No...not yet."

"Are you ever going to tell me who it is?" Minnie grinned wickedly, nudging her so hard that Georgiana almost fell at Achilles's bare feet.

Georgiana could hear Minnie's spinster aunt *tsk* in disapproval from behind them. While chaperoning them on their walk, Aunt Augusta had been *tsking* for the better part of an hour. She *tsked* so much at their behavior that Georgiana had ceased to even remember she was there, thinking a broken clock was trailing after them instead.

"There's nothing to tell," Georgiana replied, imbuing her voice with as much confidence as she could rally. "They are still negotiating. Nothing's final yet. I doubt it will lead to anything serious."

The rain finally decided to make good on its promise, and tiny drops began to fall. Georgiana didn't usually believe in signs, but it was difficult to look the other way on that one.

"Well, it sounds serious," Minnie countered, rolling her eyes at another of Aunt Augusta's *tsks*. Clearly, a rain shower was no place for two young ladies. Or perhaps they'd stayed too long gawking at the almost-naked statue. "They've been negotiating for the past month. Why are you hiding it?" Her nose scrunched up. "Is he only a baron? My father said he wouldn't settle for anything lower than an earl for me, but I know for a fact two viscounts came to speak to him last week. I was out with Mother, and he wouldn't tell me their names. He says he doesn't want me to corner them at a ball and scare them off with my conversation."

"What's wrong with your conversation?" Georgiana asked, insulted for her friend.

"Apparently there's too much of it."

Yes, that made sense.

The rain pattered down harder. Her nonverbal cues unsuccessful, Aunt Augusta was forced to speak up. "Girls, it's time to go now. You'll catch your death if we stay any longer."

"Of course, Aunt Augusta," Minnie replied before leaning into Georgiana and whispering, "The clock has spoken."

Georgiana choked back a laugh. Taking each other's arms again, the women were just about to round the statue toward the gates when insistent hooves pounded into the dirt behind them. Their skirts swirled as they turned to see an austere gentleman approach on his jet-black horse. Even through the curtain of rain,

Georgiana recognized the figure, and she froze, quite certain that her stomach would have dropped to her knees if her trusty corset hadn't been there to hold it up.

The man pulled up his animal. Immaculately—if soberly—dressed, he was resplendent in tan doeskin breeches and Hessian boots that Georgiana was positive she would see her reflection in if she deigned to bend over and look. His navy-blue jacket was expertly cut to his body, with a plain matching waistcoat underneath. No ruffles burst from his shirt, nor was there any flash to his cravat. It was all class, absent of pizazz, with his high collar as starched and unyielding as his expression.

"Miss Georgiana," he said, skimming the brim of his hat with his fingers in a perfunctory greeting. Dark brown, unruly waves of hair peeked out underneath. "It's raining."

Georgiana gritted her teeth into a tight smile. Somehow, by the grace of God, she got her mouth to move and say something *not* completely rude. "I can see that, my lord. *And* feel it."

Nothing. No response. Not even a quirk of lip at her flat remark. The man's stern features were as unwavering as the giant horse underneath him, rigidly contained.

"You should go home so you do not catch a cold."

Georgiana could feel Aunt Augusta throw her a smug nod. "Indeed, my lord. We were just on our way. How did you happen to see us? I didn't think you enjoyed rides in the park."

"I don't," he said with the overbearing conviction that Georgiana had come to expect from him. "I was on my way to a meeting with my lawyer when I saw you."

His lawyer—of course. "Oh, how"—*utterly, utterly boring*—"nice."

He nodded, as if agreeing that he was the blandest man in England. Georgiana thought to leave it at that, exiting the dull conversation with a respectable curtsey, but he continued in front of her, apparently waiting for her to entertain him further, weather be damned.

She scoured through the cordial topics in her head. "We were just discussing the Eglinton Tournament. It's fast approaching. Will you be attending?"

The man curled his lips and frowned at the rain. If a scowl could warn it away from his jacket, his could. "There's only one reason to go to Scotland in August, and that's to shoot."

Well then. "So that's a no?"

"Indeed."

Another awkward pause ensued. Why was he just sitting there on his horse? Why wouldn't he just leave?

The rain gained an unrelenting rhythm, and Georgiana knew it was only a matter of time before puddles gathered around them—not that *he* cared.

Next to Achilles—one of the noblest and most respected warriors in history—the faults in the gentleman couldn't have been any more blatant. *He* would never throw his cloak on a puddle for her to walk over like a chivalrous knight; nor would he haul her up onto his horse, charging away at full speed and tucking her in the safety of his warm embrace.

Would he?

The gentleman's dark eyes stayed on her a little too long, and Georgiana shifted her weight on her other foot.

Would he?

"I must be on my way," he said, breaking the moment with all the elegance of a sledgehammer. "I cannot be late." The gentleman gathered his reins, sparing Aunt Augusta an impatient glance before adding, "Madam, I insist you guide these women home at once."

No, he would not.

Georgiana wasn't disappointed, nor surprised. It was for the best anyway. If he behaved like a true gentleman, she might actually have to treat him like one—and she was determined never to do so.

He gifted the group another of his perfunctory nods. "I will see you tonight, then," he said to her, beginning to turn his horse.

"I doubt that, my lord."

He stopped, the arch of his eyebrow as sharp as an arrow. "Oh?"

Georgiana decided she hated those supercilious eyebrows, how he could command so much with them while barely uttering a word.

"Yes, you see, there's only one reason to go to dinner, and that's to eat. I'm afraid I've suddenly lost my appetite and don't think I'll be finding it anytime soon."

She almost slapped her hands over her mouth. What had come over her? She'd never spoken like that to him before. In all honesty, she'd never really spoken to him. Whenever he visited, she usually sulked in her seat, giving drab, one-word answers whenever her parents glared at her.

Georgiana forced herself to meet his gaze. A glint of challenge burned in his dark eyes, though his flavorless expression remained the same. The man was as vanilla as Victorian sponge cake. Georgiana knew she was being unquestionably rude, but she couldn't seem to regret her words. Why could he be curt and aloof all the time, but she couldn't? Why was the woman always held to a greater standard?

She thought he would snap back, put her in her place with a harsh rebuke, but thunder cracked across the sky, putting a decisive end to the impromptu meeting.

Surprising her, he touched his hat once more. "I will say good day to you, then," he replied before speeding away down the lane, the rain a mere nuisance to the expert rider and animal.

Georgiana could only stand there for a few heady breaths, watching him go. She had a feeling she would pay for that later. She'd have to see him. There was no way her parents would let her skip dinner, not when "the lord" was coming. She could be at death's door, and they'd still prop her up at the table like a marionette, poking and prodding her using any utensil available to form a smile on her face.

Eventually, Aunt Augusta got her to move, corralling the girls out of the park gates like cattle.

More like lambs to the slaughter, Georgiana thought disconsolately.

For once in her life, Minnie appeared to be speechless. However, it didn't take long for her to pull herself together. "Who. Was. That?"

The raindrops pelted down on Georgiana like boulders, leaving her wet and so very, very heavy. "Lord Edw—" The name lodged in her throat.

Luckily, Minnie puzzled out the rest. "Lord Edward, Marquess of Marlborough?"

"The very one."

Minnie *humphed*. "He was rather rude, although I suppose he can be, since he's a peer. To not even take off his hat in the presence of ladies..."

"We're not ladies. Your father is a banker and mine manufactures buttons."

"Correction, my dear friend. My father is an enormously *wealthy* banker, and yours is no different. Besides, we'll be ladies soon enough after we're married."

"I know." Georgiana sighed, wilting.

"And he didn't even get off his horse! He probably didn't want to ruin his boots."

Another sigh. "Probably."

"And the way he spoke to Aunt Augusta when you hadn't even introduced them. Why didn't he offer to help us find a hansom cab? Since you live close by, we don't need one, but he couldn't have known that..." She stopped in her tracks, pulling another *tsk* out of her aunt. "Wait. How *do* you know the Marquess of Marlborough? And why did he say he would see you tonight?"

Georgiana shifted uncomfortably, and it had nothing to do with the pernicious wetness permeating her clothes. "He is a friend of my father's."

"A friend?" Minnie's mouth dropped open at the word, staying there for long seconds before she continued. "Lord Edward doesn't have friends. I heard he's a bit of a grump, and from what I can tell, the gossips were right for once."

Georgiana didn't bother to respond. She could spy her door down Park Lane, and hastened her footsteps. Perhaps if she didn't say anything, Minnie would move on to a new subject.

She should have known better.

"Still..." Minnie said in stout contemplation. "He *is* handsome...has quite an air about him. He's positively horrid—but in a dashing way."

"Horrid? In a dashing way?" Georgiana squawked, tripping over her boots.

Minnie had a romantic look in her eye as she turned her cute nose up dreamily. "Don't look at me like that," she said. "He's definitely more *Castle of Otranto* than *Ivanhoe*, but...there's something there."

"His title," Georgiana remarked dryly.

"No, that's not it," Minnie said, shaking the adorable curls that were drooping at the sides of her face. "Well, that's not *only* it. High forehead, strong figure, straight nose, dark and brooding—very Mr. Darcy."

Georgiana snorted. Her friend read too many novels. They both did, for that matter. "More like Frankenstein."

"Georgiana! The man is handsome. Are you blind?"

Was she? Georgiana had never thought of Lord Edward in that way before. She'd never been given a chance. The second he was foisted upon her by her father and opened his imperious mouth to introduce himself, all her girlish fantasies had fled for the hills. They still hadn't come out from hiding.

Reaching the townhome, the girls scurried up the steps. Georgiana flung open the door in a most unladylike manner, but Aunt Augusta was obviously too cold and drenched to disapprove. Jeffrey, the butler, greeted them before hurrying to take their personal items and issuing commands for a fire to be started in the upstairs parlor.

"Of course I'm not blind," Georgiana grumbled, rubbing her

hands together to gain some warmth. Even in the middle of summer, the London rain could chill her to the bone. Or was it the subject matter? Georgiana had come to believe Lord Edward could suck the warmth from a cast-iron stove, given half the chance. "I just don't want to talk about it."

"Why not?"

"Because I just don't."

"You don't want to talk about anything."

"We've been talking for the past hour!"

"*I've* been talking. You haven't." Minnie planted her hands on her soggy hips. With her slender figure and curls, she might look harmless, but Georgiana knew Minnie could be as feisty as a fox terrier when the situation called for it. "I want to know the name of your betrothed."

"He's not my betrothed yet."

"You know what I mean."

"Girls, please," Aunt Augusta said. "Lower your voices."

Minnie threw up her hands. "This is her house."

"It doesn't matter," her aunt returned, just as testily.

Jeffrey returned down the steps to the foyer. "The fire is ready for you, Miss Georgiana."

"Thank you, Jeffrey," Georgiana said.

But when she and Aunt Augusta headed for the stairs, Minnie stayed put.

"Minnie," her aunt pleaded, "stop this now. You'll catch—"

"Yes, I know, I'll catch my death. I don't care." Minnie crossed her arms, leveling a glare at Georgiana. "You're my best friend in the world. We tell each other everything. I want to know who your betrothed is."

"Stop ordering me around," Georgiana cried from the second step, gripping the chunky handrail with both hands. "I get it from my mother and father; I don't need it from you!"

A heartbreaking look of empathy clouded Minnie's stubborn face. "I'm not ordering you! I can't stand that you're hiding things from me. I was only teasing before. It's perfectly fine if he's a baron…or even a rich merchant. Does he have bad breath? A clubbed foot? I know you have your opinions about peers…"

Georgiana rolled her eyes. Her friend made "opinions" sound like nasty diseases. Besides, she didn't have an opinion on the aristocracy—she just didn't want to marry one of them. The last thing she needed was to be shipped off to some country estate where all her ideas would die on the vine.

"The aristocracy is full of odd ducks, isn't it?" Minnie went on. "Does he have one eye? Or does one of them wander? Is he old? How old…thirty?" She walked in front of Georgiana, taking both of her hands. "It doesn't matter. Mother says wives don't really have to see their husbands much anyway. You'll have me. Always. Everything will work out."

How reasonable…and horribly unromantic. This was all becoming too real to Georgiana. And she didn't want real. She wanted dragons and ancient quests. The Eglinton Tournament was the only thing keeping her from worrying over her plan to stay unmarried this summer. It was keeping her sane, though rapidly failing. Living in her head amongst the knights and ladies was the safest place for her. A place where men treated women like the goddesses they were, and true love was nourishment for the soul.

But time—and reality—was catching up to her. Seeing him outside in plain sight added to that fact.

Minnie's fingers tightened. Georgiana focused on her friend's determined gaze but could only see her mother and father's unhinged desire that she should marry someone for position rather than sentiment. What did it matter if the soul was nourished, as long as your belly was full of the gluttonous trappings of the aristocracy?

Georgiana's voice broke. "You swear?"

Minnie nodded.

"Swear on something you hold dear."

Minnie smiled. "I swear on my signed copy of *The Bride of Lammermoor*."

Naturally, she would have to point out that she had a signed copy from Sir Walter Scott.

"Now tell me who it is. I promise, once you do, it won't seem as horrible," Minnie said, shaking Georgiana's hands. "Have I met him before?"

Georgiana gulped. "Yes."

"Did I like him?"

"I think so…maybe."

"Well, that's a good start. It can't be all that bad."

Tears began to well, and Georgiana didn't know if they would ever stop. As if the rain hadn't been enough.

But Minnie refused to relent. Georgiana loved her friend and owed her the name, yet she didn't want to give it. Saying *he* was her fiancé (or about to be) would make it true, and Georgiana was still pretending there was a chance her plan might work or that he might back out and look for someone else to marry. But deep down, she knew he wouldn't. Just as sure as she knew her father would find her tickets to the Eglinton Tournament.

"Oh, Minnie." Georgiana sobbed. "It *is* that bad. *He's* that bad." Even if he *was* dashing, he was still horrid. And haughty. And rude. And never even tried to get to know her *or* pretend he wasn't marrying her for her substantial dowry.

"Who?"

Georgiana lifted her chin, locking eyes with the person she trusted most in the world. But she still couldn't bring herself to say the name, so she blurted the next best thing.

"Frankenstein."

Aunt Augusta gasped, covering her mouth with her gloved hand.

"Not the real Frankenstein," Georgiana assured her.

"Honestly, aunt, she means Lord Edward," Minnie added drolly.

"I knew that!" Aunt Augusta snapped, not convincingly.

Minnie settled back on Georgiana, as if surveying her friend under a whole new light. "You'll be a marchioness. That's rather impressive."

"No, it's not because it's not going to happen," Georgiana answered, stomping down the staircase, where she wrapped around the polished newel post like an obstinate limpet. "He's so, so boring."

Minnie grimaced. "Yes...I caught that. But perhaps he's kind?"

Georgiana groaned. "And he doesn't love me."

"Give him time," Minnie replied. "You haven't known him that long."

"Long enough to know he loves my money."

That stumped Georgiana's friend, who finally shrugged in defeat. "Well, you have so much of it, dearest. And you had to have known he'd want your money. That's the whole point of marrying heiresses with no titles."

"I know," Georgiana grumbled. "It's just..."

"What?"

Georgiana's thick lashes fluttered over her cheeks, and her voice came out in a whisper. "It's also what he needs it for." She looked up to catch pure fascination glowing from Minnie's intrigued face and couldn't help but laugh.

"Don't you dare say you don't want to tell me," Minnie said. "You can't leave it at that. What does he want it for?"

Georgiana shook her head. "I can't. It's too ridiculous. It's too...too..."

"What? Spit it out."

"I can't! It's crude and shameful. My father told me the marquess has a notion to invest it in some scheme. Those kinds of men know nothing about business; it's bound to go badly. Honestly, I cannot imagine what he's thinking."

Aunt Augusta sucked in another ragged breath. Casting a quick eye on her aunt, Minnie warned her friend, "If you don't tell us soon, I'm afraid this one will faint at the implications. I hope you have smelling salts close by."

At the words, Jeffrey turned on his heel and left the room.

"Is it really as bad as all that?" Minnie asked, huddling close to her aunt's arm, positioning herself to catch her if the older woman spilled over.

Georgiana straightened from the post. "It's worse. It's...it's..."

CHAPTER TWO

"SHIT?" LORD CHARLES exclaimed, shaking his head at Edward. "I can't believe it. You're the only man I know to be so excited to find ancient lizard shit on his estate."

"We prefer to call it coprolites," Edward returned, nodding at his solicitor.

From behind the giant mahogany desk in his office overlooking the park, Mr. John Dawson, Esq. tilted his head confidently.

"Fossilized dung, my lord," Dawson clarified. "And it's extremely important to men in the natural sciences. Along with the bones they find, the coprolites are beginning to help them understand more about these ancient reptiles, for instance, what they used to eat—"

Charles cut him off. "And where they liked to shit."

"For God's sakes, Charles, stop using that word," Edward implored. "This is science."

Dawson cleared his throat, shuffling tidy papers into even tidier piles, his gin-blossom nose under his spectacles blooming into a darker shade of red. "Yes, where they…relieved themselves. If they used a communal commode, etc. etc."

Charles cocked an eyebrow in Edward's direction, brushing his wheat-colored hair off his forehead in an exasperated swipe. The only unfashionable thing about him, Charles's shoulder-length hair still made all the women within a mile radius swoon.

"This is science?"

Edward answered with an arrogant smile, "It is, and it's going to make me millions."

Charles snorted, lifting his straight, aristocratic nose in the air as if he could smell the coprolites all the way from Cambridgeshire.

Edward couldn't understand his friend's dubiousness and almost regretted asking Charles to meet him today. It wasn't as if Edward hadn't explained all of this before, but he and Dawson went into it again, detailing the process as best they could to someone with limited knowledge—and interest—in paleontology, highlighting the effects the fossilized dung would have on England's agricultural system. How it was recently discovered that crushed bones added to soil could help improve yields due to their high count of calcium phosphate. And England desperately needed its yields to improve. With Napoleon's threat safely in the past, the population was booming, and people needed to be fed.

However, human and animal bones weren't as easy to come by as imagined. That was where coprolites came in. Incredibly rich in phosphate content, they provided all the food and minerals plants needed to grow. And they were everywhere. Well, not everywhere, but the land on Edward's estate apparently had its fair share. All he had to do was start mining, and all his problems—the problems his father had left him—would be solved.

While Edward continued his tutorial, Charles stood up from his armchair and wandered over to a table against the wall where Dawson had set up a series of rare ammonite fossils. "Yes, yes, I remember all that," Charles said distractedly, fiddling with the hoary shells. He held one up to the sash window, swirling the iridescent specimen around in his fingers. "But I don't understand. I thought the plants couldn't use these…coprolites."

"That's exactly correct, my lord," Dawson said, practically jumping out of his seat like a child bursting with a secret. "Up until now, they were insoluble to the plants; the phosphorous couldn't be absorbed from their roots." At Charles's dubious expression, Dawson continued. "Imagine it this way: you're the plant and you're thirsty—*dying* of thirst on a deserted island. You are surrounded by water, but you obviously can't drink it. What we've done is essentially make the salt water drinkable."

"You lost me. I thought we were talking about manure."

Dawson shook his head, rubbing his eyes under his spectacles. "Sorry, yes, that was a confusing analogy. Chemists have recently discovered that if you treat the coprolites with oil of vitriol first, then the solubility can be increased, and the plants can consume the nutrients!"

"Right," Charles drawled, causing the geologist to sit slowly back in his seat, his ardor effectively doused.

Edward sighed. Respectability for this endeavor would be an upward battle in his world. It was bad enough a peer was going into business, but fertilizer business...that was beyond the pale. His own mother hadn't even spoken to him in months, and that was after he gave her the good news that he'd be able to rebuild their family fortune with this venture. A family fortune that his father had squandered while betting—and losing—on horses and cards for the majority of his profligate life. Though frowned upon, that had been perfectly acceptable to members of their crowd. That was what marquesses did.

Perhaps Edward was asking too much. Charles was his oldest friend in the world, but he was still an earl—a wealthy one—and didn't have to worry about his estates falling under. His own father had put money into their lands, investing in all the newest innovations and technologies to keep it thriving. The only heavy lifting Charles had to do was pick up his pen to write to his steward inquiring about his profits every month.

"I thought you'd show *a little* more enthusiasm," Edward remarked as Charles moved on to another fossil on the table. "This is a way to grow more and spend less. Think about all the money you allocate buying guano fertilizer."

"Oh good," Charles replied dryly, his head falling back. "We're on to your other favorite subject—bat droppings."

"*Expensive* bat droppings," Edward said, ignoring his friend's sarcastic tone. "With the coprolite fertilizer, we wouldn't have to import all the way from South America anymore. We are, quite literally, sitting on a gold mine."

Charles faced his friend, his lips curled into a genuine smile. "You mean *you* are sitting on a gold mine. I'm just here for the food. When are we going to eat, by the way? I thought we were going to the club."

"Soon," Edward growled. It was like dealing with a toddler.

Dawson rustled his papers again, bringing them back to the matter at hand. "There's no gold mine yet. The coprolites are worthless unless Lord Edward can get them out of the ground. He needs investors to fund the project—capital to set up the mine, equipment, and mill. What do they say, my lords? It takes money to make money?" He pushed away from the desk, giving his belly ample room for his chuckle.

Edward watched Charles zone in on the lawyer's sizeable girth. Remarkably fit, Charles had even less patience for sloth than he did science. "What does that mean?" he asked, clearly trying to hide his distaste.

"That means," Edward began wistfully, "that it's time for a wife."

"A wealthy one," Dawson added.

"What other kinds are there?" Charles asked drolly, dropping back into his seat. "Why don't you skip that unfortunate step and take out a loan like everyone else and be done with it?"

"No," Edward said sharply. "No loans. I'm still paying off all the loans my father took out from his friends and neighbors. I refuse to be in any more debt. I want people to believe in me— believe in this venture—as I do. I have to do this myself." *Just like everything else, damn it.*

Charles stared at him for a long time before nodding. "Of course, my friend. Now I know why you've been so insistent upon a particular heiress. How's that going, by the way? Seems to be taking a little longer than usual to get her to walk down the plank—I mean aisle."

Edward uncrossed his legs, only to cross them again. He wasn't sure why, but he didn't like Charles speaking about Georgiana in Dawson's office. This austere room, full of masculine colors and dark woods, wasn't the place for her.

Unbidden, flashes of Georgiana dripping with rain in the park ran through his mind. Up until that point he'd attempted to keep his animalistic side at bay, knowing he was courting for a wife and not a mistress. She'd been pleasing enough at the balls, decorated in innocence, and fitted in lace and bows like every other virginal young woman scouting for a husband. She'd been acceptable—no more, no less.

But in the rain…with her chestnut hair falling slick and wet down her cheeks…her eyelashes spiked with droplets, her dress molding to curves he hadn't expected… And then she'd opened her impertinent mouth.

Edward dashed Georgiana's pouting lips and nerve-tingling voice from his mind. "Her father says he will be my chief investor if only I can take her off his hands," Edward said. "With the summer almost over, we won't be able to mine until next spring anyway. Everything will work out; I'm sure of it." His eyes flickered to his friend, and he added, "She'll come along."

Regarding him warily, Charles asked, "Does the little woman know of your unhealthy zeal for reptile shit?"

"It hasn't come up in conversation."

"She still busy giving you the cold shoulder?"

That was putting it mildly. Georgiana's chilly reserve for him could freeze a lake. This afternoon was the first time he'd actually heard her string a sentence together. "She's still busy talking about your little tournament," Edward hedged. "It seems to be all she's interested in."

"Jealous?"

"Are you insane?" Edward asked.

"Are you going to answer the question? What does she think of all this?"

Edward froze in his seat, his jaw clenched. It was the only way he could keep from squirming. "I told you. It's best not to discuss it. She wouldn't find it interesting."

Most didn't. People would always be an enigma to Edward, throwing away so much energy and excitement over some silly medieval tournament when they could be focusing on modern marvels like this. How could anyone fixate on the stale past when the future was so malleable and open?

"But *you* find it interesting," Charles countered, determined not to let the subject drop, "and it would show her that you're making an effort in this courtship by letting her know something about you. If you tried a little harder, maybe you'd have a wife by now. Christ, Edward, the Season's almost over!"

"I *do* show an effort! I've come for dinner the past four weeks."

Charles arched a thick eyebrow. "That's not showing an effort, lad; that's showing you're hungry."

Feathers effectively ruffled, Edward decided it was time to leave. By this point in their friendship, he recognized the signs. Charles was hungry and getting irritable. He wouldn't stop until he had a fresh pie on his plate and a pint of ale in his hand.

Edward pulled himself up from his chair, thanking Dawson for the meeting and reassuring him that he'd have more information to share soon.

As he exited the building, he forced his upbeat performance to bolster his own inner insecurities, pushing his anxieties to the back of his mind. He might be new to business, but it was not much different from life—never let them see you sweat. Edward needed to leave Dawson with the picture of himself assured and in control. If it got back to the public that he was having a difficult time finding investors, the mine would be dead in the water. Everything was going as planned because that was the way it needed to go. Edward couldn't accept anything less. There were no secondary options. This was it.

Charles was waiting for him at the front of the building, and he heaved a disgruntled breath when Edward started walking in the opposite direction of their club.

"White's isn't that way. Now where are we going?" he whined, his long legs catching up to Edward's intent gait.

Edward's mumbles were barely audible to his own ears. "There's a pawnbroker I need to speak to. It won't take long."

Charles stopped in the middle of the lane, sighing deeply before catching up to his friend again. "Still? When are you going to be done with this? Haven't you bought back enough of your mother's jewelry? When is it going to end?"

Soon.

After his father's death three years ago, what started out as a curiosity turned into an obsession. Hellbent on getting back everything that belonged to his sisters and mother—furniture, paintings, jewelry—Edward had spent all his free time scouring London's pawnbrokers looking for everything that once called his Marlborough estate home. His father may have ruined their family in life, but Edward refused to let him do it in death.

"You know," Charles went on, "I can't help but think all the money you've poured into buying back your family's items might have paid for your mine by now. Why is this so important to you? It's just some jewelry. If this venture is going to make you as rich as you say, you'll be able to buy your mother boatloads of new diamonds, ones that don't remind her of your father's perfidy."

"It's not the same," Edward growled. Like the coprolites, this was something Charles would never understand. He'd never trusted someone so implicitly and had that trust betrayed again and again. He'd never had to go to sleep listening to his mother's sobs and wake up to ransacked rooms. Somewhere in London, his great-great-grandfather's portrait was gracing someone else's wall. Edward was just waiting for the day he attended a dinner party and found his ancestor glaring down at him as he ate a spoonful of trifle. The potential humiliation would always be there, chasing him like a starved wolf.

No doubt reacting to the harshness in Edward's tone, Charles slapped him on the back. "At least tell me you're almost done. How much longer can you go on like this?"

"Not long," Edward answered, finding some relief in the conversation. "I'm actually down to one piece of jewelry. Then everything will be back to how it was, and I can focus."

"On a wife?" Charles grinned. "I didn't mean to upset you in front of Dawson. I just think—all things considered—maybe you should put as much work into the wooing as you do this reptile shit."

"I'm wooing just fine," Edward muttered, fixing his top hat securely on his head. It had started to drizzle, and again, he thought of the husky notes in Georgiana's voice. The disdain she didn't try to hide. "And I'm not worried in the least. As I said, she'll come along. Georgiana Spence is a new breed of spoiled little rich girl who doesn't enjoy being told what to do."

"Sounds like a match made in heaven," Charles replied dryly. "Did you ever stop to think about wooing someone who might be more interested in you? You're a marquess, for Christ's sake. Even with a lack of funds, you should have nailed her down by now. Why do you keep after her? Is she the most beautiful woman you've ever seen?"

"Certainly not," Edward scoffed. Or, at least, he hadn't thought so *before*.

"Is her figure the picture of your dreams?"

"No… I don't know." Which was true. Edward didn't know, but reevaluation was in order.

Charles was stumped. Considering those were the only two reasons (other than money) to favor a woman for marriage, he was out of ideas. "Do you want a taste of her?"

"Charles! You're talking about my future marchioness!" Though that answer was easier. *Yes*. Edward unequivocally did. He hadn't a clue what she would taste like—perhaps a little bit sweet, a little bit smart—but he knew he would like it.

Charles swiped a hand over his hopeless expression. "Sorry, but I'm at a loss. Why are you spending so much time on the spoiled chit when she doesn't want you?"

"You wouldn't understand."

"I didn't understand reptile shit an hour ago, but now I feel like an expert. Try me. You can have any pick of heiress this Season, can't you?"

Much too conspicuously, Edward averted his gaze.

"*Can't you?*"

There went Edward's confidence. "It seems most men in our social group—even the untitled ones—don't wish for their daughters to be the Coprolite Queen."

Charles jerked his head forward. "Ah."

"Yes," Edward said. "Ah, indeed."

No one had had the gall to whisper the little sobriquet in his presence. His sister, Louise, had told him it was making the rounds, with some even lobbing it behind her back. He hadn't known it to be an issue at first. The first three fathers who'd turned down his offer to court their daughters had used his lack of funds as the excuse, expressing worry that he might squander any dowries as pathetically and wholly as his own father had squandered his fortune. *The apple doesn't fall far from the tree…*

Oddly enough, when Louise had told him about the rumors, he rested easier. Edward would much rather be held in contempt for his own actions rather than those of his father.

"Well, still…" Charles went on, pulling Edward from his thoughts. "There have to be others."

"You'd be surprised." Edward was so very done with this conversation. Charles was right—marquesses didn't have difficult times finding women to marry. Hell, even the Marquis de Sade found a wife! And yet here he was. Edward refused to be embarrassed by the *ton*'s collective snobbish stupidity, but if let himself dwell on it, he would feel mightily abashed.

"Don't tell me she's the only one."

Edward's lips straightened into a flat line. "Fine. I won't tell you she's the only one."

"Really?" Charles squeaked. "She's the *only* one."

Edward answered with a rueful chuckle. "It seems I misspoke before. In fact, *no one* wants their daughter to be the Coprolite Queen."

"Even if the venture takes off? Even though it makes her an incredibly wealthy marchioness?"

Edward shrugged. "It appears the ridicule is not worth the title. It doesn't matter to me. I only need one rich wife, and Georgiana Spence will do the job well enough. I just have to convince her of that fact. Her father and I have an agreement, and I will see it through."

Charles slapped him on the back again. "Well, good luck to you, my friend. I know you'll succeed. You always do. Hell, it took years, but you eventually got *me* to like you."

"Exactly. And it was lucky I did when we were younger, because, to be honest with you, I don't think I'd like you very much if I met you today."

"Ha!" Charles said. "Have you been speaking to my mother? She said the exact same thing to me just yesterday."

Edward cast him a side glance, breathing an inner sigh of relief that the conversation was over. Teasing Charles was much more enjoyable than worrying about the social and economic ruin of his entire family. "How is your mother, by the way? Handsome, rich woman that she is, I should have considered her. Is she ready for another husband?"

Like a lead balloon, Charles's grin slammed to the ground. "Don't talk about my mother, Edward. Don't even think about it."

"Fine. Just tell her I said hello and that I'm thinking of her fondly."

"Don't *think* about my mother."

Edward grinned up at the gray sky. "I think I'd like you calling me Papa."

Charles sped up, leaving Edward yards behind him. "Drop it, Edward. My mother's a saint. She's out of your league."

"Oh, I wouldn't try to deter me like that. You know how

much I love a challenge."

Which was true. Nothing in his life had ever been effortless. Even with the title, Edward had had to work to keep what was his and could only conclude that he was better for it. Jaded at an early age by the weaknesses of his fellow man, he'd become distrustful of things that came easily. Too many sunny days in a row made a man weak. *Hard* made sense. If blood and sweat and a few rain showers weren't involved, there had to be a catch.

Why would marriage be any different?

CHAPTER THREE

LATER THAT NIGHT, while sitting at the Spence family's walnut table in their elegantly appointed dining room, Edward reevaluated his personal mantra. Perhaps his character didn't *always* need to be carved by adversity. Perhaps, sometimes, especially now, the universe could grant him a break and make something just a little easier.

Like Georgiana Spence.

Because they were almost at dessert, and she'd barely strung ten words together for him, though she had plenty enough to say to everyone else.

Edward didn't know what had got into her. He'd dined with the Spence family a handful of times over the last month, and her standoffish behavior had led him to believe she was shy and retiring—a perfect lady.

Tonight, on the other hand, she was a dog with a bone. For the past fifteen minutes, she and her father had been arguing around and around over the family business—something that Edward was surprised she knew anything about.

"But Father, they say it's working in America," she argued, stabbing her fork in the air toward the patriarch sitting at the head of the ornate table. "Not only are some of the employers providing room and board for the workers, but they're also encouraging and promoting clubs to be formed for the women, and even classes and extra training for their betterment. Our workers are predominantly women. If we help them, then we help their families. Isn't that our responsibility?"

More engrossed in his pheasant than in his daughter, Robert Spence never moved his narrow face up from his monogrammed china plate. "My one and only responsibility is to make quality buttons," he responded, chewing. In a tone that led Edward to believe this wasn't a new topic, he added, "And I'd like to make some money in the meantime. I pay my workers enough; what they do with their salaries and their time is their business."

Georgiana's jaw flexed. It was a nice jaw, Edward noticed. Along with her chin. Strong. Pointed. The aristocracy was filled with weak ones that rarely reached past their noses. Edward enjoyed the prospect that his future children might inherit it. Not so much her arguing skills—though they were superior as well.

"Speaking of time," Georgiana continued, not paying heed to her father's lack of interest, "we should also consider the eight-hour workday."

"Bleh!" Spence returned, the idea apparently not justifying a real-word response.

"The man I wrote to in America just started it," Georgiana explained, keeping her temper in check. "It doesn't lower profits as you'd think. He said it's actually increased his investment by fifty percent."

Spence's chewing slowed. "He? Who is this he?"

As far as questions went, Edward thought it a good one.

Georgiana straightened in her chair, her yellow satin gown stretching across her shoulders. Cut low, her bodice sloped toward the valley of her breasts, showcasing an enchanting swath of pale, creamy skin. Thank God for the array of flowers pinned to that area, Edward had thought more than once. The temptation was too great for his roaming vision.

She cleared her throat. "M-Mr. Lawrence," she stammered. "After reading about his unconventional managerial policies, I wrote to him, asking about his motivations. He was kind enough to write back. He told me that every good leader had to learn to think outside the box."

"Write back? Write back?" Spence finally placed his fork on his plate, the indignation in his beady eyes swallowing his long, thin face. "Who said you could write a man about my business? And what boxes is he talking about? We don't make boxes."

"I just thought it could help to learn from others…" Georgiana stared at her food as if the answer could be found in her mock turtle soup and fried sole. "He manufactures buttons, like us, among other things. And I've been studying our ledgers—"

"Who said you could do that?" Spence glared at the only other gentleman at the table besides Edward—good old George.

Spence's right-hand man at the company, George, was always at the house whenever Edward visited. Handsome and intelligent in that middle-class, chip-on-his-shoulder way, he wasn't someone Edward generally worried about or paid much attention to, even though it was quite obvious he had his sights set on Georgiana. Someone had once told Edward his last name, but he never remembered, preferring just to call him George. Because it never failed to make him giggle like a small child. George! The idea was preposterous! How this young upstart thought that he could marry Georgiana when they practically shared the same name was beyond Edward's comprehension!

However, that was precisely what the industrious man thought. No one ever came out and said it, but Edward could smell the competition, especially as the businessman slavered over Georgiana, agreeing to everything that came out of her pert mouth.

He was smart, though. Edward would give him that. Under Spence's formidable scowl, George stalled for time, intent on stacking the perfect bite onto his fork tines, clearly searching for an appropriate answer.

"George didn't give me the ledgers," Georgiana hurried on, bailing the young man out. "I found them in your office one day when I was distributing charity baskets to some of the women. I just…I just wanted to show you that I could help. I have so many suggestions, if you'd only let me play with the numbers."

Spence *hmphed*, returning to his food. "My business is no place for your 'playing.' Stay out of my office. And stop writing to men in America. What will Marlborough think of you?"

The table fixed its eyes on Edward as if suddenly remembering he was there. He made it a habit not to speak too often at the family dinners. The Spence cook was spectacular, and dining was for eating—not talking, especially since he rarely allowed himself to indulge like this. However, he couldn't chew his way out of this one as George had done. And he had a good hunch Georgiana wouldn't come to his rescue either.

But she was lying about the ledgers, he was sure of it. If there was something Edward could spot without fail, it was a liar. On the other hand, calling her out wouldn't do him any favors. For some reason, Miss Georgiana could barely tolerate him. Strategically speaking, Edward should take her side—even though Spence had a point. She really did need to stop writing to Americans. Lord knew what she might learn from those backward yokels.

Edward took another route, wading around the familial waters carefully. "The lady sounds like she reads Dickens, which surprises me. I thought she only had a passion for all Sir Walter Scott's knights and ladies fair."

That got her attention. Georgiana twisted in her seat away from her father to finally meet Edward squarely in the eye, lightning all but flashing from her large green orbs. His touch had not been so deft after all.

They held each other's gaze for long seconds, a galvanizing current humming between them. He could tell she didn't want to engage. She clamped her straight teeth together a few times, widening her full lips into an illusion of a smile, as if willing herself to stand down. Luckily for Edward, he found most people couldn't stay calm around him. He didn't know if it was his delivery or what he said (probably both), but he tended to make people want to argue.

"Perhaps the *marquess*," she said, spitting out the word like milk gone bad, "doesn't realize that women are multifaceted things. We can read Dickens *and* Sir Walter Scott. We can champion causes for the poor, aid our workers, and still enjoy fantasy tales. The world is changing at a breakneck pace. Is it so wrong for people to want an escape?"

"Do you?" he asked.

Her gemstone eyes narrowed above her long nose, the only feature she shared with her father. The rest of her was short and full, round in all the right places. "Right now, yes indeed."

George snickered across the table, breaking them from their moment.

Well, Edward thought, that didn't go over quite as he'd planned. How in the world was he supposed to work on his wooing when the bloody woman wouldn't allow him to woo in the first place?

It certainly didn't help that all he had to do was look at her and be transported back to their meeting in the park. His traitorous memory had taken on a life of its own, saturating the fateful moment with a grand, dramatic flourish. In his mind's eye, the scene now included booming thunder and lightning charging across the sky, electrifying their interaction. Georgiana no longer wore a bonnet, and her light brown hair was unbound and wild, plastered to her rain-spackled skin, her chest heaving and bursting from the raw energy of nature.

And when she finally spoke to him—entrancing him with the sultry, husky tones of her low voice—it was like swimming naked in a pool of soft corduroy. Every word she uttered felt like her tongue was rasping against his skin. It was the most erotic thing he'd ever heard, and Edward wanted more of it.

Shifting in his seat, he surreptitiously rearranged himself while he listened to Mrs. Spence attempt to change the subject and tell an extraordinarily boring story about some Greek tragedy she'd attended last week at the theater. Beth Spence wasn't much of a storyteller, and the tale lost Edward's interest within seconds.

Large-boned and abnormally tall for a woman, she had a pleasant countenance and soft features, and wore her hair in the same no-nonsense, sleek style as her daughter, with braids at the temples wrapping behind to circle the neat bun at the base of the neck. No curls for the Spence women—nothing framed their faces other than thick eyebrows and forthright emerald eyes.

Sneaking a glance at Georgiana's hair, Edward wondered at its length. It appeared rather thick. Would it reach her waist? Her hips? His fingertips twitched at the thought of touching the hidden tendrils.

"What do you think about that, Marlborough?" he heard Spence ask.

Edward dropped his knife, and the heavy silver pinged off the delicate china.

"My apologies," he said to Mrs. Spence, who gave him another of her bland smiles. He could burn down the house and she'd still give him one of those blithe looks. Such was the life of a marquess who dined with the middle class. "What was that, Spence? I missed the question."

"Oh, Mrs. Spence was just telling us that she saw Camoy at dinner before the theater, and he led the line into the dining room—ahead of Lord Burrell! Can you believe that? I wish I could have seen Burrell's face. Ever since Camoy won his case in the House of Lords, everything has been upside down."

Edward tried to join in with the polite laughter, but he'd never had much patience for the rule-following hierarchy that nipped at the *ton*'s elegant heels. As far as he was concerned, Camoy had every right to be in any part of the line. The man had just fought a long and contentious battle to prove a three-hundred-year-old title in abeyance belonged to him, and the audacious bastard had actually won.

Long-forgotten peerages were all the rage at the moment. Though for every Camoy, there were a thousand other poor sods who were wrecking their fortunes paying solicitors, heralds, and scam artists to investigate their family lines, attempting to find a connection to a title. That was the true travesty, not who got to walk into dinner first.

Clearly, Spence didn't agree. His bushy eyebrows pulled together. "I don't care if he is a baron now. He's still a textile merchant, just like me. But I suppose there will be no living with him," he grumbled, taking his aggression out on his pheasant. "Every fool with a copy of *Debrett's* and a French-sounding name will be trying for the same bit of luck."

Edward opened his mouth to mutter some innocuous response, but Georgiana beat him to it.

"Why are they fools?" she asked, her thick, low voice yet again causing his chest to crackle like burned sugar. "Isn't that what you and all your friends want now that you've conquered the financial world? A title?

Edward had to hand it to the girl. When she found a weakness in someone—namely her father—she made it count. And she didn't let up.

"Didn't Grandfather say we held a distant relationship to the de Ponce family in Suffolk?"

"The ramblings of an old man, nothing more," Spence countered. "I told you not to listen to him." He chewed around a polite smile, but his eyes said something completely different, something more along the lines of: *Just wait until we're alone.* "But I will allow that you are right. Everyone wants a title. It's the high-hanging fruit, closest to the sun, free of dirt and blemishes. But I want to get it the right way." He lifted his fork to Edward, who couldn't help but wince. The Spences didn't put much stock in subtlety. "I want a title that doesn't have to be argued in Parliament. A title gained from a solid marriage is just fine for me."

Georgiana scooted to the edge of her seat as if readying for battle. Because she was looking down the table away from Edward again, he got a lovely view of her graceful neck, the long tendons branching along her healthy skin like sea-swept coral. He had an unholy desire to trace them with his tongue.

"But they aren't *all* foolish, are they?" she continued. "Wasn't Mr. Vaux able to claim an old peerage last year, and Mr. Braye the year before that?"

Spence shrugged. "They are exceptions, lucky like Camoy." He set his forearms on the table, leaning over his plate toward his argumentative daughter. "You want to know what I really find distasteful about all of this?" He didn't wait for Georgiana to respond. "*The money.* I work long and I work hard, and I've done it to pull my family up to a level of gentility I never could have imagined. It's distasteful for me to see others waste theirs so easily, all for a silly dream."

"But as we've seen, they're not all silly dreams—"

"Do you know how many heralds and solicitors are being employed right now to substantiate these claims?" Spence cut in. "Thousands. For every one person that can prove his line, hundreds of others are turned away. And yet these fools keep paying, more and more money, to find something that simply isn't there. It's a gamble. And Braye might be a baron now, as you've politely pointed out, but he spent his entire savings arguing his case. I heard he even squandered his daughters' dowries just to get that measly title. He's left with nothing, just a family crest that can barely buy him dinner."

"That's a very good point," Georgiana bit back dryly. "A poor lord..." She craned her neck to smile sweetly at Edward. Her full cheeks, her wicked, rose-tinted mouth...they almost distracted him from the blow he sensed was coming. "Who would ever want one of those?"

The air fled the room.

If it hadn't been at his expense, Edward would have appreciated that she'd gone for the kill. However, as the comment was meant to embarrass him, all he wanted to do was wring the little neck that moments ago he'd only dreamed of licking.

LORD EDWARD WANTED to strangle her. Sure, he was smiling easily enough, but his jaw was tense, his teeth hidden behind a grim line of thin lips. And his eyes...his eyes were as black as ashes. The only thing that kept Georgiana from fleeing was that the proper lord wouldn't dare buck his manners and kill her at the dinner table. It would disappoint the fawning commoners, and her mother would undoubtedly scream if anyone got blood on the linens.

Acknowledging her safety, Georgiana goaded him further. "Don't you agree, my lord?" she asked. Up until now, she had stayed quiet and docile whenever he visited—boring. But, apparently, that hadn't done the trick to turn him off. She was running out of time. Let him see the real her. Despite the ridiculous display of her parents—the hoops they jumped through to make the marquess feel comfortable—Georgiana was determined Edward know her true feelings in this farce of a courting.

By the looks of it—the tight planes of his face, the barely-there, infinitesimal intake of breath, the gripping of his long fingers around the stem of his wine glass...she was hitting her mark.

But ever the spoiler of her fun, Edward smothered his emotional fire like the repressed peer he was. Something clicked in his head. A lever was pulled, and forced animation returned to the monster.

"I heartily agree, Miss Spence," he said softly, menacingly, inching his head toward her as if they were enjoying an intimate conversation. "But why stop there? I find most lords, wealthy or not, are quite useless."

Georgiana hid her surprise at his answer; her parents' titters filled the clumsy atmosphere. They wouldn't dare argue with him, even though she knew they disagreed with him down to the marrow of their social-climbing bones. What would come of their world if they didn't have lords and ladies to aspire to?

Edward continued to hold her gaze a heated moment longer,

his features so contained and brooding she almost worried that, given the chance, he would absorb her altogether—almost. Then he broke the connection, shooting her a lazy smile before returning to his food, sighing through a bite as if he hadn't eaten a decent meal in months. By the hollowness in his cheeks, the bruised shadows under his opal eyes, she wondered if he had.

"Though I do find it interesting that someone who loves reading—what did you call them? Adventure tales?—about knights and ladies should turn her nose down at the aristocracy so decidedly," he drawled. "Another part of your multifaceted sex, I suppose?"

Georgiana contained her sneer. "I don't turn my nose down at the aristocracy. I only said we all need an escape from time to time. Besides, people have flaws, idiosyncrasies. I am no different. I daresay even you have some."

Edward patted his pockets and made a show of searching inside his crisp dinner jacket. "I haven't found any yet. Maybe you can help me look around sometime."

He thought he was being cute. He was *not* cute. Although her stomach did feel like it was full of cream in the process of being whipped.

"What do you think of the young queen?" her mother blurted, no doubt hoping to defuse the considerable tension in the room. "They say she's been heartbroken ever since Grand Duke Alexander Nikolaevich left last month. Can you imagine it? The queen marrying the heir to the Russian throne? I simply can't. I just can't."

"Why ever not?" Georgiana asked, dismissing Edward. "By all accounts, he was handsome and most attentive to her."

Edward scoffed, tearing into his bread. "Everyone's attentive to a queen, especially an unmarried one. She'll marry that German cousin of hers. Her family has planned it for years."

Georgiana continued, blatantly ignoring him. "I, for one, appreciate the fact that the queen isn't jumping into marriage just because *others* think she should. She's taking her time, waiting for her soul mate."

"Quite right, Miss Georgiana," George said, issuing her an encouraging nod. "Quite right."

Sweet George. Where would she be without him?

But his amiability was ruined by another scoff. "Soul mate, ha!" Edward muttered, making sure Georgiana was the only one who could hear him. Years of good breeding had helped perfect the art of hiding rudeness and doling it out to the correct person as efficiently and pointedly as playing cards.

Georgiana lifted her chin. "She's a shining example to the women of this country that they needn't just"—she rolled the word around her mouth like a piece of gristly meat—"*settle* just because society *or family* dictates it. We deserve better, and it's about time men realize that."

That proved to be too much. Edward sliced her with an incredulous look. "And what is 'better'? What does that mean, exactly?"

Georgiana squelched the urge to shoot back *anything other than you,* instead simply replying, "Love."

"Love." Edward dropped the word like the hand of a leper.

"Yes. Love. Ever heard of it? It's an old emotion, written about in many books if you deigned to read anything other than the *Farmer's Almanac.*"

George tittered in his hand performatively, not trying to hide his giant smile at all.

Her father placed his napkin on the table, indicating dinner was over. "Now, Georgiana—"

Edward threw up a palm, warding him off. "Please, Spence, I'm intrigued. I absolutely have to hear this. Continue, Georgiana. The *Farmer's Almanac* is a tantalizing read, by the way."

Something tugged at her chest. Had he ever said her name before? So informally? She expected bile to rise in the back of her throat, but the passage stayed clear.

"I know it's not fashionable in certain circles, such as your own," Georgiana began, "but women require more than jewels and carriages and titles. Love, passion, purpose...those are the ingredients we need to be...filled."

That slow, lazy smile returned, quirking up suggestively, though she wasn't sure what he was suggesting. "Filled?"

"Yes," she squeaked. She'd obviously meant to say *fulfilled*, but she couldn't back down now. "Filled."

"Oh, Georgiana..." her mother breathed, waving her napkin in her face like she was about to be overcome with the vapors. "This is not proper conversation."

"You brought it up!"

"I did no such thing!"

"Stop stalling," Edward interrupted, holding back a grin. Was he actually amused? By them? By their crude middle-classness? Georgiana hardly thought he could be amused by anything other than his growing bank account. He ticked the items off his fingers. "According to you, women want passion and love and purpose. Fine. But what about stability, family, and society? Do those virtues no longer count?"

Georgiana straightened her spine. He was obviously talking about all he had to offer—his title and position, nothing else. "Of course they do—"

"But just not as highly?"

"No, I don't think so. Perhaps not at first, anyway."

He shook his head, allowing his grin to run free.

"Are you laughing at me?" she asked.

"Yes."

"Why?"

"Because you're spoiled. You've wanted for nothing your entire life. Don't eat for a week and then tell me what you'd want more, excitement or a piece of bread, the *stability* of food on your table at every meal."

Georgiana didn't need time to respond, and she surely didn't need a week. "If I had to choose between you, my lord, and a piece of bread, I would always pick the bread."

"Ah-ha!

"Ah-ha, what?"

"You proved my point," he said, smugly leaning back in his chair. "You'd take the stability of bread."

Georgiana's nose itched from the laughter she was holding in. "I've proved nothing.

"And why is that?"

"Because, *my lord*," Georgiana answered, "between you and the bread, the bread *is* the exciting option."

CHAPTER FOUR

"HELLO, FAMILY," GEORGIANA sang, sailing into the dining room the following morning. As usual, the other members of the family were already seated and halfway through their breakfasts.

"Everyone hears the same bell, Georgiana," her father said from behind his newspaper, an edge of warning in his voice. "Why is it you are the only one who doesn't listen to it and come down on time?"

Georgiana halted in front of the mahogany sideboard on the far wall, taking stock of the enormity of its contents. Feeling fresh and happy for the first time in weeks, she loaded her plate with toast, bacon, and kippers before sitting across from her two brothers. Though not twins, Jasper and William, ten and nine respectively, were mirror images of their father, with their blond hair, diminutive features, and short legs. However, that never stopped them from causing giant mischief. What they lacked in height, they more than made up for in reckless imagination.

"I was recuperating from last night, Father. I needed my rest," Georgiana answered the front page of the *Morning Post*. "Besides, it's practically criminal the time you make us wake up."

Robert Spence expected the family to eat with him every morning on his schedule. Fashionable London didn't break its fast until around ten o'clock, but Robert tried to be out of the house and at his office way before then. In a compromise with his wife, he agreed to breakfast at nine, though he would have preferred it much earlier.

Luckily for all, conversation wasn't usually expected at the early hour. Georgiana's father had no qualms about reading his newspaper at the table, sharing sections with his children while his wife balanced her ledgers at the other end. The Spence family might be climbing the ladder of respectability, but middle-class habits died hard.

Robert Spence appeared to be in a talkative mood this morning, however. After a few minutes of appreciated silence, the newspaper rustled in his hands, as if he'd only then apprehended what his daughter had said. "Recuperating? Ha! It's the marquess that should be sleeping in. He'll wear the lashes of your tongue on his back for the next fortnight."

Georgiana pulled a face at her smirking brothers. *Honestly, the histrionics.* "I'm sure the marquess is just fine. No doubt he spent the night in some gaming hall drinking his money and feelings away." She cocked her head, brow comically furrowed. "Oh, wait, he doesn't have any money. Well, I'm sure he spent someone else's."

Her mother peeked up from her pages. "That doesn't sound like Lord Edward at all."

"Quite right, Mrs. Spence," said her husband. "Lord Edward is a man of resolve and vision—"

"You're only saying that because he's a peer. Lord Edward is an arrogant bore," Georgiana said, buttering her toast with unbecoming gusto. "I'm sure you don't agree, but I'm glad we won't have to see him anymore."

Finally lowering the paper, her father stared at her, freshly shaven and bewildered. His long nose twitched. "Why would you say that?"

Georgiana took a confident bite of her bread. "That I'm glad?"

"No," her father said. "That he won't be visiting us."

"Oh." She shrugged. "He left quite in a hurry last night, rushing through dessert. He was obviously ready to be away from us. I think I finally got it into that thick skull that we won't suit."

Her father's gaze narrowed, and he contemplated her with an odd look, making the back of Georgiana's neck itch.

"What?" she asked.

He sniffed. "Do you really think your acting like a shrew for a night would deter a man in need of a fortune?"

Georgiana's stomach dropped. She felt like she was walking down the stairs and had missed the last step, leaving her off balance and discombobulated. "Didn't it?"

Robert sniffed again, and Georgiana watched helplessly as her parents looked at one another with matching raised brows. They shared a pregnant pause before unloading into jabbering cackles.

"Why are you laughing at me?" Georgiana cried as the boys joined in on the fun. Even if they were natural allies against their parents, Jasper and William never missed a moment to torment their sister.

Robert wiped a tear from under his eye.

"Whatever it is, it can't be that funny," Georgiana sulked, slumping back in her chair.

The laughter died down, and her father heaved a deep breath, his face abnormally red. "Was that what you were trying to do last night? Scare him off? I might not know Lord Edward as well as I would like, but he's made of sterner stuff than that."

"My sweet, innocent girl," her mother purred patronizingly.

"But...but..." Georgiana fought to find the words. "He doesn't like me. It's obvious."

Her mother appeared equally confused. "What does liking your fiancée have to do with anything?"

Georgiana could feel her emotions run all over the place, making a goopy mess like a cracked egg. Why were they acting like her future was a comedy? They were treating her like a child who didn't know her own mind. "Don't you want me to be happy?" she implored, hoping to pull at familial heartstrings.

Her mother returned a soft smile—though it was still too condescending for her daughter's taste. "My love, of course we want you to be happy. How could you ask such a question?"

"Then why won't you trust me to marry someone of my own choice? I've told you, I don't want a stuffy peer. You got to marry for love. Why won't you let me?"

Her parents gave each other another look and broke out into gales of laughter once more. Georgiana gritted her teeth, wondering how long she'd have to sit through this caricature of family bonding.

"I couldn't stand your father," her mother choked out through hiccups. "He always talked with his mouth open and smelled like a factory. It was utterly grotesque."

The opposite of affronted, Robert Spence smiled at his wife as if charmed by the memory. "And this one," he said, pointing down the table. "I worked for her father, and he promised me his business if I married her. I thought she was an amazon with her immense height and broad shoulders. I was afraid she'd crush me if we embraced."

"Oh, don't say that." Beth giggled. "You couldn't wait to get me in your arms."

"I couldn't wait for you to pass on that height to our children."

At that moment, they turned to the boys, and Robert's laughter died as softly as a morning glory as he viewed his tiny sons.

"Give it time, Mr. Spence," Beth said stoically, reading her husband's troubled mind. "They'll grow."

"Right you are, Mrs. Spence. Right you are."

"Excuse me," Georgiana said, slapping her palm on the table. "Can you please get back to the matter at hand?

"And that is?" her father replied.

She sucked in as much breath as her tight corset would allow. "Lord Edward and me. More importantly, how there isn't going to be a Lord Edward and me."

"Oh." Robert picked up his newspaper, again blocking his

torso from view. "That reminds me. Before he left last night, he asked to escort you to the knights' practice this afternoon."

"But I'm going with Minnie and her mother!"

"Not anymore you're not. You need to make up for your behavior last night. Maybe now that you know he won't be put off by those ridiculous displays, you'll show him that you can actually be a tolerable person."

Georgiana's head fell, her face coming within inches of her buttered bread. She hated whining, absolutely hated it, but there was a time and place for everything. "It's not fair. Why are you so stuck on Lord Edward? I'm adorable. I'm sweet—when I want to be. George certainly thinks so."

Jasper choked on his milky tea.

"Are you really talking about yourself?" William asked, knocking his brother in the back. "Because that doesn't sound like you at all."

Her father dropped the newspaper back to the table. "George? Why are we talking about George?" he said with a frown, desperately trying to glare manners into his sons. "He's in no position to marry; besides, he's not good enough for you."

"George is more than good enough!" Georgiana railed. "You must think so as well, since he does everything for you!"

"He's my employee! He's supposed to do things for me. Has he made any advances on you?" her father asked, scaring her with his intensity. "The boy is brilliant, but I thought he knew his place. If he's made any untoward—"

"No, no," she said, hoping she wasn't getting the young man in trouble. "George has never acted improperly in any way. He has always been the perfect gentleman." Georgiana didn't even know why she brought him up to begin with. She supposed she was just making a point, but it was unfair to drag George into the conversation; she'd never looked at him as anything more than a friend.

Beth *tsked* from her end of the table. "He can't afford *not* to be a gentleman."

"So it's a peer or nothing at all, is that it?" Georgiana asked, shocked by her parents' snobbery. "I had no idea you were so repelled by your own class—"

"Now that's enough, Georgiana—" her father started.

"—that you would sell me to a man who wants to sink my dowry in *manure*. And he'll do it badly. You know those peers don't have a head for business. They spend and gamble their money away, and he will be no different. I want a man who will work to better himself, not use me to support his lavish lifestyle. Do you have any idea how embarrassing that is?"

"Embarrassing?" Robert's voice whipped out so harshly it even wiped the smile off the boys' faces. "He's industrious. He's forward-thinking. He's hardworking. If ten other peers came to me asking for your hand, I'd still choose him."

"Please..." Georgiana said. "You're just saying that because no one else will have him."

"No, it's true," her father insisted. "Yes, perhaps his manners are a little staid. Perhaps he doesn't smile at you as much as you'd like or laugh at your little witticisms like some of the other sycophantic men of your acquaintance—like George. But I know a good investment when I see him, and Lord Edward is a good investment. More importantly, his mine is a good investment."

Too overcome by the cage she could feel building around her, Georgiana couldn't take the snickers that had started on the other side of the table. Before she could stop herself, she picked up a piece of her bread and threw it across, striking her youngest brother square in the chest. William grabbed the morsel and pitched it into his maw.

"Boys!" Beth said. "If you can't behave like gentlemen then you can go back to the nursery."

"That's the problem, Mother," Georgiana cried. "They'll never be gentlemen. It doesn't matter how rich or high they marry; their children will never give Father what he wants—a title. Which leaves little old me to be your sacrificial lamb and bring respectability to the family." She scowled at the two.

"Thank you ever so much."

"Not at all, dear sister," William replied with a rascally grin.

"Some of us have all the luck," Jasper piped in. "Or, in your case, none at all."

With a groan, Robert tossed his newspaper in the middle of the table, just inches away from Georgiana's plate, giving her a healthy view of the morning's headlines. Just as she'd expected, another sensational story about the Eglinton Tournament ran across the top. Though she was still furious, the headline piqued her interest, and she pulled the paper in front of her so she could read it better. It featured Lord Charles. Georgiana had never spoken to the man but had seen him look charmingly aloof from across a few ballrooms. Despite his being an earl, he always impressed her with his behavior, always dancing with whatever girl was thrown at him—and pushy mothers threw a great many girls in his direction. Whatever accolades the writers gave him were surely justified. Lord Charles was a true gentleman, as pleasing of character as he was in figure.

"...I don't understand why you'd think she has no luck," her father droned on. "Georgiana is the epitome of luck. She will be a marchioness. She will dine with the queen. And what will you two have?"

William smiled, betraying a mouthful of eggs. "Boatloads of your money?"

Jasper guffawed, spraying herring over his plate. "Contentment and happiness?"

Their father waved his teacup in his sons' direction. "And what is money or happiness when you could have history, boys? Answer me that."

They couldn't. Literally. Jasper and William had stuffed their mouths again, and their mother was watching much too closely for them to try to respond. Instead, they gulped, flushing their food down their gullets.

Georgiana sighed, directing her father's attention back to her. "Even poor families have history, Father."

"Yes, my love, but not the right kind." He fluttered his fingers, indicating he wanted the newspaper back, but Georgiana pretended not to see. The article didn't have anything new to tell; however, it was better than nothing. "Honestly, darling," he continued, softening his voice, "I don't understand why you are staying so hardheaded about this. I know you're reading the Eglinton article. Can't you see I'm trying to give that to you? You could join one of those illustrious families! Do you think I would press this so hard if I didn't think it was the best for you?"

"You mean the best for you," she sulked.

"What was that?"

"Nothing."

Georgiana stared at the page, at all the words cramming together into one large black-and-white blob. Somewhere deep down, she knew her father thought he was doing right by her. It was hard to stay angry at him when he truly believed he was doing the decent thing. But his decisions betrayed his ignorance because he didn't know her. That was what hurt the most—not his ambitious plans, but the fact that he thought he was acting in her interest, and nothing could be further from the truth. One didn't become as successful as Robert Spence without having a dominant personality. When he wanted something, he put his nose to the grindstone and got it. And he wanted his grandchildren to be peers. It was that simple.

"Do you really think I'm interested in the tournament because of the lineages and families?" Georgiana asked.

"Of course," he answered gruffly. "Aren't you?"

"Maybe a little," Georgiana said. "But it's more than that." Her fingers roved delicately over Lord Charles's name in the small print. "It's the passion and the romance, the love that's invested in the time period. It's...it's..." She wasn't sure what it was. But she could *feel* it. She could sense it sizzle just underneath her skin, leaving her heated and flushed like a geyser ready to blow. It was emotion. No thought, just pure feeling. A far-off time when people weren't so hemmed in by insurmountable conditions. A life could change its course at any minute. Possibilities weren't endless, but they were at least available to the man or woman who had the courage to snatch them. But how could she explain all that to a man who made buttons for a living?

"It's make-believe," her father said gently, fluffing out his fingers again. With a harsh exhale, Georgiana tossed the papers back into his waiting hand. "Life isn't like your little storybooks. I'm going to give you the real thing. All you need to do is accept it. A title is real. Happiness and love are a state of mind, nothing more, nothing less. You can choose to be happy—it's as easy as that."

Georgiana slumped back in her seat, her corset not letting her slouch as much as her irritation wanted her to. She was just about to give up and quit the room when a servant entered with a single letter on a silver tray.

"This just came for you, Miss Georgiana," Peter said, coming to her side.

Georgiana's spine shot as straight as a lightning rod, and she snatched at the letter.

"Who is it from, dearest?" her mother asked.

Georgiana unfolded the paper and read the contents, pure joy pulsing through her blood. Her eyes ripped through the lines. She couldn't believe it. She hadn't received a letter in so long that she'd almost given up hope in her plan.

She remembered her mother had asked her something. "Oh, it's from Minnie. Her father finally found her tickets for the tournament. She's positively delirious with joy." Georgiana never knew she could lie so well. The second her mouth opened, the words just flew out, ready and willing.

"Oh, how lovely," her mother replied, back to her ledgers.

After reading it for a second time, Georgiana folded the letter tightly, holding it securely in her palm. This letter was for no one's eyes but her own. "She's having a seamstress come over today and get started on gowns for the events. Minnie's desperate to look like Anne Boleyn for the ball. Can I...call to watch?"

"Of course, dear."

Georgiana's heart beat so hard, it might have broken a rib. *Good.* She could be out of the house half the day with no one wondering about her.

She stood up from the table. "I should be going, then. Minnie will want to drown me in brocades as soon as she can."

"Take the carriage," her father said. "I don't want you late for Lord Edward when he comes."

Ugh, she'd forgotten. "Must I really? You know how special this is to me. He'll ruin it. He doesn't even care about the tournament! Didn't you hear him complain about it? He said the tournament is crowded with silly dandies who have nothing better to do than play dress-up like little girls and stick each other with the blunt ends of sticks."

"He has a point." Her father chuckled. "And it doesn't matter if he doesn't care about the tournament—he cares about you."

Georgiana groaned. "Father, please. We all know that isn't true."

He shifted in his seat. "Well, it would be true if you spent time with the man. Just be the sweet, amiable girl I know you are. He's trying. Give him a chance."

"I will try, Father," Georgiana lied, knowing full well she would treat Lord Edward with the same uncomfortable indifference he treated her. But her father didn't have to know that, nor did he have to know about the brilliant plan folded up in her palm.

Soon enough, all his dreams would come true, and it would be because of her. Then he would be proud, and it would have nothing to do with who she married. He'd forgive his daughter her impertinence then.

"Every word that comes out of my mouth will be as harmless as a snowflake. I'll be the perfect lady you want me to be."

CHAPTER FIVE

"YOU PERNICIOUS SNAKE," Georgiana seethed across the filthy table at the Coat of Arms Tavern. "How dare you charge me more money! I thought we had a deal."

No one batted an eye at the outburst. It being late morning, the tavern was full of men grabbing a quick pint before work and men grabbing a quick pint after, as well as the tired women who catered to them all, who weren't special enough for day or night shifts.

As far as drinking establishments went, it was one of the nicer ones Georgiana had slipped away to out of her parents' watchful eyes. No doubt trying for respectability, the owners had papered the ceiling with an economical lincrusta relief, and the Arabic tile floors were mopped enough for her shoes not to stick. The stained-glass windows provided a nice touch, giving the place a penitent vibe, though Georgiana was quite certain most of the frequenters weren't regular churchgoers.

The reason for her visit—Allan J. Prichard (pernicious snake and *ex*-herald)—reclined in his seat, his mouth splitting into a smarmy smile. "Oof, those aren't the words of a lady, are they? Of course, you aren't one yet, but I hear you will be one soon— unless you get stingy on me now."

Georgiana was getting quite the education today. First from her parents, and now from this repugnant ne'er-do-well. She was learning that knights in shining armor came in all shapes and sizes, and nowhere was that more evident than Prichard. For instance, the perfume he'd showered himself with acted as more of a shield than any standard-issue steel breastplate, and if his face glistened, it had more to do with his oily glands than his heroic personality. But he was helping when others wouldn't. For a fee. An *astronomical* fee that kept getting larger the more they met.

"Besides, isn't your father one of those wealthy business-men?" he continued. "I'm sure he's taught you that deals change all the time. One has to be malleable. One has to…renegotiate."

Georgiana had also learned that she didn't have to like her knight in shining armor. In fact, she downright loathed him. Unfortunately, beggars could not be choosers.

Recapturing her composure, she fixed her horseshoe-shaped poke bonnet further forward on her head. The last thing she needed was to be recognized sitting across from Prichard, and screaming at him, no less. The chances were slim, since his letter had asked her to meet him near Heralds' College on the far side of the city, but Georgiana still couldn't take any chances.

She was all out of them. She'd taken her first—and most questionable—chance when she hired Prichard a month ago to dig into her family's history. He wasn't her original choice of herald, to say the least, but he'd caught her at a low moment. Like most enterprising men, he'd been at the right place at the right time and reaped the benefits of a woman at her most desperate.

Georgiana had started that day full of hope and vigor and gone to Heralds' College to retain an active office of arms to inquire into a particular barony of writ that had fallen into abeyance over two hundred years ago. It had once belonged to an old Norman family, de Ponce, who had lived in the same area of Suffolk as her father's family for generations. To Georgiana, the little information she'd obtained from papers in her attic and the stories from her grandfather—along with a healthy dose of wishful thinking—was enough to send her on this chase to dig a little bit more, despite what her father thought. Unfortunately, the men at the college had not agreed. They'd told her they would be more than happy to look into the matter for her; she only had to come back with her husband or father so the heralds could speak with them instead.

Georgiana could only imagine how she'd looked to Prichard after leaving the college. At that serendipitous moment, he'd been exiting the tavern across the street with a healthy ale stain on his jacket, a wobble in his step, and a talent for smelling out despondent women. Teary-eyed and horribly distraught, Georgiana had been primed for the picking and would have agreed to most anything. And she had.

That wasn't to say Allan J. Prichard wasn't a real herald, or, at least, had been one before he was thrown out of the college. Though he never told her why *exactly*, Georgiana had her hunches.

To keep from touching the tacky tabletop, she placed her gloved hands demurely in her lap and tried again. "We both know I'm not stingy. You sent me a letter saying you had information for me. And now I realize you only want more payment. I told you last time, I have nothing left. I've given you all my pin money. You said it was more than enough."

Prichard fixed a watery eye on Georgiana, no doubt sizing her up to see if she was lying. She only wished she was. "You think I like asking a sweet young woman like you for more money?"

Georgiana pursed her lips. *Yes. Yes, I do.*

"Well, I don't," he said, pushing his stringy black hair across his bald head. "But it's not for nothing. I'm getting somewhere. I am. But you didn't give me an easy job, did you? A two-hundred-year-old title in abeyance? Not so easy to uncover."

Georgiana threw her hands up in the air, and they landed square on the grimy wood. *Disgusting.* "Then why did you take the job?"

"Because I'm good. That's why," he replied, tonguing one of his back molars. "And you've got a decent case. Better than most,

I'd say. Your grandfather wasn't spinning you some yarn. There's definitely a connection between the Pences and the de Ponces. The papers you gave me add up, but there isn't enough evidence for the Committee of Privileges. Not only do I need to prove your father's pedigree as the rightful heir, but I also have to prove the other claimants are dead. That's no walk in the park. And I can't do that here. I need to do some sniffing around in Suffolk…church records, things of that nature."

"Good," Georgiana said, slightly gratified. "So go do it!"

Prichard frowned, clearly affronted by her lack of regard. "I need money for all of that!"

"What did you do with the last payment?"

He lifted a finger for the barmaid, indicating he wanted another drink. "I need to live like everyone else."

Georgiana attempted to keep a rein on her temper. She wondered how much of her money had been flushed down his throat in establishments such as this one.

The maid came quickly, placing a frothy mug of ale on the table and sloshing a bit over the sides, not bothering to clean up the mess. No wonder the wood was so sticky…

Prichard took a long drink, ending with a drawn-out "Aah, that hits the spot" before wiping his mouth with his jacket sleeve. "Now, there's something else we need to talk about," he said, visibly more relaxed now that he'd had his liquid. "What do you want me to do if I get there and find nothing?"

Georgiana blinked, unsure of what he was truly asking. She fingered the lace cuffs at her wrists. "I suppose then that's the end. If you don't find anything, then there's nothing my father can present to the committee."

"Not so fast, not so fast," Prichard said, dropping his voice. "Just because you don't find something doesn't mean you don't find nothing. Your case is real. I can feel it. Your father is the true heir to the de Ponce barony."

Forgetting where she was, whom she was with, and how she was raised, Georgiana reflected his position, leaning closer. "You really think so?"

He nodded almost imperceptibly, like a predator who'd finally found his prey. "I'm the best, I tell you. And I know a winner when I see one. However"—his eyes flickered from side to side—"sometimes we heralds need to…pad the truth."

"Pad the truth?"

"Exactly. I knew you'd understand."

"I'm afraid I don't understand any of this."

Prichard took another long drink, ending with the same sloppy noises. "It means I might need to *invent* some paperwork in order to make your case airtight."

"Invent?" Georgiana hoped she would stop repeating the man soon, but she was having a difficult time finding words of her own.

"Right. Invent. Remake some of the official documents."

"Isn't that lying?"

"It's not lying if they once existed. And I think they once did."

"But how do you know?" she asked.

"I know."

"But how do you know?"

"*I know.*"

Georgiana shifted away from the table, settling her spine against her chair. When something didn't feel right, it usually wasn't. Georgiana felt as slimy as Prichard's hair.

"No," she said, shaking her head, suddenly concluding why Allan J. Prichard was an *ex*-herald. "You are talking about forging, and I won't condone it. Didn't Brydges try something similar last year? The Committee of Privileges saw right through him. It was in all the papers."

Prichard scratched his bristly chin with the back of his hand. "You read too much," he muttered.

If she had a pound for every time she heard that… Georgiana pulled her reticule closer to her chest, ready to leave. "I'm afraid we will have to do this honorably. If you can't provide me with the correct information, then I'm afraid we are done here."

He lashed out, grabbing her forearm before she could lift herself to her feet. She gasped, but his hold only intensified, imprinting her skin all the way through her muslin. Georgiana looked around the room; no one noticed the altercation, all too busy in conversation or lost in the bottom of their cups.

"Don't touch me," Georgiana said, ripping her arm out of his greasy hold. Absent-mindedly, she rubbed at the spot.

"I didn't mean to hurt you," Prichard said, without a hint of apology in his voice. "We just aren't finished yet."

"I think we are."

He leveled her with a cold stare. "The job ain't done yet. You haven't paid up."

Through all her layers and petticoats, Georgiana searched inward and found her backbone. "I am not paying for false documents."

"Fine. Fine. No false documents." He grinned mirthlessly. "Only the real thing for the Queen of Coprolites."

Georgiana's mouth would have hit the floor if she hadn't regained her senses at the last second. "What did you say?"

"The Queen of Coprolites. That's what they're calling you."

A team of wild horses could have run her over and Georgiana wouldn't have felt a thing, her shock was so strong. "How did you...? Who told you about that? No one knows."

Prichard's smile was so wide that she could count every yellow tooth. "I told you. I'm the best at what I do. I can find out anything."

She averted her eyes, playing with the strap of her reticule. "But there's nothing...there's nothing to know."

"Oh, I hear there is. I hear you're to be a marchioness soon." Prichard squinted at her, as if he were assessing her value. "This seems like an awful lot of trouble to go through when you're one 'I do' away from being a member of the *ton*."

"My father wants to be a member, not me."

"Ah, so you think finding him this barony will do the trick? Get him off your back while he enjoys his new title."

Georgiana shrugged, and her lungs constricted from the embarrassment. "Maybe."

"Not a bad plan," Prichard allowed. Did she hear a hint of appreciation in his voice? Did she *want* to hear it? "I don't think I'd want to be called the Queen of Coprolites either, marchioness or not. That's the thing about freedom, though…it always has a cost."

There. He'd done it, circled back to the matter at hand—money.

Georgiana sighed. "How much more do you need?"

The corners of his eyes crinkled. Prichard had her. He knew and she knew it. "Just a bit."

"I told you. I don't have anything, but I'm sure my father will pay the remainder once we tell him what we've found."

Prichard clucked his tongue. "Not good enough. I need to eat too, or do rich girls like yourself think that's only an upper-class luxury?"

Georgiana glared at him from under heavy lids. "What do you want?"

"Oh, I don't know. There has to be something you have that's worthy. Jewelry…trinkets and whatnot."

"I'm not much for jewelry."

"Come now, Miss Georgiana, don't play coy. There has to be something you value. Something you have *of* value. Don't you want to be free of that stuffy old marquess? Oh, yes, I know all about him. Hoity-toity, utterly rigid. Great big stick up his arse—excuse my words. Do you really want to be saddled with him for the rest of your life? Not a lot of laughter in that household, and you seem like a nice enough girl, a girl who wants to enjoy herself."

Yet again, Georgiana realized she hated Allan J. Prichard. He was a terrible human being—but a smart one. Because when she pulled a necklace out of her reticule, he accepted it at once, without a hint of surprise. It was almost as if he'd known it was in her bag all along.

"Oh, now she's a beauty, isn't she?" he purred, holding the elegant piece up so it could catch the light. Two giant sapphires sat in the center, separated by a bow shaped by diamonds. Garlands of sapphire-centered stars rounded out the rest of its length. "Steal this from your mother, did you?"

"No," Georgiana said. "It's mine." She shouldn't have brought it. But she'd known—just *known*—Prichard would ask for more. Men never seemed to have any compunction about doing that.

"Well, it's mine now, thank you very much," he said, slipping the necklace inside his jacket pocket. "This will do just fine. Just fine, indeed. I should be back in a couple of weeks. I'll come to you directly when I find something."

She nodded. "I'll most likely be in Scotland for the Eglinton Tournament. Send a message to the house as you did this morning. I will contact you when I return."

"But what if it's pressing?"

Georgiana sharpened her gaze, pinning the odious man to his seat. "*Do not* go to my father. You have to wait for me. I need to be the one who explains everything. He might take some convincing. He has very strong views about this sort of thing." That was putting it mildly.

"I doubt it," Prichard replied with a bitter chortle. "You'd be surprised how quickly men like your father turn when they think they have a chance at a peerage."

Georgiana gathered her things, desperate to get away from the shame of her actions. "You don't know my father. He's proud."

Prichard smirked. "Oh, I wouldn't be so sure. Proud men fall just like the rest of us, only harder."

⸎

RUNNING LATE AFTER meeting with Prichard, Georgiana had

thought to return home to ready herself for the knights' practice; however, she left the tavern so utterly dejected that she suddenly had a craving for a sympathetic face.

Minnie, as ever, didn't disappoint.

She was midway through a fitting and dressed in the beginnings of Tudor splendor, and her long, unfinished bell sleeves dragged along the carpet as she met her friend in the parlor. She reached for Georgiana's hands, pulling her past the piano, scattered chairs and stools, two large sofas, and floor-to-ceiling potted palms to sit on a dark green settee in the corner. Minnie's mother was an early fan of the modern bric-a-brac collecting and furniture coverings, and Georgiana's skirts nearly upset numerous trinkets and antimacassar as she slid through the cluttered room. The rules were relaxed where Minnie and Georgiana were concerned, and they were left to converse in private while Mrs. Carmichael entertained an older woman whom Georgiana had never met before.

"What's wrong?" Minnie asked, huddling her close. "You look positively spent."

Trying not to cry, Georgiana filled her friend in on the events of the morning with Prichard, even adding the part about the necklace that she'd used to pay for his continued services. She hadn't been lying when she told the ex-herald that she wasn't one for jewelry—she didn't have much. The necklace she'd given away had been a present from her father for her sixteenth birthday. Robert Spence had been so proud of the gift, telling all and sundry how it once belonged to some duchess or countess who had fallen on hard times.

Georgiana supposed it was beautiful, in the way that all garish gemstones were—however, it had clearly meant more to him than to her, and the depressing story of how it had fallen into his hands left a nasty taste in her mouth. Georgiana had never worn it, choosing smaller, simpler pieces instead.

Truth be told, she wouldn't miss it, but she had no idea what she would tell her parents if they asked about it. And she had no doubt they would. She only hoped Prichard would find what they were looking for before that time came. Perhaps she could even save up her pin money again and buy it back.

"My Lord, Georgie, you've been busy," Minnie said a little stiffly, betraying her hurt. Georgiana hadn't meant to keep her friend in the dark. Her involvement with Prichard had been like a wish she was too afraid to voice out loud, because then it wouldn't come true. "Why didn't you tell me any of that before? Oh no, don't cry. Please don't cry. I'm sure once you prove your case, your father will understand."

Georgiana nodded, relieved that Minnie had pushed her irritation aside. Quickly, she realized that she'd done the right thing coming to Minnie's house. It was difficult to stay upset when Minnie was so blissfully happy in her cascading, embroidered tunic. She looked like she'd climbed out of one of their favorite stories.

"I'm so sorry I didn't tell you. Sometimes I think I'm going crazy, and, perhaps, I didn't want you to know *how* crazy," Georgiana admitted. "Am I even doing the right thing? Should I just marry Lord Edward and be done with it?"

"That depends." Minnie tilted her head thoughtfully. "Do you really think your father is the heir?"

Georgiana wiped her eyes with the back of her hand, lifting her chin. "I do. I can't explain it, but I know something's there."

"Then you should see it through. It's what you want."

Georgiana laughed bitterly. "I don't know what I want anymore, but I know what's being offered to me isn't good enough. I want…I want…passion. And the excitement and the kind of love that Guinevere and Isolde and Juliet had."

Minnie scrunched up her nose. "That's all a bit dramatic, even for me."

"Maybe I am being dramatic, but I'll take that over polite comfortability any day."

"Isn't that what you would have if you married someone like your father's man, George?" Minnie asked, lowering her voice.

"You seem to talk about him a lot. I thought…maybe you were growing attached?"

Georgiana flinched. "George? We're friends." She bit her lower lip as the idea grew in her desperate mind. "On the other hand, with George, I'll always know where I stand. I could never love him—truly love him—but he would treat me with respect, as a real partner. *He* would give me a role in my father's company. Passion would come in the form of work."

"Georgie," Minnie groaned. "Please don't tell me you still think you're going into the button business. Your father lets you get away with a lot, but you know he'll never let you work for him—whether you marry George or not."

"You don't *know* that," Georgiana muttered, covering her face with her hands. "He might… Things are changing, and I have so many ideas for the people that work for us. Ideas that can really make a difference."

Minnie offered a tender smile. "I know you do, dear heart, but I don't think your father's changing fast enough for your ideas."

"The more I think of it," Georgiana said, her mind on a roll, her brow sunk low, "why do I even need a husband at all? If work is my passion and joy, what's the point of a man?"

"Work as passion and joy?" Minnie made a face. "Who are you right now? What have you done with my friend?"

Georgiana rolled her eyes, trying not to jump out of her seat. Her candle was lit. She was onto something here, whether Minnie wanted to hear it or not. "Look at the queen," she said. "She's not married, and she's the most powerful woman in the world."

Minnie regarded her dubiously. "You think you're the same as the queen now?"

"We are all queens when it comes to matters of our heart."

Minnie's hand flew to her chest. "Oh, that was lovely."

"I know!" Georgiana said, giving a mock bow. "Seriously, though. I'm not saying I'm against marriage. I just don't want to pin all my hopes on a union that results from a few heavily guarded meetings and lukewarm feelings."

"Do you think it will make a difference, marrying someone you love?" Minnie asked wistfully. "Mother says you aren't supposed to love your husband before you marry him because you don't know him enough yet. She said love grows with the marriage."

Remembering what her parents had told her earlier about their initial dismal thoughts of each other, Georgiana reached for the book lying on the nearby table. Just as she'd expected, it was another Sir Walter Scott novel, *Tales of My Landlord* featuring *The Bride of Lammermoor*. She flipped through the pages before tossing it back. "Minnie, you read the last page of every book first to make sure it has a happy ending. You hate waiting. How would you be able to accept waiting to see if you actually like your husband?"

Minnie spread her arms. "I suppose I'll be content being a lady," she answered. "I can leave my dreams in my books where they will never grow old or go astray and trust my parents to know what's best for me."

Georgiana's frown deepened. She loved her parents, but from what she'd learned this morning, it was safe to say she did not trust them when it came to her future.

"And you're forgetting something very important," Minnie went on, her eyes wandering back to the book on the table. "The queen *will* marry. Everyone says it's only a matter of time. And no doubt she will be able to balance her role as sovereign and wife. If work becomes your only passion, who will be the hero in your story?"

A corner of Georgiana's mouth curled up. She wouldn't keep this hope to herself. "Me," she replied matter-of-factly. "I will be the hero."

CHAPTER SIX

EDWARD KNOCKED ON the Spences' door at two o'clock sharp and was confronted by a panoply of elephant-like footsteps. The door swung open, and the brothers stood on the other end of the threshold, each nudging the other for prime space.

"Good afternoon, Lord Edward," Jasper said.

"Pleasure to see you again, Lord Edward," the younger one chimed in. William. Always the second to talk, but always the louder of the two. "Come for Georgiana? She isn't ready yet. She returned late, and Mother is driving herself—and all of us—mad getting her ready for you."

Edward checked his pocket watch. "There's no hurry." There actually was. Even if he had no interest in the knights, he hated the idea of not being on time.

A rustling of skirts alerted him, and he looked over the two short towheads to find Mrs. Spence descending the stairs with Georgiana trailing after her.

The first thing he noticed was that she was dry. And sullen. And uncommonly pretty with her light blue damask dress and matching bonnet. With its high neckline and long sleeves, there was nothing particularly alluring about the outfit, but now that Edward had a notion of what was underneath, he had a whole new appreciation for anything Georgiana wore.

"My lord," Mrs. Spence said demurely, with Georgiana dropping into a paltry curtsey next to her.

Edward bowed his head. He recognized there were things to say, light small talk for the mother while he guided the daughter out of the house, but his brain came up empty. He could only keep wondering what he had to do to get Georgiana to look at him. She rarely did, he realized. Her stony green eyes were always staring just over his shoulder or at his feet. He understood that was proper, the way things were done—only now he didn't want it to be how it was done with *them*.

"We should go," he said, offering his hand. After a moment's hesitation that grated on his nerves, Georgiana allowed Edward to escort her out the door. Jasper and William followed, taking turns gawking at his two bays and curricle.

"She is a sight, isn't she?" Jasper said. "Can I drive her?"

Edward frowned at the old curricle, unsure of why they thought it so special. It had been his father's vehicle, and he had always wanted a new model, though that need had fallen to the back of a very long list of more pressing matters. It had clearly seen better decades, and the black paint was chipping in spots, but it worked, and that was all that Edward could afford to care about.

It wasn't until he saw Jasper pass a tiny hand over the door that he realized the boy was gaping at the Marlborough crest. Even that was wearing off, but the vivid golds and reds were apparently still striking enough to turn heads.

Lost for words, Edward was saved when Georgiana's laugh cut like a freshly sharpened blade. "Don't be silly, Jasper. You'd have it turned over in a heartbeat."

"Would not."

"Would too," William chimed in.

"Would not!"

"Boys!" Mrs. Spence called from the door. That one word snapped their mouths closed.

Ignoring the banter, Edward handed Georgiana up to her seat, trying not to register the hollow ache he felt when he had to relinquish her hand. Settling in next to her, their thighs kissing, he readied the reins, only to notice the boys hadn't moved.

He stared down at them.

They stared right back up.

"What is it?" Edward asked.

Jasper switched on his youthful charm, his round eyes growing more innocent. "So…can I?"

Georgiana groaned. "For goodness' sake, Jasper, go inside."

The boy refused to budge. "Everyone has answered except Lord Edward. I'll wait for him, thank you very much."

"Lord Edward won't play with you."

All eyes centered on Edward. Except hers. He cleared his throat. His little sisters were hoydens, but they were nothing to rambunctious boys. He was sure his mother would tell him he used to be one, but he doubted it. Edward had always thought it best to fill any room he was in with the decorum his father inevitably lacked.

"That's not true," he said a little gruffly, feeling the hesitant press of her knee toward his. The unexpected sensation almost made him flinch as if he'd been stung by a bee. "I like to play as much as the next person." He ignored Georgiana's unladylike sound and addressed the boy. "Have you ever handled a pair before?" he asked, nodding toward the animals.

Jasper shook his head, trepidation leaching into his delicate features.

"We'll take it slow, then," Edward said.

Georgiana laughed. *At him*, he noticed. "How utterly responsible of you."

Edward gave her his full attention, causing her cheeks to flush. He liked those cheeks. Like two delicious apples. Why hadn't he noticed how full they were, how utterly kissable they were? "Responsible? Oh, you mean boring," he said, slapping his reins to get the horses started.

"I didn't say that."

Yes, but you meant it. "Well, that's another thing we'll have to take slow and steady, then."

"What?"

His lips twitched. "Your opinion of me."

Fifteen minutes later, Edward had them in the St. John's Wood neighborhood and pulled his curricle up to the large garden behind the Eyre Arms Tavern, where the knights had chosen to practice. On a hill, close to Regent's Park, the tavern's garden was a popular spot for archery and cricket, as well as for launching hot air balloons on calm afternoons.

To Edward's delight, they weren't late, though they were one of the last vehicles to find a respectable position next to the cordoned-off area left for the training. It seemed all of London—common or not—had turned up to watch them prepare for the fast-approaching tournament. And the knights did not disappoint their visitors.

Tiered benches had been erected along the lists to provide room for the onlookers, along with tents on either end for the combatants and distinguished guests. Edward thought he recognized the Duchess of Cambridge sitting in pride of place under a red and white striped canopy, heraldic banners waving gallantly around her.

The crowd couldn't have asked for more perfect weather. The sun shone brightly off the shiny armor as the knights rode around on their caparisoned horses. Playing it up for the event, heralds walked the fields, dressed in their tabards, and even the men who were enlisted to keep the crowds in check carried menacing halberds for dramatic effect. Edward hated to admit it, but the scene was rather impressive. He'd had no idea the fools could put it together so well, as it was only practice, after all.

Speaking of fools… Edward searched the field for Charles, but quickly concluded it was a lost cause. With the knights sporting their head-to-toe armor—including unyielding helmets that only left a narrow slit for them to see out of—deducing who was underneath proved quite the challenge. He was positive Charles had told him which knight he was playing, along with his heraldic symbol, but Edward couldn't remember. He had to admit that he probably hadn't been paying attention.

"Oh, look," Georgiana gushed, tipping forward in her seat to point at the field. "It's the railway knight I've read so much about. I do hope they put it in action. I want to see how it works."

Edward frowned at the mechanical contraption. The railway knight was perched on a wooden horse with wheels that had been installed to slide down a pair of grooves along the tilt for the knights to joust against.

"You know that's not a new idea," Edward responded, watching Georgiana look energetically over the lively scene. "It was invented three hundred years ago."

"Is that right?" she answered in a manner that made him question if she'd even been listening at all. "I hope no one gets hurt today."

Edward snorted. "How could anyone get hurt? The lances are blunted."

Georgiana heaved a sigh, inching farther away from him in the seat so their bodies were no longer touching. "I read John Campbell was injured during the first practice."

"The stupid man stood there and allowed someone to charge at him at full speed!"

"He told the newspapers he wanted to know what it would feel like to take a direct hit!"

Edward crossed his arms, brushing hers with his elbow. He wasn't entirely sure it wasn't on purpose. "Well, now he knows, doesn't he? What a complete idiot. I don't have to put my hand in a fire to know it's going to burn."

"No harm was done. They say he's fully recovered," Georgiana replied haughtily, clearly affronted for the silly knight.

Edward bit back a harsh retort. He was supposed to be wooing, and even he could admit he wasn't doing a very good job. If she slid any further away from him, she'd be riding on the wooden horse behind the railway knight.

After a painful silence, he tried again. "Beautiful day, isn't it?"

She made him wait for an answer but eventually relented. "Yes, very. I hope it's this nice for the main event."

"In Scotland?" Edward chuckled. "I doubt it."

"Do you have anything pleasant to say, my lord? I wonder why you asked to take me here if you knew you weren't going to enjoy the spectacle."

Spectacle. That was a good word for it. Well rehearsed or not, this nonsense he was being forced to watch was indeed a spectacle. Why on earth these grown men—these pinnacles of upper-class society—thought it would be a good idea to dress up as knights from centuries past, he had no idea. And he counted his best friend as one of them, which only proved that the gothic interest pervading the nation was insidiously prevalent and common. Perhaps if Edward had copious amounts of money at his disposal, with nothing better to do with his time, he might be out there in the middle of the field brandishing his ancestor's sword to cheers and whoops from the overly indulgent crowd.

No. Never. Even if he had all the money in the world, Edward couldn't see himself putting on such a display. Let men like his father crave that kind of attention. Let Charles have the adulation. Center stage had never been a comfortable place for him. There was always too much work to be done instead.

As if such thoughts had conjured his friend, Edward finally spotted Charles's golden hair in the middle of the field. He'd taken off his helmet and was stretching his legs back and forth, limbering up under the restriction of his ridiculously exacting costume. At least his armor was his own. Most of the men out there had spent a ridiculous sum on suits from as far away as Germany. Charles was English to the core, from a long line of Somerset earls.

Out of the corner of his eye, Edward saw Georgiana notice the handsome figure as well, her eyes firm and unwavering on the heroic vision Charles presented.

Though he couldn't understand it, he found he liked the joy she received from watching the idiots prance and play. He wouldn't call it infectious; however, a sense of calm fell over him at her innocent beguilement. Edward was self-aware enough to acknowledge that it was difficult for him to find pleasure in the day-to-day. Too focused on the future, he tended to skip over the intricate details of life. He wondered what it would be like to live like Georgiana, discovering tiny charms at unknowable moments, allowing the whims of chance to foster delight. It sounded horribly tiring, but also…pleasant, if one had the right partner to experience it with.

Perhaps her frustration with him was merited. He *was* being a churlish ass. He should say something—anything—to prove he wasn't jealous of the stupid men peacocking around, chasing after the windmills in their heads.

But when she continued to stare, refusing to look away from the field—from Charles's glistening handsomeness—Edward's sense of calm evaporated.

"You know, his own mother doesn't even like him."

Christ, that wasn't what he'd meant to say! *Come now, man, get it together!*

Georgiana jerked out of her daydreams, the pheasant feather atop her bonnet bobbing ferociously. "Lord Charles? How can you say that? Isn't he your friend?"

"My very best."

Her forehead creased, and Edward felt a need to run a finger between her eyes to smooth it over and release her anger toward him.

"You should be more courteous to your friends," she said. "If the mother is dissatisfied with her son—which I am sure she is not—then that is because she has high standards and knows he has the inner strength and fortitude to match them."

Edward thought of his own mother and wondered if the same could be said of her. Deciding it couldn't, he replied, "Actually, he goes whorin' too much and spends too many nights drunk on my floor."

"My lord!"

Christ, he hadn't meant to say that either! She might not be a lady in the truest sense of the word, but Georgiana Spence was a gently reared woman, and he was speaking to her like she were a common barmaid. Why was his mouth so out of control? Edward prided himself on his control, relied on it, but he felt no sense of pride now, only raw jealousy.

"My apologies," he mumbled. "That was uncalled for."

"Quite right," she said, turning her long, imperious nose up in the air, though she surprised him when a deep chuckle erupted from her chest. "And where are you when he's drunk on your floor?"

Edward snorted, enjoying the way dimples showed on the corners of her eyes, just above those luscious cheeks. "Usually drunk in my bed."

"At least you have some sense."

He grinned wolfishly. "Was that a compliment? I'll take it."

He turned back to the field only to laugh as Lord Maynard— who had been in the middle of performing lance exercises to the enamored crowd—fell off his horse into a pile of dung. Because of the weight of his armor, he couldn't move, and had to wait five whole minutes before Lord Gage spotted him and hauled him up to standing. For some insane reason, the crowd decided that feat was worthy of raucous applause.

"I don't think I've ever heard you genuinely laugh before," Georgiana said quietly, though not unkindly.

The smile stalled on Edward's face. "I laugh."

"Cleary." She smirked. "Though not enough, I think."

"Does one ever have enough of a good thing?"

"You can try."

"And you think I don't try?"

"I didn't say that."

But she'd meant it.

An awkward pause ensued. For a moment, Edward thought they were getting somewhere, but as always, it was one step forward, one step back with them.

"I'm sorry you had to come here today," Georgiana said in that calm reserve that made him bristle. Now that Edward had heard her giggle—*with him* and not *at him*—he found he would do almost anything to get it back.

Straightening his shoulders, Edward replied, "I'm not sorry—in fact, I actually think I'm enjoying myself."

"Please do not lie on my account. Let's not pretend. I think we're past that."

Forgetting the ostentatious display in front of them, Edward turned to Georgiana. Their knees kissed once more, and he watched an electric current of tension run up her body.

"Fine. Perhaps I'm not enjoying the show. It's difficult for me to look past the real men behind the sparkling façade. Gage had to sell two of his estates this year," Edward griped. "And yet here he is. And Culpepper...he only agreed to marry the Dalrymple girl if her father paid for his tournament expenses. Useless, the lot of them. For the life of me, I cannot understand what has you so enthralled."

He worried his confession would make her dismissive again; however, her features were loaded with pity. Edward decided he preferred anger.

"No," she said. "You wouldn't."

"Explain it to me, then," he said, a tad too harshly even to his own thinking.

Georgiana didn't seem to mind, or maybe she was just getting used to his rough manner. "It would only land on deaf ears," she said, tearing her attention away from the shiny toys on the field.

She studied him for a few heartbeats, and he used the time to lock her into a battle of wills, with her finally relenting.

"Oh, very well," she said, tilting her head up, as if searching the clear sky for a clear answer. Her expression melted into dreamy contemplation. "It's...magic."

"Magic?"

"There's just something special about those times, something simpler yet more visceral. Reputations won and lost within seconds, grand displays of affection... Men in armor and not corsets—"

"I don't wear a corset!" Though Edward certainly knew men that did.

Her lips curved. "There's a romanticism to it all—its symbolism and honor...things that seem quite lost today."

"Honor?" Edward spat. "You find these men honorable when they, quite literally, think your family is beneath them?"

Her dreamlike state vanished, replaced with a sour mien. Edward would have chided himself if he hadn't caught the emerald flash in her eyes that she tried to hide. It nearly blinded him. He absolutely had to find a way to make that flare happen without her being so disgusted with him.

"I didn't say I find *these* men particularly honorable; I am not naïve. I know what peers think about my father and his living and know it will not change anytime soon. But I can still applaud what they are doing, the hope and escape they are bringing to all these people. What they are trying to achieve. I can still get lost in the fantasy of what a knight represents. How it has nothing to do with whom you were born to be, but rather whom you were brave enough to become. Every man was in charge of his own fate. He only needed the strength and conviction to reach for it. It's a lovely sentiment, something I rather envy. What I could do if only my father would let me—" She stopped herself, her gaze falling to her lap.

Could that be it? Edward wondered. It wasn't merely the pretty horses and insipid false courage on display that kept her engaged? Could it really be the meritocracy of knighthood that held her captive? Did she long to be a female William Marshall who rose from obscurity to become one of the most powerful men in the realm?

As if Georgiana had realized she'd divulged too much, she straightened her spine, ignoring him for the field again, her wide bonnet acting as a screen between them. "And don't give yourself credit just because you are sitting here next to me. We both know you wouldn't find my company quite so palatable without my father's money, which makes you no different than them. You've made it quite clear."

Had he? Edward couldn't remember behaving so tactlessly, but then again, he hadn't exactly tried to get to know Georgiana either. Obviously, that had rankled her.

Mulling over her tepid opinion of him, Edward watched as she took out a simple embroidered handkerchief and dotted at her hairline.

He was transfixed by the square patch of linen, the way she patted it to her soft skin. Sweat—something that was vilified as much as thievery in their society—had never affected him so. He liked the fact that her body was warm. Was it the weather? Maybe. But he preferred to think it was him.

"I can be chivalrous," he groused, sotto voce.

"Ha!"

"I can," he insisted, latching on to an idea. He reached across her, his arm skimming her chest.

"What in the world are you doing?" she snapped.

Edward attempted to knock the handkerchief out of her hand, but she was too fast for him. "Drop your linen so I can pick it up," he ordered her.

Her stare could have rivaled Medusa's. "Absolutely not."

"Just drop it." Edward went for it again, and she elbowed him away.

"Will you stop? I'm not dropping my handkerchief. How would that be a symbol of chivalry, anyway? Chivalry is spontaneous. Chivalry lies at the very heart of a knight. Sportsmanship, scholarship, music…appreciation and acknowledgement of a good woman…those are only some of the interests he must excel at to earn the badge. And, above all else, a man of worth believes in something greater than himself."

If Edward was confused before, he was downright flabbergasted now. The enlightened man she was speaking about didn't exist. The only person Edward believed in was himself. Who had the time to waste on all that frivolity?

The clanking of steel brought him back to the field. *Oh, right. Them.*

"Fine," he said, retracting his arm, though he didn't move back into his own space. He liked his body against hers. He could feel her heat now through the thin slips of her muslin dress. And for some reason, it was important that she felt his. He jerked his chin at her hands, which were covered in her delicate lace gloves. "Give me your hand so I may kiss it."

Her voice could have bent steel. "Don't. Even. Try. It."

Edward threw up his arms. "How about a sonnet, then?"

An eyebrow rose. "*You* know a sonnet?"

"I went to Oxford," he explained. "They don't let red-blooded men leave without knowing how to write a sonnet, or a limerick, rather. Mine is awfully good, too. It takes a certain kind of brilliance to find a word that rhymes with China."

Was that a smile forming?

"You are incorrigible," she said.

"How? I'm trying to be chivalrous and appreciate you, and you're not letting me. What is left for me to do to win your esteem?"

Georgiana's mouth tightened; she *was* fighting a smile. She studied the lists for a long pause before arching an impish brow. "You can joust."

Edward felt like she'd punched him. "Never."

"Oh, come now," she purred, waving her elegant hand at the hoary tableau. "I know the suits are expensive, but I'm sure families like yours have plenty rotting away in their attics."

He tried to keep his humor up, but her statement effectively dashed away all levity. "No."

"Then I suppose we are at a stalemate," she said breathily, feigning disappointment. "Perhaps you could look for a damsel in distress to rescue on your way home. That might prove your mettle."

"Lord, woman, don't you see that's what I'm trying to do?

I'm trying to marry you. If that's not rescuing, I don't know what is."

Georgiana snorted. It was completely unladylike and absolutely adorable, and Edward couldn't stop himself from grinning in response.

"Lord Edward, I'm afraid you are confused," she said, her eyes dancing. "You need me; I don't need you. *You* are the damsel in distress in our situation, not me."

Ha! She was right, and Edward didn't care one bit. There were worse things than being rescued by a fair maiden. If she wanted to throw her arms around him and carry him off into the sunset, then he would be more than willing. Though something did nag at him.

"By the by," he said slowly. "Is that the reason why you're so against the match? The fact that I need you? My lack of funds and"—he chose his words carefully—"choice of industry?"

Georgiana grimaced, and Edward's stomach dropped. However, her answer wasn't what he expected. "Of course not! I am my father's daughter. I applaud ingenuity and hard work, despite your...chosen field. Although, I will admit, I did find it odd at first."

Edward held back a sigh of relief. But that only left one thing. "So, it's just me that's the problem? You have doubts in my ability."

Her pale face blossomed under her powder-blue bonnet. Edward would never point it out to her, but Miss Georgiana Spence was enjoying his company. "Yes, it seems only you are the problem." She laughed. "I've told you, we don't suit. I don't think a man raised as you were has the aptitude for business. Aristocrats play at it, but they lack true drive."

Edward gazed out into the field. "They are only good at pretending."

"Yes, I suppose they are."

"You don't know anything about how I was raised."

"You're right. I'm sorry, but that does not change my opinion."

"Your father does not share it."

Georgiana huffed. "My father is a businessman. He says pretty things to get what he wants. When he looks at you, he only sees your title, one that can be easily bought. Your business matters little to him, and he can't convince me otherwise. It's you he wants. You are a sure thing."

Edward chuckled ruefully, flashing her a roguish smile. "You're goddamned right I am."

CHAPTER SEVEN

How can he be so pleased with himself? Georgiana wondered. She'd basically just told the marquess that he had absolutely no chance of changing her mind regarding his intentions. And yet there he was settling back into his seat—sitting much too close to her—with a satisfied grin on his face as if she'd just gifted him the master key to her heart.

She would have laughed if she hadn't already laughed enough. For such a humorless man, he had an uncanny ability to amuse her. It made no sense.

Before she could think too deeply about the reason behind that, they heard a call from a few yards away. Georgiana followed the resonant voice to find Lord Charles striding over to the curricle.

"Edward, you came!" he said jovially.

If Georgiana thought he looked magnificent on the other side of the field, he was positively glorious in front of her. His armor molded to marble-like perfection against his well-formed body, and he stood in front of them as if he was born to wear it. He carried his helmet at his side, and his face was wet and ruddy under the unrelenting sun. But he looked happy and content, tired yet rejuvenated after a day's grueling and fulfilling work.

Edward, clearly, wasn't appreciating the picture as she was. He shook his head. "I told you I would."

If Charles could detect the hint of derision, he didn't let on. Rather, he smirked at Edward's self-righteous tone. "Yes, but the sight of you was so surprising to me, I thought it was a fever dream, not to be trusted. Miss Georgiana," he said, turning to her, "lovely to see you again. Are you enjoying our little performance?"

Georgiana attempted to maintain her stoicism, but there was just something about Charles, and she caught herself grinning like a simpleton. "Immensely," she replied, biting at her lower lip to curtail her smile. "Speaking of fever dreams, this is indeed mine."

"Then I am glad Edward brought you. Without fair maidens such as yourself, these exercises are fruitless." He placed one hand on his heart and lofted the other in the air like an old player performing at the Globe Theater. "Your cheeks with their cherry-blossomed hue, your alabaster skin as innocent as morning dew—"

"For Christ's sake, Charles, give it a rest," Edward growled.

"What?" Charles asked.

"Miss Georgiana doesn't want your inane words."

"Yes, I do," she blurted. "They're...quite lovely."

Edward twisted to her with a bewildered scowl. "I offered you poetry mere seconds ago."

Charles hung his head. "Not the China poem again?"

"It's a limerick, and it's a fine one!"

"I don't want *your* kind of poetry," Georgiana said.

"No," Charles agreed. "You most certainly do not."

Edward plopped back, crossing his arms in a huff. "Absolutely ridiculous," he muttered. "And here I thought I was being chivalrous. What is the matter with you two? I am the epitome of a well-bred gentle—Wait." He hopped to his feet. "God damn it!"

Georgiana jumped in her seat. *What on earth?* "What's wrong?" she asked.

Edward slanted toward the field, almost falling out of his vehicle. His hand flew to his forehead, acting as a visor under his hat. "Is that Jacobson out there? You didn't tell me he's a part of this!"

Charles's jovial manner dropped, and his voice hardened. "He came on late. And before you do anything rash, I'm handling it."

Edward was climbing out of the curricle before Charles finished his sentence. He shot his friend a disbelieving scowl. "If you were going to handle it, why is the bastard still standing? Never mind, she's my sister. I'll do it."

"Now?" Charles asked.

"It's as good a time as any."

Charles made an attempt to grab Edward's shoulders, but Edward shook him off easily. For all the luster of the armor, it left the knights remarkably clumsy and slow. "He's quite literally dressed for battle," Charles said.

"Please," Edward returned dryly. "Besides, I'm just going to talk to him. I won't be gone long enough to do anything *rash*."

Resigned, Charles watched Edward go, leaving a bewildered Georgiana in his wake. He hadn't even bothered to give her an explanation or apologize for deserting her. The man was an uncouth animal. And he thought a lousy poem and a kiss of the hand would change that!

Sensing her frustration, Charles said, "He's not as bad as he looks."

Georgiana *humphed*.

As he looked? To her mind, Edward's looks were the one thing he had going for him, and he had never seemed more dangerous. Next to the knights, who were merely playing at being menacing, the stone-cold expression Edward wore seemed positively frightening. And those weren't the only features that set him apart. His parlous aloofness, his purposeful stride, and his unrelenting conceitedness only added to his threatening demeanor. To his peers, who prided themselves on appearance and comportment, his unfailing ego must be a thorn in their self-conscious sides.

Lord Edward of Marlborough didn't know how to perform for a crowd. And Georgiana would bet he never wanted to learn how. The farther people were away from him, the more he liked them.

"It's a shame I couldn't convince him to take part in the tournament," Charles remarked conversationally as they waited. "Not that the others minded he opted out. He scares the hell out of them, you know. Not much of a team player."

Georgiana already knew the answer but asked anyway. "Why?"

"Because he doesn't care what they think. He puts no stock in their rules."

Losing sight of Edward, Georgiana returned her attention to the earl, who, somehow, was not as exciting as he was scant seconds before. "I doubt he's ever been one for games," she said, smiling politely.

"Oh, we used to have loads of fun. Our mothers are good friends, you know. She'd take me to visit Marlborough, and Edward and I would spend hours playing with the old swords and armor in his attic. Before his father sold it all, that is."

Georgiana had only been joking when she teased Edward about his family's armor. It seemed she'd been right. "Why did he do that?"

"Why else? Debts. The old marquess was always buying his way out of some trouble. No doubt that's why Edward acts the way he does—so, so…"

"Restrained," Georgiana whispered.

"Yes, restrained," Charles said, chuckling. "Although he isn't acting restrained right now, is he? Nevertheless, with a father like his, there was hardly room for him to be anything else. Someone had to pick up the pieces, keep the creditors at bay, pay for the, uh, other issues."

Georgiana flushed. *Other issues?* Did he mean children? "How many were there?"

Clearly pained that he'd brought it up, Charles answered the question nevertheless. "I lost count a while ago. Let's just say the marquess had healthy appetites of all kinds."

"And he left that all for his son to deal with?" she asked,

searching through the crowd of knights once more. Georgiana thought she saw a tussle of some sort at the far corner, but it was over too quickly, covered too efficiently by the others surrounding it for her to make heads or tails of the situation.

Charles nodded. "He's still cleaning it up. But all that's about to be over for him. Has he talked to you about the ancient reptiles yet?"

Georgiana hesitated. "No. I'm... To be honest, I'm not sure if I'm interested."

"Oh, you simply must. Edward is... Well, he's a different man when he's truly enamored with something. It's worth it to see. Perhaps that's why he's behaving so...unrestrained now."

"Why?"

"Because of you."

Georgiana barked out a laugh. "Lord Charles, I appreciate your kind words, but Lord Edward is not enamored with me. He's on his best behavior to try to win me over."

Charles flashed a devastating grin, the whites of his teeth almost blinding. It was the kind of grin that said he'd never had to try to win a lady over in his life. "Is it working?"

Georgiana blinked when an easy "no" didn't come out right away. Sitting on the tip of her tongue, the word simply didn't want to leave. "I...I—"

"What did I miss?"

Georgiana was saved from having to answer as Edward carved his way through the crowd to the duo. At first glance, he looked none the worse for wear, but as he lifted himself back into the curricle, Georgiana could see his cravat had been mussed and his wavy hair was slightly out of place under his hat.

Landing next to her—much too close yet again—Edward took off his hat and combed his fingers through his locks, his color high. "Anything?" he said, acting like nothing untoward had happened. Of course, untoward actions were all relative, weren't they?

"What did you do?" Charles asked. "I told you I would handle the bastard."

Georgiana flinched at the earl's indecorous word. On Edward, it fit like a well-tailored coat. She'd never seen this side of Charles, and it seemed as anachronistic as the players running the lists.

Edward smiled grimly. "I told you, I was just engaging in a friendly chat."

"Friendly?" Georgiana repeated.

He stretched his shoulders wide, expelling a deep breath. "Yes, of course. I politely asked him to keep my sister's name out of his mouth."

"And what did he say?"

"It's fuzzy," he said, battling back a smirk. "It all happened so fast. The poor viscount got punched in the face and was having a difficult time speaking after that."

Georgiana looked to Charles for outrage, but the earl was too busy admiring his friend's barbarity. "*You* punched him?" she asked, aghast.

"A broken jaw is a good deterrent for speaking out of turn."

"Very true," Charles agreed.

Georgiana felt Edward's gimlet eye on her, and she desperately wanted to take out her handkerchief again. She'd dressed coolly for the weather, and yet she kept breaking out into a sweat whenever his gaze landed on her too long.

"Why are you so upset? I thought you wanted spontaneity, passion, honor." Edward waved his hand at the fields. "This entire event is just an excuse for men to hit one another. Why is it wrong when I do it?"

Georgiana fumed at his *nearly* valid argument. But it still wasn't right. None of this was right. All of a sudden, she felt completely out of her element. "You could have taken him aside and spoken to him in a courteous manner. Is your sister nearby? She must be beside herself at your boorish behavior."

"You obviously don't know his sister," Charles interjected.

"You, my lord, are a brute, and you do not belong here,"

Georgiana stated, slamming back in her seat. She would never understand men. Never.

"Good of you to notice," was all Edward replied.

⟫⟩✦⟨⟪

GEORGIANA *DID* NOTICE. She noticed a lot that day.

Like Edward's patience—or rather, stubbornness. It matched her own. Because for the remainder of the event and the entire ride home, she gave him the silent treatment, and he gave it right back.

Surly as a bear, he sat next to her grunting and growling through the drive. He set his bays at a generous clip, and although the warm summer breeze whipped past, the air between them was as stiff and rigid as one of her horsehair petticoats.

Toward the end, Georgiana counted herself lucky. Best to not speak at all rather than end up in an argument. For some reason, it was difficult keeping a level voice when speaking with Lord Edward. More often than not, tempers flared, shouts ensued.

As he pulled into Park Lane, easing the horses to a stop outside the townhouse, Georgiana figured she was in the clear.

She readied her skirts, hinting for him to get out and help her from the curricle, but he turned to her, his frustration evident and still fresh. "Are you going to pout all afternoon?"

She lifted her chin. "That is hardly your concern anymore, seeing as how I'm finally home. Thank you for an illuminating day, my lord. Rest assured that you didn't ruin the entire time for me—only most of it."

His chest rumbled in something close to amusement.

"This isn't funny!" she said. Georgiana was so tired of people laughing at her. First her parents, and now him. "Don't you have any idea how rude you were?"

The mirthless smile froze on his face, torquing into a sneer.

"Did Charles tell you what Jacobson said about my sister?"

Georgiana sat up straighter. No, as a matter of fact, he hadn't, and she hadn't thought to ask. "What did he say?" she returned airily. "Did he remark on her beauty? Is he not good enough for the Marquess of Marlborough's sister? Perhaps it's time you men allowed a woman to decide if someone is good enough for her."

"Wrong," Edward replied, punching the word out bitterly. "It had come to my attention that last year, good old virtuous, honorable, *knightly* Lord Jacobson wanted to court my sister. She is quite beautiful, after all, and her dowry is fat again—thanks to me. However, he couldn't countenance a relationship anymore because…'the stench of her family's business was too much to bear.' Yes, those were his exact words. It doesn't take a genius to know what or who the son of a bitch was talking about."

"O-oh," Georgiana stammered. "Yes, that's… Well, that's quite dishonorable."

"You don't say," he replied, sharpening his teeth on the acerbic words. "And you want me to behave like those men? Those courtly paradigms of ethics and morality?"

"No, of course not. I didn't say that—"

"Those men who laughed and drank and gambled with my father as he threw away our future, dropping illegitimate children and IOUs in his wake? But that was fine, they said. That's what marquesses do, they said. And yet I, who have had to fight to rebuild all of it, am cast down with derision, with my sisters along for the ride. Me, who has had to place my ego to the side and rip open every single oyster I could get in order to find one measly pearl."

He shifted closer to her, the sparks of gold in his gray eyes lighting the path between them. "Well, that's fine with me. They can strike me with their limp tongues and blunt lances until they are blue in the face, but it won't hurt me where it matters the most," he said, placing his hand over his heart. "I will take care of my family. I will provide my sisters with everything they need and replace every single thing my bastard of a father sold. I will make sure my mother lives out the rest of her days in unadulter-ated luxury even if she never says another word to me. And I won't let them, *or you*, or anyone else get in my way."

Before she could stop him, he reached out and grabbed her hand, never breaking eye contact. Georgiana wasn't even sure he knew what he was doing. But she didn't pull away. She told herself he was too strong.

"That might not be the 'man of worth' you speak of," he said solemnly, his voice reduced to a rasp, "but that is honor to me. That is chivalry. That bastard will never speak against my sister, not as long as I live. Now, do you see why I had to do it?"

"Let go of my hand," Georgiana said.

His eyes continued to dig into hers, and he did not move. "Now, do you see?" he asked again.

When she didn't respond, he fell back, blinking as if waking from a trance. Quickly, he dropped her hand and got out of the curricle, rounding the front to lift her down. Georgiana couldn't understand why she was so winded; she couldn't seem to catch her breath.

Placing her firmly next to the vehicle, Edward bent over, snatching something up from the ground. Unceremoniously, he shoved it into her hands. "Here's your damn handkerchief."

Slowly, Georgiana nodded, recognizing the monogrammed linen in her trembling fingers. She hadn't noticed she'd dropped it.

Hot tears formed above her lower lids, but she managed to keep them at bay. She refused to let them cloud her vision as Edward escorted her to the door.

Because she'd noticed a lot that day and thought that maybe, just maybe, she might want to notice more.

CHAPTER EIGHT

THE STREET WAS quiet. That didn't stop Edward from pounding as hard as he could on the door.

He heard the dogs first, scratching and barking on the other side before the door whipped open and Charles faced him, incredulous and comfortable-looking in his silk paisley dressing gown.

"What the hell is the matter with you?" he asked. "Are you drunk?"

Not one for pleasantries, Edward didn't waste any here. "I need tickets," he replied, shoving past Charles across the threshold. "And no, I'm not drunk. But I need you to help me with that too."

A short time later, Charles had them both ensconced in his library, balloons of brandy in hand. Charles's mother preferred staying in the country with his younger siblings, which meant he had the townhouse to himself. When Edward had asked him why he didn't buy his own, Charles had just smiled rakishly and said he rarely slept in his own bed enough to care.

Indeed, the room held very little of Charles's personal style. A relic of the old earl's time, it was sparsely furnished with the requisite books and the occasional Greek vase. However, papers were scattered on the mahogany desktop and stacks of books were littered on various side tables. With a low fire burning in the hearth, the space maintained a lived-in feeling, convincing Edward that his friend didn't prowl the streets of London searching for a good time as much as he let on.

"Spit it out, my friend," Charles said, sinking into his plush velvet chaise. Hooking one leg over the other, he studied Edward with a quiet calm. "Let me guess. You didn't win her over today with your brotherly hysterics."

"Never mind Jacobson," Edward said before sipping on his brandy. He didn't know where to start. After dropping Georgiana off that afternoon, he'd taken his curricle home and walked for hours, lost in a contemplative daze. She'd dug underneath his skin. He hadn't even known he was heading to Charles's townhouse until he recognized the stately porch. "I suppose I need your help."

Charles's smile was so cocksure that Edward wanted to punch it off his face. "You think tickets to the tournament will win over your lady love?"

Edward glowered. He'd known Charles wasn't going to make this easy. It was too much fun for him, and Charles adored fun. "I know she wants to go to the tournament, and her father can't get tickets," Edward explained. "With your assistance, I have the means to get her there. Ergo, she will be most grateful for my help."

"Grateful enough to marry you?"

"That's the plan."

"It's a shit plan."

Edward bounded out of his chair, pacing the length of the room. "Well, what would you have me do, Charles? I've done everything I can, and the girl remains stubborn. You know how much I need her father's investment."

"I told you to woo the girl. You're not wooing correctly."

Edward stopped wearing the carpet down long enough to glare at the fire. He rarely went to others for help, and the act was making him feel all out of sorts. "You heard her today; she told me I wasn't chivalrous. Can you believe that? Me? A marquess?"

Even with his back to his friend, Edward could still feel Charles's taunting grin. "And what does she want you to do to prove your heroism and valor? Ride in on your white horse and slay all her enemies? Does she want to send you on a death-defying quest? Or does the sweet girl merely want you to pay true attention to her, send her flowers, learn what she likes, and perhaps read her some poetry?"

Edward spun around. "I *tried* to recite her poetry!"

"She doesn't want that kind of poetry, Edward. Christ, what is wrong with you? You act like you've never been in love before."

"I haven't," Edward replied matter-of-factly, sinking back into his chair. "Falling in love takes effort and time that I don't have. Nor do I want the hassle."

His mocking expression gone, Charles regarded his friend with the kind of sincere compassion that made Edward wish he'd just gone home. He came for tickets, damn it, not bloody sympathy!

"You poor boy," Charles said.

"Oh, like you've been in love," Edward snapped.

Charles chuckled. "I was in a lot of love last week, a healthy amount this week, and I'm sure I'll be up to my knees in it next week as well."

Edward grunted. "You know that's not what I'm talking about."

"Oh, I know. Boy, you've become so tetchy with age." Charles sipped his brandy, taking his time savoring it. "Honestly, though, the tickets won't solve anything. They might help— might get you in the game—but it seems to me that Miss Georgiana Spence is made of sterner stuff than that."

"So?"

"So...you're going to need to put in the effort."

"I don't know how."

Charles cocked his head. "Yes you do. You just don't want to. I'm sorry to say, mate, but if Miss Georgiana Spence wants a knight, you're going to have to give her a knight."

"What the hell does that mean?"

Charles snorted into his glass. "Well, first it means you're going to have to learn some new poems."

BROWN LIQUOR DID things to a man, like give him ideas and the unhealthy belief that he could actually see them through.

Later that night, after many more brandies, Edward had been just drunk enough to appreciate the brilliance in the lovesick youth from Verona. Climbing up to Juliet's window under the cover of darkness with parents close by? Romeo was reckless, stupid, and imbecilic! *But*…his actions had been effective. He'd got the girl, after all.

Unfortunately for Edward, his sanity didn't return until he was halfway up the drainpipe of the Spence townhouse. It had all seemed so simple from the bottom. But feet on the ground tended to make all men confident in their abilities.

The only thing he had going for him was that the Spences had covered their drainpipe with a trellis in an effort to offset the ugly appliance from their façade. So he had help in the climb. Wisteria wasn't the strongest vine, but it grew like the devil and was handling his body weight well enough.

What room was Georgiana's? A typical townhouse, the Spence abode had three stories above their basement, with the family's bedrooms at the top. Since only one of those bedroom windows had a light currently on—and it was the closest one to the drainpipe—Edward decided to rest all his hopes on it.

Muttering curses to himself, he shimmied up the remainder of the pipe, steadying his feet on the string course that ran the width of the structure. It was made of brick and just wide enough for him to balance his toes on, so he managed to slide his way across, reaching for the tiny wrought-iron balcony outside the window.

What a bloody fool, Edward thought for the hundredth time as he pulled himself onto the balcony, hearing his pants rip from the effort. He hoped to God the rip wasn't in an inappropriate area. It was bad enough showing up at Georgiana's window at this time of night. Showing up with a tennis-ball-sized hole in his crotch was a whole other story.

Like an indignant fish, he flopped over the railing, landing on his face. Hearing footsteps inside, he quickly drew himself up and plastered his back against the brick face as the sash window was unlocked.

Edward closed his eyes like a child convinced if he couldn't see, then no one could see him. *Please don't be the parents. Please don't be the parents. Please don't be the parents.* Edward's title earned him quite a lot of leeway with Mr. and Mrs. Spence, but these theatrics might be a leap too far.

The window slid up and Edward waited. And waited.

But neither a gasp nor a scream rang out. Only an acerbic huff followed by that husky voice.

"My lord, if you're thinking of killing yourself, could you please do it at your own house? I've known our servants since I was a child, and I'd hate to ask them to clean blood off the sidewalks tomorrow morning."

He cracked open an eye to find curls—long, vivacious curls—as Georgiana leaned out from the window. Not a lick of alarm on her face—she appeared amused and deeply unimpressed.

"Your hair," he stammered.

Instantly, her hand went to her head. "What about my hair?" she asked, two red spots hitting the tops of her cheeks.

"I needed to talk to you," he said, peeling himself off the brick, stumbling in the process. *Damn brown liquor!*

"About my hair?"

Edward shook his head, attempting to diffuse the brandy's concentration. "No. About us."

"Us?" She clucked her tongue behind her front teeth. "Perhaps the morning would make a more suitable time. Then you could actually come in the front door."

Edward leaned back over the balcony to frown at the main door two stories underneath him. It must have been too far for her comfort, because Georgiana snatched hold of his jacket, tugging him back.

"I don't want to come through the front door," he said, turning to her worried expression. "I wanted to surprise you. To make an effort. A point."

She pulled her robe tightly around herself before crossing her arms. For a moment, Edward was struck dumb at her ensemble. He'd never seen her look so...bare. Not naked—just bare. Covered from chin to toe with a formless white cotton nightgown, she was the picture of irritated innocence. Her nightcap was fitted tight to her head and tied under her chin, but it did very little in containing the sultry mass of hair that tangled around her like a living, breathing halo. Edward had never seen her hair let out before. Usually set in severe braids and bun, it now rained deliciously down her torso like a flood with the intent to reset life. Then and there, Edward decided he hated the current arbiters of fashion. Anyone who decided that magnificence like that should be hidden away should be shot dead and dragged for miles behind bolting horses.

"What is your point?" she asked, swinging her chestnut locks behind her shoulders as if aware of his libidinous thoughts.

Hell. What *was* his point? Edward smacked the center of his forehead. Oh, yes, that stupid twat from Verona. "Romance!"

"Romance?"

"Yes," he replied, feeling a sting of annoyance that she wasn't getting it. Why wasn't she getting it? It was so obvious! "The boy...the whiny kid from that play. The star-crossed lovers."

Georgiana lowered her chin as her brow rose. "You mean Romeo?"

"Yes, that's it! Romeo!"

Why was her frown deepening? When would this woman

look at him like he wasn't a bug crawling on her food?

"Oh, I see!" she said. *About time!* "You thought you would climb up my parents' drainpipe, knock on my window, scaring me half to death, and beguile me with soft words and the sight of your underclothes through the hole in the back of your trousers?"

Well, shit. At least now he knew where the hole was.

"Not en-entirely," Edward sputtered. "I thought—"

"You thought what? That I would jump in your arms at this ridiculous display? You thought that I was so childish and dim that I would find a drunk man one slip away from breaking his neck somehow romantic?"

Well…when she said it like that…

Edward had to get a handle on this. Like one of the new state-of-the-art trains barreling across the country, this had gone from zero to thirty in no time. He held out his hands in a placating manner. "Now, you're taking this all wrong."

"Am I?" she scoffed, her words cooler than the wind literally blowing up his arse. "Am I really? Because I think I'm seeing everything for what it is—pathetic."

"You're not pathetic."

"Not me, you dolt!" she said. "*You're* the pathetic one. This isn't romantic; it's asinine. So I will say good night now. Please, try not to fall on your way down."

She was dismissing him. Him! Before she could even hear what he'd come to say. As she twirled to vanish back in her room, all of Edward's frustration and uncertainty thundered through him. Pure, unadulterated impotence pooled in the pit of his stomach. He couldn't let her leave. He couldn't let her derail his future and the future of his family.

"You said you wanted passion and love and purpose—"

"And this, Edward, is none of those things." Her expression grew melancholic as she reached to shut the window. "Shame on me, I suppose. For a moment there, after the practice, I actually thought you had a little more substance to you."

"I've got tickets!" he blurted, stopping her hands on the window sash.

Georgiana's head popped out again. "What did you say?"

There it was. He finally had it. As precious as gold and finite as time: a woman's interest.

"You heard me," he said, straightening, his confidence bolstered. "I have tickets. To the Eglinton Tournament. You wanted them. I got them for you."

She stared at him for a long minute, her nose wrinkling up in disgust—at the fact she hadn't shut the window or at his blatant bribe for her company, he wasn't sure.

Planting her hands on the base of the windowsill, she hung her body out even more. "Let me guess, Charles?"

Edward nodded.

She appeared to consider that. Whatever she thought about him, her opinion of Charles seemed to be positive. That could only aid him in his endeavor.

"My father promised to get me tickets."

Edward shook his head. "He's out of luck—even came to me asking if I could find some."

Her eyes flared. Like seeing lightning before you heard thunder, that was a bad omen for what was about to come out of her mouth. "So now you're only helping my father—and me—for something in return?"

Edward slapped his palm over his heart. When it turned out it was the wrong hand, and the wrong side, he made the motion again with the correct one. "You think so very little of me, don't you?"

"Yes, I do."

"That was a rhetorical question!"

"Not to me, it wasn't."

Edward scowled. "I am not asking for anything in return… Well, not much, anyway. I can't make you love me, Georgiana, that is true. However, I wouldn't mind if you would try. Get to know me. Help show me what I can do to sway your mind and heart. I plan to marry you, but I can't do that on my own."

"How very astute of you," she remarked dryly.

Ignoring her jab, he went on. "Just because I don't slip on armor and joust in the fields doesn't mean I don't have merit or pride. It doesn't mean I don't have honor or courage. Hell, I'm showing you a boatload of courage right now! Do you think it was easy to come here tonight, knowing your disregard for me? I know how I look, but I am throwing myself out here so you can see another side of me."

Even Shakespeare would have approved of that soliloquy. Edward hadn't known he had it in him, and he paused for effect, admiring his fruitful words. Was she as impressed as he was?

Georgiana's eyes narrowed, but the green was still vibrating through the slits. "What do I have to do?" she said through her teeth.

Thank the Lord, they were actually getting somewhere. Catching his breath, he continued, "I want you to go to the tournament with me. I want you to spend time with me. I want...I want a chance. You say a knight has all the characteristics you look for in a man. Let me show you that I'm just as worthy as Gawain and Galahad and..." His brow furrowed. "What's the other one's name? You know, the one who ran off with his best friend's wife?"

"Lancelot?"

Edward snapped his fingers. "Yes, thank you. Lancelot. I'm *definitely* better than him."

Georgiana regarded him warily. "And in the end, when you ultimately fail, and I still say no?"

"*If* you still say no after the tournament, then we will shake hands and say we tried. I can't ask for any more than that."

Her mouth twisted as she considered, and a choir of angels belted into song in Edward's chest. "Something tells me you'd like to ask for a lot more," she said.

"Not from you, and not now. Just this and only this...your time."

Georgiana shook her head, and her bounteous curls lured

Edward into a trance. He'd just known she was hiding something under those prim hairstyles. "It won't be easy," she warned.

Edward glanced at the drop over the railing. "Nothing of value ever is."

She blew out a long breath, looking him up and down. "Fine, then," she said, a little too reluctantly for Edward's taste, and stuck out her hand. "You can come to dinner again."

He grabbed it gladly. Too gladly, pulling her halfway through the window, making their heads almost bump into each other. "I've already accepted an invitation from your mother. All I ask is you dull your fangs and promise not to bite while I enjoy your cook's delicious food."

"I promise not to draw too much blood."

"Good enough."

They held each other's gaze for long seconds. Not for the first time, Edward acknowledged he enjoyed holding her hand. She employed a firm, confident hold. Taking advantage of the fact that she wasn't wearing gloves, he grazed his thumb over her silky skin. The smoothness of her flesh—its heavenly indication of the rest of her body—was enough to make him lightheaded.

It could be the liquor. It also could be the way she was looking at him—without derision. They weren't friends by any means—and he definitely didn't plan to be her friend—but they weren't enemies either.

The only thing keeping him from kissing her was the fact that she'd probably push him over the railing if he tried—blood cleaning be damned.

"I have a feeling I'm going to regret this," she whispered, her warm breath caressing his skin.

Edward smiled. "Do you ever wonder if Juliet thought the same thing?"

CHAPTER NINE

"Tickets?" George exclaimed, his disappointment cutting her like the edge of a fresh piece of paper. "You're doing this for tickets?"

Georgiana shifted uncomfortably under his reproach, hiding her flushed face behind her teacup. "You make it seem so scandalous," she replied, her exasperation evident. "I daresay women have given much more to a man in exchange for something they wanted."

George's mouth screwed up in distaste, but he let it go, allowing them to relax into a semi-comfortable silence in the Spences' parlor.

It had been a week since Edward's proposition. Georgiana had expected him to visit sooner, but tonight's dinner party was the first he'd accepted. True to her word, Georgiana got through the courses well enough. She wasn't particularly loquacious, but she hadn't been openly hostile. When Edward asked a question, she answered it without an exasperated sneer or snide return. There could be no doubt that she was living up to her end of the bargain and putting on a good show for the two other couples invited by her parents.

Post-dinner, the party had retired to the parlor for drinks and more relaxed conversation. Perhaps too relaxed. Georgiana wasn't sure why she'd told George about her deal with Edward, and she wasn't sure why he resented it so much.

"I'm just begging you to be careful," he said, softening his expression. His compassionate eyes roamed over her, but Georgiana felt nothing except annoyance…at herself. Because loving George would make her life so much easier. She knew that her parents thought he held a candle for her, but he'd never pressed it. Georgiana wasn't sure what she would do if he ever addressed his intentions. He was so special to her, such a wonderful sounding board and friend. On the surface, he was everything she would ever want in a spouse—handsome and polite, broad, with the kind of shoulders one could always lean on. All George lacked was a fortune, though his intelligence and ingenuity would quickly make up for that fact; she had no doubt his millions would come in due time.

But still…her amorous reaction to him was lukewarm at best. He would undoubtedly make some woman happy one day, only it would not be her.

"Men like the marquess always get what they want," he added bitterly, dragging her away from her thoughts.

"I know that," Georgiana said. "But only because of what they are—not who they are. Believe me, my friend, I am as steadfast as ever in my resolve, and he is quite aware that I'm using him for the tickets. Despite what he thinks, my head will not be turned by a title and a crafty tongue."

Nevertheless, her head did turn. Laughter boomed from the other side of the room, where Edward was doing his best impression of a gentleman to the small crowd, regaling them with story after story. Georgiana watched as her parents lapped up everything he was serving them with stars glistening in their eyes.

She could hardly blame them. Edward seemed positively sparkling tonight with his ready smile and quick wit. She wouldn't call him the life of the party, but he wasn't as reserved as usual. Even she couldn't help but admire his commanding countenance and slick manners. In her mind, his form—once straight-edged and empty—was curving on the paper. Details were being drawn in, features unmasked, color added.

But Georgiana knew better. He was playing a part, just as she was.

Her shoulders sagged. She felt intolerably tired all of a sudden. Being pleasant was so draining.

Still…she could do this. It wasn't even *that* horrible. If Edward could behave, so could she, and the road to the tournament wouldn't have to be so bumpy. All she had to do was give him time and attention. With her father not letting her anywhere near his ledgers, and Prichard in Suffolk researching her family's history, she had plenty of that to give.

"How about some music?" Mrs. Spence asked excitedly, walking to the center of the room. "My Georgiana is greatly proficient on the piano. Do you enjoy music, my lord?"

Edward smiled benevolently, exuding copious amounts of charm. "As much as the next man," he replied.

Her mother gave her an impatient look and nodded toward the piano.

Georgiana sighed. It seemed her talents were being put on display for Lord Edward's appreciation. But that seemed all wrong. *He* was the one vying for her hand. Why was *she* the circus animal who had to perform?

Which gave her an idea.

In the days after, she'd been too embarrassed by what had transpired on the balcony to truly recount all that was said. She'd remembered the promise of tickets and her agreement to spend time with him without biting his head off, but not much else—however, Edward's messy soliloquy filtered back to her now. *The drunken fool.* She doubted *he* even remembered all he'd consented to.

You say a knight has all the characteristics you look for in a man. Let me show you that I'm just as worthy as Gawain and Galahad…

Lord Edward would never be a knight. That was obvious. Men of his ilk lacked the selflessness and self-control that exemplified the position. But that didn't mean she couldn't have some fun watching him flounder. It was *he* who should be impressing *her* with his courtly skills—and he should start now.

Georgiana glided to the piano, taking a seat as she had so many times in the past. She searched through her sheet music for the ideal song.

Finding the one that served her purpose, she placed it on the stand and readied her fingers on the keys. The room went silent, all waiting for her to begin. Right when she was about to strike the first note, she turned her attention toward Edward in his seat. Relaxed in the comfiest chair in the room, naturally with the tallest back, he met her gaze. There was nothing there. No smug smile, no anticipatory gleam. He sat as a man accustomed to being entertained, a man used to people falling over their feet for him.

To Georgiana, it was high time the lord gave back. *Noblesse oblige.* Edward's inner knight needed to come out and shine for the common man.

Her smile was as sweet as the almond tarts the cook had made especially for the lord—and just as sinful. "How about a duet?"

Her mother clapped louder than the Westminster bells. "Oh, what a lovely idea. My lord?" she asked an increasingly distressed-looking Edward.

He pulled himself together quickly enough. "Sadly, I do not play, which is fortunate, since now I can watch your talented daughter and enjoy her playing instead."

Georgiana's smile only grew more wicked. Of course he didn't know how to play. The piano was a woman's instrument. Men considered it inferior to the more masculine ones like the trumpet or cello, though Georgiana would have bet her bonnet he didn't play those either. Learning an instrument took patience and fortitude, other knightly characteristics she was sure he did not possess.

"Not that kind of duet," she said. "A singing duet. I'm sure you have a wonderful baritone, my lord. We'd all love to hear it."

He sat there, swirling his brandy around and around in his crystal glass, his eyes sharpening on her. Was he remembering their bargain? Was he cursing his stupidity? Georgiana certainly hoped so. What kind of a man made promises he was too proud to follow through on?

George broke the silence, setting his glass on the side table. "I'd do it. I always enjoy singing with Miss Georgiana."

"Next time, perhaps," Edward said, rising from his chair. He took a long swallow of his drink, finishing it all before placing it down. "The lady has made her choice."

Georgiana wiggled on her bench, proud of all that she was orchestrating. Mrs. Spence clapped again, and the room braced for the impromptu performance. When Edward came up to her side, Georgiana could feel the tension radiating off him, the loss of control wrecking his impenetrable façade.

"Do you know it?" Georgiana asked, pointing to the music. She wasn't sure if it was the low light of the candles or the green-papered walls, but Edward looked as sallow as a fish. She had to twist away, afraid she'd laugh and ruin the whole performance.

He leaned over her shoulder, spiraling her senses with his pine and citrus scent. "I'm going to get you for this," he replied sotto voce, providing her answer.

Again, she stifled a chuckle. "What an unchivalrous thing to say," she whispered back. Before he could respond, Georgiana struck the keys, sending the room into a somber rendition of the popular parlor song "Kathleen Mavourneen." Starting the first verse on her own, Georgiana squeaked off-key a couple of times before finding her rhythm. Singing was not her forte; Georgiana much preferred pounding the ivories, though she could hold a note.

Edward, on the other hand, could not.

When he joined her on the second verse, her hands almost slammed down on the board, so struck was she by the disastrous noises coming out of his mouth.

He got the words right, she'd give him that, but the tone was so off that she almost believed him to be playing a joke on the room. However, when she peeked up at him, his expression was anything but facetious. The poor dear was sweating like a sinner in church.

Georgiana tried to direct him, singing louder to force him on key—or drown him out—yet it was to no avail. It seemed when Lord Edward agreed to do something, he did it. There were no half measures. He was asked to sing, and he was going to *sing*, no matter how badly.

When the unholy duet concluded, Georgiana could only sit and stare at the pages before her, barely registering the unmerited and polite applause showered on them.

From his corner, George coughed a few times. "That was...something," he said, locking a stern expression in place. "Just...something."

Edward bowed, offering his hand to Georgiana so she could stand and do the same.

"Was it as bad as all that?" he asked in her ear.

Goosebumps erupted behind her sensitive lobe, and her mouth dropped open. "Did you not hear us?"

He shrugged. "It sounded fine to me. Maybe a little rusty."

A little rusty? Georgiana couldn't figure out if the man was delusional or just a normal peer—oblivious to his failings.

Something compassionate burned inside her, prodding her to guard his feelings—but still, try as she might, Georgiana couldn't mince words. "Were you trying to sing off-key the entire time?"

His eyebrows crushed together, and the bags under his eyes hung even more. "Off-key? I wasn't off-key."

"You were...*quite* terrible."

Edward's lips pressed together as he seemed to entertain the possibility. "I thought we sounded perfectly adequate."

Good Lord, he couldn't differentiate the tones. That was the only excuse for his confusion. Suddenly, Georgiana began to cackle and couldn't stop. Even the glare from her parents failed to put a stop to her rudeness.

"I'm so sorry," she said finally, holding her aching stomach. She couldn't remember the last time she'd laughed like that. "I had no idea. I wouldn't have asked you to sing if I'd known."

"Oh, sure you would have," he countered, sliding a hand through his wavy hair. The sweat on his forehead served to slick the hair back, creating a rather debonair display. "You like me at a disadvantage. Not everyone can sing like you."

"Like me?"

He nodded. "Your voice."

"What about my voice?"

That was the wrong question, because it encouraged Edward to stare at her neck, which was, unfortunately, bare. Georgiana could feel a patch of red spread over her chest like a jar of ink spilling over a blank page.

His gaze traveled back to hers. "It's…pleasant."

She swallowed. *Pleasant?* Why did the innocuous word make her feel like a powerful siren? Catching her ego, Georgiana hurried to blow cold air on the conversation. "And here I thought the only thing you liked about me was my dowry," she joked before shrugging a delicate shoulder. "It's just a voice."

Only Edward didn't laugh. If anything, the serious man became even more serious. "Trust me," he said wistfully. "It's more than just a voice. It…does things."

"To you?"

His jaw flexing, Edward didn't respond.

Georgiana had to turn away. This conversation was beyond inappropriate. And he was saying things too lovely to be believed.

She wanted to believe them, anyway.

"I didn't mean to embarrass you *that much*," Georgiana confessed, changing the subject. She reached down to caress the keys once more. "But you *did* ask me to treat you as a knight, and all knights were expected to have a knowledge of music and dancing."

"Is that so?"

"That is so."

"And am I to conclude that I failed?"

Georgiana scrunched her nose impishly. "What do you think?"

He paused. "I think every knight has a bad day."

"*He who fights and runs away may live to fight another day.* Is that it?" she teased.

He stepped closer to her, their chests almost touching. "And are we fighting, Georgiana?"

She spied her parents, who were pretending to be oblivious on the other side of the parlor. No help there. Finding herself a bundle of nerves, she bit at her lower lip. "Not at all. I thought you said you were willing to be tested."

"I think you'll find me willing to do many things with you."

"Why is that? Are you a masochist as well as tone-deaf?"

"Hardly." A grin flitted over his face. "I thought you were spoiled before, but now I know that isn't the case."

"What am I?"

"Ruthless."

"I am not!" she said.

A rumble sounded from his chest. *Was that laughter?* "Don't be upset. I like a good adversary. It provides me the motivation I need to win your challenges."

"Perhaps you should give up now, my lord. Not everyone is knight material."

"And yet that is what I must be to win your favor. Only I get to pick the next event you judge."

She was about to argue, not thinking that was fair, considering this whole thing was *her* challenge, but she backed off. The man had little hope and had been embarrassed enough. What was the harm in throwing him this bone? Besides, she'd be lying if she said she wasn't curious about what he'd come up with.

Edward stared at her mouth. His eyes naturally dipped down in the outside corners, always creating a haunted, somber effect, but they warmed when he noticed she was conceding. "What would you prefer next?" he asked. "Art? Sportsmanship?"

"You've already failed sportsmanship," she replied. "You refused to joust."

Edward placed his hand on the small of her back, and Georgiana almost jumped. It was an intimate touch, one he had no right to place on her. She had no right to like it either.

"My dear woman," Edward said, smoothly directing her away from the dastardly piano. "Surely you do not believe that playacting at the joust is the only way for men these days to exhibit their talent in competition. I also exert my manliness and chivalry on a field, but a different kind. It is a sport of integrity and glory and incalculable honor. It separates the men from the boys, the true from the wanting. An equalizer, it is a sport that transforms men into kings and reduces kings to sniveling babies."

Georgiana's focus was still on his hand and how it managed to make her entire body feel like it was roasting over a spit—in a good way. When he stopped speaking, she forced herself to find her tongue and reply. "And...and what magnificent game could possibly do all those things?" she asked.

Her heart skipped a beat as he cocked his head to the side. He was acting delightfully human; it was like she could actually see his form actualize in front of her. Even when throwing frowns at her ignorance, he was gaining color on the page. "Why, cricket," he answered. "What else?"

CHAPTER TEN

ESPITE ITS GROWING popularity, Georgiana had never been to a cricket match. With not a little bit of curiosity, she ventured to Lord's Cricket Ground later that week with Minnie and Aunt Augusta to witness Edward's honorable masculinity in action.

He'd told her it would be a friendly match between two clubs; however, when they pulled up in the carriage, Georgiana was taken aback by the number of people already crowding the grounds, guessing over a hundred people had to be there.

The premier venue to play the sport, Lord's was still rustic in its simplicity, more an open field with countryside surrounding half of it. The pavilion overlooking the field had been refurbished the previous year, and gas lighting had been added, though Georgiana still thought it looked no larger than an expensive garden shed. For the most part, the scene was provincial, with a few benches lined up around the players' oval for the fans to use.

Dressed in a light green dress with a straw bonnet and yellow parasol, Georgiana was quite certain she'd be lost in the expanse. The field was rich and verdant, and the anticipation pulsing within the crowd only encouraged the butterflies fluttering in her stomach. She couldn't remember why she'd agreed to come and watch Edward play. It had seemed so reasonable at the time, though now it felt entirely too familiar. Was she supposed to keep an eye on him the entire match? Was she supposed to clap *for* him? Those actions—innocent on the surface—felt rather intimate and threatened to expose something she wasn't sure she was ready to reveal—to herself as much as anyone else.

"Do you see him?" Minnie asked, exiting the stables with Aunt Augusta trailing respectably behind a few paces. Minnie had been overjoyed when Georgiana asked to accompany her, and she might have gone overboard in her choice of outfit. Decked out like she was attending a ball, Minnie sported a cream ensemble with a pink bow shoved in every nook and cranny, which made a *whooshing* sound every time she moved.

The women stood at the edge of the field, and Georgiana scanned the area, taking a minute to differentiate the players from the spectators. The difference was quite startling. Having never encountered men so underdressed, Georgiana was shocked to find the twenty-two players *not* wearing their jackets or waistcoats. They were proper enough with their leather shoes, high collars, cravats, and leg pads; however, seeing a man in public in only his white linen shirt and braces was something of a novel experience. She decided to leave that part out to her mother when she described the event later, just in case she ever wanted to come back and watch another match.

Eventually, Georgiana found Edward on the far side of the field. Not surprising her at all, he stood on the outskirts of a group of players and appeared to be in an intense conversation with a man old enough to be his father. Spotting her, Edward waved his hand, beckoning the trio over.

Georgiana felt Minnie pinch her arm as they drew closer. She didn't have to glance at her friend to know exactly what she was thinking. Stripped down of his usual gentleman's uniform, Edward seemed even more intimidating than usual. One would think a jacket and waistcoat would accentuate a man's form—and it did—but without it, one could make out the very essence of the masculine figure: the way the clavicle ran wide and long along the chest, the way the waist pinched in an inverted triangle where the shirt was tucked into the trousers. The backside—with no tails covering it—was all quite…illuminating.

Edward didn't greet them with an ebullient smile, but his countenance was generous, all the same.

"I'm glad you could make it," he said, and Georgiana believed him.

To her consternation, the butterflies under her corset flapped harder as if they'd eaten a whole bowl of marzipan. Was it the fact that she was so out of her comfort zone, or was it Edward's voice that did it to her, deep and as stripped down as his body, without artifice?

When her words took too long to arrive, Minnie pinched her again. "You spoke so highly of the game," Georgiana began, rubbing her forearm surreptitiously. "How could I not show up?"

"Oh, it's the greatest game the Lord ever put on this earth," the older gentleman said, cutting into the conversation. A whole head shorter than Edward, he appeared more like an elf than a player, his white eyebrows longer than the spare hair peeking out from under his hat. But his eyes twinkled when he spoke, and Georgiana couldn't help but be charmed by his enthusiastic boasting.

"God created cricket?" she asked.

The man's face turned solemn, as did his voice. "Naturally. Only something this perfect and pure could be created by the Almighty. I hear this is your first match? Well…you'll see. You'll see."

Edward grinned at the old man, whom he introduced as Lord Malbeck. He went on to explain that it was Malbeck who'd first exposed Edward to the addictive game when he was a young boy, adding he couldn't have asked for a better teacher. Malbeck had been playing cricket at Lord's back when it was housed in Dorset Square in the late 1700s.

Georgiana could see the intimacy in the easy exchange between the two men, and was confused when she found there wasn't a familial connection between them. Surely Edward's own father should have taught him cricket, though from what she'd heard about him, he might have been too busy doing more unsavory things with his time. Was this what it had been like for Edward growing up, relying on the goodwill and generosity of other men to learn activities every boy needed to flourish amongst his peers?

A raw pang of sympathy struck her as she watched the men exchange pleasantries with Minnie and Augusta. This wasn't the Edward she was used to. Unlike at her parents' dinner party, he was not putting on a show for the others, hiding behind manners or his title. This was him.

"You should have seen the boy," Malbeck said through laughter, jutting a gnarled thumb in Edward's chest. "He was all elbows and knees, couldn't walk a straight line without falling on those huge feet of his. He was like a newborn colt—couldn't bat to save his life."

"That changed rather quickly," Edward replied dryly, meeting Georgiana's eyes for a split second before she blinked and returned her gaze to the older man.

Malbeck grunted. "Not that quickly," he replied before pushing Edward forward. "Come now, Edward, be a good lad and find your nice girl a place to sit so she can watch you." He winked at Aunt Augusta. "And make sure this fine woman has me in her sights the entire time. I'm feeling mighty limber today. I think I might be able to pull a few smiles out of her."

Aunt Augusta sniffed a reproach, sticking her nose in the air, though Georgiana could have sworn she saw the hint of a shy smile.

Malbeck shoved Edward again. "Hurry now, Eddie, the game is about to start. Those benches over there are going fast."

Eddie?

Edward didn't admonish the older man, only saying, "Yes, sir," before herding the trio of women to the open seating.

He didn't touch her—not like he had that night of their musical performance. Nevertheless, her lower back flamed as if his palm lay there, and she was acutely aware of how it had made her feel…acutely aware of how she wanted to (maybe? perhaps?) feel once more.

She glanced up under her lashes to find his gaze straying to hers every few awkward seconds. "Eddie?" she asked casually, delighted to get a low chuckle out of him. What an entirely different thing to experience without his wearing his jacket and waistcoat—she could almost see it vibrate from his skin.

"He's called me that since I was eight and refuses to stop."

"You could make him stop."

"Lord Malbeck is one of the most foul-tempered men I've ever had the pleasure to know. You don't make him do anything."

Georgiana twisted her neck to catch a glimpse of the older gentleman. Standing by himself, he was busy stretching out his legs and winding his arms in large, sweeping circles like a deranged bird. "Him? Never!" she replied, incredulous.

Edward's lips pinched. "Yes, him. Don't let his sweet little act deceive you. I learned words from him that would make a convict blush. In fact," he added, settling the women in their seats, "when the game starts, I would advise you to cover your ears whenever he's involved. The man can't be trusted around ladies, and you are sitting close. You'll be able to hear and see everything."

Aunt Augusta *tsked*, but it was more halfhearted than usual. Had Malbeck made a conquest there? Georgiana wondered.

"But, my lord," Georgiana said, "what about you? Should I be worried about anything you might say? Remember, you told me cricket was an honorable pursuit."

Edward grinned, starting to back away, all swagger and arrogance in his athletic figure. "Oh, it's honorable, Georgiana. But honor is a bit more colorful on the cricket pitch."

THEY REALLY NEED to print out a rule book or a list of terms, Georgiana concluded morosely, because cricket made no sense. No sense at all.

It wasn't like she'd come into the match blind. Georgiana had asked her brothers to fill her in on the basics of the sport the day before, and although the "laws," as they called them, were complicated, they hadn't seemed out of her reach. But here, in front of her, with the sun beating down and the ball whizzing past, Georgiana was lost.

Edward's team was on the field—she understood that.

And they were bowling the ball to a batsman on the other team. Easy enough.

The batsman, holding his long, flat bat made of willow, stood in front of the wicket, which was comprised of three vertical stumps with two horizontal bails balanced on top. Yes, she got that.

The batsman's goal was to hit the ball and run to the wicket on the opposite side without getting out. Edward's team needed to get ten players from the opposing team out before their side could bat and score points. Yes, simple to comprehend.

But how the men could get out was beyond confusing. Edward's team could catch a ball hit in the air for an out. Fine. But then the men threw out words like "stumped" and "bowled" and "leg before wicket," and Georgiana's head was spinning in no time.

Which wasn't to say she wasn't enjoying herself. She could hardly remember a time when she'd had such a great time watching an event. Even the knights' tournament practice, for all its pageantry, didn't have this palpable drama. The crowd was *in it*. Like a living, breathing thing, it was in tune with every bowl, every hit, every catch and run. Georgiana loved the exuberance of it, the feeling of being able to make noises and clap (as ladylike as Aunt Augusta allowed) and cheer the players on. That was what the tournament practice had lacked. No matter the interest, the crowd was very much on the outside looking in when it came to the knights. Now, with cricket, it was almost as if the crowd was an active participant, registering the highs and lows of the game along with the players. At one heightened moment, Georgiana was afraid a spectator near her was going to jump out onto the field and make an out himself!

"You don't have to watch him the entire time, you know," Minnie whispered in her ear. Georgiana nudged her away, but Minnie fought back. "I'm not faulting you. If a man like that wanted to marry me, I'd look too, even if he is obsessed with ancient lizard dung."

Georgiana bristled, her eyes on anything other than Edward—who, by the way, was playing just off the right side of the bowler, where he'd just made a sensational one-handed catch before landing flat on his back. The crowd had gone *quite* wild.

"I'm not *only* looking at him," Georgiana groused. "I can't help it if he's so involved in the game."

Minnie snorted. "Yes, very involved, almost as if he doesn't trust anyone else to make a play. *And* he's showing off a bit."

"Edward would never show off."

"No?" Minnie teased. "I can find a little showing off. Though you might be too busy fixating on the grass stains on his knees, the sweat soaking the front of his chest, the indecent way his trousers travel up his calves, highlighting his firm, tight—"

"Minnie!" Georgiana exclaimed.

Minnie's eyes widened rounder than a cricket ball. "What? I was going to say waist. What did you think I was going to say? Your mind is in the gutter, my friend."

"It is not in the gutter. *Your* mind is in the gutter."

Minnie shrugged, a smug smile running the width of her face. "You can find the most interesting things in the gutter sometimes, kind of like mudlarking in the Thames."

Shaking her head, Georgiana went back to the match, trying desperately *not* to give Edward all her attention. But Minnie was right—it was a bit of a lost cause. Because the grass stains were enthralling in the most bewildering way, the sweat stains as hypnotic as a pagan service, the trousers... Well, they were indecent, but magnificently so. Georgiana had to remind herself there was no harm in looking. Just as Minnie's mother always told the girls when the dessert course was brought in, looking but not touching was a woman's greatest power.

Only...an apple tart was not nearly as tempting as Edward—especially when he had the ball in his hands.

The team captain shouted at Edward, ordering him to bowl the next over, which consisted of six balls to the other team. Georgiana squeezed her fingers together as Edward took over the spot twenty yards away from the batsman.

One thing she *had* learned that afternoon was that the bowler could get the batsman out on his own if he pitched the ball past him, knocking a bail off the wicket. It was a rare thing, and hadn't happened once this match, but there had been a few that had come tantalizingly close.

Edward's delivery started out similarly to the others before him. He walked toward the batsman, increasing his speed into a running jump as he launched the ball, bouncing it on the ground before it reached the batsman. What was not similar to the other bowlers was the style in which he rounded his arm ninety degrees from his body before he released it. All the other bowlers pitched the ball underhand. Edward's technique caused the ball to fly viscously faster, especially when he snapped his wrist at such a rate that made the ball spin into a nasty curve. The first two batsmen facing him popped out in the inner field, making for two quick outs.

"Is that legal?" Minnie asked, and Georgiana could only bob her shoulders inconclusively. The umpire didn't say anything, even though there were definite grumblings in his direction from the opposite team.

"He's awfully good," she heard Aunt Augusta remark, which Georgiana thought was the nicest thing she'd ever heard the woman say about someone outside the clergy.

She was right, though. Edward *was* good. Frightfully so. And it was evident in his well-formed muscles, honed by afternoons of practice and matches. It was an odd thing, seeing him here around all those people. Most of their exchanges had been in environments of her choosing. To see him let loose and stretch his body with the other players was almost like seeing a lion hunt in its native habitat.

A round of applause broke her from her musings as a new batsman braced himself in front of the wicket. Minnie gasped excitedly, informing Georgiana it was Lord Carstark, a viscount that all the young ladies were vying for this Season.

With his light brown hair and smoldering intensity, Georgiana could understand the appeal, but there was something to the viscount that turned her off. He preened to the crowd, putting on a display that wasn't necessary, demanding attention that he was already getting.

It was evident there was no love lost between the batsman and bowler. Carstark's wide grin turned insidious and taunting as he readied himself for the ball. He pointed his bat at Edward and shouted, "No funny business."

Edward didn't bother with a reply and began his bowling action, cutting through the air like lightning. The ball hit the ground and bounced up just in time for Carstark's massive swing; however, the ball changed trajectory at the last moment, sailing right by him. The crowd let out a collective cry as the ball came within an inch of the bail—shaking it, but not knocking it off the stump.

Carstark's face burned red. "I said no funny business!"

Again, Edward didn't respond, only going into his wind-up for another delivery. Once more, the ball spun off the ground, flying past the frustrated Carstark.

The viscount threw down his bat, marching down the pitch toward a bored-looking Edward, who didn't even move an eyelash. "You bastard! I told you to watch yourself!" Carstark fumed, stopping a few feet away. The other players sidled closer to referee the situation. The poor umpire had to elbow his way into the thick of it. Because of Edward's height—and the fact that the crowd had gone eerily quiet—Georgiana could make out every bit of the exchange.

"What are you talking about?" Malbeck yelled, shoving his way to the action. "There's nothing funny going on. You're just upset because you can't hit the ball!"

Murmurs of assent and dissent tumbled out of the teams and only stopped when Carstark put out his hand. "He's bowling overarm!"

"The hell he is!" Malbeck countered. "His arm's staying well below his shoulder!"

"I want to see the ball," Carstark insisted. "He's obviously tampering with it. There's no way he's making it spin like that on his own."

Still bored, almost to the point of somnambulant, Edward shook his head. "I don't have to prove myself to you. I've never tampered with a ball in my life. Now go back over there and let's continue. This is ridiculous."

"He's just afraid," Malbeck spat.

"Be quiet, old man," Carstark shot back with a menacing laugh. "No one even wants you here. You're as much of an embarrassment as Marlborough." He zeroed in on Edward. "And yes, you *do* need to prove yourself. With a father like yours…losing runs in your blood. It's why men like you cheat."

The players fell as silent as the crowd, and a current of disbelief buzzed through the field. Malbeck raged like he wanted to beat Carstark to the ground, but he stayed back, watching Edward to see what he would do.

Georgiana pressed her eyes closed, praying he didn't cause another scene like he had at the knights' practice. She could understand his *wanting* to hit the impudent man, but that didn't mean he should.

Those spoiling for a fight were left disappointed. "Go back," Edward repeated.

Carstark cocked his head. "What's wrong, Marlborough?

Where's that nasty temper of yours? Do you want to punch me like you did Jacobson? I guarantee I won't go down as easy." He glanced to the benches. "Oh, that's right. I heard you were pursuing a rich commoner to fund your little business. Is she here? She is, isn't she? Wouldn't want to show the Queen of Coprolites how low you are, would you?" he sneered. "How dirty your mining hands have become. Heiresses throw themselves at titles every day, but yours hasn't succumbed to your particular *charm* yet. I wonder why?"

It should have shamed Georgiana that Carstark was speaking about her, but she was held too tightly in Edward's grip, wondering at his next action. The tension was untenable, the scene too heightened, the behavior too intolerable.

Was that the point all along? Was Carstark trying to goad Edward into doing something silly and foul and perhaps get kicked out of the match? All because Carstark couldn't hit the stupid little ball?

After a few more heavy seconds, the crowd released a breath as Edward continued to stand his ground, not giving in to the taunts. Eventually, Carstark let his teammates prod him back over to his end of the pitch, clearly thinking they'd put Edward— and his imagined cheating—in its place.

Carstark returned to his position in front of the wicket, his pompous grin even more pronounced as he eyed Edward. For his part, Edward didn't seem to be that affected by the exchange. His brow *might* have lowered in annoyance, but Georgiana couldn't be sure. Carstark was a gnat that Edward didn't even bother to swat away.

Emotions warred within her. Carstark had tried—and failed— to make Edward into a punch line. On the one hand, she was so immensely proud of Edward's discipline. He behaved like a solid gentleman; there was much honor in that. However, she almost wished the current opinion of a man wasn't based so much on his restraint. If anyone deserved to be punched, it was Carstark. At least in medieval times, they could strike each other with lances.

It might be considered barbaric nowadays, but Georgiana guessed it was probably effective for working off aggression and putting vile men like Carstark in their place.

Because how was Edward supposed to work off his anger? Gentlemen were supposed to bear affronts, put up a stiff upper lip, and abide. Georgiana had always agreed with that. And yet, after an afternoon in the uncivilized heat with sweat running the length of her spine, clapping so hard her palms hurt, she wasn't sure she could turn the other cheek. She wanted to *do* something.

But Edward beat her to it.

And everything changed.

His wind-up was the same, his steps were the same, and his speed was the same. But this time, the delivery definitely wasn't the same.

Because when he released the ball, it hit the ground in the space it had before; however, this time when it popped up, it spun so brutally it made a direct path to Carstark's head, cracking the man square in the eye. The *smack!* was louder than cannon fire.

The players rushed the field again, arguing if the delivery was an accident or if Edward should be penalized for unsportsmanlike conduct. Disgusted by the turn of events and the length of the arguments, Aunt Augusta forced the girls to leave, not giving them time to see Edward or learn the final decision.

Georgiana spent the entire carriage ride home wondering where the lines of sportsmanship were drawn and if she would have done the same thing as Edward. Because there was no doubt in her mind that Edward had hit Carstark on purpose. Was it courage that had been behind the act, or childish stupidity?

One thing she knew for sure was that a knight would never have acted so indecorously in the field of battle. What Georgiana was less certain about was whether she cared.

CHAPTER ELEVEN

SPORTSMANSHIP WAS A bust.

Of all the knightly tests Georgiana would judge him on, Edward had been sure he would pass cricket. However, cooler heads had not prevailed—his cooler head. Damn that miserable son of a bitch Carstark!

Edward could take the taunts and the nasty quips—he was used to them. However, the second Carstark turned his vengeful eye on Malbeck, it was over. There was no way he was letting Carstark off that field without a bruised ego—and eye. The bastard had it coming. And Edward didn't regret it.

It was just rather unfortunate that Georgiana had to see it. He'd been playing so well and having a great time showing off! Alas, he'd just have to keep trying to show the woman his softer, more dignified side. And for her part, Georgiana had no lack of ideas on how he could dull his blade.

In her mind, a calming influence was needed, which was why a week later Edward found himself in a side room of a public house sitting next to her during a reading of Sir Walter Scott's *Rob Roy*.

"My God, when will it ever end?" he groaned, his harsh words tickling the raven curls of the lady seated in front of them.

Georgiana's mouth twisted before she remonstrated him. "Be quiet," she whispered. "Robin Huxley is doing a beautiful job."

"Define beautiful," Edward said, instigating one of her irritatingly disappointed looks.

If Georgiana only knew how hard he was trying, she wouldn't act half so put out. Hell, ever since the cricket fiasco—which she hadn't brought up, thank the Lord—he'd allowed her to cart him all over London in an effort to show him "the importance of art as a means for a knight to access his higher self," and he'd done so willingly with a smile on his face.

Well…mostly willing…and mostly with a smile.

He'd fallen asleep during the second half of Lord Burghersh's opera, fittingly titled *The Tournament*, though she had to give him some credit. When he woke at the end, he was definitely one of the loudest people to applaud.

He'd accompanied her to the National Gallery at Trafalgar Square, though he did grumble his way through the Royal Academy section. Just as he'd expected, practically all the artwork drew inspiration from King Arthur or the Knights Templar, making the entire excursion redundant and worthless in his eyes. Suffice it to say, they didn't stay long. Thirty minutes was plenty of time to spend at an art museum!

When she'd recommended Astley's Amphitheatre, Edward thought that might do the trick. He could appreciate art if it involved horses and death-defying acts. But, yet again, it had a twist. The owner, Andrew Ducrow, was capitalizing on the excitement over the Eglinton Tournament by staging reenactments of dramatic scenes from some of the most popular romantic books of the time. The night they'd gone to Astley's, *Ivanhoe* was on the menu.

Edward sat it out dutifully but wasted little time tossing Georgiana in his carriage to return home the second the final act ended, being sure to inform her he'd seen more death-defying feats in his sisters' playroom.

It simply could not be helped. The medieval craze failed to make a mark on him. He was impervious to its supposed charm. But he pulled up his boots and suffered through it. The whole point was to spend time with Georgiana. He didn't have to enjoy what they did; he just had to pretend like he did. Despite all the complaining, he thought he was doing a pretty good job of it too.

Unfortunately, Georgiana didn't always agree.

"What are you doing?" she whispered now, nudging him in the side. He was becoming quite used to her elbow, if no other part of her body.

"I'm trying to determine how hard I have to hit my head against the chair in order to knock myself out without giving myself permanent injury."

She answered with a sardonic smile. "I think you should give it your all and go from there."

Brat! His gaze settled on her long and hard, and Georgiana shifted in her seat. He liked that; he liked that he could make her uneasy with one of his looks. It proved she wasn't impervious and confirmed that these ridiculous trips were worthwhile.

Despite his recalcitrant behavior, Edward could feel something developing between them, though he knew she wasn't ready to admit it. He suffered no illusions—to Georgiana, he was merely a means to an end, a pet project to pass the time, but he was growing on her. He was sure of it. He might be as welcomed as weeds in a garden, but he was still climbing.

At least the room was working in his favor. It was small and packed with people, and the lack of space required the chairs to be pushed so close together that her thigh was resting alongside his. Even with all the fabric between them, Edward could still feel her skin jump whenever he moved, her blood pump, and it had nothing to do with Robin Huxley's fake Scottish brogue or the myriad props the orator fumbled with to bring the Highlands to life.

"Well, I have to do something," Edward muttered, leaning on his side closest to Georgiana as if they were old friends. The fleshy man on her other side was encroaching on her territory as well. For once, Edward was the lesser of two evils, and she angled back to him. "His accent is intolerable. I'm surprised the whole

Jacobite rebellion doesn't jump out of the book and bludgeon him to death for the effrontery."

Georgiana shook her head, ignoring him, and Edward got a whiff of her vanilla-infused perfume. His mouth watered. The woman was a veritable snack.

"Fine," she replied airily. "Whatever you do, do it quietly. I'm trying to enjoy myself."

He answered with a grunt. And tried to behave. He *really* did. He took to counting the number of times Huxley said "lass," but he laughed so hard when it hit one hundred that half the room shushed him. He tried counting the tiles on the ceiling, but he tipped so far back in his chair that he almost fell backward.

It was then he noticed the Countess of Brentwood in the front row. She'd heard his chair squeak and turned to grant him a smile, which he dutifully returned. That gave him an idea, one that didn't require anything but his trusty memory.

He relaxed in his chair, folding his hands placidly over his lap.

"Now what are you doing?" Georgiana asked.

"Counting how many women I've kissed in this room."

"What?" she squawked.

The portly man sitting on Georgiana's other side cleared his throat, shooting her a rude glare.

She sank even further into Edward's side. "What?" she repeated, quieter but with just as much intention.

Edward twisted his lips bashfully. "Well, if I have to sit here, I might as well do something useful. And I haven't always been the town pariah." He didn't feel the need to tell her that most of the innocent, exploratory kisses happened before he and the women were out of the nursery.

She paused for a beat, her mouth clamped shut as if she didn't want to say anything. Naturally, curiosity won out. "How many?" Georgiana asked. "No, don't tell me. Actually, yes, tell me."

Edward grinned, squinting straight ahead. "Nine. No, eight. The Duchess of Wentworth kissed me two times."

"How positively memorable for you."

"Oh, it was," he replied, his grin getting wider with the memory. "She was quite messy about it."

"I'm sorry."

"Don't be." He turned his smirk to her. "Messy can be good at the right times."

"Do you always have to be so—"

"Charming?"

Georgiana's neck was so tight that he thought it could snap. "Vulgar."

"Oh, please," Edward replied easily, uncrossing one of his long legs in the tight space so he could cross the other. "Don't be a hypocrite. I'm sure your George has tasted his fair share of forbidden fruit. Trust me, no woman wants a novice in the bedroom on their wedding night."

Georgiana's cheeks flamed as red as a matador's cape.

"He's not 'my George,'" she replied hotly. "And no woman wants the town rooster, either."

Edward chuckled, not offended by her comment in the least. "It's fine for your books, but the last thing you'll want is *please* and *thank yous* when the lights are off. Trust me."

"Perhaps you should be the one on the stage, Lord Edward," Georgiana replied, trying and failing to hide the bitterness in her voice. "It seems you have much to teach the audience."

Was she jealous? My God, he hoped so. Suddenly, this day was looking up. From now on, he might even think of *Rob Roy* fondly, though he doubted it.

"I only need an audience of one, sweetheart. You just let me know when you're ready to learn."

THEY LEFT THE reading soon after. Georgiana's manner had turned cold and remarkably sullen, so when she'd asked to go, Edward couldn't get up fast enough. He should have taken her straight home, but he wasn't ready to leave her yet. Instead, Edward directed them toward the park and was relieved she didn't put up a fuss.

Of course, she would have to *say* something to put up a fuss, and it seemed she was determined to freeze him out. He'd disappointed her yet again.

Baiting her hadn't been wise. He *had* kissed all those women, but that had been years ago, way before his family's fall from grace. Edward didn't know why he told her. He'd been bored, that was true, but the look on her face had been so…curious. And angry. It was the curiosity that got him. Was she curious about kissing him, or curious as to why other women had wanted to? Either way, it was an opening—one he couldn't pass up.

"Are you all right?" he asked, breaking their troublesome silence. Edward turned to study her. She was pretty in pink this afternoon, with her hair braided back against the sides of her head like a fine lace under her bonnet. However, his heart ached to see those curls again. That was truly the work of art, not these performances she brought him to. The memory of her head popping out from the window never ceased to remind of Leonardo da Vinci's unfinished masterpiece, *La Scapigliata*.

"I'm fine," she said.

"I don't know why you're so angry with me."

"I'm not angry. You have to care to be angry, and I couldn't care less about your rooster ways."

"Good."

"Yes. Good…" She kicked up a few pebbles.

Edward feigned a cough. "Awfully dusty out here today."

Georgiana grunted.

"You sure you don't have something on your mind?" he pressed, ducking his head around her huge hat, which was meant to keep out all the sun's rays and, apparently, annoy men. "Something you want to ask me?"

She scoffed. "What could I possibly want to ask you?"

In for a penny, in for a pound. "What I kiss like."

Her feet stalled as if she'd hit a brick wall. Slowly, she turned to him, her lips slightly parted, her expression the definition of aghast. Edward would have laughed if she hadn't looked so damned serious.

"I would never ask that. I couldn't care less that you've kissed half the *ton*."

"It was hardly half."

Georgiana shrugged, her feet moving again. Her brow furrowed, and she started muttering to herself. "...probably all shallow and bored, no decency or integrity, no morals to rub between them."

"Unfortunately, there was little rubbing," he quipped.

Her inhale was so loud that it startled birds out of the nearby chestnut tree. "Please, you needn't tell me any more."

"Why not?" he asked lazily. "You want to know."

"I do not!"

"Sure you do. That's why you're so angry."

Her fists clenched. "I told you, I'm not angry at you! A cad will always behave like a cad."

"Not mad *at me*," he said, taking her forearm, forcing her to stop. He waited until she lifted her chin before he continued. "You're angry at yourself because even with all my uncouth ways, my barbaric manners, the fact that I don't give one shit about all this medieval nonsense, you want me."

He'd reduced her to a trout. Her lips flopped open, but nothing came out. When the words finally flowed, they were as cold as the Atlantic. "I want nothing to do with you. If it weren't for the tickets, I wouldn't be here."

She was trying to hurt him, and he was surprised that that remark kind of did. Edward crossed his arms. "Keep telling yourself that. Just admit it. I saw you at Lord's."

"You just happened to be a part of the game I was watching!"

"You were doing more than watching," Edward said. "You were *watching*."

Georgiana flopped her arms to her sides. "Was that sentence

supposed to make sense? Besides, you literally threw a ball at a man's face. If I was transfixed, it was because of your savagery."

Edward laughed. "Oh, so now I'm a savage? Well, what does that make you? Because after all our time together, I'm absolutely certain that I'm rubbing off on you."

"Don't believe for one second you are rubbing off on me, my lord," she seethed, veins protruding from her temples. "In fact, you're failing in every way. I've given you plenty of opportunities for you to show me a nobler version of yourself, and you've failed at every turn."

Edward stepped closer, the tips of his boots brushing hers. "Perhaps it's you who's failing, because even with my disappointments, you're still falling for me."

"Falling?" she shouted. "Are you mad?"

He shook his head. "Not at all, princess. You're utterly besotted with me, and it's killing you. You want to know what it's like to kiss me, and let me just tell you...it would be fucking fantastic."

Poor thing. If Georgiana's eyes got any wider, they'd fall off her face. "How dare you speak to me this way."

"I *will* dare," he countered, raising his voice along with hers. "I've tried being chivalrous—"

"You've *literally* thrown me into your carriage countless times."

"I've made polite conversation—"

"Have you heard yourself speak? Your language consists of foul words and groans."

"I haven't tried to kiss you once—"

"Why?"

Edward blinked, coming up short. "What?"

Georgiana looked away, pulling back her shoulders. "Wh-why?" she stammered. "Why haven't you tried to...kiss me?"

Edward blew out a breath, taking off his hat to comb his hand through his hair. "I told you. I'm trying to be chivalrous."

"You're bad at it!"

"And I was trying to be respectful—"

"You call me a spoiled brat whenever you get the chance!"

"I'm trying to be the husband you want."

"Well, stop, because you'll never be!"

His eyes narrowed. "And yet you want me to kiss you."

Georgiana hesitated, her eyes darting at everything but him. Edward pressed closer, and she walked backward off the path until a weeping beech tree surrounded them on all sides with its upside-down branches, scant light dappling through. "I...I didn't say that."

He continued to stalk her. "But you meant it. And you have no idea how bloody much I want to. All I do is think about kissing you. I want to know if you taste like your tea in the morning. I want to know how soft your cheeks feel when I hold your face; I want to know if you'll whimper in my mouth or stay quiet."

Georgiana licked her lips. On any other woman, that might be an invitation, but Edward forced himself to wait. He was only going to kiss her for the first time once. He needed to make it perfect.

"You can't possibly think those things," she said.

"Oh, yes I can." He reached up to trace a path along her jaw. "With you, princess, it's quite easy. But I've been reading up on this courtly love you're so enamored with. The knights never kissed their ladies. They honored them too much for such...corporeal attentions."

"But you're not a knight," she said.

"Damn right."

Was she learning closer to him, or was his hand guiding her face toward his?

"And I'm not a lady," she whispered.

He shook his head slowly. "Not yet."

Her lips were just inches from his. He could lick them if he wanted—and oh, how he wanted.

"I will never be your lady."

Edward smiled. "That's good, because the last thing I want

you to be is my lady."

She frowned—but didn't push away. "What do you want me to be, then?"

"Just a woman. My woman."

Edward swept in, kissing her the way he wanted to kiss her, the way a woman like Georgiana Spence should be kissed—long and hard. He didn't stop to ask himself if it was right or proper or if the intensity of his desire would frighten her away. Edward only thought about how much he wanted her and how much she wanted him. Because she couldn't hide it—he refused to let her.

Holding her tight with one hand cupped behind her neck, he guided the exchange, tasting and plundering, finding a rhythm and quickly losing it. Senses were too high; inhibitions were too low. There was only an intensity to drink and know. She tasted like berries and sunshine, innocence and temptation, and all that was forbidden—the apple to Adam's desire. She was the siren to his ship, the arrow to his heel, the scissors to his hair, and he would give it all to her without rebuke because her power over him only made him feel stronger and free.

Slowly, gently, he relaxed his hold, placing long, languid kisses over her still-startled lips. He half expected her to shove him away, punching him in the process, but after a moment, the tension relaxed around her mouth and she allowed him to penetrate even further, sinking his tongue deep inside her, licking the unknown majesty that he—and only he—would ever know.

When her tongue began to mate with his, he wanted to cry so much he growled. When he felt her hands press against his back, he wanted to howl so badly he groaned. Her participation, however light, was a boon to his confidence. She may not want him. She may not *want* to want him, but damn it, she desired him. And for now, that was good enough.

Edward's fingers shook as he clasped her face, finally getting to hold the cheeks that he held in such reverence. It had been so long since Edward had let himself go, so long that he couldn't even remember a time.

There were so many things Edward yearned to say, but his mind was a tempest. Thoughts flickered in and out of sight like the beam from a lighthouse. He wanted to ask if his embrace was too tight. He wanted to tell her he'd wanted to do this from the first moment he saw her. He wanted to tell her he acted superior and aloof because he was scared on the inside and the only time he wasn't scared was when he was with her.

But mostly he wanted to tell her that for the rest of his life he would never forget the way she tasted here and now. Because it was unique and special, and there was no doubt in his mind it was created just for him. She tasted like better days. She tasted like the future, and she made him want to be man enough to deserve it.

After what felt like forever, but not nearly long enough, he lifted his head from her shiny lips, wiping his thumb over them one last time because the farther he went away, the more he wanted to touch them. Edward had never understood addiction before, and yet now had never understood anything more.

"Tha-thank you," she said, her eyes bright and wide.

Her response pulled a shy chuckle from him. "I told you," he said, tracing his fingertips down her neck under her collar to the hollow of her throat. "No one wants *thank yous* in the bedroom."

"But we're not in a bedroom. And we never will be," she said with a smile, leaving him in the shadows.

Edward straightened his jacket, wondering how she could walk so straight when he could barely stand. He'd given her his best work there, and Georgiana strolled away unaffected. Had he been wrong? Did she not desire him as much as he did her?

And then Edward heard a gasp and saw her trip as she escaped from the beech. He was on her in a second, not giving himself time to gloat. He held her upright by her waist. "Be careful," he said, meeting her shocked gaze. "Walking gets harder the more besotted you become."

All right, so he'd let himself gloat a little.

CHAPTER TWELVE

EDWARD MIGHT BE failing as a knight, but even he knew an apology was in order. He didn't regret kissing Georgiana in the park—in fact, he couldn't wait to do it again—but he allowed that the episode might not have gone as smoothly as she would have liked. Women required a certain finesse, and his woman was no different.

Which was why it took him a whole week to catch her again. Whenever he would send a letter to the Spence residence, asking for her time, he would get a curt reply saying she was busy. No other explanation—just busy. Edward had never met a woman so damn busy in his life. After the third letter, he'd decided that enough was enough. He wouldn't let her hide from him, or her feelings. They had a bargain, after all, and she would live up to it.

When Edward pulled his curricle onto the Spences' street, he was fully ready for their butler to tell him in that frosty accent that Georgiana was "out" yet again. This time he would wait like the infatuated youth she'd reduced him to. As long as it took.

However, he wasn't ready to see a determined-looking Georgiana exiting the house, her nose up in the air, her gaze sharp and focused. Following women wasn't a habit Edward partook in, but his curiosity was piqued. He parked his vehicle a few houses down from the Spence door and got out, retracing her steps and keeping his distance. Just close enough to know which way she turned—just close enough to enjoy the sway in her hips.

After half an hour of subterfuge, Edward's patience was finally rewarded, though it did nothing to relieve the swift kick in the balls at what he encountered.

George. She'd gone to meet George.

Edward watched as the friends greeted one another properly enough at the meeting of two streets, although the familiarity was throbbingly evident. There were a few moments where arms were raised toward the other, hands held in the precipice between them as if they were so very used to touching each other on different, less visible occasions. Edward was quite certain this experience would carve out space in his railing brain for the remainder of the day, although it only lasted for a few minutes. It ended anticlimactically enough, with George handing over a bag and Georgiana hugging it to her chest while granting him a profusion of apparent thanks.

George tipped his hat and exited the scene quickly, leaving Georgiana to go into the adjacent park, choosing the closest bench she could find. Instantly, she settled her skirts and began rummaging through the bag.

Edward almost hated to interrupt her solitude. He had half a mind to let her enjoy her slice of time, but the bruising in his chest smarted. The idea of leaving without knowing what was going on between the two rankled his ego too much.

Before Edward knew it, he was towering over Georgiana before she even registered he was there. His long shadow draped across the pages on her lap, causing her to squint up at her loss of light.

The only thing that salvaged his pride was the look of surprise (and not a little bit of horror) on her face when she finally recognized him. *And* the fact that she dropped the ledger at her feet. Georgiana Spence wasn't a clumsy woman, but for some reason, her limbs had a difficult time around Edward.

"Read any good books lately?" he asked, glancing at the ledger. "That doesn't look like Shakespeare."

"What...what are you doing here?" she stammered, fighting for composure.

The space closed between them, and Edward let himself drink her in. He couldn't boast of a sweet tooth, but in her light pink gown embellished with dark pink lace at the bust and elbows, Georgiana reminded him of strawberries and cream. His mouth watered at the decadent thought.

"You've been avoiding me," he said, answering in his own way.

She snorted, attempting to pick up the ledger, but he blocked her with his thigh, scraping up the pages before she could push him aside. Annoyance flaring up from her long lashes, Georgiana cocked her head. "Don't be so dramatic. Despite what you think, you don't own me. I do have things in my schedule that don't revolve around you." She fluttered her fingers in the air. "Now, give it back."

Edward hefted the journal in his hand, resisting opening it. He wanted her to tell her what was inside. "Not until you tell me why I found you—my fiancée—meeting a man who was certainly not me this afternoon."

Her eyes narrowed to slits while her arm continued to hang in the air. "I'm not your fiancée. And it is no business of yours what I do with my time."

"That's where we disagree," he replied coolly. "We have a deal, one you are not living up to. So your time is very much my business."

A battle of wills surfaced, each player calculating how long the other would hold out. The last thing Edward wanted to do was stand here all day, but he would do it.

"Why do you have to ruin everything?" she muttered, dropping her hand into her lap. She fell back on the bench, regarding him like the scum on the bottom of her shoes.

His smile was merciless. "You're just mad because I caught you in your little clandestine tryst."

"Tryst?" She *humphed*. "George agrees to meet me once a

week to hand over my father's account ledgers. I have an hour to study them, check the numbers, see what's working and what's not. It's hardly a lovers' rendezvous."

The air flew out of his sails. Edward itched to open the ledger and confirm her story. Life had made him naturally skeptical of just about anything that came out of a person's mouth, but he talked himself off the ledge. Her explanation was too odd to be a lie. He chose to trust her word. Although he wasn't sure she deserved it.

She had been lying, after all. Weeks before at dinner, she'd told her father that George had not given her the ledgers to spy on, protecting him. Clearly, he had and was still doing it. Weekly.

Alarm bells went off in Edward's head at her deception. He warned himself to be careful with this one. And then he ignored the warning altogether.

Edward released himself from his rigid pose, sitting next to her on the bench. There was plenty of room, even with her voluminous fabrics, but he still left her no space, skimming his thigh against hers as she let out a disgruntled sigh and tried to create inches between them.

"Why?" he asked through her jostling.

Georgiana didn't miss a beat. "Because I like numbers, and I won't stop until my father realizes that he can run his company more humanely without losing any money. I have to creep around in secret because he won't let me go to the factory anymore." Her words took on a bitter edge. "He calls me a distraction."

"I thought you performed charity work?"

She offered him a wary look. Edward didn't know why—he was genuinely interested. If he was being honest with himself, he had an avid interest in everything she did.

"That's one thing my father lets me do for the factory," she explained. "I meet once a week with a group of women, and we organize initiatives for some of the workers. Gift baskets, food, blankets, things like that. They spend most of the time arguing over how best to decorate the baskets. We never make real change."

Edward nodded, drumming his long fingers against the ledger's spine. "And this is the real change you seek?"

She returned a baleful glare. "Of course it is. I know it must be difficult for men like you to see from their country estates, but men and women are fed up with working to their bones day after day with nothing to show for it. Most factories barely offer a living wage, and the workhouses are veritable prisons. The time for change is now. I can't just sit by and let my father contribute to the poverty that litters London's streets."

"But what can you do?" he asked. Edward wasn't trying to be dismissive or harsh. It was a real question. Everything he'd gathered from Robert Spence was that the man wasn't a risk taker. He wanted money, and then he wanted more of it. He tended to espouse, with many others, the idea that the poor were poor by choice and not by environmental circumstance. They just didn't work hard enough to pull themselves out of the gutter. Georgiana, on the other hand, was steadfast in her notion to see the best in people, no matter the shine on their shoes.

"What can I do?" she repeated. "Everything. Anything. I've been reading so much on the subject of human working conditions—"

"Oh, yes, the American."

Georgiana's color grew high. "Yes, the American," she drawled, mimicking his dry rejoinder. "I have to learn from someone. No one wants to converse with me on the subject because I'm a woman. It's beyond frustrating."

The way she said it gave Edward pause. "Wait. Does *the American* know you're a woman?"

Her nostrils flared and she refused to meet his gaze. So that was a no.

Georgiana barreled on. "Do you know in some companies they create managers whose job it is to speak to the individual workers and ask them what they need or want for the jobs to be more effective? That kind of partnership is the future."

"How so?"

Her eyes glowed with the kind of passion that Edward had only seen in the bedroom. It rocked him off his axis. "It shows that worker and owner don't always have to be at such odds. Both sides can benefit from the exchange."

Edward attempted to keep the frown off his face but failed miserably. The woman needed to keep her fairytales to her books. "You speak of a utopia."

"I am not so naïve. I speak of an equal playing field. Like your cricket."

Edward snorted. She *was* naïve. Sides were constantly cheating in cricket to get the upper hand. His words came out in a long sigh. "As long as there are people in this world, there will always be some who want more."

Georgiana arched an eyebrow. "Like you?"

"Me?"

She nodded. "We didn't agree to meet today, and yet here you are, trying to whisk me away." She hugged her arms around her chest. "I'm too tired to spar with you today, Edward."

Oh, if she would only let him hold her! Didn't she know his shoulders were specifically made for her to rest her head? "There will be no sparring, I promise. It won't take long. Besides, I'm doing this for your benefit."

She sniffed. "And yours, no doubt."

"My God, woman, I've never met a more distrustful person!"

"I'm distrustful?" She barked a disbelieving laugh. "When you have barely told me anything about yourself. I've spent the last few weeks with you, and I still know next to nothing about you!"

That was just pure nonsense. "You know I'm a wonderful singer."

She gritted her teeth. "I don't think that was the word I used."

"You know I'm spectacular at cricket."

"You seemed to have a bit of an aim problem."

"And you know I love listening to readings of *The Bride of*

Lammermoor."

"It was *Rob Roy,* you fiend!"

Edward waved a dismissive hand in the air. "Oh, it was Scottish, close enough. The point is that you know more about me than most; now count yourself supremely lucky and come with me so I can apologize properly, damn it."

Georgiana lolled her head to the side, her brow dropping. "I don't feel particularly lucky… Oh, very well, why not?" she asked, snatching the ledger out of his hand. "I assume you won't leave me alone until I do."

"Quite right," Edward agreed.

"But can you please make it quick? I really am tired."

Edward stared straight ahead. If he had a cockstand, it would have shriveled into nothing. "Ugh, don't ever make a man promise that," he muttered.

CHAPTER THIRTEEN

THEY WAITED FOR George to reclaim the ledger. The poor man was instantly twitchy and nervous when he spotted Edward sitting next to Georgiana. Edward added to the businessman's worry when he stayed quiet, presenting a soft, menacing sneer while the transaction took place.

Edward had to commend him—George had always seemed too toothless to stand up to his boss. With no great family behind him, he had too much to lose. And yet he risked it all for Georgiana anyway. That was mostly the reason behind Edward's sneer. He never trusted altruistic men. Everyone had an angle; everyone wanted something for their troubles. George was no different. And he wanted Georgiana. Poor bastard. All this for nothing, since Georgiana would only ever be his.

They returned to his curricle, and twenty minutes later, Edward helped Georgiana step out onto the famed street where fashionable London did their shopping.

"Bond Street, my lord?" Georgiana asked with that unimpressed air that always managed to impress him. For not being born a lady, she had the tilt of her nose at just the perfect angle. His mother would adore her. His sisters, too, for that matter.

"Don't tell me you've been here before," he lamented playfully, taking her arm.

Reading his joke easily, Georgiana explained, "My mother is a fan of shopping."

"And you aren't?" he teased.

He watched as she tried to contain her smile with her bottom teeth, her adorable cheeks puffing out at the effort. It made her even more deliciously rosy.

"I like to shop, as well," she admitted as he guided her across the congested thoroughfare toward Grosvenor Street. "This is how you mean to apologize? You don't strike me as the kind of man to trail after a woman, holding her bags while she mulls over red or blue muslin."

"You're absolutely right." He sniffed. "But then again, this isn't your average shopping expedition. For starters"—he looked her up and down, causing her cheeks to flush ever more—"I'm not sure anything inside will fit you. Nevertheless, I was told it was the perfect place to take a woman such as yourself."

"Such as myself?" she repeated. "You mean someone uniquely beautiful and brilliant?"

"I was thinking uniquely stubborn and hard to please, but close enough."

Before she could utter a hot retort, Edward shoved her unceremoniously into a nondescript door, away from the other storefronts. Walking side by side through the dark corridor, it took a moment for them to get their bearings. As the room opened up, a dim light shone through the arched tracery windows on the back wall, and he could see Georgiana's lips part in a silent gasp.

"Oh, Edward," she sighed.

His balls tightened on her breathy tone, and he vowed that there would come a day when she said those words underneath him. Or on top. It really didn't matter, as long as she wasn't wearing any clothes.

"Do you like it?" he asked, banishing the visions of a naked Georgiana from his immediate mind. He had to walk, after all. He moved farther into the room, casting his arms out in the space as if showcasing the queen's jewels. To Georgiana, the room was indeed that special. "I'm surprised you've never been here before."

"To the Gothic Hall?" she whispered as if they were in a church. "I've only heard of it." He watched as she spun around slowly, her eyes attempting to take in all Samuel Pratt had to offer.

A preeminent collector and antique dealer, Pratt was a meticulous cataloger and expert illustrator. Men paid handsomely at his exhibits, purchasing arms, armor, and trinkets to add to their baronial halls. His storehouse was the place to visit if one needed to build one's medieval inventory.

In recent years, his business had expanded to such a degree that he ran out of room at his Bond Street shop and had to open a second one on Grosvenor. Designed by architect Lewis Nockalls Cottingham, it was appropriately kitted in the rich gothic style, equipped with dark, Tudor-like panel walls and high, buttressed ceilings. The atmosphere was dark and musty—hardly conducive to browsing—but the ambiance more than made up for it. Wrought-iron candelabra stretched along the expanse, highlighting bulky, intricately carved furniture and plush, gem-colored upholstery.

But all that was mere periphery. Because what everyone came for—what everyone yearned to see—was the armor.

Georgiana was no different.

It only took a second for Edward to find her camped in the middle of the room, appreciating one of Pratt's suits on display. Even worn lifelessly by a dummy, the armor was spectacularly impressive. Made in the fifteenth century, its steel was thin and shiny, expertly crafted and embellished. The sabatons worn at the feet were shapely and pointed, the pauldrons at the shoulders massive and wide, the vambraces fitted and smooth. Even Edward saw the appeal. What man didn't want to strut around in such a thing? What man's estimation of himself didn't grow when looking at his reflection in the suit? It had the ability to change a way of thinking.

Not his. Not now. But a different man's.

A patter of footsteps broke up their awed hush. "Ah, does the lady like what she sees?" a gentleman asked, coming to stand next to her. He was middle-aged and thin, and energy bounced off him in the kinds of waves that threatened to pull most people under.

Georgiana shook her head reverently at the piece, reluctant to turn away. "It is truly magnificent," she rasped. Any other person saying it would be too much for Edward, but he was utterly enchanted by her amazement.

"It's the only one I have left," the man said sadly. "The knights have completely cleaned me out."

That got her attention. Slowly, Georgiana turned to the speaker. "Are you Mr. Pratt, sir?"

He beamed, offering a courtly bow. "The one and only. And you are?"

Georgiana blinked, and Edward had to step in, making the proper introductions.

"I didn't think you would be here," Edward stated, coming to stand next to Georgiana. "So close to the event, I thought you'd be busy in Scotland putting the finishing touches on the tournament."

Pratt's face fell, and even with the diffused light, Edward could make out the bruises underneath his eyelids, the haggard expression on the tired man's face.

"I *am* incredibly busy, my lord. But when I need a place to hide and catch my breath, I like to come here. Peaceful, isn't it?"

Georgiana woke up from her trance to nod ferociously. For his part, Edward thought the hall a little too morose, but to each his own.

"Will you be leaving for Eglinton soon?" Georgiana asked. "I read in the newspapers that you are designing the entire field as well as the tents and seating. I can't imagine how you are doing it all."

Pratt smiled, but to Edward, it looked more like a grimace. "Yes, it is quite an undertaking, but I do have helpers, and we've been working for a long while. We'll be ready. We have to be!" They shared a polite laugh before he continued. "I'll be shoving off after the Sinclair ball next week. Since it's being held in honor of all the tournament's participants, they've asked me to attend."

Georgiana's face lit up. "I'm also attending the ball"—she gave Edward a begrudging look—"and we have tickets to the tournament."

"Oh, how lovely, my dear. Then I was see you at the ball as well as in Scotland." Pratt leaned toward her and tapped her hand mischievously. "Hopefully, you'll find me there in one piece."

"I'm sure I will, sir."

Edward cleared his throat, and Pratt returned to him, his features locking into business mode. "Ah, Lord Marlborough, that's right. I have something of yours, yes?"

"You've found it, then?" Edward asked, ignoring Georgiana's inquisitive expression.

"I did, just as you described it. I took the liberty of cleaning it. Looks good as new. Would you like it sent to your house in Town?"

"No, to Marlborough. As soon as you can."

"Of course, my lord. Back where it belongs," Pratt said with a dignified nod.

After a few more minutes of polite chitchat, Pratt excused himself, and it couldn't have come too soon for Georgiana, who looked like she was about to swoon from the excitement.

She turned to Edward, ducking her head, just short of laying it on his chest. What would that feel like?

"I can't believe that was Samuel Pratt!" she squealed.

Unable to help himself, Edward rubbed his hands up and down her forearms. She tensed under his touch, though didn't tell him to stop. So he didn't.

"I can't believe you almost *fainted* in front of Samuel Pratt."

She slapped his chest. A glutton starving for touch, he'd take hers any way he could. "I did not. I just can't believe it. Did you *really* not know he was going to be here?"

Of course Edward had known. He'd called ahead to make sure, though he wasn't about to tell her that.

"I had no idea," he lied easily. "Are you pleased?"

Georgiana glanced up, her eyes as wide as the night sky. "How can you ask me that? Yes, yes, I am very pleased."

"That was the plan."

"What did he find for you?" she asked. "What is 'back where it belongs'?"

Edward should have known she wouldn't miss that. He moved away to a circular oak table, expertly carved with scenes of the crucifixion. "It isn't for you, if that's what you're getting at," he replied dryly.

"I would never—"

"Besides," he cut in, "something tells me you're not the type of girl to be swayed by a string of pearls."

"Depends on the size of the pearls," Georgiana replied sotto voce.

Grinning at her retort, Edward picked up a random helmet on the shelf at their side. "Now this, on the other hand, is more your style. Put it on. I want to see how formidable you look in it."

Georgiana giggled, pushing him away. "My hair is much too thick for that."

He squinted at her head. As usual, underneath her bonnet, it was braided on either side of her forehead and swept back into a low bun at the base of her skull. With the ignorance of most men concerning such things, he merely shrugged and said, "Take it down."

Her hands flew to her head. "Take it down? My lord, you've seen how thick and unruly my hair is. You have no idea how long it will take to put back up."

He didn't care; he would relish every minute. "Let me see," he said, "like before on the balcony."

"No," she answered firmly, putting a stop to the idea. "You put it on. Besides, your head is smaller than mine."

That definitely wasn't true, though he played along. "Are you saying I have a smaller brain?"

"If the helmet fits," she shot back.

He arched one brow, stepping away. The chunky helmet was heavier than he thought it would be, close to eight pounds, he guessed. Sliding it over his head, he was overcome with darkness. The thin, rectangular opening for his eyes was severely limiting, cutting off his view of anything that wasn't straight in front of him.

Georgiana's voice came to him as if traveling through a thick fog. "Well, what do you think?"

"I think it's absolutely ridiculous," he said truthfully. Not even the centuries of triumph and blood soaked into the very life of the steel could make him feel any different. "No wonder so many men died of heat exhaustion during the tournaments. It's like a tomb in here."

Georgiana's laugh wafted up to him, and his body jerked as he felt the press of her thighs against his. Lifting on her tiptoes, she placed her palms on either side of the helmet, bringing their faces to the same plane.

Ears pounding, his breathing abnormally loud and harsh in his ears, Edward froze at her inspection. Her curious green eyes took up the entire space of his lookout slit, her lashes fanning intelligently while she stared into his eyes, as if searching for him under all the weight of the history.

She shook her head wistfully. "Cumbersome, indeed," she said softly.

Damn this infernal thing! She was so close. Edward yearned to tear it off, feel her breath on his face, taste the lips that he'd gone to bed dreaming about every night over the past week.

Suddenly, she frowned and returned to her flat feet, two high spots of red on her cheekbones.

"What is it?" Edward asked.

Georgiana averted her gaze. "Oh, it's nothing."

"Tell me," he said. "Don't make me use my knightly powers on you to get what I want."

She laughed at the ridiculous statement, her face becoming pinker. What in the world was going on in that head of hers?

"It's nothing," she said again.

He heaved a sigh, making the helmet even more hot and uncomfortable. "It's not nothing. You've become all cheeky."

Georgiana spun around in a flurry of skirts. "What did you say?"

Edward shrugged. "Cheeky…you know. When you frown, you purse your lips and then your cheeks bunch out at the sides…cheeky."

She stared at him like he was a frog she wouldn't kiss for all the kingdoms in the world. "Sounds lovely."

"It is, actually," he replied, strolling toward her, picking up a few worthless knickknacks on the way, buying himself time. "They are one of the first things I noticed about you."

"My chubby cheeks?"

Edward placed a ruby-encrusted dagger back on a bureau. "Your lovely, round cheeks. The way they fan out whenever you're excited, the way they burst through like the sun over the horizon. It's…something." He wanted to tell her that those cheeks drove him to madness, always encouraging him to kiss their soft, downy hills, but Edward held his tongue. He'd been too honest that day after the reading. He wasn't sure if she was ready for more.

Georgiana touched her cheeks, hiding them from his perusal. "They *are* something," she agreed, though, perhaps, not in the way he had meant. "You can take off the helmet now. You look ridiculous following me around with it on."

"You're the one who likes knights."

"You are not a knight, remember?"

"Very true." Edward reached for the helmet and stopped. "Not until you tell me what you were thinking about." She opened her mouth, and he stopped her. "And don't tell me nothing again."

Georgiana slapped her lips closed. "Fine." She started walking away from him once more, tracing her hands over the myriad of bric-a-brac at her sides. "I was just thinking…"

"Never a good idea."

"Be quiet. I was just thinking that it's not like the story-books."

"How so?"

She paused, a pained expression on her face, as if her next words would actually hurt. "It just struck me how unromantic it probably was."

"What?" he asked, following behind her.

"In all the books I read, there is always this crescendo of a moment when the knight wins the tournament and rushes his lady up into his arms to kiss her in front of the crowds." She stopped walking and turned back to him, a studious frown marring her face. "But the logistics seem awkward now. How would he do it with that hulking thing on his head?"

"I suppose he could take it off," Edward offered, but her disappointment deepened.

"But then he would be holding it. How would he carry her onto his noble steed while doing that?"

Edward considered this. She had really put a lot of thought into this fantasy. "He could drop the helmet, overcome with love and emotion."

"He could," she allowed, though he could tell she didn't like that option either.

Then an idea came to him. "You're forgetting something," he said. Gently, tenderly, he tipped up her chin, raising her eyes back to his. "Don't worry, Georgie. Your dream isn't dashed just yet," he said, wondering who was actually speaking. It couldn't be him. It sounded nothing like him. Was this the helmet's doing? "I would still be able to kiss you wearing this after vanquishing my foes." She huffed and pulled her chin away, starting to move on, but he stopped her. Flipping up the mouth guard, he displayed the bottom half of his face. "See?" he said. "Hinges."

The corners of her eyes crinkled as Edward swept his arms

around her, pulling her close. Initially tense, she eventually melted into his hold, as helpless and boneless as any fair damsel. Like interlocking fingers, they clung to each other for long seconds, her gaze utterly focused on his lips.

"Should I keep going?" he asked, enjoying the way her fingers clung to his jacket. Keeping him at a distance or pulling him closer, he wasn't sure of her intention.

"N-no…no, that's quite all right. I see how it's done now," she answered, rather breathlessly. All Edward needed to do was dip his head and he would be on her, licking her wine-colored lips, savoring her as he had before. Kissing her senseless surrounded by the curios of her dreams would only help latch her to him even more.

"Tell me to kiss you, Georgie. Tell me you want me."

She shook her head, her brow furrowing. "Even playing out a fantasy, you can't help but be a pompous ass."

"This isn't my fantasy," he said. He began to lift her up when he changed his mind. "But it'll do."

Slowly, Edward lowered his head and kissed her. Chastely, sweetly, they stayed that way, cinched together in a pure embrace. Edward surprised himself by not delving deeper, content to be crystallized in this innocent instance of make-believe. Georgiana whimpered in the back of her throat, but even that didn't urge him to take more. She was so supple, so intoxicating, soft as fresh butter.

A loud crash reverberated from the back room, causing Georgiana to jump out of his arms.

"Sorry! Sorry!" they heard Pratt yell, breaking the charm of the moment.

Edward let out a giant exhale, his muscles pulsing and releasing from the stress. He tore the helmet off, tossed it back on the table, and watched as Georgiana steadily walked away, hugging herself as if a cold breeze had swept into the space.

A little lost on what to do, he thought to defuse the situation, tease her back into an emotion he was familiar with. But the more he pondered ways to see those eyes flash, he found he only wanted what he'd just had: simple, real feelings.

"The helmet fit you well, as if you had some experience wearing it," Georgiana said, her voice slightly wobbly as she filled the silence. She just missed bumping her hip into a table. "Charles told me you used to play as children."

Naturally, Charles would tell her that. Edward wasn't sure if she was asking a question or not, and decided to stay quiet. He didn't know how to reply anyway. He didn't like to talk about those lost, idyllic days.

They had circled back to the armor. After giving it another long perusal, Georgina spun to face him, her expression perfectly composed. "When did you stop believing in knights?"

The answer came to him so swiftly that he didn't have time to temper his response. "When I found out their worthless steel only fetched enough to keep my father at the racetrack for one day."

Her face fell, heavy with empathy. Edward regretted being so honest. The last thing he wanted was her pity. That was not the way he intended to win her.

"I'm sorry your father did those things."

Edward shrugged, wanting to be as far away from the armor as possible. To Georgiana, it harkened back to valor and chivalry, honesty and faith. He didn't want her associating it with him and his depressing youth.

"He's gone now," he said. "There's nothing to be done about it but move on." Edward picked his proverbial heart off the floor and dusted it off before beaming her a cocky smile. "So answer me this—is a trip to the Gothic Hall enough of an apology? Are you back to being besotted with me?"

She scoffed. "Hardly. Although I appreciate your bringing me here, you didn't necessarily exhibit any of the characteristics found in a knight, besides the fact that you have a large head."

She had no idea.

Again, not an honorable thought, damn it.

"I disagree," he countered. "I was cunning. This took thought and planning."

Georgiana shot him a wary scowl. "You were already coming here to pick up something from Mr. Pratt. You merely brought me along."

Fuck, that's true.

"Fine," he allowed, steering her toward the exit. "I just wanted you to enjoy yourself. I hope this took your mind off your troubles for an afternoon."

She stopped to give the room one last look. If he could have bottled that wistful expression, he would have carried it in his pocket for the rest of his life. "It did," she replied softly. "Thank you."

Outside, the blinding sun warped their vision, forcing them to use their hands as visors. "Are you going to the ball?" she asked conversationally while he helped her back into the curricle.

"Why the hell would I go to the ball?"

"Oh, I don't know," Georgiana said, rolling her eyes. "To dance and have lovely conversations? Enjoy yourself for once. It's the last ball of the Season; it's a chance to say goodbye to people before everyone leaves for the country."

Settling next to her in his seat, Edward grimaced. "But I don't want to say goodbye to them. I never wanted to say hello to them."

Georgiana sighed, no doubt resigning herself to her unsocial companion. "You know they aren't all Carstarks and Jacobsons. It wouldn't kill you to be pleasant and spend time with people, cultivate friends. Is it because of your father? Do you resist people because of what he did to you?"

Edward felt himself blanch. Was that the reason? He always thought he stayed away because most people were disappointing arseholes.

"I have no idea what you're talking about," he said.

Georgiana returned a shrewd look. "You don't trust people. You keep them at a distance."

Edward shrugged. "I play cricket," he said, encouraging the horses to go.

"Besides Malbeck, I didn't see you speak to one person on your team."

Why the hell would he want to speak to them? They were playing. Conversation would only dilute the game. He decided to ignore that. Women, obviously, didn't know the first thing about cricket.

"And you're my friend," Edward added. "I spend time with you."

He could feel her studying him. "You barely tell me anything about yourself. You have a sister in Town, and you've never even introduced me to her. It's not the same at all. Besides, I spend time with you because you're bribing me. And we're..." She fidgeted in her seat. "We leave for Scotland after the ball, so we're... That's coming to an end as well."

He refused to let that sting. Besides, it wasn't true. It couldn't be, because he was never letting her go. She knew it just as well as he did. "Keep telling yourself that, princess," he said, leveling her with a look. Her lips were still swollen and juicy, her cheeks still pink and flushed with desire. For him. "Keep telling yourself that."

CHAPTER FOURTEEN

T HE EARL OF Sinclair's ball was the crowning send-off for the tournament. Indeed, just as Mr. Pratt had said, it seemed everyone who was taking part in Eglinton had come to show off their fancy dress for all those less fortunate in London who couldn't make the journey.

And what fancy dresses there were! Georgiana had been so excited about her own outfit, deciding to go simple with a thin emerald gown, embroidered with yellow and navy flowers along the bodice and sleeves. The only embellishments were her bell sleeves, which hung halfway to her feet, and the gold belt she wore loosely at her hips. Her hair had been the ultimate coup. After fighting with her mother, she eventually won out and was allowed to wear her curls unleashed down her back, with only a golden circlet across her forehead keeping everything tidy and in check.

Though odd at first, it felt marvelous to wear clothes with such few restrictions. No corset, no unlimited petticoats, no layer upon layer of fabric—Georgiana only wore a long cotton chemise under her gown. The ease with which she was able to move made her feel like a completely different person—free.

Minnie, on the other hand, wasn't experiencing the same emancipation.

"It's like I'm wearing a house," she groused, rearranging the boxy hooded gable on top of her head. Authenticity had been her aim, and she'd hit the bull's-eye, looking as regal and stiff as Anne Boleyn before she met the axe. "How could women wear these all the time?"

Standing on the outskirts of the crowded ballroom, Georgiana empathized with her friend while watching partners pair up for another waltz. "I suppose one gets used to it. Women of that age would probably think the same way about how tightly we cinch our corsets."

"At least those serve a purpose," Minnie replied bitterly, clawing at the pearl choker at her throat. "They are for our health."

Georgiana grunted. Their health? One night without a corset and she could safely say she felt just as supported by her own body muscles as she did wearing her silk and bone corset.

She wondered what Edward would say about that. She did that a lot lately. Most of the time Georgiana didn't even like what he had to say. But his opinion was always different, always kept her on her toes, and forced her to contemplate something from another view. Frustrating as it was, he never failed to make her think.

A rush of laughter burst from the opposite side of the room, where a group of finely dressed ladies gathered in a circle. With all their glittering jewelry and ermine capes, it didn't take Georgiana long to identify them as the Queen of Beauty and her ladies-in-waiting. Lady Seymour stood in the middle of the group, directing most of the lively conversation. Many whispered that Lady Seymour was only chosen to be the queen of the tournament because her husband was such good friends with Lord Eglinton. Some even whispered *she* was too good of friends with Lord Eglinton, but Georgiana put no stock in that. Though handsome, she wasn't the most beautiful woman or the most popular, but she had an outgoing personality, making her a brilliant fit for the signature role.

"Is that Lord Edward's sister next to Lady Seymour?" Minnie

asked, openly gawking at the group. Georgiana couldn't fault her blatant curiosity; all daughters of peers, the ladies in the group never had much time or inclination to acknowledge Georgiana or Minnie at a society gathering, which, naturally, made them prime sources of interest.

Attempting to be more discreet, Georgiana scanned the women over the twirling dancers and made a noncommittal noise. She'd never met Edward's sister, having only seen her at a distance from time to time. Lady Louise wasn't touted as the most outgoing girl, and Georgiana had been surprised when Edward told her she was selected as one of the Queen of Beauty's ladies. She certainly looked the part tonight, though she didn't appear to be enjoying it. Clad in a lovely yellow Tudor-style gown that accentuated her rich auburn hair, the poor woman stood on the outside of the fun, looking bored and ready to leave. She and her brother had much in common, Georgiana concluded. They both preferred to be on the outside of things. Why had she accepted the role if she didn't even want to be there?

"Why has he not introduced you to her?" Minnie continued, annoyed for Georgiana's sake. "You spend so much time together."

"Not that much time."

Minnie cocked her head, her hands scrambling to right the gable before it toppled over. "You spend every second with him. Honestly, Georgie, I've barely seen you in two weeks. I can't believe you're not engaged yet."

"I told you. We aren't getting engaged. He's taking me and Mother to the tournament, and he asked me to spend time with him beforehand, that's all. You're making a bigger deal out of it than it is."

"But you're obviously friends."

"We're not friends," Georgiana scoffed.

Were they? She thought back to their conversation outside the Gothic Hall, when Edward had referred to her as such. Her cheeks flamed as she remembered the thorny barb she'd thrown back at him. He pretended otherwise, but Georgiana knew she'd hurt him when she said she was only with him because he was bribing her.

She wasn't sure why she'd said it, even if it was true—they *wouldn't* be spending time together if it wasn't for the tickets. Yet these last few weeks had been some of the most fun she'd ever had. She'd be lying to herself if she said she wouldn't miss them when they were over.

But that still didn't make them friends. Friends didn't argue, and friends definitely didn't kiss. Friends didn't constantly challenge and make each other feel like the bottom was always going to drop out. Or was that just her? Georgiana was positive she didn't elicit such feelings in Edward. No doubt, for all his talking, he never listened to a word she said anyway.

"Oh, sweet Lord, he's here!" Minnie squealed, jolting Georgiana from her rambling thoughts.

"Who?"

Minnie's answer came out in one dramatic breath. "The American. Nathaniel Lawrence."

Nathaniel Lawrence! The textile manufacturer that Georgiana had corresponded with? He'd mentioned that he was coming to London, but she'd had no notion he was coming so soon. And here they were, at the same ball.

Instantly, Georgiana broke out into a sweat. She surveyed her surroundings, searching for heavy draperies, a large potted plant with enormous fronds, or even a corpulent man she could stand behind. Anything to keep her out of Lawrence's sight.

"What's wrong with you?" Minnie asked as Georgiana scooted them closer to a mammoth Swiss cheese plant next to the wall, taking a close inspection of its large, waxy leaves.

"Ah…nothing," Georgiana stammered, shuffling through believable excuses in her head. "It got hot all of a sudden. I think it's cooler by the wall." She really didn't want to tell her friend that she was somewhat acquainted with the American. The only problem was that Lawrence had no idea she'd lied to him and was, in fact, a woman. She had signed her letters as "George," insisting she was her father's eldest son.

Thankfully, Minnie accepted her excuse with a distracted nod, too enveloped in Lawrence's aura across the room.

From the safety of her frond protection, Georgiana caught a glimpse of the man when the crowd shifted. If she wasn't going to be what he expected, he certainly wasn't what she expected either. Georgiana had envisioned an elderly gentleman, one with a shock of white hair and an intellectual countenance. What she got was something quite different.

Brawny and tall, bearded and dark, Lawrence looked like he cut down apple trees with his bare hands for fun. His fashion, though not medieval, was showstopping in itself, with bold plaid pants and matching crimson jacket. Georgiana would have considered him a dandy if he didn't look like he could crush any man in the room as easily as a walnut.

She was so lost in her head, it took Georgiana a moment to realize that Minnie was still speaking.

"...he just sailed in from Boston. Apparently, he's come for the tournament, but Father says he's staying with the Duke of Wembley because they are considering going into business together. Apparently, he's also some inventor. Americans are *so* interesting, don't you think?"

By "interesting," Georgiana was certain Minnie meant handsome. And he was. Horribly so.

"I want him to ask me to dance!" her friend declared. "Maybe if I just stare at him, he'll get the hint. You don't think that's too much, do you?"

Georgiana was not going to touch that question. She continued to watch Mr. Lawrence, who was speaking to the Duke of Wembley, though he didn't appear to be paying much attention to what the duke was saying. Georgiana followed his line of vision. "He seems to only have eyes for the duke's daughter," she replied offhand.

"Everyone does, the daft cow," Minnie replied before immediately turning red and covering her mouth with her gloved hand. Forgetting herself and her subterfuge, Georgiana burst out laughing. "Forget I said that," Minnie said. "That was pure jealousy speaking."

"That's all right," Georgiana said, regarding the luminous Lady Charlotte. With her resplendent yellow hair and crimson brocaded gown, she looked like Queen Jane come back to life, ready to civilize King Henry all over again with her pious beauty. Georgiana could understand Minnie's jealousy. Everyone always stared at Lady Charlotte.

Suddenly, Minnie grabbed her arm, cutting off her circulation. "Georgie! It's working! He just looked at us."

Damn! Lawrence must have heard her laughing like a wild hyena! Georgiana averted her gaze, turning to her friend. "Stop shaking me. I know! I saw him. Stop looking at it. I don't want him to see me!"

"Why?" Minnie asked, bewildered. "Oh, it doesn't matter. He's coming over here!"

"Stop staring at him!" Georgiana hissed, trying for a modicum of pride. Why was he coming over here, and, more importantly, what was she going to do?

The noise in the ballroom became smothered as the guests held their breaths at the American's actions. It simply wasn't done for a man to go up to a woman at a ball without being introduced, though perhaps allowances would be made, since, as everyone knew, uncouth Americans—even rich ones—didn't know better.

Trying to save face, Georgiana and Minnie turned toward each other, pretending to have a conversation and look completely oblivious as Lawrence approached. Making it even more awkward and *not* normal, they didn't even glance up until he was upon them and cleared his throat twice.

"Miss Georgiana Spence?"

Georgiana could have heard a pin drop as she reluctantly lifted her chin to the stranger. She could sense the entire room spying, but Lawrence was so tall and broad, she felt like she was shaded under an oak tree, hidden from anyone's view.

She nodded, rather meekly.

Lawrence's mouth broke out into a kind smile. "Georgiana? Not George, correct?"

She swallowed a lump in her throat and nodded again when words still refused to come.

"I'm Nathaniel Lawrence. I hope you got my last letter—"

"Yes! Yes, I received it," Georgiana blurted, unwrapping Minnie's iron-clad grip from her arm. "I cannot tell you enough how sorry I am to have deceived you. You see, ever since I learned about your company, I've wanted to speak to you. I have so many more questions, and I'm afraid it can be hard to find people to take me seriously in this endeavor…"

Lawrence waved his hand in the air. "It's no matter. I enjoyed your letters. It's always welcoming to speak to people who have a similar vision of the future."

Georgiana's chest felt like it was full of fireworks, all going off at the same time.

On closer inspection, Georgiana wouldn't consider Lawrence conventionally attractive. He was much too large for that. His face was long, and his eyes were so blue they were almost devoid of color, but there was something about him. People always talked about American confidence—and he had that; however, there was more to it. His voice was strong and even. When he spoke, Georgiana wanted to listen.

"I completely appreciate what you are trying to do," Georgiana said through a tense jaw. She had to keep herself in check; if she let herself totally relax, she was afraid her excitement would carry her all the way up to the ceiling.

"I appreciate that." He laughed. "Not many people agree with you. Many still don't see the positives in treating their workers like actual people and not animals."

"I do," Minnie cut in. "I completely see it. It's as clear as day."

"Thank you," he said directly to Minnie, causing her to wince back as if his gaze had been infused with fire. Georgiana sent up a quick prayer that her friend wouldn't faint. "I don't want to take up much of your time," he went on, raising his eyebrows toward the ballroom. "I'm afraid we have quite the audience. But a mutual acquaintance told me that you would be here. After I landed, he wrote to me explaining why you'd pretended to be a man, excusing the behavior, though like I said, there's nothing to excuse. I wanted to introduce myself and ask if it would be all right for me to call on you at your home. Perhaps then we can get into all your questions, and I may pick your brain as well regarding your father's factory."

Georgiana was about to rival Minnie for giddiness when something stopped her. "Mutual acquaintance?"

"Yes, the Marquess of Marlborough. He just sent me a letter. I'd planned to find you while I was in Town; however, he hastened it." His face clouded with worry. "I hope you don't mind. He assured me you wouldn't."

Georgiana was struck dumb. "Not…not at all. That would be most welcome. I'll have to thank Edward"—she shook her head—"the marquess, for his attention to these matters."

Lawrence nodded. "Of course. Now, if you'll excuse me, ladies, I have a roomful of people wondering if I can actually speak English without embarrassing myself and if I can dance without tripping. It seems I have a whole country to represent tonight."

"Good luck," Georgiana replied, laughing.

"Yes, good luck," Minnie added. "I'm a lovely dancer, by the way."

Georgiana elbowed her friend and watched as Lawrence returned to the duke. Her thoughts swam in a dizzying pattern, so convoluted that she couldn't seem to grab one and hold on.

Edward had remembered. It had been so long ago when she mentioned her letter to Lawrence. Had she even said his name at the time? How did he know? And why did he care? Did those questions even matter? Because he *did* know, and he *did* care enough to do something about it. That was so un-Edward of him. No, that wasn't true, she thought, recalling the surprise of the Gothic Hall. It was *very* Edward of him, actually.

Georgiana started to sway, and it had nothing to do with the music.

Minnie clutched her arm again, righting her. "Georgie, are you all right?" she asked. "Do you need some punch? It did get rather hot in here, didn't it? My sweet Lord, he is a beautiful man."

Georgiana felt her forehead and her fingers came away wet. She was hot, though not because of Lawrence. "I don't feel well all of a sudden," she said. "I think I'll tell my parents I'd like to leave."

"But the night has just started!" Minnie cried, before composing herself when she saw the strained look on Georgiana's face. "I understand. I'm sorry, dearest. Yes, you do look a little peaked. Let me take you to your mother. I'll come by tomorrow and tell you about everything you missed."

Georgiana nodded, letting her friend direct her to the refreshment room, not in the least sorry for leaving. She wasn't going to miss a thing.

CHAPTER FIFTEEN

FIFTEEN MINUTES LATER, Georgiana was standing outside a door that was not her own, shielding her face with her hood. It took her three deep exhales before she gained the nerve to knock. She'd convinced her parents to let her leave the ball alone, complaining of a nasty headache, knowing they wouldn't cry off with her that early in the evening. With a room full of nobility, it would take more than a nagging megrim to drag them away.

In the carriage, she'd prepared an explanation for the butler, excusing her presence at this hour, but when the door finally opened and Edward appeared, the words died in her throat.

Dressed down in only his waistcoat and trousers, he seemed even more casual than he had on the cricket field. His expression, on the other hand, was not.

"What the hell are you doing here?" he growled, stepping past the threshold to see if anyone was watching. The street was quiet and black. "You're supposed to be at the ball."

"I left," Georgiana said.

Edward's brow lifted. "I can see that. Why?"

"Aren't you going to invite me in?"

"No."

"Why not?"

He held the door close to his body as if afraid of showing her what was inside. Georgiana had never been to Edward's home before. It took all of her resolve not to shy away, leaving him and what she'd longed to say behind on the doorstep.

"It's not proper," he answered in an autocratic tone that made her frown. After all their time together, were they back to that?

"Since when are you proper?" she asked, hands on her hips. She caught Edward's gaze flicker to her body where her thin medieval gown was visible under her light cape.

He seemed to have a difficult time finding his voice after that. "Since…a woman I'm courting showed up at my door in the middle of the night."

Georgiana craned her neck, peeking past his shoulder. "Are you hiding something"—*or someone?*—"in there?"

Edward sighed, swiping a hand over his face. "It's not safe for you here. I'm thinking of you, Georgiana, not me."

Thinking of you. Yes, that was what he was doing. And this wasn't the only time.

She was losing her nerve. Georgiana didn't expect him to make this simple for her, but she'd hoped it wouldn't be this hard.

She straightened her spine. "Fine. If you won't let me in your house, then I will say what I need to say right here."

Edward crossed his arms, leaning on the door. He locked into his customary bored expression as if her appearance was nothing more than a nuisance. "Make it quick," he said.

Georgiana paused, swallowing down a nasty retort. She wasn't exactly sure how to start. It had all made so much sense ten minutes ago. Why did he have to ruin everything with his put-upon behavior?

No, she wouldn't let him ruin this.

Before he could make her rethink her plan, Georgiana threw her arms around his neck, kissing him. It was a short kiss, with only lips, but the fact that it was initiated by her made it all the more arousing. And once she started, it took all her strength to stop.

After a few heartbeats, she pulled away, watching as his eyes stayed closed. It made what she had to say easier. "Lawrence told me what you did," she said, warmth rushing to her cheeks. "And I know you said—in moments like these—that saying thank you isn't very romantic—"

Edward's eyes flew open, and he grabbed her waist, dragging her inside the townhouse. He kicked the door closed with his boot before pinning her up against the wall in the foyer. "I don't give a damn what you say as long as you do that again," he replied before crushing his mouth to hers.

It was messy and haphazard at first, each of them trying to get everything they wanted out of the other. Kisses met half-lips and chins, teeth clashed, and tongues played hide-and-seek, but the thrill of passion almost overcame her.

Standing on her toes, Georgiana plastered herself to his front, luxuriating in the way his clothes rubbed against her breasts, feeling the tingle all the way down to her soles. His hands roamed her body, searching her, mining her for her secrets. Edward splayed his palms wide and hungry over her neck, down her back, fanning them over her behind, pushing her pelvis against his with a roughness she hadn't known she craved. But she did. This and only this was what she wanted. This push and pull, this back and forth. This wanton greed of desire and need that threatened to combust inside her.

More. She wanted more. And she wasn't exactly sure how to get it. Only the third time kissing him, Georgiana still felt like a novice, sucking on his lips without finesse, only exuberance. He growled as they each fought for supremacy, each wanting to stamp themselves on the other.

"This is the last time," Georgiana panted as Edward trailed silky kisses down her jaw. Was she arching her neck to give him greater access? When had she learned to do that?

"The last time," he agreed.

He reached her chest, resting his head in between the slope of her breasts, where he wrenched her gown lower so he could lick each side of her heated skin in turn. The feel of his raspy tongue against her flesh woke her conscience. They'd gone so far, so fast. Had she meant for this to happen? Had she anticipated this as she prepared her speech in the carriage? They were in the middle of his foyer! Where were the servants? Where was the butler?

Georgiana grabbed his head, pulling him away. "A knight would never do this, you know."

His smile was pure rake, and he placed a soft, lingering kiss on her lips, then coaxed his tongue into her mouth as if he owned it. The intimacy of it was intolerable. With such little action, all focus centered on the rawness of their skin, the edges of their lips, the spicy heat of their mingling breaths. Edward's hand crept up to palm the back of her neck, and he deepened the kiss, sliding his tongue into her with such assured skill that Georgiana thought she was swimming in a hedonistic pool, one where every slippery movement added to the pleasure in the pit of her stomach.

He traced her lips with his tongue before responding, "Of course a knight would do. Just not the knights in your stories." While he was speaking, he inched her gown higher and higher up her legs. He didn't even have to encourage her to hook one leg up over his hip. She did that all on her own. "Real knights had too much time on their hands, time to get up to no good," he said huskily as he kissed a path up her neck, only stopping to linger at her ear. The new sensations caused her pelvis to rock against his, rubbing in a ravenous rhythm. "That's why codes of chivalry had to be made, morality enforced."

His calloused fingertips seared the flesh of her bare thigh. "Right now, I'm probably the knightliest knight you've ever seen. I can't say pretty things or offer chaste remarks. All I want to do is get you naked and kiss every freckle on your skin. I want to lick the gentility off you until the heat and throbbing of your body matches mine. Are you there now?"

Georgiana had no idea what he was talking about, but she never wanted him to stop. She loved the timbre of his voice, the feral beast that lurked just below his surface, hidden in plain sight.

And then she felt it.

His fingers stretched across her sensitive skin, riding her inner thighs until he reached the center of her. His kisses stopped, his lips poised against hers, mouths open as they traded breaths, each waiting, waiting, so much waiting, to see what he would do.

Though she couldn't see his eyes, she could make out the tiniest sparks in the whites—laden with wanting, yes, but also a question.

Georgiana arched her pelvis into him—into that hand—giving him the answer.

His mouth widened into a smile, and his tongue brushed into her again, in a worshipful thanks as his fingers got to work.

Georgiana didn't know what to make of it at first, a man touching her in a place she'd only been brave enough to venture once herself. But to call this mere touching was an understatement. He stroked her with the intention of a penitent, solemn in her sacredness.

Almost shy at first, he kneaded her tentatively, giving her time to accept him, each little touch building into something she couldn't define. But her breathing increased, her thigh over his hip tightened, her toes curled, and her pelvis moved under his instruction. This was not the artful composition she'd envisioned, the knightly attention she'd sought, and yet a dance was taking place, one in which his aptitude could not be ignored.

"You do not want me yet," he whispered, "and that's fine." The pressure of his fingers increased—as if gravity was overtaking them, they circled closer and closer to the center of her very being as the planets orbited the sun. "But I want you to want this. Need this. And I want you to know that I am the only man who will ever be able to give it to you." He found a spot that made her spine jolt back against the wall. "Yes, that's it," he continued. "There. None of your gentle storybook knights would be able to handle a woman like you, but I can. I can be the gentleman you want on the outside, but here"—he pressed harder, and Georgiana felt lightning bolts strike her thighs—"here is where I will be what you need. Not some silly fool playing games, vying for your attention, but a man whose life goal is to make you feel like the fucking woman you are. To make you come and sweat and scream until you have nothing left inside you. That is messy. That is real. That is us."

Georgiana gulped, dropping away from his lips to lay her head back. Her body was working without her mind, her hips rocking in tandem with his hand until everything inside of her pulled together, stretched so tight, so tense, that there was nothing left but to snap. Suddenly, she broke so deliciously that sparks shot through her, electrifying her limbs, shocking her heart. Her breathing intensified as she tried to contain herself, but the effect was too absorbing, and she hung on to Edward, tethering herself to his ground.

When she came back down to the mortal plane, she found he'd already dropped and smoothed her skirts and was in the process of readjusting his trousers. Through the fog of her mind, she remembered where they were, and horror gripped her chest.

"Where are your servants?"

She thought she saw him tense. "Don't worry—no one saw anything," he replied.

"Oh," Georgiana said, not feeling any better. That didn't answer her question, did it? "You answered the door. Why? Is your butler asleep too?" She looked over his shoulder and noticed that the room across the hall was shrouded in white sheets, all the furniture covered. She only had a split second to spy, since he moved in front of her, blocking her view.

"What are you getting at?" he said, his tone dangerously low.

"I'm not getting at anything. I just want to make sure we were alone."

"And I already told you we were."

Getting anything out of this man was like squeezing water from a stone. So he lived minimally—what did it matter? This house was huge, and it seemed like he was the only one living here. It only made sense not to open every room. However, by the edge in his tone, Georgiana thought it best to drop it.

"Well…" she said, patting down her dress awkwardly. Why did she feel so out of place all of a sudden? "Like I said, I just came here to say thank you and—"

"You don't have to be so embarrassed, Georgiana. It was bound to happen."

"What?"

Edward shrugged. "This. Me and you."

His nonchalant tone made her want to claw out his eyes. Somehow a lever was pulled, and he was completely different. A coolness settled over his features, a barrier erected. How could he do what he did to her and then make it sound like it was so…ordinary?

Two could play that game, Georgiana decided. "There is no me and you. As I said, this will not happen again." She stuck her chin in the air. "And you agreed."

He cocked his head. "I didn't agree."

"Oh, yes you did. When we were…and you were…"

"When we were making love?"

"We were not making love!"

His mouth quirked. "We were almost making love."

"We will never make love."

"We will most definitely make love."

Georgiana pushed him off to the side, reaching for the door. "On that note, I suppose it's time for me to go. Thank you, my lord—Oh, I already said thank you—ah…" Georgiana blew air out of her mouth, making her lips rumble. "It seems we are never going to agree, and I fear I've given you false hope. This was an aberration, a momentary lapse of judgment. Things got out of hand, and I assure you, I've learned from my mistake."

His mirthless laughter trailed behind her as he placed his hands over hers on the handle. "Oh, I think you've learned a great many things tonight," he said against her ear.

Georgiana contained her shiver. "I have," she shot back. "Yet again you've shown me that getting to know the real you is fruitless. You are exactly as you seem—you do not have the qualities of a chivalrous man and will never have them."

"What about you?"

She twisted her neck to meet his gaze. "What about me?"

"You came here to take advantage of me. If I'm not chivalrous, then neither are you."

Georgiana glared at him but didn't respond. What could she say? He was right. And this wasn't the first time he'd made this point. If she was always determined to call out his inadequacies, she'd have to do it to herself as well.

By degrees, gracefully, with the calmness of a man derailed but not beaten, Edward edged away, lifting his hand off hers. Georgiana twisted the knob, but not opening the door yet. She sensed he had more to say.

Per usual, Edward didn't disappoint. "I've proved one thing, though," he said, trailing a finger over her lips.

"And what's that?" she said, before biting the finger hard enough for him to yank it away.

His chuckle was infuriatingly husky and suggestive. "You may like them between the pages, but the last thing you want between your legs is a chivalrous man."

CHAPTER SIXTEEN

EDWARD COULD HAVE handled that better. That was beyond evident. But she'd caught him off guard—not only by coming to his house but by bringing up his lack of staff. It was a sore subject with him—nevertheless, even he could admit he'd acted harshly. Georgiana had given him a gift. For the first time, she'd come to him. And he'd let it slip through his hands, as easily and carelessly as coin ever fell through his father's.

Well...he was paying for it. Edward could only be glad that she didn't pull out of the trip. He'd feared she might. In the days leading up to their departure for Scotland, Georgiana, yet again, refused to answer his letters. At the end, he only knew she and her mother were joining him because Spence sent a messenger telling Edward when they would be ready to leave.

Suffice it to say, the trip had not been a loquacious one.

He'd hoped the rush of the event would provide him with a little bit of mercy. However, if there was one thing he could say about Georgiana, it was that she had conviction. Because she stayed angry the entire journey. Oh, she was pleasant enough with her mother, but Edward got the cold shoulder. All for being a bit of an ass.

Even his mother forgave his father time and time again, and that bastard had been the worst.

Edward was hardly in his league. Sure, he'd been rather brutish about it, but all he'd done was put a mirror up to Georgiana's face, showing her what she really wanted—him. She should be thanking him. He was saving her from a lifetime of polite, boring sex with a polite, boring husband. What they'd done to each other was otherworldly. Why couldn't she just admit it? What was holding her back? Why couldn't she just admit that she wanted him?

But she refused. *The entire trip.*

Though many people were taking the new trains to Liverpool and opting for a steamer to get them to Ardrossan, Edward had insisted on his carriage. He wasn't against modernity when it came to travel, but he didn't want to be held to its whim. It took a few days longer, to be sure; however, when they reached the southern Scottish coastal town the day before the event, he was glad for his prudence. To say he was astounded by what he saw there would be an understatement.

Bodies were practically spilling over the docks while they waited for transportation to take them the eight miles to Irvine, the nearest town to the castle.

Even in his wildest dreams, Edward had no premonition that this many people would be coming. Who had? One needed a ticket to watch the event from a seat in the grandstand, but that apparently hadn't stopped thousands of others who were convinced they could enjoy the spectacle standing on the outskirts.

Edward had met Lord Eglinton on numerous occasions. He was a jovial man, more than a competent sportsman, a lover of the ponies—but, unlike Edward's father, smart enough not to gamble his entire fortune on them. He and Eglinton ran in close enough circles for Edward to know that the lord would make traveling all the way to his estate worth the people's time. However, Edward could never believe that the earl had planned for *this* many people to make the journey.

The weather was the only welcomed surprise. Sweet, salty air and blue skies greeted them in Scotland, something Edward hadn't counted on, though it was appreciated. He only hoped it held.

The group pushed on to their hotel. On the way, a looming dread continued to weigh on Edward's chest as they passed numerous crowds in the road, most walking the entire way to the town. Even the lovely countryside couldn't derail the foreboding. Just fifty miles from England, the luscious hills and moors surrounding them made it feel like they were in the rich wilds of the north. But he couldn't focus on the fantastic greens and lush heather. He only saw people. And more people. All going to the same godforsaken place.

THE EGLINTON ARMS was a Georgian-styled structure with eighteen well-appointed rooms, most of which Edward had booked weeks before. However, as they entered the hotel and Edward asked for the innkeeper, he was met with a broken-looking man who appeared to be at the end of his rope.

And the news he gave didn't look any better.

"What do you mean all the rooms are taken?" Edward asked, biting back his anger as more people plowed into the portico entrance, asking the same question he was asking.

The innkeeper's neck sagged, and he could only sigh, telling Edward—telling anyone that would listen—that every free space (even the previously occupied ones) in the hotel had been stormed and snatched up by disgruntled travelers who couldn't find a place to stay in the town.

He explained that every villager nearby had even opened their homes to the visitors, charging exorbitant rates for a measly mattress and a jug of water to wash with. Other, more adventurous, travelers had settled for a square of solitary dirt in a barn or fresh straw in a horse stall. Quite simply, there was no room at the inn—or anywhere else within a five-mile radius of the castle.

Edward swallowed down a curse and forced the crestfallen innkeeper to meet his gaze once more. "I would like for you to show us to our rooms," he repeated slowly, as if he were speaking to a child.

The innkeeper just threw up his hands, on the verge of tears, before explaining, yet again, that their rooms on the third floor were taken.

Edward felt Georgiana press into his back, no doubt shoved by someone else. It was the first time she'd touched him in days, and he appreciated the fleeting act, nevertheless. "Should we try somewhere else?" she asked.

"There is nowhere else," Edward replied, his mind working overtime. He squinted at the innkeeper. "You said the rooms were on the third floor?" The man nodded from under his shaking hands. "All right, then."

Edward made for the stairs.

"Where are you going?" Georgiana asked, running after him.

"I'm going to get our bloody rooms."

Edward took the stairs two at a time, pushing off anyone silly enough to get in his path. The third floor was slightly less chaotic than the rest of the house, with only maids scurrying back and forth through the long hallway. Too annoyed by the turn of events, Edward didn't hesitate to attack the first door he saw. Finding it unlocked, he barged in on three men in various degrees of undress, their bags and possessions scattered throughout the room.

He braced his legs in the doorway, his expression calm, yet there was no mistaking the intention as he said one word and one word only: "Out."

The three pairs of eyes blinked for a few seconds before the men looked at one another. They had no idea who Edward was, but by his arrogant demeanor and aristocratic bearing, he didn't appear to be someone they wanted to argue with. Slowly—but surely—they began to gather their things.

With a nod, Edward left the space, performing the same act

on the remaining rooms down the hall. No one argued, no one issued one peep as the marquess dominated the floor.

Edward could feel Georgiana watch him, most likely ashamed of the heavy-handed way he dealt with the situation. What did she want? To sleep out in the barn? She might not be impressed by titles, but most others definitely were. And it wasn't like he was *taking* the rooms. They were his! Bought and paid for already! The squatters were in the wrong, not him!

He waited near the staircase for the interlopers to exit the floor. As the last couple, a young man and woman, sidled by, their eyes downcast in embarrassment, Georgiana finally spoke up. "You aren't just going to kick them out," she said, aghast at the thought.

Since that was exactly what he was doing, Edward wasn't quite sure what to say. She was regarding him as if he was a monster, and he tried to temper his response with pure reason. "They stole our rooms," he pointed out.

"There was nowhere for them to go. They were just trying to enjoy the tournament, as we are."

"Then they should have booked the rooms in advance, as we had. It is not my fault they didn't plan correctly." He didn't add that the person who *really* hadn't planned correctly was Lord Eglinton.

The man and woman stopped on the staircase, eyes wide and innocent, regarding Georgiana as if she was the Patron Saint of Travelers, St. Christopher, herself. "Look at them," she implored.

He was. They looked like non-planning grifters, but since he knew that wasn't what she wanted to hear, *and* he liked the fact that she was speaking to him again, *and* he wanted to keep it that way, he replied, "Oh, very well, I'll help them find a place to stay."

Edward ambled down the stairs after the couple, Georgiana clapping happily in his wake. All he wanted to do was lie down in his bed and sleep, but at least she was pleased with him for the time being. He would see how long it lasted.

HOURS LATER, EDWARD carried himself up those very same stairs, a very different, very exhausted man. He hadn't thought that finding the couple a place to stay would be that difficult; however, he'd underestimated the situation. The innkeeper hadn't been joking when he said there was not a square inch available. Even the servants' quarters had been stolen by visitors, most sleeping on the floors, since all the mattresses were already taken.

Edward had learned the local vicar was renting out his manse, but by the time they got there, it was already filled. The only thing an enterprising person could think to do was build. With the help of a few others, Edward found planks of wood and started creating makeshift lean-tos off the sides of the hotel, hoping to give some people a chance at a dry night. It wasn't much, but it was something. With the vicar promising to provide the people with water, Edward left believing he'd accomplished enough.

Reaching the third story, tired and sore, he couldn't help but acknowledge how good it had felt spending the day outside in that manner. He'd been in London so long that he missed working his body as he normally did at his estate, where the situation there sometimes forced him to labor side by side with many of his tenants.

Not to mention the pent-up sexual frustration holding tight to every bone and muscle in his body. Though the cutting and sawing hadn't completely mitigated that need, it had helped.

Earlier, Edward had messaged Georgiana and her mother to go ahead and eat without him. The vicar had found him some bread and cheese and a bottle of wine, and he firmly intended to spend the rest of the night in their care. But as he shuffled his feet past Georgiana's hotel door, he paused, and his knuckles burned to knock.

He wasn't sure why. He didn't have anything to say, no news on the tournament, which he was sure was all Georgiana cared to hear about. And yet, despite her frosty demeanor the last few days, he'd got used to her being around. In fact, he relished seeing her every morning when he woke up and before he went to sleep. It was...nice, calming. Special. And something he was definitely looking forward to in the future. What would it be like waking up to Georgiana, deliciously tousled from the night before and ready (hopefully) to be tousled again?

He was unable to stop it—the image of Georgiana in her bedclothes that night on the balcony with her head sticking out the window came to him. Her hair, loud and waving down her back, with that ridiculous cap on her head doing absolutely nothing to contain it. He would forbid those silly caps. But he loved the nightdress, all prim and proper in its cottony abundance. He couldn't wait to get his hands on those buttons, to peel the demure clothing from her lithe body.

Edward rested his forehead against Georgiana's door, picturing her shy, sultry smile when he shed the gown, kissing her bare shoulders. Would they be spotted with freckles? He'd been too mindless to notice when she surprised him at his house. And it had been too dark. Next time he wouldn't miss the expression on her face as she came, as she gasped in his mouth from the startling fulfillment. When he truly made her his.

Edward understood that many husbands and wives didn't share the same room—Lord knew his parents didn't—but that wouldn't be the case for them. Edward was done sleeping alone. Once Georgiana took her side of his bed, she would never wish to leave it. He would make sure of it.

Suddenly, the gentle murmurs on the other side of the wood gained intensity, and Edward could hear the words more clearly.

"What do you mean we're going to his estate, Mother? You never told me that."

"Just for a week after the tournament. Your father and I thought it would be a good idea for you to see the marquess's home, get a feel for him away from London."

Edward bit back a groan. Why hadn't they told her? He'd planned the whole thing with Spence weeks ago. So much for her speaking to him. She would return to her cold treatment tomorrow, thinking he was a part of the ruse.

"I don't need to get a feel for him. I know exactly the kind of man he is," Georgiana stated.

"The kind of man who spends all night providing shelter for others?"

Thank you, Mrs. Spence! At least he had someone fighting in his corner.

"He only did that because I made him." Well, that was true. "When will you and Father give up on the idea? I don't want to marry Lord Edward. He's...he's..."

Edward pressed his ear so hard against the door that he felt the cartilage crunch.

"...cold. He's too set in his ways, too used to getting everything he wants. Life with him will be all about him. Nothing is simple with him; he makes everything so bloody difficult."

"Georgie! Don't speak like that. I've never seen the marquess act in such a pompous way around you. In fact, I find him to be a different sort of man."

Edward was rather humbled by the mother's opinion of him. Because he hadn't spoken much during their dinners together, he was surprised Mrs. Spence had seen so much. Such were mothers, he supposed.

Deciding it was best to stop eavesdropping, Edward was about to go back to his room when Georgiana's next words stopped him.

"A man can't change his nature, Mother."

Mrs. Spence took her time responding. By the time she did, Edward had already jerked his head away from the wood.

My nature?

Yes, people always seemed to have an opinion about *his nature*—the nature he'd inherited from his father. It seemed

Georgiana wasn't as above the others as she'd believed. Just like Jacobson and Carstark before her, she lumped him in the same category as the horrible man who'd borne him. "His nature" was always going to be the shield those people needed from him, the excuse to keep him at arm's distance so he could never prove himself different.

Well, he'd stopped trying to prove himself to members of the *ton* years ago, and he would stop with Georgiana now. It didn't matter how she saw him, anyway. They would still marry. And he would keep the lights off in their bedroom. After all, every-one's sins looked the same in the dark.

CHAPTER SEVENTEEN

"WHAT DO YOU mean you're not coming?" Georgiana asked a stone-faced Edward.

The morning of the tournament, they met outside their rooms on the way down to breakfast. Georgiana—too excited to wait—had already donned her medieval ensemble, with her brown hair relaxed and down her shoulders. However, relaxed wasn't the word to use for Edward. Stiff and starched, somber and cold, he regarded her with the formality of a new acquaintance.

"I told you, I am grouse hunting."

"You never told me that."

"I did," he asserted. "Back in London."

Georgiana searched their conversations (*there were so damn many!*) and came up ignorant. "I thought you were joking about that," she hedged, uncomfortable with the level of hurt she felt at his icy tone.

He barely batted an eyelash and met her expression with detached indifference. "I assure you I am not joking. Why would I want to go to the tournament?"

Because I'll be there.

Georgiana hurried for a less pathetic thing to say. "I-I thought you were becoming more"—*attached?*—"curious, is all."

"Not at all," he said, his tone as sharp as the dagger Georgiana had slipped into her belt. She felt the insane wish to use it on him now. How dare he act so unaffected, so…aloof.

From his fine, pressed clothes to his arrogant demeanor, Edward was the picture of remoteness, as if he'd erased all that had happened between them. But over the course of their journey, hadn't she been doing the same thing to him? Georgiana should be ecstatic at this shift. This Edward—the old Edward— was so much easier to dismiss from her thoughts.

Oddly enough, ecstasy was the last thing she was experiencing.

"I promised I wouldn't ruin it for you, remember?" he said, lowering his voice as if he was offering her a boon. "Besides, it's not like you've enjoyed my company of late."

She nodded meekly, firmly chastised, as he passed her to go down the stairs. She had been horrible to him. And yet when she asked him to help those people last night, he'd barely balked.

He *did* ruin so many things. She remembered that now. In fact, she was always thinking it or saying it. But try as she might, she couldn't remember one instance of him doing it.

Her mother came out of the room then and gave her daughter a look, letting her know she'd heard the entire exchange. Georgiana lifted her chin and took a fortifying breath. Let her mother defend *that* behavior. This was what she'd been trying to explain the night before. Edward's nature—the one that decreed him a marquess and a gift to mankind—would never allow him to open up to her. He was determined to keep her at arm's length.

After a paltry breakfast of bread, jam, and tea, the ladies set off in Edward's carriage toward the castle. The event was set to begin at noon, but they were encouraged to get an early start due to all the traffic believed to be on the main road.

The ladies were glad they did. Just like yesterday, the countryside was packed with people in carriages and wagons, on horses and foot. The numbers were staggering to Georgiana but also fueled her anticipation, taking her mind off Edward's callousness for a time. If this many people were coming to the event, it must be worth seeing, she thought. She'd been right to accept Edward's bargain for the tickets. This would truly be the spectacle of a lifetime!

They entered the estate a full hour before the tournament was to begin, and the sun shone beatifically on the massive castle. Though built in recent years, it was modeled on the Gothic style, with an octagonal central tower and four small turrets at its corners. It was an astonishing pile that fit Georgiana's imagination for the day. Just past the impressive structure was a quaint river that bordered the western side of the meadow, which was serving as home for the lists. As they crossed the single cast-iron bridge, the scene opened up to such a magnificent degree that Georgiana almost lost her breath.

Lord Eglinton and Samuel Pratt had spared no expense. Georgiana had never seen something so grand or so large. She'd heard the lists were going to be near six hundred feet long, but she'd had no idea what that had meant until she saw it. Six hundred feet! Bigger than any cathedral she'd ever been to. This was indeed a religious experience.

Striped tents were pitched on either side of the enclosure for the knights, each with its own set of heraldic flags and coats of arms.

For the ticket holders, a huge grandstand was constructed down the length of the lists, with enough room for four thousand people. Only the Queen of Beauty's gallery in the center had a roof, and it was decorated with ornate columns and crimson and gold cloth. The galleries on either side were open to the sun, which made Georgiana long for her bonnet.

Like everyone else, after departing the carriage, her mother sent it back to the hotel. There was no reason to ask the driver to stay all day, baking in the heat. The celebrations were meant to go on for most of the night anyway. Georgiana heard her mother tell the driver not to bother coming back until midnight, which sounded a bit too early, in her opinion.

After their fair share of maneuvering, the women managed to

find seats that were high up the grandstand, though toward the center, affording them an enviable view. The castle acted as the backdrop of the lists, and the fields sloped up around the meadow, with sheep grazing lazily across the green expanse. It was a lovely sight, and Georgiana found herself wishing Edward was there to see it. He would hate most of it, but at least he would have enjoyed the river and the sheep.

"What are you laughing at?" her mother asked, but Georgiana just shook her off. "Thank goodness for this breeze. I can't imagine how uncomfortable this would all be without it."

The breeze was welcome, that was for sure; however, it had picked up in the last hour, along with a few clouds in the sky. Georgiana remembered what Edward had said about Scottish weather. However, with only a few minutes until the jousts would begin, Georgiana assumed they were in the clear.

But those few minutes stretched. And stretched. A parade was supposed to kick everything off, but as Georgiana strained her neck toward the path to the castle, she saw it was disappointingly bare. Clearly, things of this magnitude never started on time, but the longer the crowd sat, the more restless it became. And the crowd was its own being.

Georgiana and her mother passed the time searching the seats for their acquaintances, making as much small talk as they could. Spotting Minnie and her parents as they arrived, Georgiana was disappointed when all she could do was wave as they settled at the opposite end of the grandstand, on the right side of the queen's pavilion.

If Georgiana had thought the grandstand was enthralling, the hordes of people standing on the outside of the railing surrounding the lists were positively frightening. She couldn't possibly calculate the number of spectators. When she heard a gentleman next to her guess over one hundred thousand people, she almost fell out of her seat. *One hundred thousand people?* Most of them weren't even close enough to see the lists and were sitting on each other's shoulders and scaling every available tree. It was pure and utter mania.

She felt her mother shift next to her. Georgiana caught a worried frown before her mother noticed her watching and calmed her exterior. Then she jerked again. "Oh look, is that… No. It's nothing. I thought I saw the parade."

Her mother would do that a dozen more times in the next three hours. She'd straighten her back, point straight ahead, and then fall back in her seat, convinced she'd seen something on the path from the castle. But each and every time was a false alarm, and they weren't the only people in the stands growing restless.

Like a giant balloon, the mass of people lost a little bit more air with every minute that went by. Excitement turned to boredom, which soon turned to irritation. Georgiana wasn't sure what anger looked like in a mob of a hundred thousand people but surely didn't want to find out.

To make matters worse, a steady patter of rain began to fall. Light at first—most of the spectators seated around her thought it would just blow over—but the sun, once gone, refused to come back, and the rain grew heavier.

Because her mother hadn't decided to dress up in character, she not only came equipped with her bonnet but also her lace parasol. As the rain continued, mother and daughter hunched under it, pretending it was actually saving them from the bleak wetness. Georgiana's imagination, and desire to experience this fantasy, was strong; however, after an hour of frigid water running down her back, she realized it wasn't strong enough. The parasol was useless, as was the pavilion's roof.

At first, the very important people lucky enough to have tickets in the queen's pavilion turned up their noses at the lesser ones who didn't have a canopy. Soon, those noses were just as wet as everyone else's. The boards on the roof had not been fitted together properly, merely placed next to each other before being nailed down. Streams of rain were now pouring through the cracks, making the roof as pointless as the accompanying fabric canopy that whipped uncontrollably against the hefty winds. Hats and umbrellas were flying like puffs of cotton, never to be seen again.

Teeth chattering, her mother hugged Georgiana's arm miserably after her parasol, too, took off for the fields. "Do you think they'll cancel?" she asked hopefully. Georgiana also felt a flicker of hope at the idea. Jousts weren't usually conducted in the rain; it was much too dangerous. However, how could Lord Eglinton cancel the day? Too many people had traveled here at too great an expanse. It wasn't as if he could simply reschedule, could he?

Her velvet gown stuck to her skin, and a shiver went up Georgiana's determined spine. They were sticking it out. They had no choice. For starters, they had no way to get home. No one did. All the carriages were gone. It was either they sit in the freezing rain and watch the show in misery, or they sit in the freezing rain and watch the show in cheer. Georgiana chose cheer.

She rubbed her mother's clammy hands, fighting to give her some life. "It will start soon," she said, lining her voice with confidence. "I can feel it—Oh wait, yes! Yes, there! Can you see it? They're coming! It's starting!"

It was as if the crowd took one giant exhale in relief. All stood and began clapping riotously at the sight of the procession winding from the castle.

A half a mile long, it moved slowly along the mud-caked path. Over one hundred mounted people—including musicians, pages, and squires—trudged to the lists decked out in minivered jackets, suits of gold and purple velvet, and all the pomp and ceremony they could muster under the dire circumstances. Unfortunate plumes had practically melted off many a helmet and cap, but the majesty could still be felt as Lord Glenlyon tramped forward with close to seventy men in his entourage, all wearing their Highland garb and playing their bagpipes gallantly.

Despite the rain pouring down in sheets, the tableau might have been perfect, if only Lord Londonderry hadn't ruined it. He rode in the center of the procession, holding a giant green umbrella.

Not very knightly, Georgiana thought wryly. The anachronistic picture even gained a few laughs from the crowd, though Georgiana assumed that hadn't been the lord's intent.

Hoping to capitalize on the laughs, a jester reached the center of the field and tried to do a little entertaining but was mostly met with boos. It seemed the people had no patience left for anything other than what they'd come for. The parade was four hours late. If the knights were going to joust, they better get to it.

After entering the lists, most of the procession immediately took cover in the tents, causing immediate confusion and disappointment from those in the grandstand who didn't believe they were getting their money's worth.

"Where's the Queen of Beauty?" Georgiana heard a young child ask her father a few seats down from her. "Aren't they supposed to *do* something?"

They were. A ceremony was supposed to take place commemorating the start, but Georgiana figured it must have been shelved due to the lateness and the rain. No grand herald came forward to read out the rules of the event, no Queen of Beauty rode around allowing all to witness her magnificence, and no knights rode out to the grandstand to choose ladies to give them handkerchiefs or tokens to place around their lances.

Hearing a scuffle toward the pavilion, Georgiana turned in time to see the Queen of Beauty, Lady Seymour, settle herself in the royal box along with all her ladies. Even with the roof, the pavilion appeared flooded, and someone had the grace to stand over the queen with an umbrella, though it did very little. The rest of the officers and tournament royalty found their seats, and everyone was back to waiting again.

Eventually, a herald came to the center of the field. He began shouting, but Georgiana could barely hear anything over the rain.

The crowd grew hushed as it waited for the gauntlet to be thrown, a challenge to be made—however, the knights' tents were in utter chaos. Squires were running back and forth testing equipment, entourages were moving around trying to stay dry, and the horses were pacing in their enclosures, visibly nervous in the conditions.

"What are they waiting for?" her mother asked tightly, overcome by the cold. Georgiana hugged her even closer, trying to give all the warmth she had. Unfortunately, it was next to nothing. Her own cape was drenched, as well as the gown underneath. To make matters worse, her hair hung soaked and caked to her body, making Georgiana want to crawl out of her skin from the discomfort.

And yet all of this didn't matter, she told herself. The show could go on and wow everyone. It just needed to start! Then everyone would forget their miseries. She just knew it!

But her positivity was challenged as the afternoon wore on. Because the little jousting that took place was absolutely terrible. Georgiana tried not to blame the knights. She'd seen them at practice; she knew what they were capable of. The elements simply wouldn't allow that finesse to come through.

Like a bad omen, the first two knights selected to start everything off didn't even hit each other on their first pass down the lists—nor the second. By the third pass, they were each so frustrated they punched their lances into the air, missing each other once more with such force that they almost flew off their mounts.

And that was only the beginning. The lists were growing increasingly muddy and slick. Each step for the horses was a precarious one, and the knights rode the courses slowly. Everyone understood that safety needed to be considered; however, for people who had spent the better part of their day in the blistering rain, they needed something to show for it, and it simply did not come.

It seemed to take forever for the knights to ready themselves for each pass, and only two managed to strike each other the entire afternoon. Georgiana couldn't even tell who the successful knights were. Visibility was terrible, and the heralds had not even tried to announce the knights over the blistering wind. It was like watching a silent play from the other side of a cloudy glass.

Realizing their dismal display, some knights attempted to liven up the crowd with a swordfight on foot, but even that was met with derision from the spectators. It was all too little, too late. All tolerance had been washed away by the unrelenting showers. The people had come to be entertained, but the good mood, once lost, was lost forever.

When Lord Eglinton took off his helmet and approached the pavilion, Georgiana felt her heart sink. She knew what was coming, and as much as she wanted the joust to continue, she understood calling it off was the safest decision.

"My friends," he shouted over the roar of the wind. "I am so terribly sorry for what you've encountered here today. I cannot tell you how disappointed we all are." The grandstand rustled, as if each person was leaning in to hear everything the earl had to say. "I know so many of you traveled long distances to get here, and I wish things could have been different. I've lived in Eglinton all my life, and I've never seen a storm quite like this before. That is not an excuse," he said stoically, widening his shoulders against the pummeling rain, "but I thought it important that you know. Perhaps we'll try again tomorrow, or the day after that, if the weather allows. For now, I think it best that we all disband and find shelter. I thank you for coming today and being a part of my vision. Farewell. I wish you a pleasant and successful journey home."

Then he came closer to the center pavilion, addressing the people gathered around the Queen of Beauty. His expression grew even more somber, his countenance even more apologetic. Georgiana strained to hear his speech.

"I'm afraid this also means the medieval banquet and ball have been canceled as well," he said with a grimace. He explained that he'd been made aware that the tent behind the castle, which had been built for the functions, had also been damaged by the storm. Apparently, it too had been constructed in the same shoddy manner as the roofed pavilion.

After another apology, the earl took off toward his tent, leaving the crowds in a suspended state of disbelief. No one budged. Even Georgiana, who had already guessed at what Lord Eglinton was going to say, seemed paralyzed by the decision.

That's it? It's over?

A few minutes went by without anyone moving, nor even uttering outrage. It took the controlled chaos of the knights and their entourage fleeing the lists to knock most people out of their stupors.

They were leaving. Just leaving everyone behind.

"Do you think our carriage is back?" her mother asked hopefully—and naïvely.

Georgiana twisted around to watch what everyone else was doing, but they seemed to have the same question as her mother. A few carriages were waiting, but the majority still weren't expected back for hours. As the rain continued to dump around her, Georgiana could only make out Lord Eglinton's carriage. And it was slowly receding from eyesight back to the castle, carrying the Queen of Beauty and her ladies safely within it.

"Surely the knights will come back," Georgiana muttered to herself. "They can't just...*leave* us here."

But as seconds turned into minutes and minutes into an hour, it soon became apparent that that was exactly what they'd done.

Climbing down from the waterlogged grandstand, Georgiana kept a steady arm around her mother, who was finding it difficult walking the muddy paths with her slippers. "We can't just stay here," Georgiana said, following the long line of people toward the bridge. The lists were in danger of flooding, along with the rest of the field. The river bordering the side was reaching overflowing levels.

"Come on, Mother, we have to hurry. We have to get to the high road," Georgiana said, dragging her mother behind. But once they were out of the field and onto the road, it didn't get any better. The holes from people's footsteps in front of them had left the trail slimy and mucky, causing the women to lose their balance and fall to their knees time and time again.

Her mother pulled Georgiana to a stop, eyes heavy with strain and tears. "I cannot go any further," she said.

"You have to," Georgiana ordered her. "It's only a couple of miles to the hotel. We have no choice."

"We do have a choice!" her mother cried, throwing her soaked arms in the air like a drowning bird. Her bonnet had collapsed against the torrent, and her hair, limp and messy out of its normal bun, stuck to her cheeks like weedy vines. Georgiana knew she looked the same as her mother—felt the same way too. But she couldn't afford to go easy on her. Only a tough hand would get them out of this horrible mess.

Georgiana searched their surroundings, looking for anyone familiar. She'd hoped to run into Minnie and her family while exiting, but thus far had come up empty. The rain acted as a curtain, making it difficult to see anything farther than a few yards ahead.

She reached for her mother's hand, but it got smacked away. "I'm not going," her mother declared stubbornly. "A carriage will come soon. I will wait for that."

"What carriage?" Georgiana cried hopelessly. "No one can get through…and look at what happens to the ones that can!"

Down the road, they could make out a carriage being seized by a group of frustrated people, each person clawing at the vehicle, begging it to stop so they could climb on. The driver tried to whip them away, though it did no good. When the inside was packed, people took to climbing on top and hanging off the sides as the carriage wobbled away through the mud.

"We only have each other," Georgiana said solemnly, asking for her mother's hand again. This time, her mother allowed her to take it.

They went on like that for long minutes, sharing a miserable silence, slapping one foot in front of the other, lurching them out of the quicksand-like mud, only to do it again. They moved at a snail's pace, slower than a snail's pace, and Georgiana quickly lost hope that they would reach the hotel by dark. She had no idea what time it was now, and already the sun was much too close to the horizon for her comfort.

Some people had decided to halt the exodus to Irvine altogether, attempting to find a close place to get warm and dry and run out the night. Just a half-hour before, Georgiana had passed a cowshed crowded with people who'd decided to test their fate with the bovine rather than the unyielding Scottish weather. She had wanted to ask her mother what she thought of the idea, but ultimately dismissed it. There was no way Beth Spence would bed down with cows. It was the hotel or nothing. If Georgiana had to carry her on her back the rest of the way, she would make it happen.

And that seemed incredibly likely. Slipping in the mud, her mother fell to her knees again, almost yanking Georgiana down with her. Her mother's dress, which had been so light and pretty in its mint-green glory, was now a dull and earthy brown, stained and ripped beyond repair. "Just leave me here to die!" she said dramatically.

Georgiana was too tired to roll her eyes—or argue. "Get up, Mother."

"No! Leave me. Save yourself!"

"It's just rain, Mother." Georgiana sighed. "I'll have you dry and warm in front of a fire soon enough."

"And then what? I'll still probably die of a cold. No, just leave me. Tell the boys I love them."

The time for encouraging words was over. Instead, Georgiana grabbed her mother's shaking shoulders and attempted to haul her up. She didn't expect her mother to fight, and Georgiana lost her balance, landing in the mud as well.

"Look what you did," Georgiana grumbled, lumbering up to standing. "You're making this harder than it needs to be. Now come on!"

But her mother only sagged on the ground, her tears and

cries bordering on hysterics.

"I'll carry you. Just get on my back, please."

Her mother refused to move. Like a tantrum-loving toddler, she was making her stand—or rather, her seat—in the mud.

Georgiana's last resort was to beg. "Please don't do this, Mother. You know I won't leave you. If you just try a little bit more, I promise—"

"Lord above, we're saved!"

Georgiana whipped around to find out what her mother was screaming about. A figure developed through the sheen of rain. She had to blink the water away from her eyes to make any sense of what she was witnessing, thinking it was a mirage. But there he was, riding high on his horse, water dripping over the brim of his tall hat onto his calm face.

Edward maneuvered the horse in front of Georgiana and stared down, not seeming to register the wails of gratitude coming from her mother. And even in the pandemonium surrounding them, the unholy discord they found themselves in, Georgiana felt them locked immediately in accord. Like the weaves of a basket. The fibers of a rope. Like hands in prayer.

And she found her first smile in hours, because she knew what he was going to say, and as ever with Edward, he did not disappoint.

Tipping his hat, he said, matter-of-factly, "Miss Georgiana. It's raining."

She laughed, though her mind was so addled, she might have cried as well. "I can see that, my lord. *And* feel it."

CHAPTER EIGHTEEN

EDWARD'S HEART WAS beating out of his chest. Thank fuck he'd found them. He'd been out the last few hours battling the storm, searching for any trace through the hordes of lost people. The rain had made it next to impossible to see clearly, and by the time he reached the lists, they'd already left. It was pure chance that he found them when he did—chance and his perseverance.

As he stood over Georgiana (and her screaming mother), it wasn't pride that made him appear calm and stoic—it was gut-wrenching fear. He'd simply been too relieved to get off his horse, to find that she was safe.

When Edward came to—when Georgiana's words from their past encounter in the park smashed through his befuddled daze—he sparked to action, hauling her into his arms, cradling her drowned form in front of him on the horse. Her mother climbed up quickly after.

The mother kept calling Edward a hero, shouting it through tears of joy into the back of his neck. Edward only tightened his arms around Georgiana, shuddering over the thought. The last thing he felt like was a hero. He was much too scared for that.

Even traveling slowly through the storm with the extra weight, Edward had them back at the hotel in less than an hour. He wasted little time dragging them off the mount and carrying the women, one at a time, to the hotel porch. They were covered in mud, and he refused to allow them to step in any more.

The hotel was still stirring, with the innkeeper and maids waiting near the front to greet the guests limping in. Georgiana's mother rushed to their aid, accepting their blankets and commiserations while she hurried upstairs to her room.

Edward began to walk back once Georgiana reached the threshold. He felt like he'd been holding his breath underwater for hours, and he finally took a long inhale, his lungs inflating with the calm of deliverance.

Georgiana paused. "Where are you going?"

Edward couldn't bear to look at her, and averted his gaze to his feet. Shame and guilt overwhelmed him when he stared too long at her bedraggled and exhausted figure. Her lips were blue and trembling, her shoulders sunken under the weight of the sodden, useless cape. He should have been with them. He should never have let them go by themselves.

"I'm going to go back out," he answered, retracing his steps to the horse. "I'm just going to trade mounts and be on my way."

Naturally, the stubborn woman followed him. He had a mind to throw her over his shoulder and take her to her room. She needed to get out of those clothes and in front of a fire.

"You can't go back out. It's terrible out there."

"There are too many people still on the road. I can't just leave them."

"They did," she shouted bitterly, and he knew exactly who "they" were—the knights that she held so close to her heart. He hated for her to learn it this way, but they weren't knights; they were men, plain and simple.

"At least let me go with you," she said, coming alongside him, her determined stride matching his own.

"No."

"Yes."

"Go to your room!"

"If you're going, then so am I," she said. "If we both take

mounts, we can help twice the people." She glanced at him from under her tired, heavy-lidded eyes. "You have no idea how many people are there…what it's like."

He did, but it was true, not like her. She was going to be difficult, which was nothing new; he should have known she wouldn't sit back while others less fortunate were still out there in the storm. Despite his better judgment, Edward's emotions were too wrecked—his self-control stretched too thin. He didn't have the strength to tell her no.

"Hurry and get changed into dry clothes," he said grimly, detesting his weakness. Or was it selfishness? A need to have her with him drove the decision. Nothing would ever hurt her then.

Georgiana flashed him a smile that almost took him to his knees, then made a beeline for her room. Ever the good knight, she couldn't turn her back on defenseless people. Ever the enamored man, he couldn't do the same to her.

THE MISERY OF the next couple of hours was mitigated by the fact that they made such a good team. Navigating the roads, they picked up mostly children and mothers who'd become stuck in the rot and delivered them to some kind of enclosure. They were able to help dozens, which, though not a lot when one considered the numbers of the day, was at least something. It was well past midnight, with the rain still pelting down, when Edward had to call it. The paths had become too treacherous, the visibility too opaque.

By the time Edward and Georgiana made it back to the hotel, it was shrouded in darkness. Everyone was retired and asleep after the tumultuous events.

They saw to the horses in silence, giving the animals all the love and affection they could for their tremendous hard work. They continued their quietude all the way into the hotel and up the stairs to their floor, almost afraid to break the peace that had developed between them.

After pausing for a moment at the top of the stairs, Georgiana eventually walked to her door, hand heavy on the handle, before turning back to Edward with a quizzical expression. "Mother is an uneasy sleeper," she said.

Edward could only nod.

"This was very difficult for her," Georgiana went on, as if trying to tell him something he wasn't getting. She shrugged. "I hate to wake her."

Oh. Edward fumbled for a delicate way to say what he most wanted in all the world. When he couldn't figure it out, he just let the words flow. "Do you want to sleep in my room?"

Georgiana took her time mulling over the idea, picking sections of her damp hair off her shoulders to lay down her back. "If you think it's best."

"It was a difficult day for your mother," Edward repeated. "It would be unfortunate if you wake her, especially if she's such an uneasy sleeper.

"Yes," Georgiana agreed, pursing her lips. "Quite."

Suddenly, all the weariness and bone-deep fatigue vanished from Edward like a bad dream right after waking. All he saw was Georgiana's shy little smile.

But he still couldn't move. "I have a confession to make," he said, meeting her gaze pointedly. "I don't have a butler. I only have one servant, and I rented the valet I brought with me on the trip. I don't need much; I can dress myself. Ever since my father died, I've economized so my family doesn't have to go without. That's what you saw at my home that day, why I got so angry. I'm not embarrassed. I just didn't want to see any of that yet."

"Oh," Georgiana said slowly, her hand falling from the door handle. "Thank you for telling me. Thank you for trusting me enough to tell me."

Edward exhaled, feeling he'd shed half his weight.

"I also have something to confess," she said. Her eyes wandered back to his. "I might be a little besotted."

CHAPTER NINETEEN

I T TOOK EDWARD three tries to unlock his room, his hands shook so badly. Eventually, he got them inside and stayed back, allowing Georgiana space to acclimate to the masculine surroundings—not that there were many. His valet had already been inside and started a fire, as well as laid out fresh clothes and a basin of tepid water for washing. The poor man must have stayed up all night waiting for Edward to return.

The room was cozy and warm and small—much too small for the staggering feelings cascading through him.

Edward had told himself that Georgiana wouldn't leave his bed once she found it; however, he hadn't anticipated that would begin tonight.

Trying not to gape, he watched as she idled around his bed, picking up some things before daintily putting them back down. He had no idea a gentleman's razor could cause so much interest in a woman.

"How did the grouse hunt go today?" she asked.

"What?"

She paused. "The hunt? That's why you didn't come with us, remember?"

"Oh, of course." Edward coughed, crossing the room toward the bureau, where he slipped off his wet overcoat and jacket and stacked them on top. He'd forgotten about hunting. Instead, he'd decided to drink away the afternoon, driving her from his mind. "I got halfway there and turned back."

"Because of the rain?" she asked, slightly breathless as she studied him working on his cuffs.

"Sure," he said with a wide grin, enjoying the way she fixated on his every movement, especially as she zeroed in on his neck while he unwound his cravat.

He tried to temper his burgeoning desire. What the hell was she doing in here? More importantly, what was he supposed to do with her? Naturally, he had ideas, but wasn't quite sure yet if they coincided with hers.

"Did you at least enjoy what you saw?" he asked.

She gulped, her gaze still on his neck. "What I saw?"

"At the tournament. Did you enjoy any of it?"

She blinked, suddenly coming to. "Oh, not really. It was quite"—Edward unbuttoned his waistcoat and tugged his shirttails out of his waistband—"anticlimactic."

A tremor shook Georgiana's entire body, and Edward finally snapped into action. He found one of his clean shirts and a towel, handing them to her. "You can wear this tonight," he said, nodding toward the basin. "I can leave while you wash."

Why the hell had he suggested that? He wasn't going any-where.

"No, stay," she said, dragging a relieved breath from him.

With a tight chest, he observed her as she placed the shirt on the bed and began to undress. She removed the heavy, wet cape well enough by herself, but when it came to her dress, she was at a loss. Buttons in the back—she would need his assistance to take it off.

Edward came to her before she could ask, turning her in a perfunctory manner to flick off the buttons and spread the velvet fabric wide, giving her the opportunity to slide it off her hips. Edward should have given her room, but his feet were stuck. His blood pumping, his hands poised in the air for action, he waited for her to need him again.

But she didn't. Georgiana stepped out of the gown and used the rag near the basin to begin wiping the caked mud from her skin, rearranging the chemise along her body to keep her modesty in check. Short-sleeved and wide at the neck, it afforded Edward a healthy view of the slope of her back.

He was paralyzed with want. His attention was on every silken swipe of the water across her alabaster skin, the fluidity of her movement, the gentle rustle of the cotton. Thin and flimsy, the garment gave his imagination just enough to work with; Edward's overactive appetite provided the rest to drive him damn near crazy.

"You missed a spot," he blurted, surprising no one more than himself.

Hesitating, Georgiana looked over her shoulder, her brow arched. "Where?"

Edward pointed to her neck where a smudge of dirt lay just under the chemise. "Just there."

Georgiana tried to reach back and get it, but she missed again. He shook his head, and she sighed, handing him the rag. "Can you?"

He stared at the rag dumbly. "You would let me wash you?"

Georgiana waited to respond. It was as if they both knew just how monumental her next words would be. "I daresay you would do it better than I. My fingers won't stop shaking."

"Stand next to the fire if you're cold."

"I'm not cold."

Neither was he.

Edward accepted the rag, and she turned away from him, pulling the chemise down along her shoulders. He took a deep breath—and then another. Like the heavens above, the sweet breadth of her skin seemed to go on forever. He could explore it the rest of the night and still come away knowing nothing and everything.

Gently, he caressed her, taking his time, not leaving one inch of flesh untouched. Georgiana closed her eyes, her mouth opened slightly as he worked around her, lifting and maneuvering her limbs to perform his duty. He didn't overstep; he didn't need to. This was the single most erotic thing he'd ever experienced in his life. No stranger to women's bodies, Edward was mesmerized by hers. The way her shoulder blades formed wings along her back, the way her clavicle slid across the chest, the sharp cliff that dropped from her jaw down her winding neck. Every space had a story that he wanted to read.

The trickling of the water and the brushes against her skin were the only sounds between them, though Edward was sure she could hear his heartbeat. It pounded between his ears like a marching band, only adding to the bubble they found themselves in.

Georgiana didn't speak again until he dropped to his knees. "Let me sit down, to make it easier for you," she said, her eyelashes fluttering.

Edward smiled up at her and shook his head. "I like this view."

She laughed nervously, and he picked up one of her feet, perching it on his thigh. Forgetting that he was supposed to be washing her—or just giving up on the façade—he ran both hands up her downy leg to her knee, massaging the flesh so well that he heard her groan.

"You like that?"

She didn't answer, and when he glanced up, he saw her eyes were closed again, and she bit at her lower lip. The light from the fire magnified her chemise, and he could easily make out the outline of her body, the fleshy buds of her breasts straining against the cotton. He could kiss her now—he could make love to her on the floor, joining their bodies and spirits and making something completely new and holy between them.

But he had to ask, "What are you doing here, Georgiana?"

Her eyes shot open, milky with desire and confusion. She replied softly, "I don't know."

"What do you want?"

She shook her head. "I don't know."

Edward slid his hands up her legs again, stroking all the way to her inner thighs. "Do you want to go back to your room?"

"No."

"It is dangerous for you to be here."

"With you? Never."

"Yes, with me. I want you," he said, hoping honesty would give her the strength to leave—the strength he did not have.

Georgiana removed her foot from his thigh, planting both feet on the floor. "Today has been a day of pretending…"

"What does that mean?"

Timidly, she reached out and brushed the hair off his forehead. He almost flinched at the light touch. Edward couldn't remember the last time someone had simply touched him just for the sake of touching him. Georgiana had kissed him at his house, but this was different, even more intimate.

His chest grew heavy with emotion, and something choked in his throat. Then and there he knew he was helpless against this woman. Whatever she wanted, he would give. Whatever she needed, he would provide, even if it killed him in the morning.

Her fingertips stayed on his forehead, burning little lines in his flesh. "We have tonight," she said.

"What about tomorrow?"

"I don't want to think about tomorrow."

"All because I saved you today?"

"No," Georgiana replied. She brought her other hand to his face and cupped his cheeks. "Because today you showed me…who you were." She caressed his jaw, and he turned his head to capture her thumb in his mouth. Nostrils flaring, he sucked her with all the frustration and apprehension that pulsed through his blood. She had no idea what she was asking; she couldn't. But Edward was done saving people today. He couldn't save her from herself. As he'd already told her time and time again, he was no knight.

Edward circled his arms around her, holding her arse tight as he cradled his head in her pelvis, breathing in her fecund aroma. He could smell her need—her readiness for him—and knew there was no going back.

He felt her holding the back of his neck, pressing him to her even more. "What do you want?" he repeated.

"I…I want you to make me feel like I did before."

His laugh was husky, his control in abeyance. Tilting his head up, he glanced at Georgiana and found her expression slightly worried. "Oh, I'm going to do that, but would you mind if I tried something a little different?"

The tendons around her neck flexed. "Something different?"

Edward was already lifting the chemise higher up her legs. He nodded. "Something different."

She licked her lips. "Will it…will I feel the same way?"

He nodded slowly, a wolfish grin on his face as he grabbed for more and more bare skin. When her garment reached her upper thighs, she tried to pull it down, but Edward's insistence won out. "Trust me," he purred, sliding his hands underneath the fabric to palm her behind, squeezing the luscious globes for extra measure. "You'll like it."

Her fingers had a death grip on his shoulders, emboldening him further. "If…if you think—"

"Oh, I think," he said, sliding his hands around her pelvis so he could lift the chemise the last few inches. They both inhaled a quick breath at the same moment.

Edward leaned forward and nuzzled his nose in her core, not able to stop himself from swiping his tongue along the groove of her sex. Georgiana jumped, and he clamped his hands on her hips to keep her still. But she didn't stop him.

No, she didn't stop him.

Dipping his head, he licked her again, tasting the ripe fruitiness of her body, the wet fervor that was there because of him—and only for him. He took his time, laving her folds, flicking his tongue back and forth, no rhythm to be found, keeping Georgiana quite literally on her toes. When he found the little bud under her hood, he played with it at first, waking it up, exciting it, letting her understand the source of her pleasure and power.

After that, this was no longer a solitary dance. Her nails digging into his shoulders, she began to move in tandem with his tongue, sliding her pussy against his mouth, asking without speaking, directing without ordering. She wanted that elusive feeling again and wasn't waiting for Edward to give it to her.

The undulations of her pelvis came faster, the rise and fall of her chest quicker, and Edward had to grab her arse again, providing even more friction, even more pressure as he ate from her mound. He sucked and he bit and he kissed and he stroked, loving her with every inch of his mouth until she arched back in a harsh sigh that was so erotic and beautiful he almost lost himself.

Looking up, he saw her breasts straining out of her chemise, one of her hands at her throat, and her mouth open and panting toward the ceiling. Pulsing, pumping, contracting, her body responded in so many ways to him, and Edward sat back on his haunches, wanting a front-row seat to all of it.

Sensing his gaze, Georgiana came back to him, looking exhausted in that lovely, orgasmic way. "You're still on your knees," she whispered.

"Always with you," he said.

Taking her hand, he brought her down to him, and she straddled him. He loved the way her eyes widened as her sensitive core settled along his crotch. "Was that better than before?"

She grinned wickedly. "I do not know, my lord. I might have to have it the other way again, just to be sure."

He chuckled, kissing her for the first time that night, sweeping his tongue inside in a lazy kiss that belied the throbbing insistence of his member. All he wanted to do was impale her and let her ride him until the sun came up. But he tempered that thought. Georgiana was mistaken—or just delusional—by thinking they only had tonight. They had forever. And Edward was damned good at playing the long game.

"Do you want to go into the bed?" she whispered shyly

against his neck, her pink tongue licking at his skin, causing him to shudder. He pumped his hips up while sliding her pelvis over him.

A delighted "Oh!" fell from her sultry lips. He kissed her again, light and fleeting and damned well.

"It's best to keep away from the bed for now," he said, sliding her again. Quickly, she got the hang of it, finding the rhythm, working their pelvises against one another.

He held the back of her head and kept their foreheads together, their eyes locked, their heads still as each of their bodies worked their needs out on the other. Edward hadn't meant for it to go this far, but he still had the taste of her pussy on his mouth, and his body was crying out for release. Spilling in his pants was all he would give himself tonight. He had to make her come first, though. Just one more time.

Their movements grew more forceful and aggressive. A frown played out on her face as Georgiana searched for that feeling once again. Edward was at the cusp; his balls were tight, and sweat had broken out on his brow. Her lovely breasts bobbed in front of him, and he gritted his teeth to stay with her, to give her everything she wanted. Tucking his hand between their legs, he petted the hood of her core again, giving her more. She bucked wildly then, her body taking on a life of its own. A new life. With him.

Edward tucked his head into her chest as she ground on him, relieved when he felt her still and arch, keen and cry from the base of her throat. Then Edward came hard, his motions relaxing and smoothing as they both collapsed into one another like the arch of a chapel, holding the other up.

It could have been minutes, it could have been hours—but eventually, Edward managed to pick them up from the floor and get them changed before climbing into the bed. Too exhausted and replete, Georgiana put up no fuss as he undressed her, though she did tug the new shirt on quickly enough.

She needed no coaxing into the bed, positioning herself at his side, laying her head comfortably in the cove under his shoulder. *Georgiana's cove,* Edward thought fancifully as she placed a hand over his shirt along his ribcage.

Her yawn broke him from his thoughts—as well as her giggle.

"What?" he asked, playing with her long hair, tracing the never-ending curls down as far as his arms would let him go.

"I thought you said the bed was a bad idea?"

He *humphed.* "It was."

"It's not anymore?"

He yawned. "Not anymore."

She played with a button on his shirt, twirling it over and over again like it was an errant thought in her busy mind. "I thought when I stayed that we…that we…"

"It can wait," Edward said, placing a steady palm over her hand.

She tilted her head up. "I told you: we only have tonight."

"It can wait," he said again.

Georgiana hesitated. "I would have stayed regardless, you know. Even if you hadn't helped so many people today."

"I know."

"Oh, you do? How?"

He smiled kindly, brushing a curl off her face, behind her ear. "It was as I told you before. You don't want another man. You want me. You are right where you want to be."

She collapsed back on his chest, taking the wind out of him.

Edward could feel her head spinning. When she didn't respond, he chuckled, not put out by her reserve. She was scared. So was he, for that matter. He let her fall asleep with the comfort of that silence.

It didn't matter. She'd admitted she wanted him. In a day full of knights, she'd ended up in his bed. That made him the winner of the tournament in his book.

CHAPTER TWENTY

EDWARD TOLD HER he would stay.

The following morning, Georgiana received news from the castle that the knights were going to try the tournament again. But the mystique was gone. Once she had seen the real men behind the curtain—watching out for and acting in their own interests—pretending they were chivalrous warriors of a bygone age seemed impossible. With the rain washing it away, Georgiana's imagination bled into the fields.

Instead, with her mother in tow, they set out for Edward's estate, reaching it two days later. The storm had petered out, and the journey was uneventful enough, with the pair's interactions vastly different. There were no more frosty, one-word answers between Edward and Georgiana, although conversation was still stilted.

After fleeing his arms the morning after the storm, Georgiana was unsure how to treat him. How could she look him in the eye after he'd performed something so magically personal to her? Especially with her mother so close?

Edward's behavior couldn't be more proper, but the moment her mother looked the other way, he'd convey something that would make Georgiana blush for hours. A shy smile, an arresting stare, a show of teeth, and she was one slippery memory away from swooning. He was teasing her, forcing her to come to terms with what they'd done, and she was absolutely lost on what it all meant. Georgiana had given him the night and knew he wanted more. The question was…did she?

She didn't regret it. How could one regret something so profound? She'd once likened herself to Andromeda, with Edward being the sea monster. She was her father's ultimate sacrifice, but she'd had no Perseus to fly in and save her on his winged horse. While in her chains, waiting for the rescuer who would never come, Georgiana got to know the beast and realized that, perhaps, he wasn't the worst thing to come out of the ocean. Even a monster's cold touch warmed in time.

Sat on the shores of Ipswich in southeast England, Marlborough House was a classic Jacobean-style pile with a flat, broad exterior constructed of red brick. Crenellations spiked along the top center of the main building, with turrets on either side and mullioned windows throughout. The smell of the sea combined with wildflowers to give the air a wind-swept freshness that was so different from London that Georgiana wondered why Edward ever came to the city at all. It was a home steeped in history and secrets, with the types of poky halls and dark corridors that Georgiana had lost many an afternoon reading about. It was also the kind of home where a boy could wear generations-old armor and pretend to be a knight.

As the carriage approached, Georgiana was about to remark on the house's beauty when three little girls ran out from the entrance, standing on the front steps, bobbing up and down in their excitement.

From the corner of her eye, Georgiana saw Edward smile at the domestic scene, and when the carriage stopped, he didn't hesitate to join the girls, giving each one a large hug, lifting their tiny, dainty feet off the steps. Georgiana never thought she'd see the day where Edward would elicit any kind of bumbling laughter from three red-headed girls, yet here they were.

Remembering Georgiana and her mother, Edward introduced his younger sisters, the eldest of whom couldn't be more than twelve. Eugenie, Caroline, and Bess lived full-time in Marlborough and, due to his efforts in London, hadn't seen their brother in over two months.

Even with the commotion over the arrivals, the girls behaved properly, greeting Georgiana and her mother with impeccable manners and just a little of the haughty reserve that Edward showed on occasion. The love between the siblings was evident, along with a camaraderie that all the restraint and good breeding in the world couldn't disguise. Georgiana liked the girls right away, especially when they swarmed her, taking her hands and dragging her into the house after the introductions had been made.

For long minutes, Georgiana couldn't get a word in as they bombarded her with questions, statements, and all-around inane chitchat. Edward merely looked on helplessly, leaving her to the insatiable harpies.

"You're Edward's fiancée?"

"Is everyone wearing braids so tight in London?"

"How was the tournament?"

"Did you see Louise?"

"Did she stab someone?"

"Was Mother very angry?"

After the promise of gifts to come, Edward managed to whisk Georgiana away from the information-hungry girls, while the housekeeper took her mother up to her room. Holding her hand, Edward led her up the stairs as well; however, when her mother and the housekeeper reached the floor of rooms and turned left down the corridor, Edward turned right.

"I hope you like it," he said, opening the door to a large bedroom richly appointed in seafoam-green silks. Georgiana waded in, taking in the splendor of the furnishings—old, no doubt, but lovingly cared for and as enchanting as anything that could be found in the greatest homes in the country.

"It's beautiful," she said, turning back to Edward. He'd stayed at the threshold, leaning against the doorframe.

"My room is next door," he explained.

Oh.

"Oh," she said. "I suppose that means I'll be seeing a lot of you while we're visiting."

"I certainly hope so." He chuckled easily enough, though Georgiana couldn't help but notice the tightness that had overtaken his features. Was he thinking of their night together? Did he do it all the time, as she did?

After a few more moments of palpable silence, Edward straightened, running his hand along the doorframe a few times as if searching for what to say. "Tell Agnes if you need anything. I want you to enjoy your time here."

Deducing Agnes was the housekeeper, Georgiana circled the room a final time, a wide smile breaking out on her face. "I'm sure I will; I can't think of anything more that I would need. It's so lovely, Edward. Like a dream."

He nodded, fighting a proud grin. "It wasn't always like this. Just a few years ago it was quite bare, nothing like you see now." His expression became serious as he stared off. "It took me longer than I liked, but I got everything back. Every little thing he sold."

A flood of sympathy overtook her. Georgiana wanted to wrap her arms around the man who had sacrificed so much for his family. This place was nothing like the townhouse in London, where he lived so starkly. The sisters appeared to want for nothing, and she wondered how much of their father's perfidy they'd had to experience, or if Edward had sheltered them from the worst of it. Did they even know how he lived in London?

"Your mother must be incredibly grateful to have her things returned."

He snorted. "I assume she is. I wouldn't know."

"Because she doesn't speak to you?"

Edward tried to smile through a grimace. "She is proud. As she should be."

"She should be proud of you."

"Perhaps," he allowed. "I thought you'd get a chance to meet her, but it turns out she accompanied my sister to the tournament."

"Are they—"

"They're fine," he reassured her. "They had rooms at the castle. I doubt my mother let one drop of rain land on her head. Hopefully, they'll return before we leave."

Georgiana didn't share his hope. From the stories he'd told, his mother seemed absolutely frightening. She wasn't sure how to behave in front of the marchioness, especially since she still had no idea who or what she wanted to be to the woman's son. An uncomfortable conversation ahead was all Georgiana could see.

"I'll leave you to rest," Edward went on. "Again, let me know if you need anything. I want you to feel…at home here."

When he left, Georgiana was the only person to hear herself say, "I'm afraid I will."

⤜⤜⤜⬥⤛⤛⤛

AS ONE ALWAYS said but truly needed to experience to understand, life in the country was so vastly different from life in the city, and it took Georgiana a few days to acclimate. For one, everything was earlier, from waking times to eating times. It wasn't a huge deal for her, though her mother had a difficult time of it, always needing her maid to rouse her from sleep and prod her on her way.

Georgiana needed no such help. She loved sitting in the chair by her window, savoring the sparkle of the manicured gardens as the sunlight kissed the estate every morning. Sensing the need for a shield around her heart, Georgiana started off the week repeatedly telling herself to enjoy it without getting used to it. Environments like this were usually too good to be true.

Nor did she want to get used to the version of Edward that the country brought out. She wouldn't say he was entirely changed, but the surroundings relaxed him in a way she hadn't experienced. From his lighthearted quips to the simple way he carried himself, he seemed lighter, more at home, both literally and within his own skin. Which wasn't to say he wasn't busy. The moment they arrived, he'd begun flying around his estate like a man possessed. His exertions were not forced or unwilling. From the sidelines, Georgiana could tell he loved getting into the minutiae, finding problems, and solving them with breakneck speed.

It was true, Georgiana's knowledge of the aristocracy was limited, but from what she'd seen in London, she'd always believed they had people—so many people—to deal with the everyday so they could sit back and be...aristocratic. Above it. It appeared that no one had told Edward about this. He worked just as hard as her father in his factory, riding out to speak to his tenants every morning, conversing with his steward and estate manager for hours at a time. The house was infused with light and voices, seemingly comfortable in knowing what it was. And that had nothing to do with the paintings and rugs and silver that had only recently found their way back. Georgiana had no doubt that, down to its bones, Marlborough House would show life. Because it held Edward's heart.

But did she?

At first, Georgiana had been a little confused by his inattentiveness to her. Wasn't she there so he could persuade her to his suit? She'd fully expected him to come to her room that first night, since they were situated so closely—however, he'd played the perfect gentleman, saying good night to her and her mother as they retired. What had been the point of the room if he hadn't meant to finish what they started in Scotland?

As the week wore on, Georgiana told herself she didn't care. It was for the best. All of her free time gave her a chance to be with his sisters and explore the grounds at her leisure. Jumping into bed with a man she was mildly besotted with was destined to lead to ruin—quite literally.

She had to remind herself that this home, however majestic,

was the place women like her went to die. After marrying her, Edward would ship her to the country while he got on with running his businesses and their lives, most likely from London. She would be left with the children and the charities, the organizing of staff, and all the other trivialities that went along with running an estate. It would be overwhelming at first, maybe even exciting in its newness, but the rose's bloom would fade quickly. Capable as she was, Georgiana would get a quick handle on things and the boredom would set in. She could see it as clear as day. This sort of life boasted of pretty, sparkly things to turn women's heads; however, in the end, they always came back straight. Georgiana allowed herself to appreciate it at a distance, though at a distance was where she had to stay.

But by the middle of the week, Edward's distance continued to confuse her. Georgiana wasn't exactly bombarding him with come-hither looks. She was, on the other hand, providing a decent amount of situations where they could be alone.

One night, after a robust dinner of pheasant and root vegetables, she announced that she'd be taking a light walk before bedtime. Her mother politely declined to join, having had one too many trips to Edward's substantial wine cellar. Georgiana had expected that; however, she hadn't expected Edward to wish her a pleasant walk and warn her to stick to the gardens.

With a tight smile, Georgiana trudged out into the mazelike hedges, wondering what she had done to encourage his neglect. He'd wanted her before, hadn't he? He'd made enough comments about his desire for her to believe he wasn't playing her false. What had changed? What hot-blooded man wouldn't want a chance with a woman in the garden with no one watching?

Georgiana kept herself out as long as she could, though the coolness in the autumn air had her marching back to the house with nothing but a pink nose and more questions swirling around her head. The house was cavernous, and her footsteps echoed up the staircase. Not ready to spend the remainder of the night bored in her room, Georgiana didn't stop when she reached her floor. She kept going to the third, where she assumed the nursery was placed. When she reached the top, she was rewarded with giggles and a deep, low voice, which she followed down the hallway to a half-opened door. Using it to shield herself, Georgiana peeked through the crack to find an unexpected scene.

"I want to read that part! Why does Bess get to?" Caroline cried, hopping onto a four-poster bed where her two sisters were snuggled up to their brother's sides.

Edward gave her a stern look and turned the page of the book in his lap. "Because Bess needs to work on her reading out loud, and I want to hear how much better she's doing," he explained patiently, causing ten-year-old Caroline to flop on the bed over a multitude of pillows.

Not wanting to miss a prime opportunity, the eldest of the three, Eugenie, picked up one of the pillows and slapped her surly sister soundly on the stomach. "You can do the next part, when King Richard and Robin of Locksley save Ivanhoe from the burning castle," she explained.

"Oh, all right," Caroline grumbled. "I suppose that's a good part."

"They're all good parts," Eugenie replied breathlessly.

Georgiana stifled an amused snort. She wondered if she sounded that enthralled when she discussed the book.

Edward groaned. "Can we please continue? I don't think I can handle this nonsense much longer."

The girls laughed at their brother, who looked completely at curmudgeonly ease between them, his jacket off and cravat unwound, sitting in the pink bed with his head on a lacy pillow and his long legs out and crossed at the ankles in front of him, dangling off the end of the bed.

It seemed Georgiana's knight could appreciate art after all; he only needed the right inspiration.

"Go on, Bess," he said as the seven-year-old lifted the book close to her face. Edward picked up her long, carrot-colored hair, swiping it away from her face. It was a loving gesture, and clearly made many times before. Georgiana doubted he even knew he did it.

Bess took a deep breath, opening and closing her mouth a few times before beginning. Her start was littered with a rash of stutters as she fumbled over the words. Only Georgiana could see Edward's lips moving along with hers, sounding out the difficult words for his little sister, encouraging her over her insecure speech.

Georgiana didn't recognize she was crying until she felt a solitary tear fall down her cheek.

When Bess finished the page, the entire group clapped, her older sisters throwing in a couple of extra cheers for the effort.

"Wonderful, Bess, truly wonderful," Edward said, hugging the little girl close. "You've come so far since I was here last."

"I always read better when you're here," she said, biting her bottom lip shyly at the attention. "I wish you could stay longer."

Edward sighed, turning the page. "I know, dear girl. I know. But it won't be much longer now."

"Why can't you just get married and come home?" Caroline asked in her direct manner. Of the little girls, it was no surprise which one took after Edward in his bluntness. "What's taking so long?"

Edward didn't seem to object to the questioning, nor did he evade it as Georgiana thought he would. A smart man knew when he'd met his match. "Oh, you remember, don't you?" he said, lifting up the tome. "I need to convince the fair lady I am as dashing and good-hearted as Ivanhoe."

Caroline hugged a pillow to her chest, answering with a sarcastic laugh, "No wonder it's taking so long."

Bess grinned and snuggled into her brother's side even more. "It shouldn't take long at all," she said, going back to her book. "You're better than Ivanhoe."

A barely-there smile flitted over Edward's face. "High praise indeed. Why do you think that?"

Bess tapped her finger on the open page. "Because you're real," she said.

CHAPTER TWENTY-ONE

E DWARD WAS JUST about to mount his horse the next morning when Georgiana stormed up to him.

"I want to see the coprolites," she demanded, brushing a few errant tendrils off her face. Ever since they'd been away from London, her mother had apparently relaxed her stringent hair laws, and Georgiana's curls were more and more noticeable. Either that or she wasn't listening to her mother anymore, which Edward found just as plausible.

He hadn't allowed himself to be alone with Georgiana since they arrived at Marlborough, and Edward had to resist the temptation to pull her in his arms and kiss the life out of her. He was so damned thirsty for her. And she was definitely a temptation with her wind-swept features and light blue dress, which showed off the delicate neckline that he had slavered over only days before.

That was why he'd stayed away—well, one of the reasons.

He wanted to give her time to get to know his home without his influence. Edward yearned for her to see him, but he forced himself to get out of his own way and let the estate work its fairytale magic. And he didn't want to debauch her in every shadowed corner. Edward was determined to be Richard the Lionheart in this fantasy, not his lecherous brother.

"Why did you wear your hair so tight in London?" he asked,

not knowing he was saying the words until they came out. "Always in braids. I had no hint of your curls until that night at your window."

Georgiana flushed, pushing more of the brown locks out of her face. "She—my mother—strives for decorum. My curls remind her of her mother's, the poverty they lived in when she was young. In some odd way, my hair is everything my parents have strived to leave behind."

Edward reached for a lock, playing with it thoughtfully between his fingers. "Do you want to know what I see when it's down, Georgiana?"

She licked her lips.

"I see you. Who you are and who you are going to be. And I want to be a part of all of it."

"Then let me see *you*," she said, taking the wisps of her hair out of his hand. "Take me to the mines. That's where you're going, isn't it? I want to see what you've been haggling me for."

"Haggling?"

"Yes, you know…why you've been so keen for me."

Edward placed his hands on his hips, towering over the misinformed woman. "I think I've made it quite clear why I've been so 'keen' for you."

"Not lately," she muttered.

What in the world was the silly girl talking about? Didn't she know? Couldn't she tell he could barely spend more than a few seconds in her presence without sprouting a cockstand? Christ, he had to constantly excuse himself so as not to embarrass himself in front of her mother.

However, he caught something else in Georgiana's words; something he'd wanted but hadn't dared hope for. "Am I to understand that you *miss* me?"

Suddenly, she found the horse incredibly interesting.

"Am I?" he repeated, harsher than he'd expected.

"I'm just asking to see the mines," she said. "Don't make me beg."

He grinned. "We'll save that for later, then."

"What—"

Edward untethered his restraint and pulled Georgiana against his chest, covering her mouth with his, slanting his lips across hers in a kiss that had been haunting his nights. Georgiana wasn't surprised for long, kissing him back with matching fervor, knocking his hat to the ground to slide her fingers in his hair, holding him so close he could feel her heartbeat. Or was that his?

They stayed at it for long minutes. Edward penetrated her mouth to such a degree that he could no longer taste the tea she'd drunk that morning. He could only taste Georgiana.

A cough brought him back to attention, and Edward noticed his groom readying another horse. He broke away reluctantly, mystified at how the woman could make him forget himself so easily. For a man who had lived with a single purpose these last few years, it was astonishing *and* disconcerting, to say the least.

He wiped away the sheen from her rosy lower lip before letting his hand drop to rest on her rising chest. Exactly where he wanted to lay his head and die a happy man.

However, that would have to wait.

"Mount up," he said, to her delight, though he had to kiss her two more times before he actually let her go to the horse.

It was a relaxed ride to the far end of the estate, but when they reached the would-be mine pits, Edward didn't stop. Instead, he continued toward the shore. The mines weren't a safe place for her, nor were they that interesting to see—not until they were functional, at least. If she wanted to know who he was— everything he was working toward—then Edward could only think of one place to take her. It was the one place that had captured his soul early in his childhood and had yet to release it.

They left the horses near the top of the cliff and traveled the rest of the way to the beach on foot. It wasn't particularly treacherous, though Edward kept an arm on Georgiana as she navigated her heavy skirts down the rocky path. On such a brilliant blue day, the shore was calmer than normal, and low tide revealed the pebbled beach in all its multicolored glory.

"This is my favorite place in all the world," he said at Georgiana's questioning gaze. Edward squared himself to the water, letting the breeze wash him clean and make him whole, as it always did. "I would come here when I was a child when I needed to get away from the house. My father would be home for a time and my mother would be so ecstatic, preening under his attention. But I knew better. I knew he would just stay home long enough for the devil to rise in him again and get that itch. Then he would find something to sell, and he'd be off for no one knew how long. I would stay here for hours, searching through the rocks for anything that resembled the jewelry that he stole from my mother and try to fashion something for her."

"What a lovely thing to do."

He grimaced bashfully as he picked up a deep green stone that, to the untrained eye, looked as extravagant as any emerald. "She'd keep them for a time and then throw them away when she thought I'd forgotten, so I started collecting them in my room. I noticed some had odd ridges in them, like snails' shells. I didn't know what to make of them, until one day a man on the beach saw a basket of my jewelry and told me what I was actually finding. That's when I first discovered ammonites and coprolites. And I was hooked. The idea that I could actually find something so old and so mysterious... It was like..." Edward touched his hand to his heart. That same current of discovery pulled him into its insistent grip just as it had years ago.

"Stepping back in time?" Georgiana offered.

"Yes, yes, exactly. Like stepping back in time."

Georgiana reached for the rock, tossing it up and catching it a few times. "Is this an ammonite?"

"No. That's just a rock." He laughed at her frown. "You want to find a real one?"

"Yes, please!" she said. Before he could direct her, Georgiana was already hiking up her skirts, marching toward the cliffs. "Do I have to climb?" she said, pointing at the intimidating rockface.

"What? Hell no, don't go over there. You'll hurt yourself. You can find them on the beach. Usually, there are plenty after a storm, so we should be able to find a few. Maybe, if the lady is lucky, she'll even find a few precious medieval coins."

Georgiana popped her head up from scouring the ground. "You really think so?"

Why did he feel as powerful as a warlord? Save his sisters, Edward had never taken anyone here before, and certainly never told them about his love for scavenging. If anything, he'd expected to feel embarrassed, and not a little bit raw, but Georgiana's lack of judgment and exuberance took all those insecurities away. Sharing his love with her just made sense.

Edward desperately wanted to find her something, but his focus continued to be yanked away. The childlike wonder she took in tackling their task kept his attention firmly in her grasp. It didn't help that every few seconds she'd pick something up and yell, "Is this one?" before throwing it back down when he shook his head. He was completely spellbound by her—the way she unabashedly took to the fun, throwing herself into the adventure of the unknown. The way she accepted his dream and wanted to be a part of it.

Over the course of the morning, Edward did find two small ammonites that he pocketed. He planned to give them to Georgiana if she didn't come up with something herself. With the sun moving higher in the sky and his lower back aching, he was just about to call it a day when he heard her squeal.

"Edward! Come over here quick!"

Her bonnet half flying off her head and her hair falling out of her bun like the gangly arms of an octopus, Georgiana was a fantasy come to life. She would never know how right she looked to him at that moment, nor would she ever believe him. To have her in this place, fitting like a key to a lost treasure chest, nearly took his breath away.

"Edward! Please!" she whined, running toward him, hand outstretched. "This has to be something!"

Sure enough, when she opened her palm, he saw a spiraling ammonite.

"Was I right?" she said, giddy with anticipation and pride.

He brushed the sand away with his thumbs. "You were," he replied, smiling over her exuberance. "It's a button ammonite."

"A button?"

"Yes, you see here?" He showed her the fossil encased in its own matrix, as smooth and transparent as amber. "See how round and perfect it is? The same shape as a button. The fossil sits inside, frozen forever in its history. I have bags of them at home I'll give you, if you would like."

"I suppose it's appropriate for a button maker's daughter," she replied, her cheeks rosy and wet with spray and sweat. "Is this one special?"

Edward forgot the ammonite then. Gently reaching out to hold one of those cheeks, he brought her closer to place a sweet kiss on her salt-stained mouth. "Yes," he said softly. "It is very special."

Her lips twisted up wryly. "We're not talking about the same thing, are we?"

Edward shook his head. "No, we're not." He cocked his head. "Do you mind?"

Her smile was as bright as the sun's reflection on the water. "I guess not." Squinting over the horizon, watching the waves beat into the shore, Georgiana took a deep breath. "I can see why you love it here. It's a paradise. We're not so different after all, are we?"

"How's that?"

Georgiana glanced at her ammonite. "We both love history, just different kinds. Both histories are romantic, having a pull that captivates the dreamer."

Edward had never thought of it that way before. "I'm a dreamer?" he asked.

"Oh, yes. And more than that—you're a man on a quest, searching for ancient dragons in the stones."

There she was, comparing him to a knight again.

"I'm ready to make my dream a reality, though," he countered. "The mines would open up so many possibilities for the people."

"And here I thought you just wanted to make money." She grinned. However, there was a confrontation in her tone, an underlying question of his character.

He wouldn't let her down this time. But he couldn't mislead her either.

"I'd be lying if I said I didn't," Edward said. "My father left a trail of debt in his wake, debt I'm only now starting to climb out of. His betrayal, perfidy, and selfishness almost crippled us, and I never want to go through that again, being beholden to others, taking their loans and scraping by as they watched gleefully for us to fall." He gripped her shoulders, forcing her to stay with him. "But it's more than that. The mine would bring in better-paying jobs. Men wouldn't have to be relegated to farming anymore. More people would come to this place, meaning housing would develop, more towns, more industry. People wouldn't have to leave their families for London, working their lives away in those dour factories."

"Like my father's factories."

Edward didn't respond, leaving the truth unsaid.

"I had no idea my dowry could mean so much," she went on quietly.

"*You*, Georgiana. Not your dowry. Not your father's investment. You could help make all that happen."

Her gaze wandered back out into the sea where so many men and women had looked before, to contemplate their futures in its limitless depths. "You would let me? Help, I mean."

"Why the hell do you think I wrote to the American telling him you'd be at that ball? That was pure selfishness. I'd let you control the whole damn thing if you promised to stay." Edward laughed, tugging her against him.

And that was true. He'd listened to her enough to understand her passion. While he wasn't a complete convert, Edward recognized the change that had to take place. If he was going to make the mines a success, what better way to usher in the future than with the practices she preached about? And who better to institute them than her? Just because Edward had worked alone for so long didn't mean he couldn't see the competence in others. No one could miss hers.

"We have the chance to create something truly great here," he said.

"That's quite a bribe, Edward," she said against his chest.

"I've never said I was above it."

Georgiana pulled back, her features wrought with consternation. "It's a lot to think about."

"I just thought you should know that you're needed. Even more than your money."

She looked out at the ocean again, her hesitation carving a chasm straight to his heart. Edward hadn't known her response would affect him so much, but that was an understatement. It affected *everything* about him. The man he was. The man he wanted to be.

Because he loved her. The knowledge was at once crushing and comforting, as perilous and stimulating as the waves crashing at their feet. Years of hiding himself away from the disappointment of others did nothing to lessen the blow. The blow that his life, and everything he'd worked for, would cease to have meaning without her in it.

"I want to believe you," she finally said.

Edward sucked in a trembling breath. Belief was such a fragile thing. But he would never give her cause to regret her belief in him. After all, he was real, damn it. He was real.

CHAPTER TWENTY-TWO

AFTER THE ILLUMINATING day at the sea, Georgiana was tired—tired of waiting. The decision hadn't come to her lightly, though once it had, she didn't quibble with it.

She waited until the household was down for the night, and when she heard Edward finally retire to his room, she made her move.

Georgiana had once told him she couldn't speak to tomorrow, but that was over. Stepping into the past together had shown her that a future was possible with this man. It was as clear as the generations weathered in one of his fossils.

Putting on her robe, she left her room and tiptoed the short path in the hallway to Edward's doorway. Too much of a coward to knock, she turned the knob, relieved to find he left it unlocked, and tucked herself inside.

"I hope you aren't going to blame your mother's uneasy sleeping habits this time for coming to my room," a deep voice said from the bed.

Georgiana spotted him relaxed and leaning on his pillows, one leg crossed over the other as if he was expecting her. An Argand lamp cast his figure in soft light, bronzing him like a statue, while throwing the rest of the room in various degrees of shadow.

Georgiana prayed for confidence. Planning on seducing a

man was monumentally easier than actually doing it. She unglued her legs and carried herself across the room, stopping at the foot of his bed. Georgiana couldn't tell if it was larger than hers or only looked that way because he was in it.

Still dressed in his dinner clothes, Edward was handsome and annoyingly contained as he waited for her response.

"No, I won't blame her," Georgiana said, slipping off her robe. She tried to do it slowly, flirtatiously, planning to throw it suggestively on his chair—however, it fell out of her trembling fingers, falling gracelessly on the floor. So much for seduction. "I blame you."

"Me?"

"Yes, you," she said, growing more insecure the longer he lay there.

He appeared quite at ease, his chest rising and falling in an even manner. Was this a usual occurrence for him? Were women always stealing off into his room? Everything Georgiana had wanted to say flew out of her head at once, leaving her discombobulated and empty, like a book with the last few chapters torn out.

"Yes, well…" She twisted her fingers around her nightgown, pulling it tight across her front. "It seems you won't come to me, so I must come to you."

Edward took more than a few seconds to respond. "Come to me for what?"

Oh, he was just being cruel now. Georgiana threw up her hands. "You know what!"

He shook his head, slowly and mercilessly. "I do not. Unless you've come to propose to me, then I have no idea what could bring you to my bed in the middle of the night."

"Stop ruining this!"

Edward slid his legs off the bed to stand. "Ruin? For once, woman, I'm not trying to ruin anything—especially you. You have no idea how much I am holding it all together. You think I don't want you? I want you so much I can't see straight. I want you so much I can't be in the same room with you."

He was on her now, his expression fierce, his body tight and agitated. He passed a hand over his face, frustration evident in his beach-rock-gray eyes. "I'm trying to give you space. I'm trying to be a gentleman."

Hadn't she already told him to stop all that? It wasn't for him. Though, to be honest, he was getting better at it by the day.

"I have no need for knights," Georgiana replied. "Besides, I've seen enough chivalry to last me a lifetime."

A curtain dropped over his face. "From the tournament?" he asked caustically.

Stupid man. "No," she said, placing her hands on his chest, working his buttons loose. She heard his breath hitch, but his hands stayed at his sides. "Not from the tournament. Here. With. You."

Concentrating on the buttons, Georgiana didn't catch the note of surprise overtake Edward, nor did she see the acceptance. But she felt it. A waterfall of recognition flowed through his body, and Georgiana knew that she'd won.

"I...I—" Edward placed his hands over hers, stopping her from pulling his shirt wide. Lifting her chin, he forced her to lock eyes with his. "I'm not the knight you were looking for."

His countenance—filled with such concern and caution— made her smile warmly back at him. "No, you're not," she agreed. "But you're the knight I've found. Like one of the rocks on your beach, I don't know exactly what you are, but I don't want to throw you back."

"You're keeping me?" he asked.

Her smile turned impish. "Let's see how the night goes."

Tilting his head back, Edward looked down his nose. "Another test?"

"Perhaps," Georgiana said, wiggling her hands free to pull his shirt open. Her eyes widened at the incredible maleness that confronted her. Though they'd done intimate things, Georgiana hadn't seen any intimate parts of Edward. She didn't think it would make that big of a difference. But standing face to chest was like encountering an entirely different person, and Georgiana was struck by her naiveté.

Kissing had never done them wrong in the past. At least she was confident in that ability. So she did the only thing she knew how to do and placed her lips in the center of his chest. In the middle of a patch of curly, dark hair, she laid claim to the man who was quickly becoming her everything. The man that moved her like no other.

His skin was hot and smelled like the outdoors, salt mixed with earth, so elemental. He was delicious, and she couldn't help but kiss him again, a light and feathery action that made his stomach clench and draw in tight. She traced the indentations of his muscles with the pads of her fingers, discovering the width of him, admiring the way life had molded him, every part of him necessary and filled with promise.

"What's my test, Georgiana?" she heard him ask, the gravelly tone rushing heat in between her legs.

She kissed his nipples, only able to lick the hard nubs once before Edward wrapped his hands around her hair, pulling her head away so she could look at him. His features were ferocious, tied up and stitched together, with nothing to do but break. She had the power to do this to him.

"My test?" he said again.

Standing as tall as she could, she brought their lips so close that they grazed. "I want you to make love to me."

His hands relaxed in her hair. "That's it?"

Confusion peeked through Georgiana's confidence. "Is there anything else?"

Edward held her face lovingly. "Oh yes," he rasped. "Because I'm going to love you so hard that you will never think of leaving me. I'm going to love you so well that any man who sees you will know instantly that you belong to me. I'm going to love you so madly that you won't remember a time before you met me."

"Yes, let's do that."

Then Edward kissed her, and it was unlike any kiss he'd ever given her before. As if all doubt had been conquered between them, the kiss was soft and pillowy, unrushed. Like they had all the time in the world.

And with his lips on hers, Georgiana believed it wholeheartedly. She swam in the deep pool of hope, accepting that, with Edward, anything was possible—including a love of equals, where two people took care of each other without taking advantage. A love where no one was greater than the other.

Edward doted on her, sliding his tongue in and out of her with a sensual languidness that made her knees weak. She wasn't sure when or how her clothes came off, but soon they were both naked, and the feel of skin on skin was as luxurious as the finest fur. She rubbed up and down against him, turned on by the fever-like sensation that enveloped her.

Typical with them, the simmer did not last long, and soon they were grabbing at one other, dragging each other closer. She wanted to touch every part of him: the hair on his legs, the sinewy flesh of his arms, the soles of his feet. But something trumped all of that.

Without announcing her intent, Georgiana let her arm float between them, making enough space to wander to his manhood, which was grazing her lower belly.

Her fingers hovered over his tip when she heard him stop breathing. She looked up at his shuttered eyes. "Do you mind?" she asked.

He barked out a laugh, shaking his head wildly. "No, never. Not from you."

"But you'd mind with someone else?"

"No other woman will ever touch me again," he replied solemnly.

Immensely liking that answer, Georgiana returned to the matter. After pausing for a few more seconds, she felt Edward take her hand and place it on his shaft, causing him to hiss— though it must have been a good hiss, since he didn't ask her to stop. "Up and down, slowly," he said.

She did as he said, eliciting more groans, and he rested his chin lightly on the top of her crown. Georgiana adored the satiny feel of him, the raw energy just under her palms. She tested what he liked, going slow and then fast, hard and then soft, coming away with the conclusion that he liked all of it. Edward was many things, but she'd never considered him easily pleased. Perhaps he was only that way with her.

"That's enough," he said, brushing her hand aside. Before she could balk, he swept her into his arms, laying her down on the bed and covering her body with his. "Damn, that feels amazing. Better than I ever dreamed," Edward said, almost like he was speaking to himself, placing fleeting, insistent kisses down her neck.

Georgiana was finding it harder and harder to hold on to a thought, but she nabbed the question from the air and asked it. "When did you dream about this?"

Edward picked up his head from the valley of her breasts and grinned wickedly. "Since the moment I found you walking in the park in the rain."

"Ha! You mean the moment you left me in the park in the rain."

"I was late for a meeting, and you were close to home."

She played with the hair across his forehead. "It wasn't very courteous."

"Oh, I guess not," he said nonchalantly, palming her belly, taking his achingly sweet time to cradle her between her legs. By this point, Georgiana knew what he was about, but that didn't make her any less hungry for it. She spread her legs apart in hopeless anticipation of what he was about to do.

And he didn't disappoint. Edward rubbed his fingers through the hair of her mound, smiling when they came away wet. "But I already told you—you don't want a chivalrous man between your legs."

As he pressed one of his long fingers inside her, Georgiana

dug her heels into the bed, arching her upper body in pleasure. He did it again, pulsing inside her gently, making her body crest and wave. Keeping his fingers inside her, he situated himself higher, finally taking a nipple in his mouth. The sensation lit Georgiana like a fire, and she cried out at the tingles building deep inside.

How could a man she barely knew know her so well? He played her body like an instrument, his hands calloused and worn, making her respond in keens and whimpers that frightened her. Her body was no longer hers, but his, working in accord with his needs.

"Do you know what I thought when I saw you in the rain, dripping wet that day?" he asked.

Too overcome by the pressure, Georgiana could only shake her head, biting her lip so hard she thought it might bleed.

He replied with a hoarse laugh. "I thought about this, about fucking you, about watching you writhe in front of me."

Georgiana licked at her poor lips as sparks of electricity began to climb up her inner thighs. He'd moved on to the other nipple now, and took turns biting it and loving it, licking as his fingers continued their torment.

"You shouldn't say such things," she breathed.

"Why? Because I'm a gentleman? I'm your knight? No...I am only a man—your man," he said, ducking his head to lick between her legs, to kiss the keystone of her need. Georgiana grabbed his head, bucking wildly at the attention. "And your man likes to get dirty, use his hands and build and scrape and love and fuck. I'm sorry, my lady, but that's what you got. I'm not the knight you were looking for, but I'm the one you found, remember?"

She nodded again, wanting to jump out of her skin. That feeling—that blessed feeling—was so close, and he continued to toy with her, bringing her to the precipice before falling away. Sweat-slicked and frustrated, she rocked against his finger, hoping to bring her there herself, but he pulled back then, climbing on top of her and wrapping her legs around his lower body.

"I can't wait any longer, my love," he said before kissing her swollen lips.

"And you think I can?" she replied.

He returned a pinched laugh, fixing his shaft at her entrance, holding her gaze as he moved in, one paralyzing inch by inch. "Don't tense up," he said.

"I'm not tense. You're tense."

"I'm not tense," he ground out. "I'm trying not to hurt you."

Georgiana cradled his face, finding the truth and worry in his overcast eyes. "Stop being so honorable."

"I'm not trying to be honorable," he said, flexing more, sweat beading off his forehead. "I'm a selfish bastard. I plan on making love to you three more times tonight, so I'm trying to go easy."

She laughed then, and at that moment he thrust, implanting himself deep inside, fracturing her amusement. They sealed themselves together for a lingering minute, each adapting to the other.

So this is what all the fuss is about, Georgiana thought as she adjusted her body, exploring all the different avenues of their connectedness.

"What do you think?" he asked haggardly, as if he'd finished a long run.

Did he want honesty? "It's…interesting," Georgiana hedged. Could she ask him to still do the other things that he'd done before? Those had been much better, though it seemed *he* really liked this. Georgiana decided she didn't have the heart to speak up. And he wanted to do it three more times?

"Interesting, huh?"

It probably didn't help that her eyes were shiny with tears. Georgiana hoped her smile was as convincing as she thought it was.

It wasn't.

Placing his elbows on either side of her head, Edward stared down at her, adorably disgruntled. "Interesting is a fine start, but not nearly good enough."

"Should I be doing something?"

He kissed both of her eyelids, causing her tears to fall. "Just tell me what feels good."

She couldn't possibly do that! "Don't men just…know?"

The twinge between her legs had begun to lessen, and Georgiana could feel his throbbing inside of her. It was still interesting, and yet…maybe a little bit more?

Edward pulled out a little, only to thrust back inside. Now, *that* was more than interesting, though she still didn't know if she liked it.

"I'm not a mind reader," he teased, nipping along her jaw up to her earlobe. "This isn't a one-man show. I need your help. I can only go where you lead." He thrust again, eliciting a tiny gasp. "Now how's it feel?"

Georgiana frowned. "It's…something."

Edward hung his head. "We went from 'interesting' to 'something.' I feel like I'm going backwards."

"No, no," Georgiana cried, grasping his shoulders to pull him down to her again. "Don't give up. I'm new to this, is all."

He shot her an incredulous look. "Honey, I'm not giving up. We're just getting started."

"We are?"

He grinned. "Oh, yes. But let's try something different."

A shock of frigid air splashed her as Edward lifted himself off her. On his haunches, he froze while admiring the stiff pucker of her nipples before turning Georgiana on her side, away from him. Starting at the base of her spine, he licked up the curves of her back, not stopping until he'd contoured himself along her, settling his head in the groove of her shoulder. "I need you to pick your leg up, my love," he said, maneuvering her top leg back and on top of his own.

Georgiana tensed, not knowing what he had in mind. "Is this normal?" she asked.

"Normal for us," he replied, caressing the expanse of her arse.

She felt his rod at her entrance as he tipped her a little forward. Slowly, he entered her again, and the sensations were much as they'd been before. Only this time, his arm went around her side, hugging her to him in an embrace that made her heart melt. When he moved, he spoke in her ear, whispering things that she would never have the courage to repeat, salacious things, erotic things about how she made him feel, what her body did to him, things she couldn't believe but desperately wanted to.

All the while he pumped into her, he moved his hand down to cup her mound, letting the movement of his hips slide her nub against his palm. And eventually, by some holy accord, she began to respond; her body began to sing. His pace quickened, and Georgiana realized he wasn't the only one moving. She was pressing back against him, meeting him halfway. It was still *interesting*, still *something*, but now, also everything.

His hands never stopped, overloading her inhibitions as one worked her pearl and the other tweaked at her nipple. Never had she been held so captive and felt so free. His thrusts grew frenzied and rougher, and harder; she pushed him, needing to sheathe the length of him. Edward bit at her neck as he squeezed her so tight, his shaft no longer left her body, instead plunging to her limit.

"Fuck, I need you to come, my love. If you have any mercy for me, you'll come now," he growled, pumping wildly.

Georgiana was absorbed in his maelstrom, chasing the end as quickly as she could. She covered his hand with hers, moving his fingers at her core in frantic circles, becoming more excited by the uninhibited, erotic sounds coming from his throat. His excitement added to her own, along with the visceral sounds of their lovemaking—the slap of their skin, the wet suction of the give and take.

She reached behind for his neck and twisted to kiss him with every inch of her being. Stretched so thin, she felt something explode inside her, shards of light cutting every shadow of her body. But that still wasn't the end. Both hands on her hips, Edward pounded into her. One. Two. Three times, and then he shouted with such force, and Georgiana felt him gain release, making her own that much more awe-inspiring.

After a time, being in no hurry, they both returned from their heightened plane. Edward slipped out of her, but still held her from behind, draping a lazy leg over the top of hers like a giant blanket.

Georgiana hugged his arm across her chest, resting her chin on it as she tried to recount what had just taken place. Try as she might, she couldn't. Perhaps it was the novice in her, or maybe making love was something that could only be experienced in the moment, any and all descriptions of it after the fact coming up woefully short.

That was fine by her. According to Edward, she had three more times to experience it that night—surely, by then, she could better come to terms with what had transpired between them. Or maybe not. She was too tired to worry.

So was Edward, it seemed. Giving her one last squeeze, he yawned, stretching his legs out along hers in a decadent display of ownership and satedness. "I should carry you back to your room," he murmured lazily against her sweat-drenched skin. "You don't need me to pant all over you all night. You'll be exhausted in the morning."

"I thought you wanted to be selfish."

"I have my moments of civility."

She kissed his arm. "Well, lose them. I don't want to go any-where tonight. Like I said, I've had enough of chivalry."

CHAPTER TWENTY-THREE

Unfortunately for Georgiana, Edward was just getting started, though her ideas of chivalry continued to bewilder him for the remainder of their week.

Edward didn't think he'd changed—however, the more time they spent together, the more Georgiana accused him of honorable behavior. She threw the word at him as if unloading a chamber pot. He tried to tell her he wasn't doing anything different, but she continued to hold him accountable.

Georgiana accused him of knightly behavior at every turn.

When Edward danced with his sisters during their lessons, she'd watched from the sidelines and gleefully stated he was showing a distinct characteristic of one who appreciated the fine arts. Flabbergasted, he'd countered that he was the only person around to play the man's role for the dance, but she refused to hear his argument. The woman was resolute. She saw the best in him.

Like when he participated in the village's cricket match, playing on the same team as his tenant farmers, and she applauded his sportsmanship. Edward didn't care whom he played with as long as they were good, and men from Marlborough were wickedly good. But she wouldn't listen to him. She even congratulated him when he finished the game without starting a fight or curving the ball into someone's face. Either the poor woman's standards had lowered that badly or she was determined to see him through rose-colored glasses.

But the absolute worst was when Georgiana caught him reading with the girls at the end of one night. She appeared as if she'd known he would be there, and even demanded a space on the bed so she could listen to Bess's reading. He counted himself lucky that she didn't harass him over the fact that they were reading *Ivanhoe*. She waited until later that night to do it in bed. And then she asserted that he was an aesthete who should never be ashamed of his love for Sir Walter Scott. He had to peel off her clothes just to get her to stop laughing at him.

There was still no talk about marriage. From the first night they'd made love, Edward assumed it was implied. It was going to happen, though neither of them brought it up, almost afraid to break the bubble of happiness they'd forged around themselves. But if Edward knew anything, it was that it would break. It always did. Returning to London would only bring the old issues to a head again. Edward still needed the money from her dowry, and there was no getting around the snobbishness that would follow him and his business venture for the rest of his life. Marrying him would not be easy—even for one as capable as Georgiana. He almost didn't want to put her through it—almost. He could only hope the bond they were creating at Marlborough was strong enough to see them through.

The day before the party was to return to London, Edward couldn't find Georgiana anywhere, which wasn't that unusual. The nosy woman spent most of her days exploring and enjoying the estate. She'd got it into her head that Marlborough House must have been the inspiration for one of the gothic novels she'd read, old and falling down, lovely and ruinous in its hidden mysteries. To Edward, it was just a house—a very large house that needed a large sum of money to maintain. Though if she wanted to see it for its beauty instead of its ever-increasing issues, he would let her. Wasn't she doing the same to him?

After an hour of searching the grounds, Edward set his sights on the attic. He was only annoyed he hadn't thought of it sooner. Cobwebs and dusty furniture, ancient trunks full of answers, and even more questions about the people who'd once lived there—where else would she be?

Edward climbed the narrow staircase quickly and buoyantly, remembering a time when he and Charles played in the same space. It had been years since those memories drummed up anything but resentment in him. And it was all Georgiana's doing.

Reaching the top, he was vindicated when he saw her lone figure on the opposite side of the room. "I thought I'd find you here," he said, ambling across the dusty floorboards.

Slowly, she turned to him, and he stopped, noticing what had held her attention.

The armor—his knight's armor—was propped up in the corner, standing proudly in all its grandeur. Not only had Pratt delivered it, but he had delivered on his promise. Surrounded by shadows and the earthly colors of possessions come to die, the suit shone with elegance and pride, like it could walk out of the home at that moment and spear ten dragons.

"This was what you'd been speaking to Pratt about?" Georgiana said, cutting through the lifetime of memories. "Why we went to the Gothic Hall that day?"

Edward nodded, a lump stuck in his throat. It had taken him so long to find it, and when he did, he had to pay out his ear to keep it away from the ridiculous men who wanted to wear it in the tournament. Its condition and authenticity made it extremely valuable in their eyes, but Edward refused to let anyone else have it. His family's heirloom would never be on the back of pretender knights.

"Your father sold it, and you bought it back. Why?"

"It was mine," he replied. "It belongs here."

Georgiana seemed to contemplate this, regarding the armor again.

Edward had forgotten how huge it was, how utterly magnificent it felt to stand next to it knowing that someone who shared the same blood as him once wore it. He'd had so few men in his life that he could look up to when he was younger; his father could never fill the role of mentor. That knight had been his confidant, his playmate, his shoulder to cry on when things became too tough for the young Edward. It was silly to think of now, but they shared many conversations in this dull space. Edward almost expected the knight to say something, ask him how he'd been.

"What?" Georgiana asked, giving him a strange look.

"It's nothing," Edward replied, moving closer. "Just odd thoughts."

She let it drop, moving to stand at his side. She wrapped an arm around his waist, hugging him against her hip. Her body, so warm and soft, was nothing like the formidable steel in front of them, and yet provided all the security and protection he would ever need. Love, it seemed, was even stronger than metal, able to be bent and burned, dented and lost without ever being broken.

"I knew you believed."

"In what?"

"Knights."

"It's hard not to when you're ten."

She sniffed. "It's more than that."

Edward stayed quiet. *Perhaps it is.*

"You should put it downstairs," she said, offering him another squeeze. "Show it off. It's too beautiful to hide up here."

He smiled down at her. "Are you redecorating my home already?"

"Isn't that what wives do?"

Edward blinked, his mind moving at a glacial pace. He found so much hope in the shy smile she gave him. "Wife?"

Her mouth twisted, as if she was trying to contain a dam of joy waiting to spill out. "If you don't mind, that is."

"Why would I mind?"

"Well…" she said, walking out of his arms, perusing the room. "Wives tend to make a lot of changes."

Edward crossed his arms, feigning irritation. "What kinds of changes?"

Georgiana ran her fingers along the sides of an old birdcage. "I might need to hire more servants, open more windows, let in more light—especially in our London home."

Edward frowned, playing disgruntled. "That seems unnecessary, but I think I can handle it."

"Brace yourself, there's more," she replied, continuing her stroll, leaving the floor behind her clean where her skirts swept up the dust. "I would want to be involved in the day-to-day decisions of the mine, and also make sure the workers are given fair wages and humane hours."

Edward flexed his jaw. He thought he'd already promised her that, though he understood she might need more reassurances based on her experience with her father. "Seems reasonable."

"Oh, I'm not done yet." Georgiana laughed. "I would hire a decent cook and force you to sit and eat every meal of the day. I'd fatten you up."

"Like a lamb to slaughter?" he quipped.

"Is marriage such a sacrifice?" she asked, making her way back toward him. All of a sudden, Edward was finding it difficult to concentrate on the conversation. The sway of her hips, the determination on her face, the sexy pout of her mouth…he would have promised anything to hear her call herself his wife again. Because in his attic full of forgotten treasures, his home filled with all his father had lost and Edward had found, he only wanted one thing, and money couldn't buy her.

Georgiana stopped in front of him. "Steel yourself, my good man. You've done well enough thus far, but the last change I plan to make might make you rethink all of it."

Her voice, lyrical and husky, overwhelmed him with possibilities. "I'm ready," he rasped.

Georgiana's smile was full of empathy. "I'm going to make you happy. You're going to be so blissfully happy you won't know what to do with yourself. It might even drive you mad."

"You already have," he said, then silenced her with his mouth. It was the only thing he could think of to do. He couldn't take any more. This woman—*his woman*—wanted him to be happy. And he was beyond grateful and humbled. As a man, he prided himself on paying off his debts. But this was a gift he would never be able to, because it was free, and it meant more than the world.

The intensity of that thought took hold, and something snapped inside him. Lifting Georgiana in his arms, he ushered his soul into her, creating more love and memories in an attic that seemed big enough to hold it all. Big enough to hold the secrets and disappointments of the past and the aspirations of the future. Together they baptized themselves in the fire of their passion, only to be born again in the hunger of their love.

"Thank you, thank you, thank you," Edward said in a litany as he traced a path down her neck, massaging the taut nipples underneath her gown. She hummed as he ruthlessly took one in his mouth, feasting on her body like a man enthralled, a man loved.

He heard her shudder out a laugh. "I thought a bedroom was no place for *thank yous*."

Edward bit the tiny bud. "This isn't a bedroom. Besides, that was a stupid thing to say. From now on, every time I'm in between your thighs, I will say thank you so you know how grateful I am. How grateful I will always be."

Georgiana placed her hand on his shoulder, gently directing him down. "I will accept your thanks," she said with a definite twinkle in her eye. "Now kneel, good sir, so I can fully make a knight out of you."

He chuckled as his knees hit the floor, giving the deed the focus it deserved. Hiking her skirts, he lost himself underneath the petticoats, in the warm humidity of her desire that was more intoxicating than the choicest liquors. He found the opening of her drawers and licked her seam, long and languorously. He would earn his knighthood today.

In no time, he had her panting and writhing, clutching at her belly, curling her toes in her slippers. He knew the pleasure he was giving her, but it was nothing compared to the sensations whipping through him, the pure, unadulterated satisfaction he gained from making his woman come.

When she shouted with release, he licked her from his lips, ready to find the nearest wall and impale himself in her, but she had other ideas. Released from his skirts, he looked up to see a knowing, content grin on her flushed face.

"Now rise, Sir Knight," she said playfully.

At a loss, Edward did as she said—he would always do as she said—and didn't catch on until he felt her hands at his waist as she dropped to her knees in front of him.

He covered her fingers, stopping them.

"Let me," she said, allowing no argument. "You've earned this. I have put you through trials, and you've come back victorious and unscathed."

Edward wasn't sure how unscathed he'd be if he let her do what she wanted to do.

"I've earned nothing," he said, his chest pumping. "My only goal was to serve you. Forever and always."

"Then let us both be noble today, since that is my goal as well."

Edward dropped his hands away as she unbuttoned his trousers then nudged them down his hips. For a long moment, there was nothing, only the bite of air and the heady anticipation of need. He knew better than to look down. Seeing Georgiana on her knees in front of him had the potential to unleash something in him he wasn't sure he could control. And he needed control now to allow her to love him the way she saw fit.

Still...nothing could have prepared him for the gossamer-light kiss she placed on his shaft, the ways she attempted to fill her mouth when she took him inside.

Edward clenched his fists, filling his lungs, praying his knees didn't buckle. With one hand circled around his manhood, she swallowed him…not knowing quite what to do after that. Their lovemaking aside, Edward guessed Georgiana's imagination had run its course—and her imagination was considerable—but Christ, he needed her to move.

Slowly, Edward pulled himself out of her, only to flex his hips and enter her sweet mouth once more. Her tongue, up until then a willing bystander, seemed to grow bored, and lapped up the side of his manhood, as her mouth began to massage his length. Before he could stop himself, Edward covered her hand with his, tightening her hold on him while he pumped.

His tutorial didn't last long. Ever the capable leader, Georgiana took over, working his shaft, sucking him so hard he couldn't see straight. The last thing he wanted to do was spill in her mouth, though the luscious thought only made his balls squeeze more. Not that they were left out. Edward didn't know where she'd heard of it—didn't fucking care—but when she cupped his balls, he almost shouted to the rafters. He had to make her stop. It was too much; he could feel his control slipping. But the sexy, wet sounds she was making with her mouth, the way her throat narrowed when she took him an inch too deep, paralyzed him with yearning. A yearning to claim her, a yearning to place his mark on her, a yearning to fill her with his seed.

Suddenly—carefully—Edward released his shaft, hissing as his tip caught the edge of her teeth.

"I'm sorry! Did I hurt you?" she exclaimed as he jolted her up to standing.

Finding a sofa just steps away, he was about to throw her down on it when the state of it brought him up short. Stained, ripped, and over one hundred years old, it wasn't the place for her.

Instead, Edward brought her to her knees again, this time joining her, positioning her toward the arm of the furniture.

Her voice came out shaky and, as ever, deliciously curious. "What are you doing?"

"Honoring you," Edward stated, flicking up her skirts and

yanking down her drawers. Her luscious arse looked back at him, and, unable to help himself, he palmed it back and forth with the reverence of a sinner. She was his altar. She was his holy shrine.

"Haven't you honored me enough?" she asked, her laughter containing a tinge of nervousness.

"How could you ask that of a knight?" he said, bending her forward, watching the pink flesh of her flower open up to him from behind, never in his life seeing something more breathtaking. He swiped his hand over her seam. "There will never be enough between us," he said, placing a finger inside, feeling her muscles welcome him, encourage him deeper. Her shoulder dipped, her back arching like a well-used saddle. "A knight's oath is for his life, is it not?" When she dropped her head, he inserted another finger. "Is it not?"

"Yes," she sighed.

"Now tell me to ride you," he said, slowly gaining rhythm. "Tell me now, before it's too late. If I make you come with my fingers, I'll just keep going until you do it again."

He sensed her indecision.

"Oh, that's what you want?" he asked.

"Is that such a bad thing?"

He chuckled. "Not at all, my lady. I am a lucky man indeed."

Edward made good on his threat. Only a few minutes later, he had her creaming on his fingers, and as he promised, he didn't give her time to contain herself before adjusting his cock at her entrance and thrusting forward. With control no longer in abeyance, his thrusts were quick and hard; he needed to tease out another release before he came. Georgina was completely open to him, and he passed inside her slick passage with thirsty ease, rising higher and higher as they crashed into one another. He cursed himself for not taking off their clothes. He longed to see her naked back, her bouncing breasts, the freckles that dotted her body like specks of vanilla bean in a dessert. But the idea that he could have her again, later, and again after that, only fueled his inner storm. She was his. This was theirs. And the fact that it was only beginning between them made him so hard and thick that he thought he grazed her womb. The womb that would one day grow his family.

Suddenly off-kilter, he leaned over, holding her hair away so he could kiss her neck. She keened underneath him, twisting her head to meet him for the kind of kiss that was too real for her storybooks. The pressure built at the bottom of his spine, and the moment he felt her squeeze around him, he finally allowed himself his release, crying out into her mouth, his eyes closed to the phenomenon that had taken place.

They stayed in that position so long that Edward's knees began to throb. The couple was either too content to leave the position or afraid of what might happen when they broke apart. Edward was certain his legs wouldn't be able to carry him for a while longer, so boneless did he feel.

Georgiana shifted underneath him, and his exhausted cock only twitched, as if telling him it could go another round if Edward could.

"Should we apologize?" Georgiana said lazily, nodding to the armor.

Edward stared at it, barking out an airy laugh. The damn thing *did* look like it was watching. Probably enjoyed the show, too. "I don't think so," he said, resting his head on Georgiana's back. "I'm sure he's seen much more debauchery than this."

"Too bad. We'll just have to try again later."

Edward picked up his head. "Later?"

Her muscles clenched him as if testing his endurance. "Not so later?"

Edward was pleased to find his knees no longer hurt. In fact, when he began to move, he felt like a new, happy man.

LATER, MUCH LATER, the couple lay together on the floor,

Georgiana curled into her spot under Edward's arm, her exhausted body draped over his chest. They watched in peaceful silence as the sun drifted lower in the sky, the shards of light retreating from the floorboards, leaving the room and their knight to their shadows.

"Thank you again," she whispered against him. "For bringing me here, for taking me to your home."

"*Our* home."

He could feel her lips widening into a smile. "Our home."

"Will you marry me, then, Georgiana? I'd get down on my knees, but I'm afraid if I do, I'll never get back up."

She giggled, leaning on her elbow to look at him, and placed a short, chaste kiss on his mouth. "Of course I'll marry you. You're everything I've ever wanted in a man."

Her eyes glistening with tears, she laid her head back down, releasing a deep breath that seemed to possess the weight of the unknown.

It was done.

Edward believed again. Not only in knights, but in happily-ever-afters.

CHAPTER TWENTY-FOUR

T HEY WOULDN'T LET her leave.

Edward's trio of sisters clung to Georgiana as she made her goodbyes, assuring them she would return soon. She had come to love the girls dearly, but even she was taken aback by the outpouring of emotion that greeted her outside Marlborough House as she was readying to return to London.

She began to realize that it wasn't so much her as what she represented to these little girls. Life in the country could be a lonely one, and with their father dying and Edward spending so much of his time in Town, Georgiana's presence was a symbol of what could be. For so long their existence had been encumbered by their father's actions, their mother's grief, even Edward's unwavering determination to fix it all. Something new was in the wind, and children, being most sensitive to change, could feel its wondrous pull.

"It's such a shame you couldn't meet Louise," Bess sobbed on Georgiana's shoulder, refusing to relinquish her hold.

Georgiana patted her back, meeting Eugenie and Caroline's amused looks. "I will meet her properly in London. I'm sure we'll get along as well as I have with you."

Bess shifted away, rubbing her red nose. "No, you won't."

"Louise doesn't get along with anyone," Eugenie said.

"Oh." Georgiana wasn't exactly sure how to respond to that.

"Perhaps she'll like you," Eugenie said hopefully.

"It could happen," Bess added.

Caroline *hmphed*. "I doubt it."

"Well, you like me, and that's all that matters."

Three forlorn faces nodded back.

"And you didn't meet Mother," Bess said. "She's still not speaking to Edward, but she might talk to you."

Yes, that was a problem. Edward had expected Louise and his mother to arrive by the time they'd left; however, he'd received a letter saying they were going to be staying in Scotland indefinitely, giving a cryptically vague reason as to why.

Georgiana conceded that it seemed odd to be joining a family when she hadn't met half of the members—one might say, the most important members.

But she couldn't hide the relief she'd felt when she heard she would be missing them. If Louise sounded prickly, Edward's mother seemed absolutely formidable. What kind of mother stopped talking to her only son? Especially over something as silly as commerce.

"I'll send for Mother as soon she's ready to travel," Edward told the girls, coming up beside them. He gave each of his sisters a perfunctory kiss, ruffling their hair for good measure. "And when she meets Georgiana, she'll be so thrilled that I'm getting married she'll completely forget why she was ever mad at me in the first place. You just wait."

Caroline, ever the pessimist, returned a dubious look. "I doubt it," she said once more.

THEY MADE IT back to London by the end of the day. Edward planned to drop Georgiana and her mother off at their home and speak to her father at once. After the week they'd spent together, the idea of waiting to marry sounded ridiculous. The cart was indeed before the horse. With everything they'd talked about, all of their plans, Georgiana didn't want to wait anymore.

She steeled herself for her father's smug expression, the boasting, the all-knowing attitude that he would peacock around when she and Edward told him the news. Her mother, for her part, had been quietly triumphant. She hadn't asked many questions on the ride, content to merely bask in the victory of Georgiana's capitulation. It grated, Georgiana wouldn't pretend that it didn't, though she did appreciate that it was subdued.

Her father had never been subdued in his entire life. He'd probably run out to the newspapers the second Edward left, letting everyone know his daughter was to be a marchioness.

A marchioness.

Georgiana couldn't believe it. *How the mighty have fallen,* she joked to herself as the carriage made its way through familiar neighborhoods, and the repugnant smells of the city already made her miss Marlborough. She didn't know the first thing about being a marchioness. Yes, she had the manners down. She could dance and sing and hold a polite conversation. She was well versed in the ins and outs of propriety. But peerage was a being, a way of life she'd never considered, despite her parents' machinations.

What would Minnie think? What would George think? What about the *ton*? No doubt it would snicker and gossip that Lord Edward had finally convinced the button maker's daughter to be his Coprolite Queen.

Well, let them laugh. Georgiana was proud of Edward's ambition and would do everything in her power to see it fulfilled. This was the purpose she'd envisioned. This was the business she could build from the ground up. She and Edward would make excellent partners. In this fast-paced world, the stability of their family would be the rock they built their dreams upon.

She glanced at Edward. He was looking out the carriage window, frowning over whatever was going through his mind. He must have felt her staring, because he glanced at her then and offered a simple smile, as if he recognized the anxieties she was battling. Whatever they faced, they would face it together, Georgiana told herself. How could they fail when they had each other?

Their carriage pulled up to the townhouse just before the dinner hour. A knot immediately began to form in Georgiana's stomach when she noticed a small group of men entering the home. Her father rarely brought work home from the office, so she couldn't understand the flurry of somberly dressed men. For a moment, she thought her father had already started the celebrations for the wedding, though that couldn't be the case. There was no way her mother could have delivered the information to him so soon. The only people who could have given him the news were them.

Jeffrey greeted them politely at the threshold before leading them inside, his expression not giving anything away. "Mr. Spence requested that you join him in his study as soon as you arrived," he said to a visibly perplexed Mrs. Spence.

"Is everything all right?" she asked. "The boys?"

"The boys are quite fine," Jeffrey answered soberly. "They almost broke a window yesterday. They are intact as ever, even if the house is not."

Her mother let out a sigh of relief, a hand dramatically held at her throat. Georgiana and Edward followed dutifully, if a little dazed by the commotion.

"Do you know what's going on?" she whispered.

Edward shook his head. "I was hoping you did," he returned sotto voce. "I imagine it must have something to do with the business. Maybe he's taking your ideas to heart after all."

That was doubtful. There was too much energy in the air. Her father, nor his people, would never be this animated about spending money, only earning it.

They entered the study to find Robert Spence, nose down, scanning at least four open books in front of him. Men flittered around him, dropping ledgers and loose papers on his desk for his examination. Georgiana recognized his solicitor but was at a loss for the others. Whoever they were, they had terrible manners, not acknowledging the newcomers.

"Mr. Spence?" her mother said tentatively, as taken aback as Georgiana by the harried scene.

Slowly, her father lifted his eyes, blinking like an owl, taking a few seconds too long to recognize his family. Eventually, a smile broke out on his face, and he jumped from his chair.

Arms out wide, he lunged for his wife. "Oh, Mrs. Spence. I'm so glad you're home!" he cried, enveloping her in a back-breaking hug. The woman bore it as well as she could; however, the moment she tried to get her confused limbs, around him, he'd already let go, holding her at arm's length. "I've missed you so," he said, shaking his increasingly discombobulated wife. "So much has happened. So much."

Her expression was alight under the warm attention, though Georgiana could tell her mother was still stupefied by what was happening. She couldn't remember a time when she'd ever seen her parents touch. Hugging was completely alien.

"I can see that," her mother replied. "You must tell us at once. Who are all these people?"

"What? Oh, lawyers, lawyers, and more lawyers, as well as— There she is!" Robert shouted, cutting off his own train of thought. His wandering gaze had landed on Georgiana.

She immediately tensed, hoping she wouldn't be another recipient of one of those bruising hugs.

Too late. Pushing Edward off to the side, her father crushed her, causing a few of her vertebrae to pop during the embrace.

"Father, I can't breathe," Georgiana stammered, pounding him on the shoulder until he let her go.

"Yes, yes, my apologies. I'm just so happy to see you, daughter. My wonderful daughter," he said, finally breaking away. He continued to stare at Georgiana as if she was covered in gold. Maybe he did know about the proposal? What other reason would he have to look at her so fondly?

Her father dipped his chin, playing at a glare. "Although I should be angry at you. You're always going behind my back doing things, never leaving well enough alone," he said, wagging his finger in her face, before bopping her nose. "But you're just like me—determined. You saw something I didn't, and you went for it. I will never doubt you again, my beautiful girl. Never."

Georgiana shook her head, feeling as if the floor was tilting under her feet. Had her father had too much to drink? Taken a mysterious tonic? There was no accounting for this behavior. She'd never seen him so happy, not even when the Duke of Wembley once shook his hand and got his name halfway right, calling him Mr. Robin Spoke.

She glanced helplessly at Edward, who merely lifted his brows, before saying, "Father, I don't understand. What has made you so pleased with me? Did you hear about the engagement?"

The word seemed to knock him out of his ecstatic stupor. As if noticing Edward for the first time, Robert issued a curt bow. "Marlborough."

Edward nodded back, though he didn't otherwise respond. Georgiana felt him take her hand, and that touch was enough to balance her feet safely on the ground.

"Don't play coy," Robert said, returning to his daughter. "You know exactly what you did."

"Of course she does," a voice broke in behind her. "She orchestrated the whole thing, after all."

Even if Georgiana didn't recognize the voice, the smell was more than enough to tip her off. Allan J. Prichard's putridly sweet perfume could be his calling card in any room.

Slowly, so very, *very* slowly, Georgiana faced the ex-herald, wishing, hoping she was wrong.

But there he was, standing at the entrance of her father's study, in all his flamboyant and oily glory. Like a cat who'd got the cream. Or a herald who'd found his long-lost lord.

The words were out of her mouth before she could reel them back in. "You were supposed to wait."

His smarmy grin speared her chest. "Some things can't hold, Miss Georgiana. You know what they say. Tides—and glad tidings—wait for no man."

⇶⫷

GEORGIANA MASSAGED HER temples, staring at the scattered papers on her father's desk. She'd made him explain to her three times already, and she still was having a difficult time understanding all that had unfolded while she was gone. "What do you mean he has a case?"

"Just as I said," Prichard replied, pointing to the documents in front of her. She couldn't make any sense of them. Her mind was too warped; everything she read looked like it was written in Greek. "I followed your lead and went to Suffolk. I found plenty of evidence that your father is the heir to the de Pence baronry. It will take time, more researching and"—his eyes gleamed—"more money, but I think we can have a case in front of the House of Lords in only a few months."

"A few months!" her mother exclaimed, flopping unceremoniously into a chair.

"You surprise me, Miss Georgiana. I thought you'd be more excited than you are," Prichard said, not batting an eye at her mother's histrionics. "You are the one who started this, are you not?"

Edward's voice slashed across the room like a freshly sharpened blade. "Who are you again?" he asked acerbically. "And how do you know my fiancée?"

"Allan J. Prichard, at your service," Prichard said, bowing so low it was borderline offensive. "Your...*fiancée* sought me out months ago. Being a herald—"

"Ex-herald," Georgiana said.

Prichard acknowledged her with a tight smile. "Soon to be full herald again, I think. She came to me asking for my services.

We…*negotiated*," he said, adding a suggestive verve to the word that made Georgiana want to hit her head up against the wall. "I know you asked me to wait for you, miss, if I found something— however, I had to take it to your father right away. News like this is simply too important. This barony has sat in abeyance too long. I'd hate to make it sit a day more."

"And I'm so glad he did," her father said, fanning one of the papers in his wife's face as she remained splayed out on the chair. "I'm not too big to admit it. I was wrong and afraid before. I didn't want to search for something that I wasn't sure about. I didn't want to look like those other fools chasing nothing. You were the bigger person, daughter. You had courage when I faltered. You listened to your grandfather and saw beyond his little stories."

"Well, I'm happy for you, Father," Georgiana said…because she didn't know what else to be. To be honest, over the last few weeks, she'd forgotten all about Prichard and the wild goose chase she'd put him on. But this was her father's concern now. Whether he took his claim to the courts or not had nothing to do with her. The life she was starting with Edward would hardly be affected by it. It would cause headlines, that was obvious, and Georgiana knew Edward to be a private person, but it wasn't anything they couldn't handle.

Though she wasn't sure he looked at it the same way. Throughout the explanations, he still held her hand, but he could have been a statue for how cold and lifeless he felt. Naturally, Georgiana had some explaining to do, though she wasn't *that* nervous. He might even think it funny that this all happened because of her initial abhorrence of marrying him. It could be something they looked back on and chuckled about.

Some day. Only not today. There was nothing in his countenance that hinted at joviality at the moment.

"You mentioned money for the case," Edward began slowly, his voice composed and bitterly staid. "How much money?"

Her father stopped fanning his wife, dropping the paper on

the table. Georgiana's stomach squeezed at her father's sheepish expression. Robert Pence was never sheepish.

"Yes, ah, Marlborough, that is something we're going to have to discuss," her father said. "We should probably take this into another room…away from the women."

"I don't think that's necessary," Edward drawled.

Her father's guilty eyes darted from Georgiana to her mother. "Fine," he said, his chest swelling. "We have to talk about the mining investment."

For some reason, Edward smiled, and that grim, lifeless line made Georgiana shiver. "And why is that?" he asked.

Her father's face hardened with resolve, the businessman always ready to do what needed to be done to keep afloat. Knowing the signs, Georgiana felt her heart sink. *Please don't do this, Father. Please don't do this.*

"I'm afraid now isn't the right time," he said, lifting his chin, which didn't look as strong as it usually did. "I have to point all my resources towards winning this case. Obviously"—he waved his hand between Georgiana and Edward—"this need not go any further."

"Need not go any further?" Georgiana repeated.

"Need not go any further," her father agreed, balancing his weight on his toes as if he actually thought he was doing her a favor.

She turned her attention to Edward, waiting for him to… She didn't know what he would do. Surely he would wrap his arms around her and inform her father that he didn't need nor want his money anyway. That Georgiana was and would always be enough for him.

She would even accept the other side of Edward—a punch to her father's jaw, a cricket ball to the face, a biting remark that could make a grown man cry. Something, anything, that showed he was as incensed as her.

Fight. She needed to see him fight.

But when he opened his mouth, something altogether different came out. "Where did you get that?"

Georgiana frowned. She'd never heard him sound like that before, like his voice was physically being taken from his throat. His eyes had turned milky, his expression utterly lost. She followed his gaze to her father's table. She hadn't noticed it before, since it was half hidden under the pile of papers, but she recognized those blue sapphire stars right away.

Her necklace.

No, not hers anymore.

The necklace she'd given Prichard in payment.

"Oh," her father said, swiping the detritus out of the way to hand the jewelry back to Georgiana. "I can't believe you sold this to pay the herald. How could you do that? That was a gift from us. I couldn't have you sacrifice it for me, sweetheart. You're always so giving, always thinking of others before yourself."

Georgiana held the cold metal in her hand, not remembering it being half as cumbersome before. But it was Edward who made her body feel the true weight. His wounded expression tugged at her consciousness until it came to her—her father had said the piece once belonged to a duchess who had fallen on hard times. Could it have come from a marchioness instead? A marchioness whose husband had a nasty predilection for stealing and selling her things?

Finding courage, she peeked at Edward, who was transfixed by the necklace, his nostrils flaring. Instantly, she was doused in shame and the truth. She was the reason Edward hadn't been able to track it down. It had sat in her jewelry box for the past two years. It had only seen the light of day because she sold it under her family's nose—just as his father had done.

And it had all led to this.

Hope slipped from Georgiana as quickly as the sand in an hourglass. Edward would never forgive her. He would only see this as a betrayal of his trust, yet another reason to pull away from people and live within the cave of himself.

Not able to touch it anymore, Georgiana placed the necklace

back on the table, barely registering that Edward was speaking again.

"What about the dowry?" he asked, his voice stripped of emotion.

Tears filled Georgiana's eyes. She couldn't believe they were back to this. Nothing had changed. Edward would take her—for the right price.

Her father rubbed his forehead, and Georgiana noticed how tired he looked. Beyond manic, he probably hadn't slept in days. The bags under his eyes made his face even longer, giving him the appearance of a basset hound after a day's hunting.

"We'll need to talk about that as well," he stated. "I might need some of it for the case. Not all!" he hurriedly added when he saw Georgiana open her mouth. "But some. It's only temporary. I'll make it all back. Besides, soon, Georgiana will be the daughter of a baron. She won't have need of such an exorbitant dowry. Many men would gladly take her for much less."

Many men. But clearly not Edward.

"Father," Georgiana said softly, not hiding the pain trembling through her. "What are you doing to me?"

Her father scowled, retreating behind his desk, his business veneer firmly in place. "You didn't even want to marry him anyway. Too boring and set in his ways, you said. Only wanted you for your money, you said."

Georgiana wondered if he'd lost his mind saying this in front of Edward, or if he was trying to make Edward so angry that he'd leave without looking back. As far as plans went, it was a sound one.

Edward took the hint. "This is a family matter," he declared, straightening away from Georgiana. She glanced down at her hand. At some point—she didn't know when—he'd stopped holding it. "I should leave you to it."

"But Edward—" Georgiana's words clogged in her throat. His blank expression, his icy demeanor, made anything she was going to say unnecessary. He wouldn't hear it. Not now. Too much damage had been done. All because of her.

Without saying anything further, he slid past her, taking the necklace off the table and placing it in his pocket. "For my troubles," he said, his long strides carrying him out of the room.

"Wait!" Georgiana said, chasing behind. Edward didn't stop; he didn't even turn back until she weaved in front of the front door, blocking his exit. "You can't go. You can't just leave."

His eyes were flinty and cold, a blank slate, as he glanced down at her. Georgiana had never registered such disparity in their heights until now.

"Why not?" he asked. "It's what you what, isn't it?" He stared at the necklace still clutched in his hand. "It's what you wanted all along."

Georgiana slammed her eyes shut, racking her brain to explain her way out of this mess. "That was before—"

"Was any of it real? Or was it all just a lie? Were you always just biding time?"

She shook her head, lamenting her lack of speech. She couldn't seem to find the right words, couldn't put her thoughts in order so he could understand. "It was like that at first, but then I fell in love with you."

He sniffed, straightening even more away as if avoiding a slap. "Believe it or not, I had my reservations at the beginning as well. Your lying, your duplicity with George, the stealing of your father's ledgers out from under his nose in plain sight. I disregarded all of them. And all the while I was just another piece in your chess game with your father."

"No—"

Edward cut her off, his words stabbing through the air directly to her heart. "And the hoops you made me jump through to prove to you that I was a decent man. When all along, you were the untrustworthy one. You had the gall to call yourself a knight in our situation. Tell me, Georgiana, what about your actions screams chivalry to you? Was it the lying? Or the hypocrisy?"

"Why are you being so harsh?" she cried. "I'm sorry about the investment. I will fix this, I swear. But you act like I am some criminal just because I took my life into my own hands. I didn't hurt anyone—"

Edward's calm façade vanished. "Me!" he screamed, finally breaking the chasm between them, pressing his chest up against hers. Georgiana could see his pulse flicker at the side of his float. "Me," he said again, lowering the pitch of his voice without losing any of its ire. "You hurt *me*."

Georgiana's throat locked. She hadn't meant for any of this to happen. His pain lanced through her. She reached out, but he evaded her touch again. "Just give me a chance," she said. "Don't leave. Please don't leave. This can't be over."

For a moment, she thought he might listen. His eyes found hers, and she thought she saw the muscles around them soften. But he only said, "I don't know what this is, but I need to go," giving her a wide berth before closing the door gently behind him.

That quiet catching of the latch reverberated down her spine as if gongs had been banged inside her head. The fact that he didn't even bother to slam the door stung more than anything.

"Let him go," she heard her father say as he came up behind her to put his arm around her shoulder. He walked her back to his study, and she hated herself all over again. Because she lacked the strength to throw him off. "You don't want a man like that anyway, someone only interested in your money. Just wait and see what's going to happen for us. It's like one of those stories you like to read. Anything can happen now."

Tears fell hard and fast down her cheeks. With the chaos around her—the solicitors, the heralds, her parents' unmitigated ambition—no one noticed. They didn't even hear her when she said, "Life is nothing like the storybooks."

CHAPTER TWENTY-FIVE

H IS MIND ROLLING, his heart raw, Edward wasted no time going straight to his solicitor's residence. He couldn't care less that the workday was over and that the poor man was most likely looking forward to sitting down to a restorative meal with his family. Edward's life had just fallen apart in front of his eyes, and he needed a new plan.

John Dawson knew Edward well enough that when he saw him standing in his foyer, feral and on edge, he didn't hesitate, saying to his butler, "Tell my wife to eat without me."

Dawson's wife would eat without her husband for the next three days. In those lonely hours, Dawson and Edward pored over the Marlborough accounts, shaking every tree to find anything resembling currency.

Economize, Edward told himself time and time again when his brain felt like mush and his eyes burned from squinting at all the tiny black print. But where? How? His properties were already working under skeleton staffs; everything that wasn't entailed had been sold long ago. Raising the rents on his tenants seemed unconscionable, since the farmers were barely making ends meet as it was. But still, he persisted. Did he really need his own carriage? What of the signet ring he never wore? Surely he could rent horses instead of keeping his bays. Those tiny luxuries—the only ones he'd allowed himself—meant nothing. Everything revolved around making the mine functional.

However, after seventy-two hours, it took Dawson, taking off his spectacles so he could massage his weary eyes next to the flickering gas light in his office, to confirm the inevitable. "I'm so sorry, Marlborough, but it's not enough. It's simply not enough."

Edward slumped back in his seat, pushing himself away from the desk. His neck ached, and whenever he tried to straighten it, he got shooting pains in his jaw. His shoulders were as rounded as any hunchback's. No one cared for defeat, but when one's whole life was centered around keeping one measly step ahead, it hurt even more.

"What do you suggest?"

The solicitor scratched at his stubble. "You might have time. We could look for another investor. Your estate is in dire need of funds, but I think you can stretch out another year doing what you've been doing. The mine can hold."

"No," Edward stated firmly. "It can't wait. There's a boom waiting to happen. I'm at the forefront of something big; I know it. We have to be one of the first to mine for coprolites. I'm tired of waiting. It has to be now."

"All right," Dawson said carefully, slightly cowed by Edward's ferocity. "I haven't mentioned it because I didn't know if I should…" He regarded his client cautiously. "The button maker's daughter. The dowry?"

"Gone," Edward said, his single word saying so much and yet so little.

Dawson's reticence only increased, but he plowed ahead with the difficult conversation. It was what he was paid to do, after all. "There's still time to find another lady. I know of a few American girls who are new to Town…might be of interest—"

"What? No," Edward replied, his neck snapping up so fast his sore vertebrae *popped!* "The dowry is gone, but the woman isn't. We just have to work around it."

"Oh!" Relief shone on the older man's face, though his confusion didn't abate. "I didn't know. I'm afraid I don't understand. I thought it was over."

Over? Why on earth would it be over? Edward had told Georgiana he'd needed to think—that was it. He never said anything was over. To be honest, he didn't remember exactly what he'd said in Spence's foyer, but he definitely hadn't said *that*. He'd been furious, not delusional. Georgiana most have recognized that; she knew him. Edward had told her the truth when he said he needed her more than her money—though life would have been so much easier with both.

There was that word again—*easy*. Edward should have known better.

He dragged himself back to the table. "There's nothing to understand. I'm to be married; however, the investment that was hinted at is no longer available. And the dowry will be significantly less. Didn't I explain that? I thought I explained that."

"You did...you did," Dawson said. "I suppose I just didn't understand. Even with the new *arrangement*, you're still getting married?"

"That's what I said!" Edward returned irritably. "Plans will begin immediately once I get this"—he waved his hands toward the papers on the table—"figured out."

With shaking, sleep-deprived fingers, Dawson put his spectacles back over his bulbous nose. "Congratulations, then," he said. "I'm sure the lady is quite thrilled."

"She is," Edward grumbled down into the ledger. Wasn't she? She *had* been before they came back to Town. Even after that, when they stood in her father's study and watched the stupid man make a muck of things, Edward had still felt the warm certainty of her hand in his. But then he remembered something else—the crestfallen expression on her face when he'd left. The choked flurry of rage that he'd seen simmering as he turned tail and fled.

It had all happened so fast. He'd had to get out of that room. If he'd stayed one more minute, he would have been in danger of ripping it apart. His anger had become too big, the study way too small. The necklace on the table too damning.

Surely she could understand that? After all Georgiana had done—unintentional as it was—she could spare him a little leeway in this regard. He'd needed time to rebound from Spence's insult, to figure out where they would go from there.

But as Edward looked out on the swarm of disappointing numbers in front of him, there was only one conclusion to be drawn. As usual, he let the lawyer deliver the bad news.

"A loan is your only option," Dawson said, seeming to read his mind. "You tried, my boy. You really did. Chin up. It isn't the worst thing in the world. The business will be such a success that you'll be able to pay it off quickly—along with your father's debt. In a few years, you won't even remember you needed the help to begin with."

Edward stared at the man, letting resignation seep in. Like sap on a tree, it coated him slowly, inch by inch smothering the hopes he'd once had. Of being a better man than his father. Of thinking he could outrun, outsmart, outmaneuver the old man's sins.

"So be it," he said, rising from the table. "Draw up the papers."

FOR THE FIRST time in days, Edward went home.

At least a decision had been made, even if it wasn't the one he wanted. He felt like celebrating—or, rather, drowning himself in his misery. Too bad Charles wasn't back in Town. For some reason, the silly bastard still hadn't returned from the tournament. He was the only person who would be able to handle Edward's brand of celebrating. Because he was allowing himself a good, long wallow. His emotions were much too close to the surface to ignore, and Edward was going to let them win. He was going to toast to their persistence and then toast again and toast again.

When he eventually woke up—sobered up—he would take the next steps and sign away his dignity. He'd never felt as much like his sire as he did at that moment.

A knock sounded at the door. Edward took another sip of his brandy, waiting for his butler to answer it and send the person away. It took three more knocks for him to remember *he* was the butler.

"Go away!" he yelled from his study, situated in the back of the house on the ground floor. There was no way the person could hear him, but it felt good to yell anyway, so he did it again. The knocking persisted for a few more minutes before it went quiet.

Edward lounged back in his seat, content that he was alone again, when he heard the telltale creak of a door opening. *What the hell?* Good luck trying to rob him, he thought, scanning his desolate room. Unlike the country house, he'd never gone through the trouble of restocking the townhouse after his father's perfidy. Never saw the point. The empty bookcases, bare shelves, and naked floor—which once was covered by a grand Axminster rug—always provided inspiration. The frugality had been all the nourishment he needed to keep going, keep trying. Not anymore.

Edward took another drink as footsteps tapped down the hall. Whoever it was, they weren't much for searching, instead coming straight for him.

A shadowy figure loomed in the entrance to the study, solitary and contained. "This is a picture no mother ever wants to see."

Even though Edward hadn't heard his mother speak in close to a year, he still felt the words like a light summer rain on a blistering day—so fucking refreshing.

"Hello, Mother," he said, lifting his crystal glass in a toast. "I thought you were in Scotland."

"I'm back," she said, wading into the room. Her thin body moved like a sailboat with the wind at its back, seamlessly cutting through the water. "I must have just missed you at home; the girls told me that my son was engaged."

"Proud of me?"

"I'm always proud of you."

He snorted in his glass. "I wouldn't have known."

Lady Delilah crept closer, sitting on the edge opposite Edward on the settee. He tried not to look at her, feigning disinterest, but that lasted less than a minute. Sons and mothers were plagued with the kind of relationship that could never be broken or ignored.

Her thick red hair had dulled with age, though white strands were still sparse. She was small like his sisters, but equally as fierce. Years of being pitied by the *ton* over her husband's foolishness had not diminished her strength. Edward's father forgot himself time and time again, but his mother never did.

Her lovely gray eyes took their fill, measuring him as easily as they always had.

"So, why are you here?" he asked bitterly. "I know you didn't come at this time of night to wish me congratulations."

Her slender hands tightened along her reticule. "A letter was waiting for me when I got into Town...from Dawson."

Of course. The man should have new cards made. Good solicitor. Spectacular busybody. "So you know everything, then. You know I'm going into the family business of borrowing, just like dear old Papa."

"Your father never had any intention of paying back what he borrowed," she replied softly. "You do."

"And yet the result is the same." Edward laughed. "Debt, debt, and more debt for our children and our children's children."

"Don't say that," his mother said. She reached out as if to touch him, but retreated at the last second, returning her hand to her lap.

They were only inches from one another, but it could have been miles.

After a pause, she lifted her chin. "I can see you're in the mood to argue and feel sorry for yourself, Edward, but believe it or not, that's not the reason why I—"

"Actually, it's good that you're here," Edward said, fumbling in his pocket. He hadn't changed his clothes in days. He took out his mother's sapphire necklace and tossed it on the cushion next to her. "I got it. The last one. Found it in an unusual spot, but Father never seemed to have qualms about whom he sold to. He was a snob about many things, but never that."

Stock-still, Delilah regarded the piece, her hands never leaving her bag.

"Take it," Edward snapped. "If I can do one thing right, let it be this. Everything from Marlborough has been returned."

"I don't want it."

Edward's gaze sharpened. Even perpetually put together, his mother looked as tired as he felt. Sympathy and shame for his brutish behavior crushed his drunken haze, and his voice broke, losing its stubborn ire. "Why?"

His mother sighed, so much pity and sadness soaked into the lonely sound. "I know I was wrong to stop speaking to you. I suppose I should have explained myself. I was just so…disappointed."

Edward's head dropped. He already knew all this; hearing it from her lips was like rubbing salt into a wound.

She edged closer, careful not to touch the necklace. "You were so proud every time you returned something to the house—no more so when it was my jewelry. But I hated that you kept buying me back these jewels. They only reminded me of the horrible things your father did."

Spellbound, Edward watched as she flicked a fingertip under her eye, casting off an errant tear.

"He betrayed me. So many times I stopped counting. And yet I loved him…very much. I loved him the moment I first saw him when I was sixteen. He was so dashing and tall, so regal. You look so much like him. I know you don't like to hear that, but you do. Every time he would come home after one of his…episodes, I would forget everything he did. Just like that. It was a special skill

I had, like embroidery or riding. He was all I ever wanted, not the things he took, the jewelry he stole. It's amazing what love can do. And that's what I choose to remember."

Finally, she picked up the necklace, dangling the blue stars reflecting the light from the hearth. "But when you started buying all these things, all I could see was what he'd done, what I was supposed to hate about him. I don't want to live the rest of my life that way."

Edward hunched over, cradling his head in his hands. "How can you still love him? He made our lives miserable."

Her eyes turned down, though she tried to smile. "I can't defend him. But you know what he was like. So energized and full of life. People congregated around him like he was the center of the world, always ready for his grand gestures and exciting behavior. When he was in those moods, I would do anything to have his attention. It was like the sun shining down."

"And then he ruined everything."

His mother's face fell, like the memory had cut to black in front of her. "That sort of energy can't sustain itself. He was sick."

"He wasn't sick. He was careless, the *ton*'s dancing jester. And all the people who congregated around him stayed there to laugh and encourage all his bad decisions." Edward's gaze flashed to the necklace. "Christ, Mother, I don't understand. It's *your* jewelry. Some of it was given to you by your own family. How can you just let it go?"

Slowly, she placed it back on the cushion. "The same way you can live in this old townhouse with nothing but a chair and a couch. The same way you can get by with one maid and one meal a day. You really need to start eating more, my love." Finally, she reached out, taking his hand away from his head and holding it firmly, squeezing him until he squeezed her back. "Life is about people, my son, not things. You know that."

With her free hand, Delilah placed her reticule between them, dumping out its contents. All her jewelry—everything he'd painstakingly searched for over the past three years—came rushing out. "It's yours now," she said. "Sell it. Pay for your mine. It probably won't cover all of it, but it will help."

Edward shook his head, a sob escaping his chest. Equal amounts of power and shame and failure surged in him. "Mother, I can't do that. Then I would truly be like him."

"No," she said, her voice stronger than the metals in front of her. "You will never be like him, so stop trying so hard *not* to be. Your father is dead. Let him rest now, and live your life. These jewels are your birthright; use them to create a birthright for your children, so their father will leave them something other than debt and disappointment in his wake."

They reached for each other at the same time, and Edward let his mother fold her arms around him, providing a shoulder he didn't know he needed. A shoulder he'd never allowed himself to miss. "I don't know if I can," he whispered. Edward didn't know if he was talking about living his own life or selling the jewels.

"Don't forget," she said. "You were raised by me. You are my son and can do anything."

Edward *had* forgotten that. He was his mother's child just as much as his father's. And along with the memories of her weeping and falling into her bed whenever his father deserted them, there were also the memories of her picking herself back up and teaching Edward how to be a man, and finding others like Malbeck to fill in the rest. Why had he lost sight of that? What would Edward's life be like if he wasn't always trying to prove he was better than his father?

In an answer, a picture formed in his head. A picture of Georgiana and him standing on the rocks near the ocean, happy and laughing, running through afternoons, like the world was a good book and they were lost in it together.

SEEING AS HOW his accommodations were less than suitable, his mother left soon after to stay with a friend. Edward, though bone-weary, couldn't sleep. She'd left him too much to think about, and she'd made her point. In the morning, he would go to all the pawnshops and jewelers and resell the pieces. Like his mother had said, it wouldn't be nearly enough to compensate for losing Georgiana's father's investment, but it would make a dent. And as Edward had come to learn over the last few years, every little bit helped.

He contemplated going to Georgiana, but it was much too late. Besides, what would he say? He'd been a selfish ass. Hell, he hadn't contacted her in four days. What must she be thinking? It was one thing to need time and space to clear one's head; it was quite another to be a self-centered bastard. He didn't have to ruminate hard on where she'd currently lump him.

Thinking it could only help him sleep, Edward was about to open a second bottle of brandy when he heard another knock on the door. *Christ!* He hasn't been this popular in…forever.

Edward couldn't guess who it could be this time. With Charles away and his mother already gone, there was no one else—unless… Georgiana had come to his home in the middle of the night before… It could be her, ready and waiting to give him a swift punch to the face, and he'd take it willingly—and then he'd kiss her.

Edward left the alcohol behind, running to the entrance. He threw open the door, and what he found on the other side stopped him cold.

"What the hell do you want?" he asked.

George *Whateverhisname* lifted his square jaw. "We need to talk."

Edward started to shut the door. "I'm all talked out tonight, I'm afraid. Try again tomorrow."

George stuck his boot in the door, stopping Edward from slamming it on him. "I need a job," he said plainly.

Edward eyed him warily, a harsh chuckle breaking through. "I don't give a damn what you need. Shouldn't you be with your master, searching old texts for old clues?"

George's courage wavered, his face flushing. "Things have become tenuous there."

Edward's whole life had become tenuous. What was new? But now that his rational senses had returned, Edward was desperate to hear anything to do with Georgiana.

"One drink," he said, backing away to allow George inside. "And it better be good."

"I assure you," George said, "it is not."

Three drinks later, Edward realized that George was not exaggerating. Robert Spence had officially gone overboard. Just like the men he once sneered about, he'd become obsessed with finding all the ties that linked him with the de Pence family, snatching up all the solicitors and heralds his money could buy to plead his case. George explained it wasn't as foolproof as Prichard had initially let on. When Spence eventually went before the House of Lords, it would be a drawn-out fight—an expensive one.

"You've seen the documents. What do you think?" Edward asked.

George took his time answering, something Edward was starting to admire—albeit begrudgingly—about the young man. "It looks valid to me, but I'm no expert. Prichard searched the church records and found credible archives. At least, they look credible. You never know these days." He scratched at his chin. "In the meantime, everything else is going to hell. He doesn't even ask about the factory, never comes into the office. He needs to keep making money if he's going to finance this case, and yet he doesn't seem to care. It's not what I signed up for."

Edward's brow rose. "And so now you want to work for me."

"Georgiana told me your plans for the mines. It sounds like you're on the cusp of something great."

Flattery. Edward wasn't used to it, but he found he liked it just fine. "What do you know about coprolites?"

"Not a fucking thing," George said without missing a beat.

"I didn't think you knew that word." Clean-cut, polite George always seemed so strait-laced.

"There's a lot I didn't show you from the other side of the Spences' dinner table," George said wryly. "My blood might not be blue, but my mother taught me manners. I can run a business, create a favorable bottom line. Numbers are all I know."

George loved numbers. But did he still love Georgiana? Despite all the damage he'd done over the past few days, Edward was positive Georgiana could never love the young man; however, any lingering affections on *his* part would only court trouble in the future.

"Can you get over your feelings for Georgiana? It wouldn't have worked out anyway. You know that, right? You have the same damn name."

"Already done."

Well, that was to the point. Edward had to remind himself that young men were always falling in and out of love. It was no different with George. Edward just had to hope he wasn't as fickle in business as he was in love.

He turned a shrewd eye on the youth. "I would need you to stay with Spence until this blows over, doing everything you can to keep the ship afloat. I've already sat by and watched one father piss away his family's fortune; I won't watch another. My brothers-in-law deserve an inheritance."

George's jaw clenched, but he eventually replied, "Fine."

"And Georgiana? I have to ask again. I can't have you following behind her waiting to sweep in every time I make a mistake. Because I will make mistakes. A lot. I'm making a mistake right now, as a matter of fact. But she will never turn to you. You have to know that now."

George drank the dark liquor, hiding a sheepish smile in his glass. "It isn't what you think. I mean, maybe I played with the idea at one time, but it became obvious that Georgiana never saw me in that way, especially when you came sniffing around."

Edward was reminded of his mother. Her powdery perfume

still infiltrated the room. "I will never understand women or why they love the men they do."

George shrugged. "Money has always made more sense to me."

Edward chuckled. "Yes, but it doesn't keep you warm at night."

"Wait until you have more of it," George replied.

Edward lifted his glass, pointing at the man. "And that's why I know this will work. You must have never loved her if you can say things like that."

George frowned. "I love her in my own way."

"And now that's done," Edward said, hooking one leg over the other, finally feeling a semblance of peace. "It's time for me to love her in mine."

CHAPTER TWENTY-SIX

THE FOLLOWING NIGHT, Georgiana lay in bed, silently—and not so silently—simmering. She'd gone the desolate route, giving herself a full day to cry and mourn her relationship with Edward. Then eventually, like bone stacked with layer upon layer of sediment, that sadness fossilized and was packed away, leaving room for pure, unadulterated fury.

How dare he?

Yes, she'd put things into play that negatively affected his life. But she hadn't meant to do it. She hadn't meant to ruin everything. And he should have known that. Their blissful time together should have served in defense of her misguided actions.

But he hadn't stayed to listen. He'd left her, as easily and completely as everyone else in his life. Like he was throwing away a gutted candle, he'd deemed she had nothing more to give him.

Georgiana's fingers itched. She wanted to strangle him…and then kiss him. Ask for his forgiveness and then yell until his ears rang. But he had to be here, with her, for those things, and he most decidedly was not.

Over the last flurry of days, she'd had to watch her entire life turn upside down, listen to her father as he made rash decisions, console her brothers through their confusion, hold her tongue as her mother envisioned a new, better life with heraldic banners and signet rings.

Through it all, she'd yearned for Edward. She hadn't even wanted him to pat her hand and tell her everything would be all right—she was a practical kind of girl, after all. But a dry remark would have been nice, an awkward, badly timed joke, an exasperated look across the room that reminded her that she wasn't the only one viewing the madness from a front-row seat. And perhaps would be for a long time to come.

A scraping noise caught her attention. Still warm despite summer being officially over, she'd been leaving her window open while she slept. The sounds of the street had died down hours before, and the annoying scraping broke up the monotony. She dismissed it quickly, assuming it was some furry creature climbing up the drainpipe, but when she heard a remarkably colorful curse, she threw her covers aside and hopped out of bed.

It couldn't be, could it?

Did the bastard actually think that playing Romeo for a second time was original or romantic?

A sweet chorus of foul words floated past the windowsill into her room.

Yes, he probably did.

Warring emotions battled for supremacy. The immediate onslaught of glee was quickly replaced by indignation. Georgiana didn't want him to climb; she wanted him to grovel. In excruciating pain, if possible.

She could do something to facilitate that.

Spying the bag of Edward's ammonites she'd brought back from Marlborough, she took up a post at the window. She stuck her head out to find Edward was indeed climbing—badly—and had already made it halfway up to her room. He thought he was a knight. Bleh. Edward only enjoyed playing knight when it was easy for him. He thought he could storm her castle and that would be that. How…basic.

They aren't arrows, but let's see how he fares with some well-placed projectiles.

From inside her room, Georgiana lobbed one of the larger ammonite buttons over the railing, knowing she'd hit her mark when she heard an outraged *"What the bloody hell!"*

She snickered, throwing another, and another and another, a fresh curse welcoming her every time.

"Damn it, Georgina! Are you trying to kill me? Stop it at once!"

She leaned out the window, seeing he hadn't made much progress. "No! You left me; you deserve every minute of this."

He sighed wearily, crying out as another ammonite struck true. "Surely there's a better use for those buttons," he gritted out, heaving himself higher. A few more pulls and he'd be at her railing.

Georgiana cradled the ammonite in her hand. Such a beautiful, ethereal thing, baby-skin smooth from years of being hidden away, first by the ocean and then by Edward.

Now that she thought of it, it did have better uses. Probably very lucrative uses… But she could spare one more.

The second she saw Edward lumber over the top of the wrought iron, she slammed the ammonite into his chest. His reflexes were surprisingly good; he caged his body with his arms, and the ammonite bounced off with minimal damage, settling at his boots.

He gave her a vexed look. "Was that really necessary?"

"So very, very necessary."

Edward's mouth snapped shut and his shoulders slumped, as if he'd only just realized the climb up the drainpipe was going to be the least difficult part of his night. He raked a hand through his hair, causing the waves to spring out like overstretched coils. "Look, I know I was an ass. I know what I did was selfish and wrong. I thought… I don't know what I thought." He took a step toward the window, but Georgiana lifted another ammonite, threatening him. "But I'm here now. That's got to count for something."

A tidal wave of resentment and fear swept through Georgiana. He was right. It did count, though she wasn't sure how much.

"You walked away without even looking at me," she seethed.

"I know."

"You left me with my insane parents."

"I know."

"You didn't write. For days I wondered if you were ever going to come back. You can't just leave and return when you feel like it! You're not your father!"

"I know!" he growled. Anguish lit his features, and Georgiana could finally see the toll the past week had taken. Whether due to their separation or her father's news—most likely both—Edward was clearly not eating. He always had a malnourished look to him, but his cheeks were even gaunter, the shadows under his eyes even more pronounced. A dragging weight seemed to follow him, and yet there was an undercurrent of energy. Like a hungry lion pacing inside a cage, Edward was still something to be admired and feared.

"I understand it's been difficult—for me as well," he went on, stating the obvious. "But that's why I'm here."

Georgiana lifted her hands to her sides, putting herself on display. Edward's gaze licked over her in her nightgown, and she had to fan the flame of her anger. Just because their bodies hungered for each other, that didn't mean he could be forgiven so quickly.

Her mouth turned dry, and she maneuvered the words out carefully. "I'm not some silly maiden, starving myself to death over your desertion. As you can see, I'm fine. More than fine. Healthy as a horse, actually. My appetite has not been affected."

His shuttered eyes contemplated her, registering everything she was trying to say. "I'm glad," he returned. "So very glad." He turned away from her, clutching the rail as he looked down the barren street. Suddenly, he twisted around, his expression completely changed and open. "Well, I am not fine. Not at all. I must be one of those silly maidens, because I can't eat. I can't sleep."

She huffed. "Because of your lost money."

"No," he said, shaking his head. "No. Because of you. None of it matters without you."

Georgiana could feel her resolve melting. *Damn it, girl. Stay strong!*

"Well...good," she stammered. "I hope you're withering away in shame. You asked me to marry you. You"—Georgiana blushed—"loved me and then you left."

"I was upset—"

"You were only thinking about yourself!" she said. "*Your* feelings. *Your* life. While I've been here thinking of ways to fix the problem."

"There's nothing to fix," he said. "I have an appointment with the bank in the morning. I will take out a loan, and that's it."

He was trying to be confident for her sake, but Georgiana could tell how much it pained him to say the words.

Her resolve was now a puddle at her feet. She relaxed her grip, almost dropping the ammonite. "That can't be it. You can marry someone else."

Edward snapped his head up, and his countenance was as ferocious as she'd ever seen it. "Stop it. There's no one else, and you know that. Ever since I saw you in the park that one day and let you walk home in the rain, I've known that you're the only woman I'll ever want."

"You know, that story does not get more romantic the more you tell it."

His lips twitched. "I don't care. It's our story. I'm goddamned beside myself, Georgiana. I need you with me. I can't do this without you. You want a courtly, grand gesture? You want a public display of affection?" He raised his hands high and wide. "Here it is."

Georgiana watched him, incredulous, craning her neck out the window again to look behind him. "What public display? We're the only ones out here."

Edward dropped his arms, deflated. "You know what I mean."

"You haven't changed at all. The first time you kissed me was under the cover of trees… You proposed to me in an attic!"

"I enjoy privacy. And I thought you loved our time in the attic!"

"I did!" Georgiana cried. "I'm just pointing out the pattern!"

Edward's chest pumped, and the tired line under his eyes etched deeper into his skin. She didn't know what she was playing at. She'd already forgiven him—the moment she saw him on that drainpipe, she knew she would give him all of her. And yet she kept arguing. As a defense mechanism, it was better than crying.

"Fine," he said. "You want a public display of affection? Then hear this." He cupped his hands around his mouth and turned out into the street. He took a deep breath, ballooning his chest, and was just about to release a bellow when Georgiana grabbed his jacket, pulling him back over the windowsill.

"You fool! I'm not asking you to wake the entire neighborhood," she said as they clamored to the floor.

Untangling their limbs, Edward twisted, ducking his head close to hers. "It's what you want. And I will give you everything you want, Georgiana. You have to know that. Anything for our future together."

She lost herself in his eyes. She'd once considered those fathomless pools of darkness mercurial and frightening. How could she ever have been such a coward? They were the storm that tucked you in at night, the ink that manifested your thoughts on the page, making them come to life.

"I don't want that," she said, caressing his hair out of his face, luxuriating in the way he closed those eyes, embracing the touch like a docile kitten.

"Then what do you want? Just name it. The moon? The stars? What?"

A giggle burst through as his lyrical words reminded her of one of their earlier conversations. She didn't know if she would regret asking, but she did it anyway. "A poem."

A smile blossomed on his face. "A poem?"

Georgiana nodded, scraping her nails over his cheeks, loving the sound they made against his stubble. Beards were not the fashionable thing; however, she wondered if he would grow one for her. Maybe Vikings would be her next obsession.

Edward lifted his chin, his lips almost skimming her own. Slowly, he leaned toward her, bending her back against the floor, draping himself over her while leaning his elbows on either side of her head. "So you're in the mood to be properly wooed, are you?" he asked, his voice as silky as the stockings she wished he'd peel off her. With his teeth.

He untied her cap and threw it to the side, then fanned her hair out in a halo on the hard floor. He stared at it so long that Georgiana was afraid he would go no further. Then he blinked, and his smile turned positively rakish. "My talents are great. Prepare to fall in love, woman."

"I already have."

His kiss was light, gentle, crushing her soul and piecing it back together in seconds. As if they weren't lying in her childhood room with her parents just down the hall, there was no sense of hurry or clandestine anxiety. There was only them. And a new promise being made.

His tongue laid siege to her mouth; his caresses stormed her defenses. She was the holy land that Edward was determined to bring back under his care and devotion.

They unbuttoned, unclasped, untied quietly, their breaths the only noise in the room. It heightened the experience to such a startling degree, and Georgiana felt every touch magnified. Her skin was the only thing screaming, demanding to be matched with his skin, yearning for the missing puzzle piece.

When they were both naked, Edward sat back on his haunches, tracing the sensitive flesh around her nipples, the hilly planes of her stomach, the indentations of her ribcage. Around and around he went, the simple touch making her crazed with need.

She watched his hooded eyes, heard his shallow breaths, sensed the weight around his neck disappearing with each pass.

"I could stare at you forever," he said in his gravelly, hushed tone that only made her inner thighs pulse more.

"Please don't."

He chuckled, bending over to take one of her nipples in his mouth, licking it lightly. The action was so fleeting that Georgiana broke out into a sweat.

She lifted her arms, coaxing him over her to no avail.

He shook his head. "I owe you a poem."

"Let your body say it," she replied, her frustration growing with each ache-filled second.

Finally, he allowed himself to be cajoled back into position, laying his body over every spare inch of hers. Georgiana trembled. The feeling of his warm flesh throbbing with heat so close to the surface was as close to heaven as she knew she would ever experience on this earth.

Edward dug his nose into her neck, breathing her in as his fingers traveled down her side, tickling and tugging, re-staking their claim. His large hands gripped her hipbones, following the curved ridges.

Feeling it necessary to move him along, Georgiana shifted her hips greedily until his hand was settled correctly in the basin of her thighs, rolling back and forth rhythmically to her need.

He picked up his head then, keeping his weight on his elbow at her side. "There once was a lady from China…"

Despite the driving force of desire, Georgiana released a giant belly laugh. His fingers entered her, and the laugh stuck in her throat, morphing into an exhale of exquisite relief.

"How did I know it would begin like that?" she said, licking her lips. He then licked them for her, starting another mind-blowing kiss that she hoped would never end. His fingers still working, his thumb circling her delicate bud, their bodies began to dance. Two people. One fluid movement toward the same goal.

Edward sucked on the skin just below her jaw, his lips more and more insistent, his motions more and more hectic. She liked this Edward, the one that lost all his buttoned-up composure for her.

"Do you want more?"

"More of this," she answered, reaching down to stroke his hard length. "No more poems for today."

He laughed against her neck, withdrawing his hand from her slick passage to claim his shaft. With barely contained energy, he placed it at her entrance and thrust home with such purpose and need that Georgiana was surprised she didn't come right then and there. But it wouldn't be much longer. She was too overwrought, too overwhelmed. She didn't know how he held himself back. His body rocked with hers in a cadence that belied their passion. Slow and steady, just as he'd said long ago she would one day appreciate. She could feel every edge of him, feel every ridge working to create the friction they needed.

Her feet curled around his hip, taking him deeper. Her toes curled; her fingers curled; her mind curled. This was how it would be with them. Forever and ever.

The languid pushing and pulling, the lazy ins and outs. She wanted more, but he pinned her down with his weight, forcing her to take in every lengthy movement. They couldn't have been on the floor for very long, but it felt like an eternity with all the glories of life condensed in one shattering slice of time.

When he sensed she was ready to come, when the feeling swept up and swallowed her in a split second of surprise, Edward drank the cry from her mouth, protecting their moment.

He pumped into her two more times and found his release, sinking into the cushion of her body like a man who hadn't allowed himself to rest in years.

But even then, Edward had to move. His head between her breasts, he reached for her hand, holding it out to the side of them, tickling it over and over. He brushed her knuckles, the insides of her fingers, tracing the lines of her palms like a traveling fortune teller. Georgiana wanted to ask him what he saw but realized she didn't need his answer. She saw everything as clear as day.

With her other hand, Georgiana massaged his head, wading through the chestnut waves, rewarded as his body became even more boneless on top of her. She could handle it—she could handle him.

"Maybe we'll save your poem for another time," she said, tugging gently on his hair. "I am properly wooed at the moment."

He blew out a deep breath, before balancing himself on his elbows again. The look he gave her was so full of love and peace that Georgiana felt tears begin to gather along her lower lids.

"Finally," he said. "My battle is won."

CHAPTER TWENTY-SEVEN

J UST MINUTES FROM dawn, Edward jolted awake, alerted to the fact that he was in a room that was not his own. He would be marrying Georgiana posthaste; however, getting caught in her bed wasn't a good look for the in-laws.

Funny enough, that didn't stop him from reaching for her, hoping for a little more than a goodbye kiss. Lazily, he extended his arms, searching for luscious hips and a magnificently plump behind, but came away grossly disappointed.

He opened his eyes.

A pink and vanilla sky was just breaking through the bruising purples and blues of night, and Georgiana was nowhere to be found. He was alone.

She'd left him.

Of course. Point well made, madam.

Suddenly, there was no time to dawdle. Edward dressed and fumbled his way down the pipe, throwing a quick thanks to his maker that no one saw him flail at the last moment and drop to his knees on the sidewalk. Hopefully, he wouldn't have to be doing that again anytime soon, though he supposed that depended on how fast they could marry. Now that he'd become used to a partner in his bed, a return to celibacy didn't seem to agree with him particularly well—nor her, he was quite sure.

The plan was to meet with Dawson and the bankers first

thing. Edward had just enough time to get home and bathe and throw on a set of fresh, unwrinkled clothes before signing on the dotted line. He expected to be nervous—agitated, even—but found he didn't have the energy for it. His night with Georgiana had revived him. Whatever came of today would be for the best because it was the only way forward. And forward led to his wife and their future together.

Even the grim atmosphere in Dawson's office did nothing to stifle his calm acceptance. Edward greeted the trio of stone-faced bankers in the dark-green-papered room with hearty resolve, nodding at each one before taking his seat across from Dawson. His gaze wandered to the solicitor's stack of fossils near the window, and despite himself, a smile drifted on his face while he rubbed a sore spot on the side of his neck where Georgiana had pelted him the night before. In her defense, she had kissed it to make it better while reminding him that he'd deserved it and more, but it still smarted.

"Very good, my lord," said a tall, older man with a shock of white sideburns that traveled all the way down to his sunken chin. "We're glad you could come in today, although, as we told Mr. Dawson, it was most unnecessary. We could have sent the papers to your home to sign so you wouldn't suffer an inconvenience."

"No inconvenience at all," Edward replied tersely. "Can we start?"

"Of course," the man replied stiffly, lightly touching the papers in front of him, fiddling until all the corners and edges lined up. "We have the loan already drawn out and have gone over the particulars with your man. This should be over in a matter of minutes." His sideburns twitched. "You'll barely feel a thing."

Edward stared back, unwilling to respond outwardly to the banker's warped sense of humor. The stupid man knew nothing. Edward might not feel anything now, but he was sure to feel it later. Banks were making big business by bailing out aristocrats. This was nothing new. By giving the landed gentry safety in the form of these loans, all they did was contribute to the notion that the peerage wouldn't have to change with the times. The landed class could continue to sit on their estates, spending money they never seriously contemplated returning in any timely fashion, hoping for their farms to pay off again as they had in the past. These bankers smiled prettily at their "betters," commiserated like friends, but all they were doing was issuing golden handcuffs to a group of people too proud to realize that shackles were still shackles, regardless of the pretty metal used to forge them.

Dawson handed Edward a pen while they waited.

After five minutes had come and gone, Edward was ready to bark at them to hurry up when he heard a commotion outside the office door.

"No, no, they're expecting me," a low female voice insistently declared as the door swung open. Before his wits had a chance to rebound, Georgiana sailed in, hair tightly plaited, her skirts bouncing and her face pink and flushed, as if she'd just run the entire way from her house. She made a decent show of surveying the room from end to end until her focus landed on Edward and the corner of her lips lifted in what he could only assume was triumph. "Wonderful. I'm not late."

Her lips widened so generously that Edward almost forgot to wonder what the hell she thought she was doing.

Taking advantage of his paralyzed tongue, Georgiana appropriated the seat next to him, settling her petticoats assiduously like they were back at the opera, readying for the entertainment to start. The men across openly gawked at her, thinking the same thing, since *she* was obviously the entertainment.

"And y-y-you are, miss?" the second banker inquired with a noticeable stutter. Edward didn't know if it was a real affliction or if the man was truly taken off guard. With her butter-yellow dress and a flower-stacked bonnet that looked large enough to eat a small dog, Georgiana was not only arresting but wholly intimidating. There was also the matter of her pointy chin stuck high in the air. The woman had control of the room and was loving every minute of it.

"I'm Georgiana Spence—Edward's partner in this endeavor." She gave him a firm nod before adding, "Oh, and his fiancée."

"Ah, I s-see" the stuttering banker replied, leaning back in his chair, sharing baffled looks with the others, too good-natured—or stunned—to point out that he did not, in fact, "see."

Sideburns didn't have that problem. He threw Georgiana a politely condescending smile. "This is just a formality, Miss Spence. If you would wait out in the hallway there, Lord Edward will be ready to take you on your walk in no time. The meeting is almost over."

Edward noticed Georgiana clawing the chair's arms, the first sign of unchecked emotion. The banker was lucky she didn't have any ammonite buttons on her; she obviously didn't appreciate being made to sound like an anxious invalid dog.

Smoothing her long fingers on the wood, Georgiana spoke as sweetly as her husky voice would allow. "I'm afraid you don't understand. That's why I'm here, to tell Edward that the meeting is already over."

"Over?" Dawson asked, straightening the spectacles on his nose.

"Quite. You see, we have a new investor and have no more need of a loan. We appreciate your time and are most sorry for the inconvenience of bringing you out today." Georgiana rose, turning to Edward. "Are you ready, my love?" she said as easily as if she were asking if he'd like another helping of poached salmon.

Still a little dumbstruck by the whirlwind of activity, Edward found his way to his feet, hoping he didn't look as lost as he felt. He contemplated stopping her, asking what she was about, but, by the glint in her eye, he understood that she would never forgive him for doing that in front of the men. It would ruin her moment.

He waited until they were outside the building, the second the door clicked shut behind them.

"Why the hell weren't you in bed when I woke up this morning?" he asked, spinning her around to face him. *Well, hell.* That certainly wasn't what he'd meant to say. However, now that he'd voiced it, he realized it was equally important, if not more so.

Georgiana's brow furrowed. She might have been ready for any number of questions, but obviously not that one. She blinked a few times and patted the rope of hair at the side of her head. "You gave me a lot to think about last night. I couldn't sleep, so I went down to the study. Besides"—she squinted—"it's not like you needed me to show you how to climb down the drainpipe."

She evidently hadn't heard him when he fell the last few feet this morning. "Still," he said, "you shouldn't have left."

Georgiana's smile released the pain from his chest. "I won't ever leave you again."

"Good," he said gruffly. Taking her arm, Edward started them down the street toward her home. "Now what was all that back there? You better have good news, because if I have to make another appointment with those bankers…"

"Oh! The very best news," Georgiana exclaimed, leaning into his side. They were much too close—even for an engaged couple. But Edward wouldn't have pointed that out to her for all the world. Let everyone see how much they loved each other, how she grinned at him, how he reveled in her attention. Why should he care?

"It was what you said about the buttons."

"The buttons?"

Without taking a breath, Georgiana filled him on her morning. Pacing her father's study, she'd racked her brain thinking of a way to make up for the loss of her father's investment. She'd remembered the ammonites, how Edward told her that they must have better uses than making craters in his head. After Edward had made his escape, she'd carried them to the Duke of Wembley's townhouse, where she spoke with Mr. Nathaniel Lawrence.

"Lawrence?" Edward sneered, taken aback by his visceral reaction to the name. "Why the hell did you think of him?"

Georgiana made a point to pat his arm, making *him* feel like the anxious invalid dog. "Because he's the one who mentioned that I needed to think outside the box. I offered the ammonites to his company to make specialized buttons for clothing, knowing my father would never use them, especially while his mind is taken up with other things. Lawrence absolutely loved the idea—and gave me a very good price, I might add."

When she told him the amount, Edward, *begrudgingly*, had to admit…it was a good price. Damn fair. But still not enough. He hated to tell her that. She looked so proud of herself. However, his stomach couldn't help but constrict as the truth settled in. He would have to swallow his pride and call the bankers back in the morning to set up another meeting, after all.

"And then we got to talking," she continued.

"Talking?"

"Yes," she said, ignoring the flinty tone in his voice. "I told him all about the mining business—about the coprolites. Apparently, he's oddly interested in manure and wants to be a part of it. That's why I was late. He kept going on and on about guano droppings."

Of course the intelligent man did! Because it's so very interesting!

She went on, "He asked me if there was still time to invest, and I told him to speak to you today."

Edward was stunned. His knees went weak as if the sidewalk had begun to wobble, and he leaned on Georgiana like she were a crutch. "Invest? With me?"

"With us," Georgiana corrected him, nodding so hard that one of her braids fell loose from her bun. "I explained how we plan to treat our workers completely different, more respectfully, like the humans they are, and he was hooked. I told him about my father and how much he'd initially offered, and Lawrence matched it. He said it'll probably be the best investment he's ever made. He believes in your vision. He believes in you."

Now, Edward had to stop. If he leaned on her any more, Georgiana would be crippled from the stress. He stumbled away, collapsing against the guardrail next to a terrace house, going over everything she'd said. Could it be true? Could it all be over just like that? So easily?

Eventually, his flabbergasted expression made its way back to her. Georgiana's smile was gone, and she watched him expectantly, biting her bottom lip. When he shook his head sullenly, her mouth drooped.

"You're wrong," he said, inflating his chest with air and the undeniable truth. "He's not investing in my vision. He's investing in you. He believes in *you*. You saved me."

It wasn't accusatory, far from it, though a different woman might have taken the statement as such. Women were taught to be anything other than forthright or boastful. If "taking credit" was anywhere in the etiquette rule books, it could only be found in the "what not to do" column.

But his woman was different. He'd known that from the very beginning. So Edward wasn't astonished in the least when she matched his humble assertion with a sly grin. "I told you I was the knight in this relationship."

Edward laughed, so long and so hard that he hugged his stomach. In the middle of the sidewalk, with the early-morning bustle sailing by, he let loose, his body convulsing with pleasure, eyes filling with tears.

If people gawked at the frightening spectacle, he didn't notice—or didn't care. Besides, his attention was solely on one person—the one that had irrevocably taken his life and molded it to her will. Like Prometheus, Georgiana had seen something in this lowly human and perfected it.

She had forced him to look outside himself, given him the gift of fire and taught him there had never been anything to fear.

And he'd returned the gift by loving her the only way he knew how. As she'd reminded him, he'd kissed her under the shadow of boughs, blended their souls among the cast-away items long forgotten. He'd loved her the best he could.

But he could do better.

Pulling himself straight, Edward took her hand, leading her down the pavement.

"What are you doing?" she asked. "My home is the other way."

"We aren't going to your home," he replied, stopping to look both directions for traffic before crossing the street with her firmly in tow.

They were quiet for a few minutes, Georgiana's fluttering steps and her fast breathing the only sounds mixing with the waking London. Servants hurried into back entrances; men slogged to the pub to get to their pre-work pint. A circus could have rambled down Park Lane and Edward wouldn't have blinked an eye. He only had one place on his mind.

"The park?" Georgiana asked, pulling Edward up short on the gates.

He nudged her forward. "Don't stop now, my love. We've got a little bit more to go."

Edward moved once more, ignoring the brow she raised. He didn't stop until he reached the statue. The one he'd found Georgiana at that fateful day a month ago when the rain began to fall around them. Like a curtain closing at the end of a show, that rain had signaled the end of him, the end of a person he could never imagine being again.

No clouds above them now—the day was opening with every hope of being fine and pleasant. An auspicious beginning if he ever saw one.

"Achilles?" Georgiana asked. "Why Achilles?"

Edward regarded the massive statue standing at attention. "You know...I've never really looked at it before. I suppose it is Achilles."

"Did you really have no idea?"

He shrugged. "No. I just know it as the point where I told you to walk home in the rain."

"Again," she said, her nose scrunched up. "Not romantic on the third telling."

"I was an ass, yes, I know, but it was how our story began, so it will always be romantic to me," he replied, searching around them, nearly missing the way his words made her grin. The park wasn't loaded with people like it would be later in the afternoon, but there was a healthy amount of traffic. Enough to make his point. Maybe he'd bring her back later to make it again, though.

Like a cake topper, the ancient warrior was stacked on two layers of a stone display. Edward climbed up the first layer, glancing at the bronze symbol of heroism. Then he frowned. "It's a rather small fig leaf, isn't it?" he asked. "I'm afraid they did old Achilles wrong."

Georgiana's lips tightened, and she squinted at the statue with ferocious intensity, as if they were debating the merits of the Sistine Chapel. "You know…I didn't think so before, but I do believe you're right. Rather small indeed." Her head lolled to the side as she directed her attention back to him. "Is that what you dragged me here for? To discuss Achilles'…blade?"

Edward passed a hand over his face. "What? Christ no. Although remind me later, because I have a feeling it would make for scintillating conversation."

Georgiana stayed quiet at that, and Edward noticed her clutching nervously at her stomach, a note of apprehension in her expression. One of her braids still hung along her cheeks, giving her an adorably bedraggled look, much like the last time he spotted her here.

Edward's heart swelled so large and full it felt like it would break every rib in his chest in order to escape. He offered her a reassuring smile. "No, my love. I came to do this."

Cupping his hands around his mouth, Edward filled his lungs and released his heart into the open air. "I have come here today as a lowly servant."

"No shit, mate," a man piped up as he walked past them, not even slowing his steps for his comment.

Edward's brow lowered, but he kept going, not to be deterred. "I've come here today to tell one and all that I absolutely love this woman," he shouted.

"Oi! We get it," another member of a gathering mob lobbed at him. This man had the courtesy to stop, though he nudged a friend in the ribs before adding, "Though if I loved a woman, I'd tell her under the covers at this time of day rather than out and about, harassing good people."

Edward stared dumbly. This was why he didn't like people.

He tried to ignore the man; he truly did. His declaration was for Georgiana and Georgiana alone. Doing it out in the open was just to prove a point. This token of his love was for her edification.

But the prick was being an arsehole. "I'm trying to tell my lady that I love her," Edward returned gallantly.

An older woman cackled from the back of the pack. "Go on and tell her, then, before you make all of our ears bleed."

Edward's shoulders slumped. He wasn't even sure if this could be counted as romantic anymore. The stress had vanished from Georgiana's features, though; in fact, her countenance was impishly gleeful as she regarded the proceedings.

Feeling more than a little harassed and horribly foolish, Edward threw up his arms. "I love you," he said. "I'll love you forever or however long you'll let me. I am yours, and no matter what I do in my life, no matter what we create or accomplish, being your husband is all I'll ever want to be. That is the value I will carry with me. That will be my greatest success."

Tears spilled down her face, coating her downy cheeks.

That's enough. Edward bent over, about to let himself down from his pedestal when the old woman's voice cut through the crowd.

"That's it?" she asked, starting up another round of murmurs from the audience.

"Should there be more?" Edward couldn't help but ask. Georgiana seemed to think it was perfectly adequate. Was she merely humoring him, knowing he wasn't adept at this sort of thing?

The old woman flung her long gray braid over her shoulder, scratching at the crown of her head before inspecting her fingers. "A swell gentleman like you should have more to offer... Do you promise to keep her in the lap of luxury?"

Edward huffed, bewildered at the turn of events. He almost waved his hand at the woman, dismissing her question, but he noticed a sea of people waiting to hear what he had to say. He couldn't contemplate them too long, since this amount of attention and scrutiny was pretty much his nightmare come to life.

"I hardly have money for 'lap of luxury'," he replied indignantly. "I will house her in an appropriate manner."

That got a snort. "Where are the pretty words now?" the woman spat to the other onlookers. "Will you commit yourself with all your might, do everything in your power to keep this lady from having to debase herself with work?"

"I would think not," Edward exclaimed, fists now firmly planted on his hips. "I will expect her to work just as hard as me when building our businesses." He sliced a hand through the air. "No more, no less. Marriage to me is not a free ride."

Blank expressions, mixed with a healthy dose of incredulity, stared back at him.

"What about jewels?" someone shouted.

"Oh, I sold all those today," Edward returned.

"A fancy house?"

"I have one of those, although it hasn't any furniture, and I have no money to buy any soon."

"A country house?"

"Yes!" Edward yelled to some encouraging claps. "But my four sisters live there, along with my mother."

A collective groan vibrated around him. Edward's ego was shot. It seemed London agreed: he didn't have much to offer.

Did he care? Not one fucking bit.

"How about a poem?" someone called out.

"No!" Georgiana cut in, an apology written all over her face.

"You don't want that."

"A song?" someone else added.

Georgiana shook her head dismally. "You definitely don't want that either."

A man with a neck the size of a tire gave Georgiana a frightfully pathetic look. "Are you sure this one's for you? He's not much," he stated, jutting a thumb toward Edward. "It's never too late to back out, you know?"

Georgiana furrowed her brow, seeming to consider this. "You have a good point," she remarked before raising her voice. "You all do."

That brought about more self-congratulatory nodding from the crowd, as if everyone was proud that they were saving the nice lady from the very unworthy man.

This was not going like Edward had planned—not that he'd planned it. That was half the problem. Edward wasn't a by-the-seat-of-his-pants type of man. Clearly, he wouldn't be making any impromptu speeches again anytime soon.

Well, too goddamned bad for her. Georgiana had already accepted him; she couldn't back out now.

Edward was about to jump down and throw her over his shoulder when her next words stopped him.

"I know how it all looks and sounds," she told the spectators with the kind of unwavering bravery that would have definitely won her a spot at any round table. "But you don't know him or me, and you certainly don't know that he just said the most poetic and beautiful words that I've ever heard."

"Go on with you," the old woman shouted.

Georgiana's eyes widened at the command, but she kept going. "No, it's true. That man up there is the strongest, most courageous character in my life."

Thick Neck grimaced. "You mean the statue?"

"No, not the statue!" Georgiana countered, losing her cool. "The man, the man up there, not the statue. Why on earth would I be talking about the statue?"

Edward decided it was time to get down and take his woman home. He was on the right side of her praise and—knowing himself well enough—understood that wouldn't always be the case. Best to take advantage now.

As the crowd spread for him, her green eyes found his, flashing with warmth and unwavering love, the kind that would keep them safe when times were rough, place a blanket around them when the winds grew cold. It was a love based on respect and trust and not a little bit of lust.

And it wasn't easy getting to this place. Edward took heart in that.

"I'm sorry," he said, stopping in front of her, taking the time to glare at a few interlopers on their way. "You deserved better. I thought to make one of your fantasies come to life, when the knight dramatically declares his love to his lady." He twisted around to watch the disappointed crowd. "It obviously didn't go as smoothly as I would have liked."

Georgiana ate up the space between them, cupping his cheek. "My dear Edward, you got the lady, didn't you? How much smoother could it have gone?"

He shrugged, turning his face to kiss the inside of her palm, letting his head rest in its safe haven. From handling the ammonites all morning, her skin smelled like the sea, and just like that, his sheepish uncertainty vanished. "I wouldn't have minded terribly if they'd have seen that I'm the only man for you. But they didn't ask the most important question."

"And what is that?"

Edward circled his arms around her waist. "They never asked me what I believe in. My greater good."

"If I remember correctly, you don't believe in one," Georgiana replied, pressing closer.

"That was before. I am a changed man."

She gave him a lovely pout. "I hope not *that* changed."

He kissed her long and hard, the way a woman like Georgiana Spence should always be kissed. "Just enough to realize that your love is my greater good."

"Our love," she corrected him.

"Our love," he agreed, heading her out of the gates. "Now let's go get married so I can put you to work."

Georgiana fanned herself with her hand. "My Lord Edward, you're starting to sound as silver-tongued as one of the heroes in my books."

"I hope not." He laughed. "Life isn't like your storybooks, my dear."

"You're right, my love," she answered with a contented sigh. "It's better."

About the Author

Margaux Thorne is a lifelong reader of romance novels. Some of her earliest memories are sneaking into her mom's room at night and stealing any books she could find.

After moving around quite a bit, she's finally put down roots in New England with her two sons and husband. She's always been a writer, starting out in newspapers, but it wasn't until her sons began going to school full-time that she began working towards her dream of becoming a romance author.

She enjoys crocheting toys for her kids, hiking with her Saint Bernard, watching all the Real Housewives franchises on the couch with her very old and very fat pugs, and the rush of feeling she gets *after* she finishes a long run (though not a second before).